Jezebel Street

Jezebel Street

Irene Roberts

PIATKUS

Copyright © 1994 by Irene Roberts

First published in Great Britain in 1994 by
Judy Piatkus (Publishers) Ltd of
5 Windmill Street, London W1P 1HF

**The moral right of the author
has been asserted**

*A catalogue record for this book is available
from the British Library*

ISBN 0-7499-0264-7

Phototypeset in 11/12pt Times by
Computerset, Harmondsworth, Middlesex
Printed and bound in Great Britain by
Biddles Ltd, Guildford & Kings Lynn

To dear Tim, whose kind patience and expertise helped me to come to terms with a word processor that seemed to have a mind of its own.

Chapter One

'You pull faces at me again, Poppy Ashton, an' I'll clip your bloody ear!'

'Don't care!' Thirteen-year-old Poppy's cheeks were as red as her hair, her green eyes were tiger-bright.

'Why, you little – ' Mrs Liz Parker, sharp-nosed and skinny, took a menacing step forwards and Poppy didn't wait. She ran hell for leather down Jezebel Street, into Skelton Street, along it and into the school playground. Old Mother Parker wouldn't dare touch her in here. No one would. School was hell anyway. Most folk would drop dead before wanting to set foot in rotten Skelton School.

'Wotcher, Poppy,' mousy Jessica Davies said with her mouth full, then grinned a grin edged with crumbs and jam. 'You been running away from poopy Parker again?'

'Like a blue-arse fly, if you must know. What's it to you?'

'Nothing. Where's Ros?'

'Staying home today.'

'Bloody hell. Not going to turn up her toes, is she?' Jessica's voice was worried, even though she tried to sound casual. 'You might 'ave let me know.'

'Nothing to tell,' Poppy said and ran off to pull Sandy Swift's hair. He swung round fast and thumped her one. She flew at him, furious because he'd called her cousin Ros a misery-guts, only the day before. She loathed him and all boys, and the whole stinking world, because Ros was sick again. It was scary: early this morning Ros had looked like death.

Poppy and Sandy were going at it hammer and tongs when

1

the whistle went and they had to break away, glaring. Sandy hared off to the boys' part next door; Poppy went to stand in line.

Miss called the register and when she came to Rosemary Eden, Poppy held up her hand.

'Please, Miss, my cousin's sick again and Dr Fox said that she's to stay in bed.'

Mrs Bowden, plump, dark-haired and distant, nodded and continued in a crisp, matter-of-fact way.

'Just think,' Poppy hissed to Jessica, who sat next to her, 'Ros likes her!'

'Old cow! She could have at least pretended to be sorry. I bet – ' Jess froze as a near-black gimlet gaze turned in her direction.

After that it was morning prayers and then lessons. Bored already, but not daring to do otherwise, Poppy took up paper and pencil, and obediently wrote, as instructed, 26 October 1920.

Poppy let the teacher drone on. Her mind was on other things, not bothering with lessons. Her imagination was huge. She daydreamed that she was rich and had taken Ros and Aunt Nan off to the warm climate that Doc Fox said Ros needed. Ros's stay in hospital the previous year had frightened Poppy no end. The only persons worth worrying about in the whole world were Ros, Charlie and Aunt Nan, of course. Still, Nan was about as loving as a cat's arse.

Aunt Nan had come up the hard way, having had Ros at just seventeen. Nick Eden had married her, a proven rotter. It was said that acting right by Nan had been the only decent thing he'd done in his life. Nan had learned some lessons over the years and these lessons she passed on to her girls.

'It's never no crime to be poor,' she would state crisply. 'But it is a crime to let other people know you're poor. If they find out you're having it hard, they'll treat you with contempt. Another thing – and this is for you in particular, Poppy – it's no crime to like books and a quiet life, if you can get it. But it is round here! In Jezebel Street you've got to act like me. You've got to let the world see you as someone full of stuffing. Let them all know you won't never be put on. That you'll stand up for yourself no matter what.' She had looked from Poppy to Ros, then added, 'But when all's said and done, you two have got to be polite and act like ladies as best you can. I'd swing for the pair of you if you ever bought shame to my house.'

She had meant that, they could tell by her fiery expression. These days Aunt Nan's eyes always seemed to be blazing and keeping company with her tongue. Nan was a goer and a doer and God help anyone who got in her way. Unlike her brother Charlie, who was Poppy's father, though he refused to admit to the fact.

Charlie Ashton owned the greengrocer's shop at the top end of the street. He was a cheery, decent sort most of the time, but he could be hard. It was Poppy's dearest wish that one day he would actually get to like her – loving her was out of the question, of course.

The greengrocer had disowned her from the moment she had been born. He had passed her on to his sister Nan. Just as if a baby could be got rid of as easily as the rubbish he chucked into the nearest bin! He had told Nan that Poppy was to call him Charlie, as did 'the rest of the cheeky little sods down the street. Never, ever Dad!'

It all had something to do with Poppy's 'whore of a mother'. That was how Nan always referred to her. Poppy knew that if she ever met her mother, not that she wanted to, she would hate her on sight. On the other hand, she loved and idolised Charlie.

'Pay attention, Ashton!'

Poppy gave the teacher a withering look before she obediently knuckled down to work.

Playtime meant fighting tooth and claw with Sandy Swift and losing, and calling him all the things she wouldn't dare give tongue to and front of Nan. At dinnertime she hurried back home, only to find Ros asleep upstairs. Poppy clattered down the lino-covered stairs again to the scullery, where Nan had left some bread and dripping. Poppy took it outside and sat on the doorstep.

Flossie Wells, her buxom body dressed in navy blue, came out from the next house. Nice, warm-hearted Flossie, who loved her parents and most of the world, was a dab hand at sewing and knitting and earned her living that way. She was

3

near Nan's age and they were friends. Now her round, rosy, blue-eyed face beamed down at Poppy and she crossed her plump arms over her bosom saying, 'Hello, ducks. All right?'

'Yes, thanks, Floss. Are you looking out for your mum and dad?'

'Yes. I've got a surprise for them. Bought a nice oil stove for their bedroom. They'll love to have some warmth. Got it cheap at Berriman's Second-Hand.'

Poppy was genuinely pleased. Fred and Em Wells were nice old people and used the downstairs front as bedroom and living room combined. They would walk to Dondu's Corner Shop or Charlie's, but never much further. They were two of the very few people in Jezebel Street who could read, and, like Poppy, they all but devoured books. It was her weekly delight to go all the way to the library near Leyton Town Hall and change their books for them.

'Won't be bad for Daniel above them, neither,' Flossie said, 'since they reckon as how heat rises.' She threw back her fair, frizzy head and laughed in her rousing way. 'Think I'll charge the young sod more rent. Oh, look! Here they come, my two dear old ducks.'

Almost whinnying in her pleasure, Flossie hurried down the street to meet them.

Still sitting on the doorstep, Poppy, with her mouth full and spitting crumbs, began a shouted conversation with little Lenny Jacobs, who was hunched up on the step opposite. Lenny was very young, but he had an old face and he was thin and weedy.

'Cold today!' Poppy called out. 'You cold, Lenny?'

'Freezing,' he replied in a reedy voice.

'You sitting on something warm?'

'I'm on a rug. I'm all right.'

'Want a bit of bread and dripping?'

'No.'

'Where's your coat?'

'Indoors.'

'Shall I get it for you?'

Lenny's cheeks went pink. 'No!'

'Bet you haven't got a coat! I have, Lenny, but it's not worth wearing it yet. You sure you don't want me to fetch

4

you something warmer to wear? You can have a lend of my coat if you like.'

Lenny shook his head.

'Suit yourself. Oh, shit! Old Parker's coming. I'm off!'

Waving, with a half-eaten doorstep of bread still in her hand, Poppy tore towards the school.

At four sharp the school doors opened and children poured out like freed prisoners, laughing and shouting at the tops of their voices. Poppy walked a few steps along with Jessica, who lived nearby in Skelton Street. Deep down Poppy did not like Jess, but Ros did. Jessica had been there one playtime when a bullyboy had pushed Ros. Jessica had stepped in and bashed him. Poppy, having been kept in writing lines about not answering back, knew nothing about it till later on. From then on, Jess was Ros's best ever friend. Jealous, Poppy had accused Ros of being a traitor. Her cousin had smiled.

'Don't be silly! We're almost the twins everyone takes us for, and I'll always love you best of all.'

Even now Poppy remembered how Ros had looked when she said that, all soft and glowing. And her own relief had cut into her heart like a shaft of light.

'She's going to be all right, ain't she?' Jessica asked in an offhand way.

''Course she is!' Poppy flashed a quick, frightened look at her and ran.

She went up the stairs two at a time and burst into the door of the bedroom. It was small, cold and sparsely furnished. The curtains were thin and washed-out yellow for all they had been dipped in dolly dye many times. The distempered walls were pink and had home-made pictures pinned on them. Everything was scrupulously clean – Nan saw to that!

Ros was there, leaning back on the pillow. Her outline under the skimpy bedclothes showed that her legs were long and thin. There was a definite family likeness, for Ros seemed to be a pale replica of her cousin. Ros's hair was a cloud of pale orange, while Poppy's was red. She had large, gentle, grey-green eyes, whereas Poppy's were emerald and blazed like Nan's. Her haunting face was alabaster-pale,

5

whereas Poppy's cheeks burned even rosier than usual because she had run so fast.

Ros was nursing Josh and Jo, two small tabby cats who shouldn't have been in the room, let alone on the bed. She looked at Poppy and smiled.

'Hello,' she said quietly. 'Right old racer, aren't you?' I bet you'll be first in school sports again next year.'

'And when we break up next autumn I'll know it'll be just one more term and freedom from school for ever.'

'Oh, don't go on,' Ros pleaded. 'You're lucky to be able to run races and do hurdling. And staying off school isn't much fun, Poppy.'

''Course it isn't.' Poppy looked contrite. 'Don't matter, though, does it? How you feeling now?'

'All right. And I'm looking forward to eating a little dinner. These turns never last too long.'

Poppy wrinkled her nose. 'I can smell yesterday's cabbage stew and I know we've got the same tonight.'

'For which we must be grateful.' Ros's smile became slightly more pronounced as she gently mimicked her mother. 'Since God helped it to grow.'

'White cabbages are like weeds in Charlie's shop. I think Nan ought to thank him and not God.'

'And I think you might have something to do with it, too, eh, Poppy?' Ros teased. 'Don't stand there in the door – come and sit with me on the bed. You don't have to run errands for anyone. Mum's doing the shopping on her way home, just so that you can stay with me. Isn't that kind?'

Poppy raised her eyes to the ceiling. 'Thank you, God, and thank you, Aunt Nan!' She plonked herself on the brass-knobbed bed that she and Ross shared. The two cats opened their eyes, stretched, then slept again. 'What you been doing with yourself today, then?'

'Reading a little, but mostly just lying here and dreaming dreams.'

'Of being rich enough to go round the world? And being all posh and wearing jewels and – '

'No, Poppy,' Ros interrupted. 'Of living in a garden and being near flowers that smell nice. Lovely flowers of all colours, like the ones in the picture book of the countryside

6

Miss showed us at school. It must be lovely to live in the country, Poppy, and smell grass and see lots of trees and pick wild flowers. Then go and have tea in a country garden like the Winthrop children did in Mrs Bowden's book.'

'We had boring stuff about history today and I reckon Miss should have told us about the gunpowder plot instead. I wish old Guy could have got away with it. Not blowing up Parliament, though, just Skelton School!'

It worked! Ros was beginning to laugh even though it was a painful thing to do, her chest being what it was.

'Oh, shut up, Poppy! You – you are a one, you really are! What am I going to do with you?'

'You're going to be quiet now,' Poppy commanded. 'You're getting out of breath again. Tell you what, I'll read you some of my library book. It's all about this heiress who lost out on love.'

'I think Sandy Swift loves me,' Ros said softly. 'That's why he's always saying things and getting at me. He thinks I wouldn't notice him else. I always would because he's so handsome, daring and –'

'Don't be daft! He's nothing but a rotten bully. When I'm old enough I'm going to marry a millionaire.'

'And not Daniel?'

'He's too old. Besides, who'd want to marry someone who likes Jezebel Street? Don't talk any more, just keep comfy and rest while I read to you. You can go to sleep if you want.'

Poppy's tone was tender. It was an unwritten law that one was always kind and protective towards Ros who was so frail. This was Poppy's own law, made and kept faithfully. It was Nan's to be brisk and efficient at all times, to be bossy and down to earth. Her forthright, no-nonsense attitude fell like a mantle over her frightened, motherly concern. The girls understood this and were devoted to her. To please her, they kept themselves clean and decent and spoke nicely when she was about.

It was impossible, Poppy thought wickedly, to survive in a sweet and saintly manner. Or to act toffee-nosed about the lice-ridden inhabitants of the top end of Jezebel Street, especially the hordes of feuding Lambs and Kings, who were all out-and-out rogues. She quite liked some of the girls who

7

hardly had a rag to their backs. Getting stuck up in Jezebel Street? What a laugh! 'Sides, wouldn't be no fun in that! But, in front of Nan, who had strait-laced ideas about being poor but honest, and, above all, respectable, she had to behave or else!

Poppy fetched her book from the rickety chest of drawers, opened it and began to read aloud. In a very short time, engrossed and unmindful that Ros now slept, she entered into the world of the beautiful young heiress who had lost out on love . . .

It was a raw Saturday night and Jezebel Street, Leyton E.10. seemed to huddle in the shadows and wait. It was a thin, poor road flanked on either side by small houses, two up and two down with a scullery and outside lavatory apiece. As many as twelve people crammed into some of the buildings, living in squalor, clannish, lying, laughing, loud-mouthed, quarrelsome, all eking out their existences as best they could. Bottles would fly, knives come out, enmity be declared, but white flags were hoisted and they all stuck together like glue when Copper Noaks strolled into view. Unaided Noaksy and the rent man could bring about almost total emptiness in Jezebel Street. Neighbours would knock on the thin walls in times of stress: twice for the rent man, three times for Noaks. Among the kids the big policeman was feared for his strength. To get cuffed round the ears by Copper Noaks was to know it, not half!

The lower end, where Poppy lived, held houses not quite so crammed, but that was the only difference. The same green-painted lampposts sent sombre gaslight against railings, door knockers and paint-peeling front doors. The only oddity, shining dully against the horse dung outside number seven, was a petrol patch from Reggie Parker's motorbike. Rich and posh in his suit and tie he was, and in work!

Suddenly Jezebel Street was awake and quivering under its usual nightly onslaught. Liz Parker's button nose was uptilted in her small-featured face, overshadowed by the large, outrageously feathered hat she wore. Her eyes glittered like glass beads as she stormed a few paces ahead of her Spanish-looking husband.

'You're a bastard,' she called over her shoulder. 'And you're drunk. Stinking lousy drunk!'

'Why don't you shut your mouth, you stupid bitch?' Vic bawled. 'Button it before I do it for you.'

'Why should I? You're a silly old sod, making eyes at that brazen hussy what's half your age. I'm glad I blacked her eye.'

'Hark at her!' Vic yelled to the seeming emptiness about him. 'She's as ladylike as my arse.'

'Ladylike?' Liz screamed. 'Like that painted-up whore? Old as the hills she was – and no natural blonde neither.'

'She was only half me age a minute ago, and as for being natural, you're not natural at nothing. You're just a skinny, mouthy old cow!'

Liz Parker turned, swung her handbag high and brought it down with as much force as possible on Vic's cloth cap. He let out a roar and clumped her one back. She screeched at him, laying her tongue to every foul name she could think of until they reached number seven. She marched up to the front door, furiously kicked it open and stormed in, followed by the tipsily lurching head of the Parker household.

On the opposite side of the road, Poppy turned away from the curtains she'd been peeping behind. Her movement made the candle flutter and sent shadows dancing on the wall. She grinned at Ros who had stayed in bed. The cats, wrapped in her cardigan, were contentedly asleep at her side.

'Wouldn't be Saturday night without them having a go, would it? The Peels will be next, and poor little Clem will feel the ten-ton weight of Aggie's hand. Still, the Parkers and Peels aren't too bad. They rub along all right when they're not drunk. It's old man Jacobs that really scares me.'

'Poppy, come back to bed, you'll freeze!'

'I just want to watch for old man Jacobs. They say he bashes Mrs Jacobs something cruel. What poor little Lenny thinks about it all, I dread to think.'

'Poppy dear, please come back to bed,' Ros said quietly. 'I know you like watching the goings-on, but if you get your cold feet anywhere near me I think I'll curl up.'

9

'Don't say that!' Poppy's grin faded and was replaced with swift concern. 'Don't ever say that again, Ros. You know I can't bear the thought of you getting ill any more, let alone –'

'I'm sorry, dear,' Ros said. 'I didn't mean . . . Just come back to bed and cuddle me. I can't seem to get warm.'

'Wait a minute.' Poppy padded quickly over to the corner cupboard and got out her precious coat. She put it over the thin blanket for extra warmth. 'Here, this'll help.' She squeezed into the bed, carefully keeping her feet away from Ros. 'Are you sleepy or shall we talk?'

'Talk.'

'What about?'

'Anything you like. Best blow the candle out first, though. You know how Mum is about saving on candles.'

'What she don't know can't –'

'Poppy!'

'Oh, I'll read a bit, to justify the candle.' Poppy leaned over and picked up her book. 'Not that I can for too long. I've got to get up earlier tomorrow. Nan said I don't help enough, so that means I'll be handed the scrubbing brush first thing – after Charlie's, of course.'

'You don't have to go to Charlie's so regular.'

'Oh, I don't mind, not really. And every little helps.'

'Know something, Poppy?' Ros said quietly and reached out to take Poppy's hand. 'You try to act all hard and tough, but you're really kind and sweet and warm.'

'Come off it. I'm freezing cold!'

'Then cuddle up to me.'

'And turn you into a block of ice too? Don't be daft.' She smiled as Ros snuggled up and closed her eyes. Poppy opened her library book and forgot about everything else. The fictional world was full of sunshine, riches and beautiful places as different from Jezebel Street as chalk from cheese.

Every so often, reality intruded. It was cold, even with the coat on top of the blanket. Anxiously Poppy looked over at Ros, who was lying on her back and breathing more harshly. Her lovely face was too thin. Impulsively, Poppy leaned over and kissed her sleeping cousin on the forehead. 'Sweet dreams, Ros,' she whispered. 'I hope as how you're walking among all them beautiful flowers you like so much.'

10

A dog barked in the distance; a cat yowled like a banshee and Poppy sighed, relieved that Josh and Jo were safe inside. A train thundered over the railway arch that spanned Leyton High Road, and far in the distance there came the clattering noises of trains being shunted in Temple Mills Yard. Then the hate-filled, raucous voice of Mike Jacobs cut through the night like razor blades.

Poppy shivered, put down her book and blew the candle out. 'I hate it,' she whispered. 'One day I'll be rich and get you away from here, Ros. Just you wait and see.'

She nudged the sleeping girl just hard enough to make her turn. Mercifully the laboured breathing became easier. Poppy tried to concentrate on the glamorous pictures left in her mind by the book. But it was fiction and suddenly fiction was not enough.

Next morning Poppy went downstairs to the kitchen, where Aunt Nan was already kneeling before the grate sifting cinders. Nan looked older than her thirty-one years. She had worked as a skivvy from the time she had been old enough to carry buckets of coal. The life had made her tough. Her aqua eyes could glare as hard as glass. Her ginger hair was pulled back from her handsome face and pinned in a bun on the top of her head. There were few people with courage enough to mess with Nan, and the whole world knew it when her blood was up. She had the Irish paddy from her grandfolks, people said, and she didn't need no gin to help her say her piece neither. Her brother Charlie was a good'un, but Nan!

Nan looked across the room at Poppy. 'Is she asleep?'

'Yes, and breathing easy. Aunt Nan, sometimes I look at her and . . . and –'

'Stop that nonsense,' Nan said fiercely. 'Work it off, that's best. And don't give me that down-in-the-mouth look. Pull yourself together, girl. Doc Fox says she can go back to school tomorrow, so that shows she's all right.'

'I want to stay at home and not go to Charlie's this morning. I want to be with Ros – if you don't mind.'

'Mind? Why should I? You're a good girl and you do your best, and no one can do more. Ros likes you to be near when she's not been too well. She reckons you cheer her up. Proper

11

peas in a pod, you two are. Mind you, if you don't stop acting like you're scared for her and pull yourself together, I'll give you the back of my hand. She needs a smiling face, not two penn'orth of cold cod.'

When Ros came down there was a fire burning in the grate, freshly dolly-dyed curtains at the kitchen window and the smell of lavender polish that had made a gleaming mirror of the lino on the floor. The orange chrysanthemums on the wallpaper seemed to glow.

Laughing and chatting while she whisked about doing chores, Poppy tried to blot the fear from her mind. Ros's breathing the night before had been awful to listen to, yet the fear that the rattling might stop had been even worse. As she scuttled past her cousin, black polish for the range in her hand, Ros caught hold of her. 'Stop it, Poppy,' she said, too quietly for Nan to hear. 'You're wearing yourself out with all your thoughts.'

'I can't help it. It's sums on Mondays,' Poppy lied, 'and you know how I hate divisions and mental arithmetic. I always get the answers wrong. I can't wait to reach fourteen and leave school!'

'I'm all right, Poppy,' Ros said in her breathless, earnest way. 'I'm like a creaking gate, and every one knows they last longest and best. Doc Fox says I'm all better now, and I really am. Cheer up! I want you to sit and help me with the darning after dinner, and tell me all about that posh mansion you mean to live in one day.'

'Posh mansions need cleaning,' Nan said tartly as she came in from the scullery. 'And it's hard enough to get you two scrubbing and polishing this place, let alone mansions. Don't have idle hands, Ros. The way you go about things, the darning will take all day.'

Nan's normal brusque manner was so reassuring that Poppy started singing as she went about completing her chores.

Poppy swung towards her father's shop early on Monday morning. She was in a rage and it suited her. It sent her chin high and added sparkle to her eyes. Tossing her head made her mane of shining hair fly out. The bedroom had been

12

freezing all night and she had found herself almost hating Flossie for buying that oil stove. Much better if it had been bought for Ros. It was always hard for Ros to breathe this time of the year. It was wicked being poor, wicked!

I hate being poverty-stricken, Poppy thought, anger mixed with anguish as she remembered Doc Fox going on about Ros's health and the need for a warmer climate. He knew as well as they did how out of the question that was. Of course Ros needed pure, warm air to breathe! Of course she needed to be pampered and spoiled! But she was a child of Jezebel Street and luxuries were out.

As Poppy made to turn into Charlie's back yard, which was situated at the end of the road, she collided with Daniel Devere, who lodged with Flossie. Tall, dark-haired and bearded, Daniel was good-looking and had extraordinarily blue eyes. He worked on the railway and had done so for six years since he'd left school at fourteen. An orphan, Daniel had once been known as the boy from the Home.

Poppy and Daniel had a love–hate relationship. She was still a kid, he a grown man. She loathed him when he ignored her, admired him when she saw him poring over clever-dick books, quite liked him most times, but this was Monday and hate day. She glared up at him and, making only the sketchiest of apologies, flounced through the wooden gate that was hanging drunkenly on its hinges.

The smell of stale cabbage leaves, overripe fruit, wooden crates and sawdust filled her nostrils. Her mouth turned down at the corners as she went into the yard. When she had cleaned it up, everything looked fine, but her father just didn't care. The biting wind was scuffling up the small coloured tissue squares that oranges had been wrapped in. Straw, dust and small strips of paper packing were flying through the air.

'Charlie,' she called out to her father, 'when are you going to keep this lot tidy? Charlie! Do you hear me, Charlie?'

Her father, stringy-looking and weather-worn with thinning light-brown hair, opened the heavily peeling back door and grinned amiably. He was wearing a brown check cloth cap, a dark shabby overcoat and trousers that were very shiny and baggy at the knees. His boots had holes in the soles

13

and had never seen a lick of polish. Charlie's feet pained him at times, but, as he said, 'it weren't all bad' since they'd kept him out of the war.

'Keep your hair on, ducky,' he said. 'They can hear you yelling all down bloody Beaumont Lane.'

'I don't care, Charlie,' she flared at him. 'You told me to clean up and I did. I think you enjoy just throwing things down and mucking up everything I do. Look at this place. It's knee deep!'

His easy grin flashed out again. 'Cor, you don't half flap your lip. Only thirteen, yet you're going on like a proper bloody fishwife. You watch it, ducky. I might just tan your arse for you.'

'And then you wouldn't see me for dust.' She bent down, impatiently grabbing at a tattered sheet of newspaper that had swirled round her legs. 'What would you do then, eh? I don't know who else would half kill themselves doing what I do. Slave labour, that's me.'

'For Christ's sake put a sock in it, Poppy. I've just got back from Stratford and I want me cuppa. Gawd, you don't half go on! Like a dripping tap you are. You're getting to be too big for your boots, like Nan.'

'And why shouldn't I be?' Poppy's hands were on her hips now. 'She brought me up, didn't she?' She stepped fiercely towards him. 'And what's more, I'll tell you this. Number two Jezebel Street's never been the pigsty this is.'

'I'll clip your ear if you don't shut up,' Charlie warned without malice. 'If you upset my Clary, I swear I'll take my belt to you, old as you are – and don't glare. Them stinking looks you're so good at don't cut no ice with me. Now come on in, or else sod off. It's up to you.'

He turned his back and went inside. Poppy followed, liking him enormously, for all his sister Nan was wont to call him rough and uncouth. Charlie would shout and carry on, and threaten all sorts of terrible things. Quite a waste of time really, since he wouldn't harm a fly. He was a good sort, and closed his eyes to the fact that hordes of Lamb and King kids habitually raided his back yard to rifle through his bins of waste. An orange going off, a bruised apple, outer cabbage leaves that had been stripped, cauliflower greens, anything

14

and everything edible was niftily spirited away and handed over to sallow-cheeked mums. Poppy liked Charlie's girlfriend Clary, too, big, blowsy and buxom, with twinkling eyes and straight mouse-coloured hair.

Charlie flopped down onto a wooden chair by the fire in the small back kitchen, not bothering to take off cap or coat. Poppy winced inwardly. Nan would have had Charlie's cap off his head so fast he'd wonder what hit him. But Nan was on her hands and knees, scrubbing the floors of the children's home that was situated almost opposite Skelton School.

Charlie was a law unto himself. Perhaps he could be forgiven. After all, Poppy thought, he'd been up since five and it had taken him nearly two hours to push his laden barrow back from Stratford Market.

Rags, Charlie's black and grey mongrel, padded in from the scullery. Rags had long hair that moulted all over the place, but no one seemed to mind. The dog flopped down at Charlie's feet and rested his head on splodgy paws. Clary came bustling in. On her battered tin tray were mugs of hot sweet tea and a plate of doorstep-thick slices of toast oozing with fresh-roll margarine. She plonked the tray down on the table and wiped her reddened hands on her flowered pinafore.

'Here you are, get this down you – and Poppy, stop glaring at your dad like that. Gawd, it's monkey's outside. I can't say as how I'm looking forward to sorting out them cabbages. Choked up with ice, they are.'

'I'll help,' Poppy offered, biting into a slice. 'Clary, you don't half make nice toast.'

'And you don't half go on,' Clary said fondly. 'Anyone would think they don't make it in your house.'

'We don't have all that much time,' Poppy explained. 'Kneeling in front of the range is cosy evening-times, with Ros and me taking turns with the toasting fork. But it takes too long in the mornings. You're lucky to have a gas stove with a grill.'

'Oh, my Gawd!' The older woman laughed and went out to the scullery that had a chipped stone sink full of dirty crockery, a copper full of washing waiting to be done, and a huge pan of beetroot bubbling away on the stove. There was muddle everywhere. Drawers were spilling over with raffia, elastic bands, sheets of white tissue and balls of string. Charlie always came back from the market with flowers at weekends. Sunday mornings would find him outside Whips Cross Hospital gates, selling his wares. He did a roaring trade and was well known for his humour. 'Charlie's always the same,' his customers said.

'Come on, Poppy, move that rabbit's bum of your'n,' Charlie hustled. 'We ain't got all day and I want to get this lot sorted before Bill gets here with them potted chrysanths he grows so nice.'

'Has he said much, Charlie?' Poppy asked.

'What, about his dad dropping dead? No. Bill Bannerman's never been a one for words, but you can tell how cut up he is. Still, he's been running that small holding alone for years, so he won't be working no harder on account of not having his old man around.'

Charlie, lugging a sack of potatoes, followed the carrot-bearing Poppy into the shop. Clary staggered in behind them, holding net bags full of brussels sprouts. They worked together in companionable silence. Filling bins, stripping cabbages of their yellowing outer leaves, sorting over the fruit. It was a comfy little shop with green paintwork and strips of fake grass covering the shelves. Bill Bannerman's potted ferns at sixpence a time made things look cheery, and the scales were polished and burnished until they looked like gold. The lead weights stood one on top of the other, making a little pyramid, ready and waiting for use. In the private domain behind was one thing, but the shop was something else. Here everything was colourful and scrupulously clean.

Bill Bannerman turned up, carefully setting down his barrow in the kerb. Watching him through the window, Poppy liked what she saw. Bill was tall and spare and gentle in manner. He had greying hair and eyes that looked like those of a sailor who had been gazing into faraway seas. Bill's face was craggy and weathered, his hands large and capable. He had always been a solitary man. He and his father had been close, had shut themselves in together in grief when Mrs Bannerman died many years before. Now old Zeb Bannerman was gone, too, and pondering on death, the fear of losing someone dear, made Poppy begin to shake inside. Outwardly busy, polishing apples, she remembered how it was that she had come to work for Charlie.

It had been a year ago and the weather had been spiteful, too freezing even for the children of Jezebel Street to play outside. Poppy had stood on the step watching Dr Fox's car turning the corner. Ros had been inside the car, and Aunt Nan. There had been no time to lose, for Ros was at death's door with rheumatic fever, they said. She had been ill a very long time. She had needed extra things, and it had been arranged that Poppy should help Charlie, the money she earned going direct to Nan. Poppy had leaped at the chance, needing to help in any way she could, and also to have an excuse to be near her dad. These days Ros was well enough to go back to school. She attended classes on and off, but her illness had left her with a weak and unstable heart.

'Hurry it up, ducks!' Charlie's voice broke in on her thoughts. 'I don't want no bloody school-board bloke after me.'

'I'd back you against him any day,' she quipped. 'Ta-ta for now then.'

She waved a quick goodbye to Clary and left.

Chapter Two

The dull light made Jezebel Street look meaner than usual. Poppy began to run home and hurried inside, straight upstairs to see Ros. Ros was still in bed, lovingly stroking Josh and Jo, who sneaked into the bedroom at every opportunity. The two girls winked at each other – as always, at one. Like twin souls, Ros said, and Poppy wholeheartedly agreed. It was then that Nan's voice rang out.

'If you don't get down here fast, I'll be up after you. D'you hear me?'

'Won't be a minute,' Poppy called. As Ros eased herself out of the bed and the cats jumped down, Poppy quickly pulled the bedclothes straight.

'I mean it, you two!'

Ros was brushing her navy-blue cardigan, which the cats had slept on. She was beginning to breathe too quickly, her face growing pink with effort.

'Here, give it to me,' Poppy said and snatched the cardigan away. 'She'll be up here, all guns blazing, in a minute. I hate it when she goes on about Josh and Jo. Don't stand there! I'll sort this lot out. I've got more knack at it than you.'

'But she'll – '

'Hop it!'

Ros raised her hands in an exaggerated gesture, then went downstairs to face her mother, who was never happy first thing.

Nan sat before the bravely glowing kitchen range. The two cats were now lovingly weaving round her feet. She was frowning and her eyes looked fuzzy, as they always did when her head ached. But she sat straight-backed; her down-at-heel shoes were neatly polished, and her feet set square on the orange and green coconut matting. No matter now often it was taken up, shaken and brushed, it always had a pattern of dust on the dark-green lino under it. The wooden table in the centre of the room was covered with a brown velvet cloth that boasted a bobble fringe. The built-in dresser held Nan's prized pieces of china, things that Ros was terrified of dropping when she cleaned and polished the pretty plates and ornaments Nan had picked up second-hand over the years. Ros 'did' the dresser once a week. It was Poppy's chore to black-lead the kitchen range and rub the fender with emery paper till it gleamed like silver in the light. Both girls shared the polishing of chairs and the corner table that held the aspidistra. Big and splendid, the plant was, and Nan wiped its leaves and made them shine. The bowl it stood in was green china with daisy pattern, the flowers echoing the hearth that had been stoned pristine white.

'It's worry that kills,' Nan always said, 'not hard work. You work for what you want in this world, and every little thing that you bring home is like a gift from God.'

Nan's 'gift from God' was to have the best, the prettiest, and most certainly the cleanest house in Jezebel Street. And she was determined to keep it that way.

'You'll be late and have to rush,' Nan said through gritted teeth. 'Where's Poppy? She got her nose stuck in her book again?'

'No, Mum. She'll be down soon. Don't get so worked up about things. Oh, dear, you've got one of your heads, I can tell.'

'It's no good trying to soft-soap me, my girl. Where's your woolly? Envy of everyone round here, them woollies are. No wonder they call us the toffs of Jezebel Street.' Nan smiled frostily. 'Though a few more as I could mention could dress their kids better than they do. You can get an almost decent skirt for a penny up Ginny's Old Clothes, and there's always plenty of good bits in them to cut out and use for make do and mend. But the women of this street are too busy, like most of their men, getting sodden with beer to waste even a penny on something as boring as making their kids look clean and decent.'

Hard work and making do was Nan's hobbyhorse. Her Coleman's mustard tins had been labelled by the girls, each with a coloured sticker to show the money they held: blue for the rent, black for the coal, and so on. Distinct colours were necessary, for Nan couldn't read.

'I'd hate to count how many doorsteps I've scrubbed how and much washing I've taken in to pay for them woollies,' Nan went on. 'Took me all of a year to save up for – ' suddenly she stopped speaking, narrowed her emerald eyes and looked animal-fierce. 'Where is it? If you've lost it or had it pinched, I'll kill you!'

Unperturbed, Ros smoothed down her clean but threadbare grey dress and admitted, 'Poppy's brushing it.'

'You've had the cats up there again!' Nan exploded. 'Fleas and all. You've had them on the bed! I'll limb the pair of you before I'm through, and I'll wring their scraggy necks while I'm at it.'

'Mum, you love them as much as we do,' Ros pointed out and smiled. 'And they certainly make a great fuss of you. Just look at them!'

'They know what side their bread's buttered, that's why,' Nan snapped. 'You pamper them, I'll grant, but it's me that pays for their food and cleans up after them if they make a mess. Oh yes, the nasty bits are left to me all right. And don't you try to change the subject, miss! You should look after your woolly like it's made of gold. You'll die the death else. It's freezing outside.'

'Mum, why are you carrying on so?' Ros asked gently. 'You're moaning and groaning, and not stopping to take breath, and making your headache a million times worse. As for the cold, it looks as though it's you that'll freeze. Look at yourself!'

It was a long speech for Ros and Nan pulled herself up short. She tucked her black cotton blouse inside the waistband of her ankle-length black skirt with quick impatience.

'The rate I work,' she said tartly, 'I'll be sweating hot in two shakes.' She got up from her chair and took a furious step towards the green-painted kitchen door, 'Poppy!'

Poppy's feet pounded down the stairs. She burst into the kitchen and threw the long cardigan to Ros asking blithely, 'Can I have a slice? I'm starving.'

'You don't look like you're fading away,' Nan replied. 'And it's a pound to a penny that you've been stuffing yourself with toast.'

'Nan!'

'All right! The things are set out and ready – and hurry up. You know Ros gets breathless if she has to rush. Don't forget to go easy on the marge.'

'Can I have jam?'

'If you go without margarine. We're not made of money, you know.'

Poppy went into the scullery. There was half a loaf on the scrubbed wooden table, half a cup of jam, tea already made in a blue enamel pot, a tin of condensed milk and three white enamel mugs. Poppy poured tea, added a teaspoonful of condensed milk and took their mugs into Ros and Nan. While they began to drink she went back into the scullery, cut a generous slice of bread and spread it with apricot jam. Jam was purchased from Dondu's Corner Shop at a penny a cupful. That or a quarter of bright pink fish paste was a luxury. Sometimes Nan bought fish paste for Sunday tea.

'I hope you don't make a mess with crumbs. I've just cleaned up out there,' Nan called. 'And get a move on. The tea's all but cold, but the kettle's reached to boiling point in here. Hurry up!'

Poppy took the dishcloth from the old stone sink and wiped up the crumbs. She liked the scullery with its stone floor; she liked to see the blue enamel saucepans hanging on the whitewashed walls, and the colander and the heavy old black frying pan. She drank her tea and wrapped the slice of bread in a sheet of paper, hiding it under the bosom of her cardigan. Nan had paid Flossie to knit a replica of Ros's one, warm, long and thick. The woollies were treasures and saved wear and tear on the girls' coats – coats that were used mainly for Sunday best.

'Poppy!' Nan was near to exploding.

21

'I'm here!' Poppy called blithely and stepped back into the kitchen, innocence itself.

Once outside, Poppy and Ros crossed the street, slowing as they reached little Lenny, who was already sitting hunched up on the step, his newly mended crutches leaning against the door behind him. He had thrown them at the King boy who had been seeing how far away he could stand and still hit him with his wee. Poppy had stopped all that, and clumped the King kid round the head so hard he'd blubbed.

As always, Lenny looked pinch-faced and cold. His cheek was grazed. Lenny never moaned even though his life was tougher than most simply because he couldn't fight back.

'Is she looking?' Poppy whispered.

Ros shook her head. Poppy gave the slice of bread and jam to Lenny.

'Here,' she said casually. 'It was left over from breakfast and I didn't want to give it to the cats. Anyway they hate jam.'

Lenny's cheeks went pink, but his small clawlike hands reached out to snatch Poppy's offering.

The two girls left him sitting there. Walking arm in arm, they turned into Skelton Street, past a few dilapidated houses, to the school. Running behind the school, at the High Road end, stretched Lowerie's jam factory. There was the mica works further on, and the stained-glass place. Workers used the alleyway in Skelton Street to get to their jobs, so it was usually full of people coming and going to school or work.

'Oh! Is that the nine-o'clock train?' Ros was startled by a noise from the railway line.

'Don't start rushing.' Poppy's voice held quick alarm. 'It's not the nine-o'clock and it wouldn't be the end of the world if it was. There are too many people about for us to be late.'

'Listen!'

Poppy obediently remained silent while Ros strained her ears. To the north, crossing the High Road, towered the railway arch. The sound of train engines, wheels click-clacking over the rails, the hissing of steam and showers of sparks were part and parcel of everyday life. The area all round the railway arch was poor. Some of the small houses were appallingly wretched, but the hordes of scruffy children did not seem to mind.

'I told you! We've got bags of time, Ros.' She pointed to the young people ambling along. Some of the boys were kicking against the pavement, making the metal blakeys on their boots send out sparks. Others, grinning, dropped cap-bangers behind the girls, making them shriek. There were a great many vulgar remarks flying around.

'Don't walk so quick, Ros.' Poppy was unable to hide her fear. 'There's no need.'

Ros wasn't listening. Her eyes were hurt, her lips trembled. 'Look at that, Poppy. My best friend, who didn't even bother to call for me. She must have passed our house to knock for Grant Parker!'

'Come off it,' Poppy replied. 'Girls don't knock for boys. They've probably just met up.'

'Jessica has knocked for him. I saw her when I was being kept home. She knocked when all the Parkers were at work and – and she went in!'

'Just wait till playtime,' Poppy said darkly. 'I ain't half going to thump her one for upsetting you.'

'For goodness' sake!'

'I thought she was your best friend. To think she passed and didn't give us a knock. She's not even looking round to see if we're coming. She's always busy making sheep's eyes at the boys and Grant Parker takes after his dad where looks and women are concerned.'

'It doesn't matter, Poppy!'

'It does! 'Cos it matters to you! And who cares about boys anyway? Making a fool of herself, she is. Why she can't wait to go to work at Lowerie's, I'll never know. They say they're regular matchmakers up there. I wonder who you'll choose, Ros?' Poppy was working hard, trying to take the hurt away from Ros's eyes. 'Sandy Swift?'

'I won't be working in a factory, Mum told me,' Ros said tiredly. 'Perhaps I could manage to serve in a shop. Jessica will really resent me then. You know she's always believed you and me to be too la-di-da for words. She thinks we're rich because Mum keeps the house so spic-and-span, and we have curtains.'

23

'I don't think we'll ever be that, whatever we do,' Poppy burst out. 'And that's a fact! There won't be no diamonds and furs for the likes of us.' Poppy's cheeks burned with frustration. 'Being poor but honest and working like dogs is all very well, but Jess never seems to wear stockings with darns. Her heels are always as smooth as glass.'

'She's not heavy on her stockings, that's all.'

'Ha! She gets farthings and sometimes even halfpennies for sweets off the boys – and we all know how! Letting them feel inside her drawers and – '

'All fibs! She's not like her sister, Poppy, and she hates her terrible old dad. In any case – '

'Now you're sticking up for her as usual.' Poppy groaned. 'Why you're so fond of her I'll never know.'

Ros was not listening. She was beginning to breathe too heavily and Poppy slowed her pace, letting others run past them.

They reached the playground just as the whistle blew and took their places in line. Jessica was standing in front. Poppy leaned forward and pulled her hair hard.

'You cow!' Jessica's small dark eyes flashed as she swung round, her clenched hand raised.

'Upset Ros again,' Poppy said, coldly and quietly, 'and I'll kill you.'

Black eyes glinted into furious green. It was Jessica who turned away.

'I don't want you to fight my battles for me.' Ros's tone was pained. 'Honestly, Poppy, she can't help the way she is.'

As she went to her seat, Poppy wanted to burst with indignation. Ros was almost cross with her, and sticking up for Jess! It hurt so much that she was glad that Miss had Ros sitting quietly in the front of class, where she could keep a kind eye on her. Ros had suffered bad turns in school before, nothing too much, but Miss thought it best to be on the safe side.

At dinner time the girls, privileged on account of Ros's heart, were allowed to stay in the school hall to eat their dinner. It was bread and onion dripping. Nan made it once a week, rendering down scraps of fat from the butcher's and cooking onions in it – very tasty it was too. Jessica sat with them and wolfed down the half-slice that Ros left. In spite of Ros's determination to bring Poppy into their conversation, she felt left out.

Poppy was glad when four o'clock came and freedom at last. Ros decided to stay at Jessica's house, so Poppy ran home alone, having refused point-blank to join them. She placed the doormat on the step, so that her skirt wouldn't get heathstone stains, and sat down to read. Although it was warmer in the kitchen, she felt it was the least she could do, to sit opposite Lenny in a silent, companionable way.

Lenny waved and she waved back, thinking that he looked as though he had not moved. However, she knew that Mrs Jacobs ran all the way home from the wash-house every day to see to him. Then the poor down-trodden woman went back to work, and did not return for good until after five o'clock. She had never been accepted by the Jacobs crew on account of her Polack blood, and for the same reason Lenny was ignored by the whole bunch of them.

There were many women on their doorsteps, gossiping or rowing as the mood took them. They wore cloth caps and hessian aprons or wrap-round overalls. Some had rags in their hair to make it frizz out, others had tied it in tight little brown-paper screws to get an even better effect. Most had merely bound their locks in untidy bunches on the tops of their heads, ends hanging loose.

Suddenly fat Mrs Peel from top end bawled out, 'Stop that, 'Arry! You leave her alone!'

Poppy rested her book on her knees and watched and listened with interest. Harry, near Poppy's age, pasty-faced, skinny and with ferrety eyes, glared and shouted back.

'She pulled my hair.'

'Julie's smaller than you.'

'I don't care. She pulled my hair and kicked me up the arse.'

'Lip me again, you little perisher' – Mrs Peel was clomping steadily down the street towards him – 'and you won't have no arse left to kick.'

Harry thumped his sister hard and ran off laughing while Julie lay in the middle of the road and screamed. Aggie Peel stomped over, her massive weight full behind her hand as she lifted her daughter and smacked her backside.

'Kick him again and I'll knock your block off, d'you hear?'

'But he – '

'Shut your gob, Julie, I've had about enough for one day.' She looked over and saw Poppy. 'Keep an eye on her for me, ducks. I've gotta get up the High Road to the shops – and if that little bleeder comes back while I'm gone, you tell him his father's going to hear all about this!'

Poppy sighed and waited while the now quiet Julie joined her. Mrs Peel waddled off and Julie poked out her tongue at her mother's back and hissed, 'Old cow!' Then she looked up, smirking. 'You're a soft touch, ain't you? You stick up for that stupid cripple kid opposite, and change the Wellses' library books for nothing and' – here Julie's smirk all but twisted her face in half – 'an' on top of that you look after me when Mum asks, and don't tell me to bugger off the moment her back's turned.' She shivered. 'Oi! It'll freeze the feathers off a duck's arse out here. Can I come in your house?'

To have her in would be in direct defiance of Aunt Nan's orders about riffraff entering her home. Poppy sighed and closed her book. She was not specially fond of Julie, but she knew that Mrs Peel would be gone for hours. She began wishing that she had let go of her own stupid pride and gone to Jessica's place with Ros. She waved to Lenny and opened the street door.

'Nice in here, ain't it?' Julie said as they walked through the passage and entered the kitchen. 'All posh like. We've got newspaper on our'n.' She took a swipe at the table cloth to make the bobbles swing. 'My house is nice as yours anyway. Got table and chairs, we have, and coal in the grate, which is more'n than them rotten Kings and Lambs have. I hate them all. They get drunk and pick on my dad when he's too boozed to stand up to them. I hate 'em all, 'specially their farting kids at school. I hate school! I hate everyone. Do you?'

'I don't like Reverend Rawlins very much,' Poppy admitted.

'I like Sunday School. Oi! Can't you put the poker in the fire? It's almost out.'

26

'No, it isn't. It's kept like that, just smouldering till Nan gets back.'

'What she don't know . . .' Julie had made herself comfortable in Nan's chair set near the range. Poppy poked the fire, then, using the iron prod, lifted the circular lid on top of the range and shovelled in a few knobs of coal. She replaced the small shovel in the matching brass scuttle standing at the side of the hearth. 'That's nice!' Julie's brown eyes reflected the flames as her thin face relaxed in a smile, then, 'Why don't you like Rev Rawlins? He says what God loves everyone, even us! I reckon as how God's a good'un.'

Poppy could not explain to Julie that when it boiled down to it, she was rather afraid of God. She thought Him cruel with all that talk about an eye for an eye. It didn't add up to that bit about turning the other cheek at all. Then again, all the begats didn't go along with Adam and Eve getting it in the neck for eating the apple and putting on clothes! Surely wearing clothes was part of the fun? Because getting one's knickers pulled down by boys was a sure way of begatting, if all the whispers at school were true.

God had a hawk-nosed, skinny face like Rev Rawlins, she was sure of it. The tall pompous old Reverend went on and on about God forgiving sins and dishing out mercy. Aunt Nan couldn't give a brass farthing about mercy. All she had needed was an extra shilling or two to buy more coal to keep things warm and comfy for Ros. God was a bit of a flop Poppy thought, especially since as well as little sparrows He was also responsible for everyone in Jezebel Street . . .

It was a raw evening blanketed by mist. Lights from High Road shop windows sent pathways of light into darkness, but deep impenetrable black shrouded the warrenlike alley beside the Coach and Horses. The pub's forecourt held a group of the rougher kids from Jezebel Street. They were begging, their guy a small spindly thing with a terrible slit-eyed brown-paper face. Thick black lashes had been painted all round the eyes and a red mouth ran crookedly from ear to ear. An old cloth cap perched on top of the guy's head, its lower half covered with an old sack. It was sitting in a barrow made from an orange box on wheels. Tonight was pay night

27

for some, and there might be a hand-out – it was worth a try. An ancient grey-bearded organ grinder hoped so too. He shuffled into position near the door, his heavy instrument slung round his neck. His rheumy fingers began to turn the handle. Only a spindly note or two emerged before Harry Peel sauntered over, hands in pockets, leering in an evil way.

'Sod off!' he said.

The organ grinder stayed where he was.

'I said' – Harry stepped even nearer and jutted out his chin menacingly – 'sod off!'

The children behind him began to snigger. Their leader was not going to have his own way, it seemed. Incensed, Harry took the one further step necessary and kicked the old man hard on his shin. The old man groaned and began to weep, and the children clustered round him, jeering and catcalling, leaving their guy hunched up in the barrow that held the legend, 'CRIPPEL FROM THE WAR'.

'You leave him alone!' A fierce cry stung like a whiplash through the hubbub they were making. 'D'you hear me? Leave him alone!'

Poppy, with her arms full of library books, ran up to them, her eyes brilliant in her fury. 'You rotten cowards, leave him alone!'

'Who d'yer think you are?' Harry, almost as tall as she, turned away from the organ grinder to glare into her angry face. His thin lips went down. 'I'll kick your arse for you if you don't watch out.'

'I dare you!' she taunted. 'You're only good for hitting old men and little sisters, but you haven't got the guts to try anything on me.'

'Wanna bet?' Harry was bolstered up by the presence of his minions and he was not going to give an inch. 'It'd be easy to flatten you and your'n. Nan Eden's a snot, and as for that half-dead cousin of your'n, I reckon – '

With an impassioned shriek, Poppy let her library books fall and she was on to Harry like a ball of fury. But she was one, his gang many, and she was getting hit and pushed back helplessly against the wall. The organ grinder shuffled along, slipped round the corner and into the alley, out of harm's way. Poppy gasped as someone hit her hard. She wanted to

28

cry with rage. Then she heard someone yell out, 'You rotters, let her be!'

A tall, well-made youth with sandy hair was wading in. The teasing, twinkling arrogance he had when he and Poppy battled at school was gone from his nice-looking face. Now his expression was set, cold and angry.

'Get aht of it,' Harry bawled. 'This ain't nothing to do with you.'

A well-aimed punch at Harry's nose showed that Sandy Swift thought it had plenty to do with him. In an instant, new bedlam was breaking loose on the forecourt. And then Daniel Devere came up, a stern young man who looked ready for business. It was too much. Harry Peel and his gang of ragamuffins fled.

'I want to go home!' Lenny's reedy wail came from behind the brown-paper face. 'I want me mum.'

'That does it!' Poppy lifted a furious face into Daniel's. 'Just wait till I see Aggie Peel.' She ran over to Lenny, almost sobbing in anguish when she saw what they had done to him. He had been tied into the orange box too tightly to move, the coarse string biting into his thin, twisted legs. 'Don't stand there, Daniel. Help me!'

Daniel looked down at her, bemused. She was so young and sweet. Oh yes, he understood her very well and always had. While reading or thinking, when relaxed, the real Poppy showed through. The fiery youngster most people saw was Poppy fighting against the world, always battling against the hurt and humiliation of being unwanted by her father. Poppy standing toe to toe with life in the only way she knew. In fact, Poppy had a chip on her shoulder a mile high. One day, he promised himself, when she's old enough, I'll take care of her. There cannot and never will be anyone else.

'Daniel!' All her exasperation showed through.

'*I* will,' Sandy Swift said quickly. 'Or I'll go after them if you like.'

'It's all right,' Poppy replied. 'I'll sort it – and Sandy, thanks!'

'Don't matter,' he said casually. 'I owed Harry Peel one, that's all.'

Poppy watched as he walked away towards the turning

29

into Beaumont Lane. He walked with a springy step, wide-shouldered, slim-hipped, rather like his good-looking dad who spent long months away in the merchant navy. Freddy Swift always seemed to be laughing and joking when he came home, but he could and often did down a pint a minute in the pub. And one day Sandy was going to go into the merchant navy, too, and be just like his father.

'I'll carry the poor little devil,' Daniel said. 'It might help to get him warm. Put your books in the cart and bring it back with you. Stop mooning after Sandy. I thought you called him "Bullyboy" and hated him on sight?' He was smiling as he lifted the frozen Lenny out of the cart.

Poppy was still lost in thought.

'Come on, Poppy, don't stand there gawping,' Daniel prompted. 'This young whippersnapper's all but dead with the cold.'

Poppy hastily gathered up her books and took hold of the orange-box barrow.

'I wonder who this belongs to?' she asked as she began to drag it along behind her so that she could walk alongside Daniel. 'It's only a rough old home-made thing. I mean, oughtn't we to leave it here? Just in case?'

'In case Mr Tilsby asks for it?' he teased.

'Yes.' She played up to him. 'Wouldn't want him to go broke, would we?' Poppy was smiling rosily now, and twinkling up into Daniel's blue eyes. 'Poor old Mr Tilsby!'

Everyone knew how rich Mr Tilsby was. He owned a taxi firm and still had two hansom cabs in use, but the motorcar was the modern and by far the posher thing. It was Poppy's dream to have a ride in a motor vehicle, but Mr Tilsby charged the earth. Reggie Parker was his top driver, having been a dispatch rider in the war. Unlike Liz and Vic Parker, their eldest son did not drink. In his free time he just went off for rides in the country on his motorcycle. The neighbours thought the war had left him a bit strange. Nothing made him laugh and he never even went to the pictures. Only someone round the bend would pass up the chance of seeing stars like Charlie Chaplin and Laurel and Hardy.

There came a sob muffled against Daniel's work-blackened jacket. 'They made me do it,' Lenny wept. 'I didn't want to, but they made me!'

'Never mind, matey,' Daniel told him. 'I'll get you warmed up and with a cuppa inside you. Perhaps we'll even find you a slice of bread and jam. Then, when you're all safe and sound, I'll take you back to your mum. Poppy will go and tell her where you are.'

'Oh, but – ' she began, but he smiled down at her.

'Don't worry, Poppy, his dad's not there and neither are the rest of the Jacobses. I know because I saw them outside the Blackbirds pub as I came home.'

'Don't want no bread,' Lenny wailed. 'I want me mum!'

'All right, old son,' Daniel told him. 'I'll take you to her right away.'

On the corner that turned into Jezebel Street there was another group of young people with a guy. This one was bigger and better than poor Lenny had been, and sporting one of Liz's feathered hats. Poppy saw that Harry Peel and some of the others had now joined up with Grant. With them, watching, were Ros and Jess. Just then Vic came by, his face and hands black with his day's work of delivering coal.

Grant shrank back, but Harry Peel was made of sterner stuff. He rattled a cocoa tin that had a slit cut in its lid and yelled, 'Gotta penny for the guy, mister? Gotta penny for the guy?'

Vic glared and hunched his shoulders against a sudden gust of cold air. A pall of thick, dark mist began to swirl round. It would be a peasouper soon and no mistake. Of all things, Vic hated fog. Harry tried again, fiercely rattling the button in his tin and saying in an ingratiating way, 'A ha'penny will do. Only a ha'penny for the guy, mister? A ha'penny will do.'

'Buzz off!' Vic growled.

'Cor! You're an 'ard one, mister. How abart a farthing then?' The cocoa tin was now being waved almost under Vic's nose and Vic lost his temper.

'I'll clump you round the ear'ole, you little perisher!' he yelled, and his eyes, ringed with coal dust, glared ferociously. 'I told yer, sod off!'

Harry backed away, scowling, as Vic marched into Jezebel Street. Julie came out of the darkened shop doorway where

31

she had been hiding. She was sniggering, her dark eyes sparking with malicious delight. Daniel, ignoring them all, had continued on the way home. Harry jutted out his chin and told the rest of the grinning or gawping watchers, 'Well, at least I asked, which is more'n most of you'd dare do. Stingy ol' swine, I've a good mind to chuck something through his letter box. Something that'll stink the place out. I'd do it too if — '

'If it wasn't for the fact that your mum's threatened to throttle you if you get into any more trouble,' Poppy said sweetly. 'And don't think she's not going to hear what's happened to Lenny, neither.'

'Girls!' Grant exploded contemptuously. 'You're more trouble than you're worth. It couldn't have killed Lenny to stay with them for a while. After all, it couldn't have been as cold in that barrow as it is on that bloody step.'

'He's right, Poppy,' Jess agreed.

'And while they wanted him as their guy,' Grant warmed to his theme, 'At least the King kids weren't holding competitions as to who could stand furthest away and hit him with their pee.'

The sniggering changed into guffaws.

'Which you all think very funny,' Poppy snapped. 'Just like they did until I turned up and showed them what for! It might interest you to know that they forced him to be the guy, and they tied him down into that cart so hard that his poor little legs are all bruised and bleeding. Sitting on steps don't do that!' She swung back to face her cousin's best friend. 'How can you stand here with such nasty-minded, rotten little weeds, Jess? You're as bad as they are.'

'Poppy,' Ros said quietly, 'you're right, we none of us knew that. We thought Lenny had gone in the hope of getting a penny or two.' She shivered. 'Now please be a dear and walk back home with me. I–I don't think I can stand much more of this cold.'

Without a word, Poppy took her books from the cart, then left it with Harry. She put her free arm round Ros's waist and together they began the walk home. Jess and Grant stayed where they were, scuffing their toes in the gutter. Greg said something rude and Jess giggled, the sound high and stupid.

Poppy glanced quickly at Ros, fearing that her feelings were hurt. But Ros was intent only on getting in the warm, safe back indoors.

As they progressed, Poppy began telling Ros that it had been Sandy Swift who had been the first on the scene to rescue Lenny.

'He's not half so bad as I thought, Ros,' she said. 'And as for Daniel! That lot of rotters took one look at his stern face and that was that! I tell you, they're not all lousy round here. Perhaps not saints, but certainly not the black sinners I believed. Sometimes I think our street's not so awful after all.'

'It needs flowers,' Ros gasped. 'Lots of lovely flowers, everywhere.'

'We'll even stick a rose behind Vic Parker's ear, eh?' Poppy joked. Beyond laughing, Ros just smiled.

It was tea time. Poppy sat smiling at Charlie, who was as usual leaning back in his chair with Rags at his feet. Clary came bustling in holding her laden tray.

'Gawd help us,' she said, 'it's getting worse. They'll all be after carrot and onion today, for stew.'

'That's what I fancy myself, ducks,' Charlie said, 'with a nice bit of rabbit.'

Clary put the tray on the table, then her hands on her hips, and beamed at Poppy. 'What will we do with him, eh? He'll get his rabbit stew, like he gets everything he wants. Treat him like a mother, I do.'

'You're a very good mum,' Charlie replied waggishly and winked.

'Unlike mine.' Poppy was now scowling, then shrugged away the sense of betrayal and hurt that had been with her for as long as she could remember. She bit into the toast and changed the subject. 'I reckon that fireworks will be thin on the ground. They weren't getting much money outside the Coach last night.'

'I hope as how the little so-and-sos get nothing,' Charlie growled. 'Going to block up the letterbox, ain't we, Clary? The little swines chucked a banger through it last year and the shock of it nearly did for ol' Rags.'

33

He looked so worried that Clary walked over and squeezed his shoulder.

'Don't you worry, Charlie. I'll see to it as how Rags stays safe. He won't mind the bangs so much if I cuddle him. Make a right old fuss of him, I will.'

'What a dear old Dutch you are,' Charlies said fondly. 'Stick by me through thick and thin, don't you? Gawd, is that the time? We can't sit here like two of eels waiting for liquor. Let's get on with it, you know what Saturdays are like.'

Poppy unlocked the door in time for Flossie's frail, grey-haired old mum. A nice, friendly lady she was, too, in her long black clothes and small hat decorated with flowers and real-looking grapes. She always smiled, a small, twinkly smile that danced in her faded blue eyes.

'A pound of pot herbs, love,' Mrs Wells said in her thin, high voice, then, anxiously, 'and could you weigh me just three smallish potatoes?'

'I'll weigh you just one potato if that's what you want.' Poppy smiled and weighed a pound of mixed carrot, onion and turnip, then for good measure, as Charlie wasn't looking, added a small swede.

Other customers began to pile in. Clary was right: everyone, it seemed, had decided on stew. As she popped the vegetables into wicker baskets, Poppy noted the packets of pearl barley nearly every one held. Good and nourishing, she thought, and hoped that Nan made the same. No one could better Aunt Nan's pearl-barley stew. Even Ros lapped it up.

'My Gawd,' Charlie said as he lugged in fresh bags of pot herbs, 'today's going to be a bleeder.'

'I wish you wouldn't swear in the shop,' Poppy snapped. 'It's not necessary.'

'I ain't no gent, Poppy,' Charlie observed. 'And I ain't seen you taking much notice of your Aunt Nan, either.'

'I know when I can give tongue and when to shut up, Charlie.'

'You're right about that.' Charlie grinned and looked her over in a casually approving way. 'An' just you keep it up. You're growing up and you've got good looks. You want to be posh and I don't blame yer. But one thing ladies have, ducks, is dignity, like what Ros's got. Fishwives ain't got no dignity. You get some dignity and you'll go far.'

'Who says?'

'Nan.' His cheerful grin spread over his face. 'Don't think I know stuff like that, do you? I'm telling you what Nan says, an' she knows about such things.'

'She believes I'll go far?' Poppy's eyes were wide with pleasure. 'She reckons I've got looks?'

'Gawd, I shouldn't have opened my mouth. Stop looking like a stuck pig and get on with it.'

Apart from an isolated bonfire, a banger or sparkler or two, Guy Fawkes Night was a washout in Jezebel Street.

It grew colder and on Saturday, in between running errands and tidying the bedroom, Poppy found time to stand on the step to keep an eye open for Lenny. He was watching the boys flicking cigarette cards against the wall. Harry as usual sparred up when Sandy Swift came by, but Sandy ignored him. He looked at Poppy.

'How's Ros today?'

'Staying in bed, at least for a while.'

'I see Lenny's all right.'

'No thanks to Harry Peel!'

'Want me to bash his head in?'

'Oh, he'll behave for a day or two. Daniel went and had a word with his dad.'

'That's all right then. Ta-ta.'

''Bye, Sandy – and thanks.'

'Think nothing of it, Poppy.'

He walked on. Poppy ran inside to tell Ros that Sandy had come to ask after her, but Ros was sleeping. She had had a bad night, so Poppy tiptoed downstairs again.

The day went whizzing by. Nan made pearl-barley stew again, which was a wonderful change from cabbage. Now it was Poppy's favourite time when she pulled up a chair and sat by the range to read her book. Ros complained of a headache and, refusing all company except the cats, went to bed. Nan shrugged, saw Poppy busily turning the pages of her romance, looked grim and went next door to have chinwag with Flossie Wells.

35

Time was getting on when Poppy regretfully put down her book. She had to hurry to get through her last chore before Nan came home. Nan knew all about work and how to handle it right. 'Get it out of the way before you put your feet up,' she'd say. But Poppy always put her reading first and then had to make a mad dash of her work, knowing that if Nan came back early there would be hell to pay. Nan had been much younger than Poppy when she had slaved for people in a posh house in Woodford. Nowadays Nan still slaved. Nothing ever changed. She still scrubbed stone floors with the aid of hard yellow soap, a handful of soda to make the water soft, and bags of elbow grease. She expected Poppy to do her fair and rightful share, and Poppy duly obliged. Ros had, too, until she became ill. Ros was excused most things these days.

Placing the zinc bath on the scullery table, Poppy filled it with the water that had boiled in the saucepans on top of the range. She began washing the coloureds, her regular chore. On Mondays the copper fire was lit and the whites were boiled. Nan whisked through the house on Mondays, searching for everything washable in sight.

It took time to get the washing clean, rinsed and put through the mangle that stood out in the yard. Poppy's hands were sore from catching her knuckles on the metal ribs of the washboard, but it was the cold she minded most. She was shivering as she pegged the things out to dry by the faint gleam of the streetlamp that reared its head above the back wall.

Back inside, she cleaned everything away, swabbing the scullery floor, filled the cats' water dish, then drank a mug of scalding tea. She took some up to Ros, who was breathing unevenly again. Ros smiled at her in her gentle loving way but refused the tea.

Concerned, Poppy got ready for bed, then crept between the sheets and lay very still. Ros had closed her eyes, but her slender fingers clung round Poppy's hand. And the love and care and sense of sharing Poppy felt in that fragile grasp made tears sting against her lids. Apart from their entwined fingers, Poppy was careful not to touch Ros, especially not with her feet, which felt like blocks of ice. Ros's breathing sounded a little less laboured at last and she seemed to be sleeping. Poppy relaxed and closed her eyes.

Some time later Poppy woke with a start. She thought she heard someone sawing wood. Sawing, at this hour? Befuddled, suddenly palpitating and filled with unknown dread, she tried to pull herself together. The man was sawing again and the sound was horrible, frightening. Her senses reeled as she became fully awake. Ros was making that noise. Ros was gasping, wheezing and choking. Her eyes were wide open, but she saw nothing. Nothing at all.

'Nan!' Poppy screamed. 'Aunt Nan, for God's sake, come quick!'

Poppy huddled in the passage, lost and alone, waiting, shivering and deathly afraid. They had been fortunate to get Ros admitted into a specialist hospital, Doc Fox said. There would be no better care in the world. Providing Ros's heart held out, she might get well again quite soon. So they had taken Ros away and left Poppy screaming in her heart and mind and soul. They had taken her a long way away, to Brentwood, and life would be unbearable from now on.

Night was through and life was carrying on as usual when Nan finally arrived home. Her face was grey and washed out. Poppy's fear for Ros grew. She ran to her aunt, arms outstretched, but Nan's head was aching and above everything she needed a cup of tea. The kettle was boiling and Poppy hurried outside to fetch the tray with its white mugs and condensed milk and screw of tea ready and waiting in the blue enamel pot. Nan's face was set as she took Ros's mug away and put it on the dresser with the rest of her precious things. Her voice was bleak as she said, 'Why Ros? In God's name, why couldn't it have been –'

'Why couldn't it have been me?' Poppy asked in a small, shaky voice. 'Don't you think I've not asked myself that question over and over, Nan?'

Nan's cat's eyes opened wide, but she said nothing.

Poppy went on, her voice throbbing with pain. 'It's plain as plain what you meant, Nan. And for what it's worth, I know Charlie never did want me neither. It's common knowledge that my mum walked out on me when I was three weeks old, and I suppose it's hardly worth having me barging round all the time, reminding –'

Nan let go then. 'Shut up! Don't you dare come out with such rubbish, never again, d'you hear? I was thinking about all the evil rotters that thrive round here, not you. Never you! I need you and you need me. We need each other, d'you hear?'

They fell into each other's arms, weeping.

Chapter Three

Life had to go on. Poppy walked to school after Charlie's, feeling sick. Seeing Jessica mincing along with Grant, she hurried to pass them, turned and stuck out her tongue.

'That's for Ros,' she called out. 'Rotters!'

'Wait for me,' Jess shouted and ran after her. 'Oi! What's up with you, misery-guts?'

'Nothing. Go away!'

Jessica narrowed her eyes, knowing by the expression on Poppy's face that something was very much up. 'Hold on, Poppy. Where's the bloody fire?'

Because she sounded concerned, Poppy began taking her time. She felt an aching hole in her heart because she was without Ros, and fear was making her stomach all knotted and churned up inside. She flinched when the abandoned Grant tugged her hair as he loped by. In the far distance she heard the rumble of a train.

'Told you so.' Jessica's tone held triumph. ''S not even five minutes to yet.' Because Poppy remained silent, Jess's face went whiter and more glinty-eyed than usual. 'Look at them perishers teasing them girls! They won't half get what for in a minute. Beth Hastings can take on three at a time. Still, bashing boys don't do no good. You have a go at Sandy all regular like but he still comes back for more. You have to know a trick or two to get boys eating out of your hands. 'Sides, old Sand only mucks about with you. He never has a real go. If he did, he'd knock you into the middle of next week.'

They began to hurry and entered the school gates glaring

at one another. Then Poppy said sarcastically, 'If you mean one of the tricks to get boys eating out of your hands is to let them feel inside your drawers, no thank you! I'll leave that sort of filthy thing to the likes of you.'

'Thought you were going to get rich one day?' Jess jeered.

'You've got some hopes! Well, let me tell you something, Poppy Ashton. I bet a pound to a penny that I'll be out of this stinking shit a damned sight quicker than you. And I'll get Ros to them hot foreign countries what you're always on about.'

'Shut up!' Poppy angrily brushed tears away from her face. 'Where's Ros?'

'In . . . hospital again. And . . . it's not all that good.'

'Oh, my good Gawd!'

The whistle blew and they hurried to take their place in line. Poppy's face was scarlet and she was again fighting her tears. Life had to go on, Nan said, but . . . what if Ros's life didn't go on? Her mouth went dry and there seemed to be a great pulsing lump in her throat.

'Jess,' she gasped, 'I'm afraid.'

'No, you ain't. Not old blood-nut you! Cheer up, we've got English today. Your favourite. And tonight's your library night. Think of all them love stories you'll choose. Much better than the weekend stint when you do the sorting-out for them old Wellses, eh?'

'I visit the library lots of nights,' Poppy replied sadly. 'It's all go, isn't it?'

''S right. All bloody go.'

'I might see Daniel there and who knows' – she tried to laugh – 'he might even sink so low as to talk to me. He mostly groans and tells me to buzz off.'

'He wouldn't be such a shit if you let him – '

'Someone ought to rub your mouth out with carbolic soap, Jess.'

'Silence at the back!' came the sharp order. Miss raised the whistle to her lips, blew one sharp blast and they all filed in.

That evening Poppy began the long walk along Leyton High Road. Eventually she passed the picture house and the Coronation Gardens. She came at length to the imposing

Town Hall on the corner of a busy main road that led eventually to the Leyton Marshes. In season Bill Bannerman gathered mushrooms from the marshes, put them in boxes and sold them to Charlie. Very good they were, too. Ros never ate mushrooms. She swore they could be poison, like toadstools. In any case, who wanted to eat something that cooked black?

Poppy entered the library, returned the books she had read, and began to browse along the aisles. It was silent inside, like a cathedral, and within these exalted confines Poppy felt awed, excited, almost greedy. Miss said that the whole world could be found in the library, that there wasn't a subject, a thing or a place that someone somewhere hadn't written about. The pity was that Ros had never been convinced. Ros liked sewing and knitting, and had often helped Flossie to get an order out. Had Nan got some money to spare to get Ros some wool? Perhaps Poppy could work longer at Charlie's to get some wool money? That was a good idea.

She saw Daniel in the nonfiction section and went and stood beside him, nice and quiet. He ignored her. She noticed he held a book about politics in his hand and whispered, 'Are you a rebel, Daniel?'

He looked down at her, surprised, then asked sotto voce, 'Why?'

'Flossie says you carry on about things,' she whispered. 'Reckons you're so full of Labour talk that – oh, you know!'

'No, I don't.'

'Are you a Bolshy?'

'Do you know what a Bolshevik is?'

'A man that wears a tall black hat, is ugly and throws round black bombs about. Who spies on people and runs and hides when the going gets bad. Flossie reckons that – '

'That I'd go in all guns blazing, given half the chance?' His dark eyes were alive and dancing with silent laughter because it was so obvious that Poppy had no idea what she was talking about. The girl's head was filled with strange notions, Flossie said. 'Sorry! I can't do too much,' he whispered, 'on account of my gammy leg.' He was reminding her of a limp so slight that no one noticed it any more. 'And my beard

41

hides a scar on my neck, it's not to disguise my face. Unlike what some of the busybodies round here might think – boo!'

His swift movement towards her and the sharp, explosive sound made her jump; she gave a little shriek and chuckled out loud. A librarian came to see what the noise was all about, glaring over the rim of her spectacles in a terrible way. Poppy froze. Her cheeks flamed scarlet with guilt as she hastily looked down at her toes.

'It was my fault,' Daniel said easily. 'It won't happen again.' As the woman walked away, Daniel whispered, 'Fancy making a row in such hallowed halls, Poppy. They'll chop your head off next, and Ros wouldn't want that!'

He was the first person who had mentioned Ros since the news had leaked out, without sounding as though her cousin was dead. Poppy smiled up at Daniel so warmly that he raised one finely arched brow in surprise. His teeth flashed white as he grinned.

'Watch out, Poppy. A chap could get ideas when you look at him like that.'

Confused, she grabbed a book entitled *Kitchener* and pretended to read. They spent a companionable ten minutes browsing together, then Poppy went off to the romantic-novel section. She made her choice with care, waved goodbye to Daniel and left.

Just as she was passing the picture house she came face to face with Jessica. A real tarted-up Jessica, too. Her face was smothered with face powder and her lips were twin orange-red slashes of Tangee lipstick. She reeked of Woolworth's famous Ashes of Roses scent.

'Wotcher, Poppy. Been to the library, I see. Going back home?'

'Yes. Where are you off to?'

'See my gran. They've put her in an old folks' home. I hear as how it's like some kind of prison. Something like what you'd read about in horror books, they say. I want to see if it's true.'

'Then why are you dolled up like a dog's dinner?'

Jess winked in a knowing way. 'Don't know who I might meet up with on the way home, do I? Here, why don't you come along with me? That's if you've got nothing better to do. I'm going because my dad asked me, but I don't really want to go.'

'Are you scared of going into the Home?'

Jess jutted out her chin. 'What's that got to do with it?'

'All right, I'll come. How far is it?'

'Not too bad – as the crow flies. Heard anything about Ros?'

'Aunt Nan telephoned. They let her use that one at the Home. They reckon Ros is holding her own. Jess, what's going to happen if that old people's place is as bad as they say?'

'If it's as bad as they say, Dad's going up there to read the riot act. Gran's his ma and I think she's the only living creature he's cared about. He's an old bleeder, but he ain't afraid of no marm-stink Home people. I'll give him that at least, but I can't stand him, Poppy! What's more, I almost hate my mum for putting up with him. I can't wait to leave school and then I'll bugger off for good. . . .'

It was late when Poppy arrived back home. She found Nan sitting bolt upright in her chair. Her eyes were flashing like beacons, she was so furious.

'Where do you think you've been till this time of night?'

'Can't you guess?' Poppy put the library books on the kitchen table in a slow, exaggerated way.

'Don't you give me any sauce,' Nan was unrelenting. 'The library closed hours ago. What have you been up to, eh?' Nan leaped up and stood over Poppy. 'Answer me!'

'Give over,' Poppy said quietly. 'I've not had a nice time of it. I . . . went with Jessica Davies to see her gran in a Home. It was a real horrible place. There was brown paint everywhere, it was dark and damp and cold. The old people were all shrivelled up, hungry-looking, and they had sad eyes. Aunt Nan, I promise you this: I'd never let you go into a place like that.' She drew in a deep, aching sob. 'I swear it. They'd take you over my dead body!'

'Since when have I needed you to look out for me?' Nan asked grimly. 'And don't think going to that place excuses you for worrying me to death. As for ever getting all

43

shrivelled up and sad, I'd never allow myself to get like that. Work till I drop, I will.'

'But they . . . Most of them could hardly stand up, let alone work and – '

'You can't judge things by how you found old Grandma Davies! She's not all there and never has been for years. Drunk her brains out, she did. Times were hard, but they've been hard for most of us and we don't have to let ourselves go.'

'We don't do we, Aunt Nan?'

'No! We have to fight tooth and nail to keep this place clean and decent, and free of bugs. We keep ourselves washed and wholesome. We hold on to our dignity as best we can. We work hard and save our pennies. Mind you, there ain't nothing wrong with being poor, but it's a sin to let anyone know about it! That'd allow others to look down on you and act like snobs. I prefer to let 'em all think it's us that's the better off. So that's why we keep our end up in number two. Always have and always will.'

For the first time, Poppy understood the way Nan thought. Why she worked and fought as she did. Why it was important to have pride and dignity. Admiring her aunt more than ever before, wishing to be like her in every respect, she decided to tell Nan of her idea.

'Nan, I was thinking –'

Nan was in her stride, able to let go of her anger now Poppy was home safe. She warmed to her theme.

'It would be easy enough to let things go. Remember what I'm telling you. Fight! And the nearer your back is to the wall, think about that story my Sunday-school teacher told me about. Of the walls of Jericho tumbling down. It was no siege what done it. It wasn't no soldiers swords neither. It was the God-awful row everyone made. Drums and trumpets and shouting and yelling.'

'But I'd really rather –'

'Stick your nose in a book? Fat lot of good that'll do. No, round here the one that shouts loudest, who seems ready to have a go no matter what, wins the argument. Left to yourself, Poppy Ashton, the world would walk right over you and not even notice the pieces.'

'Aunt Nan, I try and –'

'And something else! I'd top myself before I'd let this place get to be like the pigsty Clary keeps. As for that mother of yours, the whore who cut and run as fast as her legs could carry her, I –'

'So I'm getting that thrown in my face again!' Poppy was now back to square one and sick with hurt. 'Reminding me all over again that I'm a castoff? Well, you're no shining light. And for someone who's just been told she'll be looked after like gold dust in her old age, you can't half mouth on! I was thinking of asking Charlie for an extra hour or two in the shop to get some wool money for –'

Nan stopped her. She was jutting out her chin in a pugnacious way. 'What d'you mean, castoff? Let me tell you, miss, you're more mine than most and don't you forget it. This even though you was one of the ugliest babies I've ever laid eyes on. I remember looking at you and thinking, My Gawd! No wonder her mother ran off.'

'Don't, Nan!' Poppy's voice held pain. 'Please?'

Nan glared. The world was a cold, ugly place and she was done in. Didn't know which way to turn, in fact, and she wanted to hit back. Poppy was the whipping boy. Poppy always was.

'Getting thin-skinned, are we?' she snapped. 'Can't stand to hear the truth? Well, like it or lump it, you mum was a hot-arse from the word go. Went off, she did, with a bloke that swore he'd give the earth. He let her down, there's no doubt of it. She's probably round somewhere, flogging her lot. If there's anything left to flog, that is.'

Poppy's face was beetroot red. She stepped forward furiously. 'Have you any idea how like a shrew you sound? Dignified? Not you! Why do you always have to spoil things, eh? After hearing all about Jess's family, how her dad is, not to mention the witless mother and her snotty-nosed kids, I was beginning to think what a wonder you are. But you're hard and spiteful-tongued and – and I'm going to bed!'

Poppy's flying feet made the stair rods dance. She flung open the bedroom door and went in. It was freezing cold; her teeth were chattering as she undressed. Only after her head was hidden under the bedclothes did she allow the tears to fall.

Life was a rotten bad egg without Ros, she grieved. Good old Ros, the one person who had always stuck up for her, no matter who or what her mother was. Ros would be well now if they'd been rich enough to take her to a warm and sunny place. Why couldn't her own wayward mother have run off with a millionaire, and then come back and kissed and cuddled her all warm and loving like? And tell her that she'd come to take her and Ros away from Jezebel Street, and that everyone was to live in the lap of luxury from then on?

Poppy cried herself to sleep.

In the early hours, Poppy woke and jumped out of bed, shivering as she poured cold water out of the jug and into the basin set on the washstand. She cleaned herself quickly. She and Ros had always reckoned that Nan enjoyed seeing them suffer.

'Cleanliness is next to godliness,' she always said in her firm, strong way. 'And if either of you ever let me down, I'll swing for you.'

'She don't half carry on!' Ros would explode.

'Yes, on and on and on!' Poppy would agree and they sniggered together, dreading Friday nights even so.

Friday nights were perhaps the worst of the week. It was then that Nan went over their heads, almost strand by strand, looking for fleas or nits.

'No nit-nurse is going to have my girls' heads shaved,' she vowed. 'I'd strangle them first.'

Not waiting to hear if Nan was up, Poppy pulled on her woolly and made her way to Charlie's. Her father had left at four to get to the market; Poppy hoped that he would get back soon. Then Clary would make toast. Nice old easy-going Clary who never reared up like Nan, never mentioned things about the past, who was happy to take each day as it came. Clary seemed to like everyone, even the Kings and the Lambs. She had looked as lost and empty as Poppy felt when she had heard about Ros. Cowlike, Nan had called Clary.

Well, Poppy thought feelingly, sometimes cows were far nicer than fiery bantam cocks who weren't above pecking a person's feelings to death.

46

Charlie wasn't back yet, but Clary, taking one look at Poppy's face, made toast just the same, and a large mug full of hot tea sweetened with condensed milk.

'Don't worry, ducks,' she said easily. 'Our Ros is tougher than she looks. Who knows, perhaps you'll get a letter from her today.'

'Yes!' Poppy felt a load lifting from her shoulders. 'Of course she is, Clary, really strong in heart and spirit.' She brightened even more. 'Ros fought all this off before, didn't she? She will again, I know it! I can't wait for her to sort herself out and start writing to me. She'll be back in no time at all.' She threw her arms round the older woman and kissed her. 'Trust you to make everything right.'

Nan took to making the long journey to the hospital once a week. It was hard going and she walked part of the way in order to save fares. She had arranged to do her scrubbing at night to make up the work she had left. The Home people agreed. She came back, eyes alight, her voice full of confidence and hope.

'Our girl's holding her own,' she said. 'She can't wait to get back, but I keep telling her that she's best off where she is. She's got colour in her face now. She's weak, Poppy, but on the mend.'

Nan bought Ros stamps, notepaper and envelopes. Flossie sent a bagful of tiny leftover balls of wool, so that Ros could knit squares. These would eventually be sewn together to make a blanket like her 'dear old ducks' had on their bed. Poppy, having asked Charlie if she could scrub and polish the shop in exchange for one of Bill Bannerman's potted chrysanths, knew that Ros would at least have some flowers. When Charlie wasn't looking, Clary slipped four oranges into Nan's bag. Charlie watched the pennies, always had and always would.

It was a surprise when Sandy Swift had the courage to knock on the door. He had a pennyworth of bull's-eyes in a bag and handed them to Poppy with a shamefaced air.

'For Ros?' she asked him, amazed.

He looked down, almost as tall as Daniel, his cheeks tinged

red. 'If you like,' he said quietly, 'but I bought them for you because I thought they might cheer you up.'

'Oh, thank you,' Poppy replied, liking him. 'But I don't need cheering up, honestly! Ros is getting better by the day, and she'll be home soon. Can I give them to Nan to take to her?'

'If you like.'

With no more ado, Sandy was off and away. After that he ignored her completely. Poppy, understanding, didn't mind. Confident now, certain that Nan was right and that Ros would get well enough to be home soon, she got on with her life.

There were books to read and through them she lived in other worlds. There was dear old Daniel to talk to, she met him often and they would go to the library together and talk all the way there and back. And there was Nan to please, and Charlie to slog herself to death for.

'Why do you do it, matey?' Daniel asked her once as they were walking home. 'You don't have to half kill yourself, you know.'

'It passes the time,' she replied cheerfully, 'until Ros comes back to where she belongs. Oh, Daniel, I've made so many plans!'

'I know,' he teased. 'To get rich and to treat your family to all the luxuries you think they deserve.'

'Well? What's wrong with that?'

'Nothing at all. I was wondering, though, don't you ever want to get rich just for yourself?'

'Wouldn't be much point to it just for that,' she replied gravely, and rewarded him with the sweet smile few saw. 'But believe me, I'd know how to blow a mountain of money if I could lay my hands on it. For a start, I think I'm happy with books. Oh yes, if I were rich, that's what I'd buy. Millions of lovely books to read. What would you do?'

'Marry you,' he told her.

'Now I know you're having me on!' she jibed, not believing him for an instant. 'You tell me to buzz off more times than I can count. I'm just a kid to you, Daniel. You've told me that often enough.'

'I'm just waiting for you to grow up, matey. Didn't you know that?'

'Now I'm positive you're joking.' She laughed, flattered and pleased even so. 'Get away with you, Daniel Devere.' Suddenly daring, she blew him a kiss, and as they rounded the corner into Jezebel Street, she turned on her heels, laughing, and ran all the way home. Soppy old Daniel, she thought, hugging herself. He was like a brother or an uncle, anything else was just silly dreams.

After that, things seemed to get better. Ros was having a thin time, but that would pass. And Daniel continued to be nice, which made a change. Another surprise was that Sandy was often there, in the background. He went to the boys' part of Skelton School, but he was often outside, near the gates, at coming-home times. Sandy was the strong, silent type. He read books, but only to learn things. He had to pass exams or something, to get on the ships. Still, he was a dab hand at defending himself, and if Nan was right, that was all that counted round here. He's sweet on Ros, he really is, she thought, pleased. I bet that will make her smile! I'll write to her tonight and tell her how moony he is.

Within three weeks Poppy received a plaintive letter from Ros. As usual, she read it aloud to Nan.

'What's that?' Nan asked sharply. 'She wants to come home? Back here to Jezebel Street? She never said as much to me.'

'She misses us. She's bored being all that way away. She ... she wants to see me!'

'What an ungrateful little devil,' Nan spluttered. 'After all they're trying to do for her, too. She's in her right and proper place and she's got to stay there for a while, they said. I could shake her, I really could! I've been paying a fortune to the HSA for her care, and care she's going to get!'

'She'll settle down soon. It's all strange to her, I expect.' Poppy avoided looking into Nan's tear-bright eyes. 'Ros is a good girl and she'll get to accept what's right and best.'

Poppy began putting her heart and soul in rehearsing the part of Joseph in the school's nativity play. She ran errands, got on with household chores, and went backwards and forwards to the library. Life was good and full of fun, and Jessica Davies was wanting to be friends.

Ros did not settle down. Her letters showed that she was

49

homesick. That was natural, seeing it was just about the best time of the year. Poppy could almost feel her cousin's frustration and despair. Ros should be thinking about getting well and strong, she thought, and not be moaning all the time. Of course she missed everyone, just as everyone missed her! But the really rotten weather was making the bedroom cold anyway. There would be no joy for Ros up there! Nan was right. Ros must wait until the doctors told her that she was quite all right.

There was excitement in the air. School classrooms were hung with paper chains and tinsel wound round lampshades. Even Mrs Bowden began to smile as if she meant it. Who wouldn't?

Suddenly, blessedly, it was the end of term. The last day and school had broken up. Sandy waved Poppy goodbye and went off to his nice house. Quite posh it was, at the better end of Beaumont Road. It had new paint on the door and lace curtains and all. But most people reckoned Sandy's gran was a cow and nothing like her son, Sandy's dad, who was a right'un. No one knew very much about Sandy's mum; she seemed a bit fragile and very nice.

Left to herself, feeling bliss, Poppy curled up in Nan's chair by the kitchen range and read to her heart's content.

Christmas Eve arrived. Nan had scraped the fare together for both Poppy and herself. Armed with flowers and fruit, a bar of chocolate and a new nightdress sprigged with roses and forget-me-nots, Poppy and Nan went to the Green Line stop to catch a single-decker. Poppy looked out of the window in awe. This was to live like royalty!

The first sight of Ros came as a shock. Her eyes seemed too large and she was very thin.

'I won't be a tick,' Nan said briskly. 'You two have a talk while I have a word with the doctor. Want to stick my nose in, I do.'

She marched off, stiff-backed, her head held high to hide her fear and pain.

'At last you're here,' Ros whispered. 'Oh, crumbs, Poppy, it seems like years.'

'Hundreds of years,' Poppy agreed brightly. 'So hurry up and get well. I can't stand Jezebel Street without you.'

'And I can't stand this place without you.' Ros's transparent fingers were curled round Poppy's work-roughed hands. 'Mum asked me what I wanted most of all for Christmas and I said . . . I said I wanted to see you.'

'That's funny. I said the same – that I wanted to see you – and here I am!' Poppy smiled a falsely bright smile, the kind reserved for patients in hospital. 'Proper pair of chumps, aren't we? Especially when you'll be back home in two shakes.'

'I wish Mum hadn't gone to see the doctor,' Ros said quietly. 'He'll tell her that it's only a matter of time for me.'

'Really? Playing for sympathy now, are we?' Poppy teased, then added in a more serious vein, 'Don't say things like that, Ros! You're being a right old droopy-drawers. They've told Aunt Nan you're doing nicely, thank you very much. Oh, come on! They wouldn't lie to your own mum.'

'I heard them speaking when they thought me asleep, Poppy.'

'You must have nodded off and been dreaming!'

Suddenly uneasy because Ros did seem frail, and not in the least how she had expected, Poppy leaned over and cuddled her cousin.

'You've got to promise to get me back home,' Ros whispered desperately. 'Just in case. I'm scared I wasn't dreaming, Poppy! I'd hate it if – Oh, God, Poppy, don't you understand? If I wasn't dozing, and if in the next few months I'm going to get worse, I don't want it to happen here.'

'You don't know what you're saying,' Poppy objected fiercely. 'You're not doing yourself any good, talking like this.'

'I do know what I'm saying! I'll get better if they let me go home. I won't get better here, I know it. I feel it in my bones. Everything here is sick and sorry and scary. Someone else died last night. They put the screens round and . . . and she wasn't in her bed this morning. She was a nice old girl, too.' Tears rolled down Ros's cheeks. 'It's happened several times in this ward. Death Ward, I call it. I tell you, Poppy, I've got to get out of this dump and back home.'

'Stop it!' Poppy warned sternly. 'You're having a funny

turn, that's all. You're thinking all the wrong things and making yourself ill and –'

Ros wasn't listening.

'Mum will have to sign a form for my release, so you've got to get her to make her mark. Tell her she's agreeing to new treatment for me, anything! I'm serious, Poppy. I won't get better here. The place stinks, and know something? Death smells like lemons. Yes, it does! I can't stand it. You've got to make Mum write down her cross!'

'I can't do something so wicked and underhand,' Poppy whispered, feeling a twinge of uncertainty. 'It'd be a sin to lie to Nan. I can't!'

'You can and will, Poppy.' Ros's voice grew stronger. 'Because I hate this place and I think things are against me here. And . . . and if I wasn't dreaming, you wouldn't let me die without you being with me, would you?'

'Oh, shut up!' Poppy's mouth was dry. 'Look what you're doing to me with all your stupid talk. I'm a bunch of nerves! Let's unwrap your presents.'

'It isn't Christmas until tomorrow.' Ros leaned back against her pillow and seemed too fed up to care.

Nan clumped back, her face stern. 'Couldn't see no doctor,' she said tartly. 'Seems he's busy elsewhere. But Matron says you're doing very well, and the Sister agrees. So, if you keep this up, Ros, we'll be having you home in no time.'

'That's nice, Mum.' Ros's smile was warm and melting as she looked directly into her mother's eyes. 'I really miss you. Even your nagging's not half so bad as Sister's. Besides, I . . . We . . .'

'We're blood, my girl, and blood's thicker than water. Right?'

A faint twinkle came into Ros's eyes. 'I was going to say that me and Poppy agree there's nothing on earth that's nicer – than your pearl-barley stew.'

'We'll bring some with us next time.' Nan's work-reddened hand reached out to stroke Ros's pale-marigold hair. 'Now you go and close your eyes and have a sleep. When you wake we'll be gone. It's a long haul to where we have to catch that Green Line, you know. We daren't miss it because it'd take us about a year to walk home.'

'You'll come again soon?' Ros's eyes were wide and anxious. 'You promise?'

'From now on me and Poppy will take turns. Will that do?'

Ros nodded, exhausted, and closed her eyes.

Going home, Nan was as silent as the grave.

Christmas had come and gone and the world seemed grey, as old and cold and washed out as Jezebel Street. It was Sunday night and Poppy was on her way home from visiting Ros. There was a bitter wind blowing and a steady downpour of rain. Wet and shivering, glad to be back at last, Poppy turned the corner and entered the street. She hurried straight along, passing by number two, where she knew Nan was waiting, and crossed the road.

Poppy was hardly aware of the puddles of light the streetlamps made, or the sharp clean odour of new-washed paving stones. All she felt was an ocean-deep dread. Ros was rapidly fading, Poppy had sensed it. Their conversation had been a series of words barely breathed, all mixed up somehow with the smell of disinfectant and the tang of the unwanted orange that Poppy had peeled. Funny, Poppy grieved, how she hated the smell of oranges now. She swallowed fiercely, knowing that she herself would give up in that horrible place, with its dark-green walls, dingy lights, and sisters and matrons as fierce and sharp-eyed as hawks. You disobeyed them at your peril.

Yet, for all their brisk bossy ways, acting like the biggest know-alls on earth, the people they looked after seemed to be dying like flies. That was what Ros said. Still, Poppy tried to comfort herself, it was worth remembering that Ros always had been adept at getting her own way. Ros would do and say anything to get back to Jezebel Street.

To that end, Poppy knew that she must beard Liz Parker in her den. And after her, Nan!

She marched onto the step of number seven and knocked on the door hard. It took courage to disturb Liz, for the woman's drunken outbursts were well known. The trouble with Liz was, you never knew how she'd turn.

53

The house was dark and seemed empty. Poppy knocked again, sharply, as demanding as the rent man, and waited, her heart in her mouth. She heard Liz bawling out, 'All right. All right! Keep your bloody hair on!'

The door was flung open. The hall was dark. Poppy could smell cats' urine and the kippers the Parkers had eaten. The gleam from the streetlamps outside enabled her to see the blur of Liz's face and the outline of rag curlers sticking out like lamb's tails all over her head.

'It's me, Liz. Poppy!'

'What d'yer want? Banging on my door at this unearthly hour? Can't a body have no peace?'

'Is Reggie there, please?'

'No, he ain't.'

'It's very important that I speak to Reggie. I stopped by Tilsby's office, but it was closed and empty. I . . . I'm desperate, Liz!'

A sardonic gleam flashed in Liz's eyes. 'Gone into cradle-snatching, has he? Blimey, they say how the quiet ones are the worst.'

Poppy's cheeks flared in the gloom. She fought back tears.

'Now you're being really horrible, Liz,' she said tightly. 'And blackening my name as well as Reggie's! For what it's worth, your Reggie –'

'Ain't a wick-dipper?' Liz laughed sourly. 'A lot you know. All the same, the Parkers are, and young Grant takes after his dad as sure as eggs is eggs. I could tell you a thing or two about Vic's brother that'd make your ears curl. I'm speaking about the one what lives down Beaumont Lane. Another thing –'

Poppy held herself in check, remembering what Nan said about dignity. 'Please, Liz,' she cut in quietly. 'Tell Reggie that Ros is coming home tomorrow. I only learned about it myself a little while ago. She's signed herself out, and said that Nan had put her mark on the form. Ros is very weak, Liz, and she'll need to be driven home. She couldn't possibly manage the long walk to the Green Line stop. I . . . I thought Reggie might, that he could –'

'Oh, my Gawd, you're after freemans! Do you want to get my Reggie the sack? Sod off!'

Liz took one furious step forwards and shoved Poppy in the chest hard. Poppy winced, but stood her ground. Inwardly she felt sick. She had hoped that Liz would be on her side; had prayed that Reggie would work a miracle and get Ros home for free.

It was whispered that quiet old Reg wasn't above doing some diddling. He was bitter and twisted, and out to get his own back on all the nobs of the world. And Mr Tilsby was a very rich nob indeed. The kind who treated his workers like slaves, ignoring the fact that some, like Reggie, were supposed to be war heroes. So it was that Reg gave extra drives when the mood took him to take a swipe at his boss. It was a source of wonder that he was always able to make the petrol up somehow.

Poppy's heart sank. Quite clearly, Liz was not going to put in a word for Ros to Reggie. Liz was acting all hateful and getting ready to try to shove Poppy off the doorstep again.

'Tell Reggie that this is all on the straight,' Poppy said firmly. 'He will be paid. I want him to be here in good time to get to Brentwood Hospital by eleven o'clock sharp. It is important that he's here on time. Half past nine at the latest.'

Liz seemed to puff up to twice her size. 'Don't get all high and mighty with me. And no, I'm not daft! Probably had it off with him in the back of his motor more than once, eh? Now you want a favour in return? Stone me! I know what you're really hoping for! I'll have your guts for garters before I –'

'Half past nine, Liz. I mean it.' Poppy threw down her challenge. 'Oh, and if I wanted to be as horrible as you, I could tell Mr Tilsby that everyone knows that Reggie hangs on to his tips instead of giving them in. I could also tell him that Reggie makes a shilling or two on the sly by working hand in glove with all the whores round here.'

'Lies. All rotten lies!'

'Prove it! Don't forget, Liz, half past nine sharp.'

Leaving Liz open-mouthed and spluttering, Poppy crossed the road to number two. She knew that Reggie would be there on time. Liz was not that drunk!

Nan was waiting in the kitchen. Her face was strained. As

55

usual, she sat bolt upright in her chair, her arms folded against her chest. The cats were curled up at her feet.

'Well?' she demanded as Poppy took off her soaking wet coat and hung it carefully on the hook on the scullery door to dry. 'What did she think of the chocolates?'

'She was very pleased, Nan.' Poppy's face was white with stress. 'She ate the ones with pink centres and said that they tasted like the pink roses on the box. She loves the pink roses, Nan.'

'I paid good money for chocolates and she went on about the picture on the box? Fancy that! I don't think I'll ever understand you girls.'

'Nan, I've got to tell you something.' Tired out, Poppy sank down on a chair by the table. 'Ros isn't getting any better simply because she hates it in there. She's getting to truly believe she'll die! Yes, die the death no matter what they say! Ros thinks, I mean, she wants so much to . . .' Poppy drew in a deep breath. 'She's set on coming home.'

'That's daft! They know what they're doing, don't they? She's in the best place, isn't she? I reckon –'

'No, Nan,' Poppy said quietly. 'There's not much anyone can do for Ros while she's thinking as she is now. You know how she is! She sees people dying behind screens all the time, and believes she'll be the next one to go.'

'Rubbish!'

'It isn't. It isn't, Nan! She's making herself really and truly ill, and today she looked as though she was at death's door. She's so scared! I don't think she can stand much more. She won't let them help her at all, and –'

'Where's all this leading to?' Nan asked sharply.

Poppy gulped and then had to tell the truth.

'That paper you put a cross on a while ago said that you agreed they wouldn't be responsible if – if Ros comes home. Ros gave it to them and – Nan, she's so desperate to be back. She won't give in! She back-answers them and that makes her lose her breath, you know how she is! Keeps telling them, she does. All them that argue with her.'

'Who argues with a sick child?' Nan was looking dangerous now.

'Them up there! Matron gets cross with Ros for wanting to

come back to this old place, and . . . And Ros was so rude to Sister once that she really lost her temper and said Jezebel Street was a slum.'

Poppy tried to laugh, but there were tears in her eyes.

'Well, I never did!' Nan said waspishly. 'They want to look inside this house for a start. Soon see we're as good as them any day!'

Poppy was openly weeping now. 'Ros told them we grow flowers in our yard, and that there's pretty front gardens in our street. She's lied through her teeth, and told them everywhere smells sweet with the scent of roses and carnations in the summer! That she won't rest until they let her go. She went hysterical, Nan! Made herself in such a state that when I got there I had to go to the office and I –'

'What have you done, girl?' Nan asked very quietly. 'Poppy, what have you done?'

'Told them that it was the truth, that you wanted Ros home, and that you had already signed the form.'

'Did you indeed?'

'Yes. But they didn't believe me. They also got very ratty, in the end. Then they told me you're to go up there. That Ros can come home tomorrow if you'll sign another form – in front of them. It's got to be official, you see.'

Nan snorted. Poppy heard herself pleading.

'I . . . I wouldn't have behaved so badly if I hadn't been sure that Ros meant what she said. She's made up her mind she'll never get better in that place. She says she'll die in there – and, what makes it a million times worse, she believes it!'

'I see.' Nan's eyes held anguish, but her tone was angrily brisk and efficient as she made up her mind. 'What time do we get her?'

'Eleven.' Poppy gasped with relief. 'I've left a message for Reggie to pick us up at half past nine. Liz and me had a bit of a slanging match, but it's all right now. I told her we'd pay Reggie. We've got to, Nan. Ros isn't strong enough to get to the bus stop. It's going to cost a fortune, but –'

'We'll pay. I don't know how, but we will!'

'I'm going to cadge off Charlie in the morning.'

'No, you're not.'

'Yes, I am. I can work on the barrow outside Whips Cross on Sunday mornings, or all day, comes to that. I can –'

'You'll be no costermonger, not even for Ros.'

'I don't care what I'm called. All I know is that Ros is coming home the easy way. It's all arranged.'

'What about the coal money?' Nan said. 'We'll use that.'

'Ros is always cold these days,' Poppy pointed out. 'So she's going to need a fire burning night and day to keep her warm.'

'Well, the insurance money can go towards it. Ted's not too bad, and we can use the rent and I'll –'

'We owe the insurance three weeks already and we've been warned about leaving the rent – since we've used the money to go and visit Ros once or twice before this. Nan, Ros has got to have a roof over her head! I'm seeing Charlie first thing and that's a fact. And now I'm going to bed, because I'm tired and my feet are wet, and I'm freezing cold. Even worse, I'm wild with myself for not being able to make Ros see sense.'

'You've done well,' her aunt told her. 'Even though we shouldn't have given in to her, you did your best. No one can do more.'

Poppy lay in bed unable to get warm. Her feet were still freezing after the soaking they'd received on the journey home. She stared at the shadows on the ceiling. They flickered and danced every time the wind rattled the window frame. They looked evil, she thought, watching the shapes moving silently over the cracked plaster, like phantoms of death. Phantoms that Ros believed in, no matter what they said. They had to get her home. Had to!

Poppy was still shivering at dawn next morning. She dressed and went downstairs, only to find Nan had beaten her to it. The kitchen seemed to be caught in time, very still, waiting, the only sound being the hissing of the gas glowing through the pipe and turning the mantle white. Nan was sitting at the table, her hands clasped before her, her face wan. Had Poppy not known better, she would have believed her aunt had been praying. That would have made Rev Rawlins's day!

'Couldn't you sleep, girl?' her aunt asked. 'Nippy in bed,

wasn't it? And there's plenty else to bother us. But don't you fret. Ros has got us to look after her, and she'll make great strides once she's back where she belongs.'

'Oh yes, Aunt Nan, she's got to!'

'We all live long on my side. Like cats we are, got nine lives – oh, and I've fed our two already. There'll be hairs all over the bed from now on, but I don't care. She loves Josh and Jo, and they'll keep her company. Yes, she'll get better, you'll see. Get to ripe old ages, us lot do.'

'Nan, Uncle Nick died in prison, didn't he?'

'What's that got to do with it?' Nan asked sternly. 'He got GBH slung at him. Serves him right. He was always a bad lot. Pity was, I didn't know it at the time. Only thing was, he at least tackled blokes as big as himself. Unlike that wife-beating scum Davies. Why do you ask?'

'He . . . his heart gave out, didn't it?'

Green eyes glared. 'I'll have none of that. Pull yourself together, girl. My old man went off this earth with a busted jaw, broken ribs and two lovely black eyes. A cellmate he cheated done him over while he slept. I reckon Nick died of shock as much as anything. By the way, I've never told Ros what a rotter her dad was, so keep your lip buttoned, all right.'

'But he did have a –'

'A dicky heart? Perhaps he did, but it never stopped him in his tracks, the old devil. If you must know, I grew to hate him. The more he pulled us down, the more I fought to keep us up. The only good thing that came out of it all was Ros.'

'Nan, I didn't mean –'

'Ros is all we've got to think about. And them up there! I hate all them authorities. Make you feel like dirt, they do. But if Ros is thinking the way she is, we'll fight them all if we have to. And get her home! Yes, even if we are stony-broke.' Nan lifted her chin in a defiant way. 'And that's why I changed my mind. Yes, you go and touch that tight-fisted devil of a brother of mine. Touch him for every penny he's got.'

'He's not mean, Nan,' Poppy protested. 'Only very careful and –'

'What do you know about it?' Nan snapped. 'Charlie's a

59

stingy man. Are you so half-witted that you can't see through him? Of course you are. You've got your nose stuck in books most of the time. Well, let me tell you this. My brother's never given me a brass farthing for your keep these last thirteen years.'

Poppy felt the blood drain away from her face. A sense of shame made her hunch her shoulders. Humiliation and hurt shone in her eyes.

'You mean,' she whispered, 'he hasn't given you *anything* for me? Not ever?'

'Only the pittance you slave yourself to death for. Don't look like you've been whipped.' Nan shrugged impatiently. 'He forgot, I suppose. And you know me! Too proud for my own good. But he's not getting away with it from now on.'

'No!' Poppy's throat was tight with emotion. 'You can bet your sweet life he's not. What a rotter he is! He washed his hands of me right from the start, didn't he? He just didn't care that you had to fight and struggle to bring Ros and me up on your own. That you had to work all hours on your hands and knees just to make ends meet. You've looked out for me all along, haven't you? Well, I'll never forget what you've done for as long as I live.'

'Don't upset yourself, there's no need.' Nan looked worried; Poppy's tone had been so passionate, so wild with heartbreak. 'It's never bothered me until now, and that's the truth. My pride kept me from asking him before. Always made out I was doing fine, I did. But now it's a different kettle of fish and we need him. You go up to the shop and do the asking, while I'll let Flossie know what's going on and then give everything here a final spit and polish. Oh, and tell him I'll be up to see him myself once we've got Ros back safe and sound.'

Jezebel Street was grey, cold and unfriendly when Poppy left the house. She had gone halfway down the street when she met up with Daniel, who'd been on night shift.

'Morning, matey,' he said and grinned. 'Cheer up!'

'I'm all right.'

'Think I know you better than that, Poppy. What's up?'

'Ros is coming home.' Her voice was cold with fury. 'And instead of walking ten foot tall I feel lower than a snake's belly. Even worse, I've got to ask the most rotten man in the world for help. If only you knew what something like this does to me and Nan. At least before we had some dignity.

He was staring down at her, puzzled by her tormented expression. He about-faced and began walking alongside her. 'Come on, sprat,' he said. 'You might just as well tell me the rest.'

Just then Sandy came along. His blue eyes were very direct as he looked from Daniel to Poppy, then enquired, 'How's Ros?'

'Don't ask!' Poppy replied pithily, then, seeing his look of consternation, she smiled in a brilliant way. 'But she's coming home! You've got to come and see her, and cheer her up. We've to do everything we can to make her forget that rotten hospital they put her in. Like a morgue, it is. You'll come?'

'All right,' Sandy replied in an offhand way. 'I'll be seeing you.' He gave Daniel a quick look, then walked on.

'And now,' Daniel said evenly, 'let's get down to brass tacks.'

Chapter Four

Haltingly, the tears plain to see, Poppy told Daniel about Ros being without hope. That she and Nan were about to fetch her home, but Ros was too frail to walk to the coach stop, which left her with the problem of Charlie.

'Poppy,' he said quietly, 'there are people up there to help you, you know. The hospital must have an ambulance. I know Nan's got her pride and all that rot, but the world's not such a hard place as that.'

'I'm with Nan,' she said fiercely. 'I get by on my own steam, like Nan. It's important that I get the money for a taxi from Charlie.'

'Money for the taxi. Blow me, mate, is that what this is about? There's nothing to it. I'll help.'

'No, thanks.' Poppy's expression became pinched and bitter. 'Nan and me are just asking for a little of what Charlie owes. Know something? I've just learned that my dad's not paid Nan a single brass farthing for my keep from the day she took me in. Nan's footed all the bills and slogged herself to death to keep Ros and me.'

He was frowning, unsure. 'What a fiery cock sparrow you are, Poppy. I'm sure Charlie forgot. He's a damned good bloke and I don't see him short-changing his own.'

'Really?' Poppy tried to laugh, but there was ocean-deep pain in her eyes. 'Not even when you consider he was hard enough to give me to Nan when I was three weeks old? I come a very low fourth in his book. First there's himself, then Clary, then Rags. A long way after that, there's me. So now

62

he's going to dig deep in his pocket for once. He's going to pay for our taxi.'

Before Daniel could reply, Poppy left him and ran the last few paces to the yard. Seeing no one, she entered the shop, which was empty. There was the tang of fruit in the air, and crisp icy whiffs coming from freshly cut cabbage. The front door of the shop opened into Beaumont Lane, which in its turn led into the High Road. Charlie's barrow was parked against the kerb and he was unloading. He came in, humping a sack of greens, saw Poppy and gave her a saucy wink.

'Gawd, you're early. Got a squib up your arse?'

'I want a heap of money, Charlie,' she said evenly. 'And I want it now.'

'And I want the moon,' he replied easily and dumped the sack. 'And I've got about as much chance of getting it.'

'You owe us, Charlie,' she flared at him. Her eyes were blazing now, her cheeks red. 'And you're going to pay something off what you should have handed out years ago.'

'Do what? Charlie jutted out his chin and looked very much like Nan. 'What the hell's got into you?'

'The truth, that's what. And don't think you're going to get out of this little lot. I won't let you!'

Charlie pushed his cap to the back of his head. Clary came in, took in the situation and about-faced sharply. Charlie was screwing up his eyes, his lips turned down. His breath came out of his mouth in a little puff of white. He was mad, unusual for him, his tone hard. 'Buzz off,' he snapped impatiently. 'Go on, skedaddle out of my sight, you saucy little moo.'

She leaped at him and grabbed hold of his arm. 'I'm not going, Charlie,' she yelled. 'This is for Ros, your niece, and in case you've forgotten, I'm your daughter. How's that for a laugh?'

He shrugged her hand away, his eyes puzzled, his expression hard. 'I don't know what you're going on about, and I don't want to. Are you crackers or something? And you needn't glare like that. Them stinking looks of yours don't cut no ice with me. Buzz off!'

'I told you. I'm not leaving until you hand over –'

63

'If you want money, bloody well get busy and start earning it, you cheeky little bitch.'

He turned his back on her, but she grabbed hold of his arm again, so that he swung round to face her.

'Listen here, Charlie,' she shouted, beside herself. 'I'm going to have at least thirty bob off you because Ros needs a taxi to come home in today. What's more, she's going to need a lot of things and you're going to pay for them. You've got away with not paying for my keep, but you're going to make up for it by helping Nan out now. You're a stinking, mean, rotten old swine!'

She had reached home at last. His hands shot out, took her by the shoulders and shook her hard. She was as helpless as a rag doll in his grasp. She was shocked but not afraid, knowing instinctively that he'd never harm her. But she had never seen him so angry before. His face was white, his eyes blazed and he shook her unrelentingly with every word he now spat out.

'Don't – you – ever – talk – to – me – like – that – again!'

'I will, I will!'

'I've done my best and I always have,' he said through gritted teeth. 'I've helped Nan out where and when I could. You've never gone short of a veggy stew, have you? Always had plenty of wood to light your fire. It was Nan's choice to take you on, and bloody good luck! In those days I didn't know which way to turn. She insisted, Nan did, when I wanted to have you stuck in a Home!'

Horrified, unbelieving, she stuttered, 'A – a Home?'

'Let's get this straight here and now, ducky,' he rasped. 'You ain't my kid and never was. Your mother buggered off and left her dirty washing on my doorstep. Of course I didn't want to know. Who would? I'd be off my chump to go out of my way to keep someone else's bastard.'

'No, Charlie,' she wept, chilled to the core. 'No!'

'Yes, ducky, too right!' he yelled. 'You'd have been in the Home if Nan hadn't carried on at me. Bloody fool she was and always has been. Her with her Madam marm-stink airs, and forever going on about what's right and wrong.'

Poppy went numb from head to toe and she felt her soul dying, her heart splintering into little bits. She wasn't even

Charlie's. She wasn't Nan's. She had been sired by a faceless stranger to a mother who, so Nan said, was nothing but a whore.

Shocked, ashen-faced, she stared up at Charlie, who now, ashamed, was muttering to himself as he strode over to the till. He took out two ten-shilling notes and shoved them into her nerveless hand.

'This'll do it,' he said roughly. 'But I'm warning you, it'll be curtains if you ever go calling me a stinking old swine again.'

Unable to speak because her lips were trembling so, her eyes wide in her face, she clutched at the money with a fierce desperation. When she did not reply he went on in a cold, bitter way.

'Your mum took me for every last farthing, girl. Stripped me bare, she did. Never put the takings away like I thought, oh no! It all went into her own little money box, and nothing had been paid. Nothing! And if you must know, I sponged on Nan, too. Had to, to bloody well keep this shop. It's taken me all these years of eighteen hours a day slogging to pay my debts and get back on even keel. Want to know something else?'

'No!' she whispered tragically and clasped her hands over her ears. 'No!'

'I'll fight tooth and nail to pay for this place,' he continued, regardless. 'Yes, the home what your aunt so charmingly calls a pigsty! And if you're lucky, and keep your trap shut in future, one day you'll be able to take it over, lock, stock and barrel. It'll be yours.'

'I don't want your business,' she gasped out, agonised. 'And I don't care tuppence about all your hard work. You wouldn't have done it if you hadn't wanted to. And since I'm not yours, you can – can go and do the other thing with this palace!'

'Come off it, Poppy,' Charlie said quickly. 'I didn't mean to mouth on at you. It ain't your fault, and I shouldn't have –'

He was speaking to thin air. Poppy had wheeled round and dashed outside. She saw that Daniel had waited, and that he had heard every word. He looked down into her wide-eyed, agonised face.

'I know how it is, matey,' he said quietly. 'I've been there myself. From now on everything's going to be under control. Cut off home and tell Nan so. All right?'

She nodded and broke away from him, running like a wild thing down Jezebel Street. She slowed only when she entered the house and carefully placed the two ten-shilling notes on the kitchen table.

'Didn't you get no flowers and fruit for when she gets home?' Nan asked and sniffed contemptuously. 'Go back and tell Charlie –'

'No! I won't!'

Nan folded her arms and jutted out her chin. 'D'you think you're too big to feel the back of my hand? Do as you're told, girl, and don't waste time.'

'Go on,' Poppy said stonily. 'Give me the back of your hand, or why don't you try shoving me off the step like Liz Parker did last night? Or you could at least try to shake me to bits! It won't be the first time today.'

'What?' Nan's eyes were wide and green and killingly angry. 'Who's dared to –'

'Charlie. Oh, you don't need to take on! I asked for it. I barged in, calling him names and telling him to cough up for Ros's taxi. I accused him of not paying for . . . for my keep. He told me the truth, Nan. I'm not his!' Poppy's voice was harsh with trying to get the words past the lump in her throat. 'In fact, I don't belong to anyone.'

'Stuff and nonsense!' Nan spat our fiercely. 'He only needs to look at you, listen to you, see your hair and eyes to know your blood's the same as his and mine.'

'He . . . he said. He believes –'

'It's just that he had such a shock over that whore of a mother of yours that he finished up by not believing a single word she said.' Nan was in full flow now and nothing and no one would stop her from saying her piece. 'Charlie's tight with money because he's had to be. And if you must know, I shouldn't go on about him. He's worked miracles to keep his place, and he's as pig-headed as me about not giving in. You're the same as us, Poppy. You'll work and slave to get what you want out of life. You're no whiner and no slouch. You'll go far, and me and Charlie will be as proud as Punch.'

'If . . . if you'd seen his face, Nan. He –'

'None of that matters for the moment. The chips are down, and Charlie's not getting away with giving us a paltry pound. If he's so ready to upset you, he'll have to put up with me upsetting him. I want flowers for Ros, and I want some of them blood oranges that he's got. Flossie said as how they're nice and sweet. What's more –'

'No!' Poppy was panic-stricken. 'Don't ask me to go back up there, Nan. At least not today.'

Nan's eyes glittered. She undid her pinafore and folded it neatly, placing it in the dresser drawer.

'You're going to stay here and make me a cuppa, girl. I'm the one what's off to see Charlie – and God help him!'

She put her coat on and marched out like a turkey cock.

Poppy made the tea and waited, terrified that they'd be late after all. She was almost sick with relief when she heard Nan slam the front door and come bustling along the passage and into the kitchen. She came in with a potted chrysanthemum, buttery yellow, the colour of spring. There was also a brown-paper bag holding oranges and rosy-red apples. Nan was looking sourly triumphant.

'Took the apples from the front, I did. Wouldn't be put off with the soft ones at the back. I'm up to all his old tricks! I told him a few home truths while I was at it. Gave him a right old earful. He'll never lay hands on you again, my girl. Where's my cuppa?'

'It's made, but do we have time? I think the clock's stopped. It's a long ride and –'

'The clock's going, and it's only because you keep looking at it every second that it seems to stand still. Don't worry! Reggie will be here in two shakes and at least we don't have to grovel to the likes of him. I met Daniel, who's seeing to everything, including our fare. We'll keep Charlie's oncer for a rainy day. Make him pay for shaking you, know what I mean? Oh, and guess what?' There was a devilish gleam in Nan's eyes now. 'I just happened to bump into Liz Parker. I mentioned as how I like my girls treated polite, like the ladies they are, I did. Like a lamb she was. A nice, very sober little lamb!'

Poppy tried to smile and poured out the tea. They emptied

their cups. Poppy could hear herself swallowing, hear her own miserable heart, hear the go-slow clock beating life away. The kitchen was still, waiting, but the world had stopped. There was only the ocean-deep misery and bottomless dread.

Poppy was just beginning to think the waiting would never end when Reggie knocked on the door. All posh he looked, in his jacket with brass buttons, his white shirt and striped tie. He was sharp-featured and looked a bit like Liz. His air was quiet, distantly polite. But Poppy had eyes only for Daniel, who was with him, and so did Nan.

'You tell him we don't want no funny stuff, Daniel,' she ordered. 'Me and my girl want to get to the hospital in one piece. She marched out to where the car stood in the kerb. 'We'll get in the back, Daniel. You sit next to the driver and keep your eye on him. We don't want our necks broke. I've heard tales and –'

'Reggie hasn't lost a passenger yet.' Daniel nudged Reggie in the ribs and grinned. 'Or if he has, he's kept it under his hat. Isn't that so, Reg?'

''Sright.' Reggie Parker's tone was as empty as his face.

'There, you see?' Daniel was trying hard to make it seem like partytime. 'Just make yourselves easy and leave the rest to Reg and me.'

This isn't happening, Poppy thought, it's a nightmare about how Ros is, and that I don't belong to anyone. It's all a terrible dream and I've got to wake up.

Once they had left the more open road, the landscape became kinder. Gradually greenery took over, and there were nice houses set in their own grounds. It was all very different from home, yet Jezebel Street was where Ros wanted to be. 'I'll ask Bill Bannerman what seeds to buy for the back yard,' Poppy whispered to herself. 'I'll dig it all up again and ask Bill about the right time for putting the seeds in. Ros's nasturtiums and marigolds did fine last year, but they haven't a nice smell like roses. Roses have thorns and would be better at keeping Josh and Jo in check. I wonder if Bill can get me some pink roses cheap? Like the ones Ros loves to look at on her chocolate box. I'll make Ros a lovely garden and ask Bill which flowers smell nice. I wonder if sweet peas will grow up our fence?'

She came out of her reverie as Nan snapped, 'Look out, Reggie! You nearly run up the back of that cart.'

'As long as the horse lives,' Daniel said easily, 'who cares about a cart full of coal? Cheer up, Mrs Eden, we were miles away from the coalie. Reggie came safe through Flanders, so it's a pound to a penny he can get us to the hospital and back.'

They reached Brentwood Hospital at last, and Reggie swung his taxi smoothly through the gates. He stopped where he saw other cars standing. Not waiting to be helped, Nan left the taxi and marched off, head held high, defiantly determined to face and do down anyone in authority. Especially ones wanting to argue about Ros going home. You couldn't budge Nan once she'd made up her mind.

'You go in and find your Ros,' Daniel told Poppy easily. 'I'll wait here. If you or your aunt need help, just come and get me. All right?'

'I don't think I'll ever be able to thank you enough, Daniel,' she whispered. 'You're being so kind, and you must be tired out after working all night. Daniel, I –'

'Go on, matey, cut off,' he said, and got out to help her down as if she were a lady. Then he spoiled it by ruffling her hair in a kind but clumsy gesture. 'Don't look so scared.'

'Daniel . . . Daniel, she's so ill! What if she –'

'Don't be silly. She's in there waiting for you, Poppy. Don't keep her in suspense.'

She gave him one last melting smile and walked towards the massive hospital reception area. She felt a moment of blind terror, seeing Ros's ward bed empty, then wanted to weep with relief when she was shown to a small side room. Ros was there, resting on top of the bed. She was dressed, but her clothes were now miles too big for her. She looked wan-faced and feather-light, then scared because she did not see Nan.

'Cheer up,' Poppy told her in a falsely bright way. 'No one's let you down. Nan's gone to see them in the office. Heaven help anyone daring to try and cross her path! We'll have you out of here in no time.'

Weak tears oozed silently down Ros's cheeks. She could

69

not speak, so she and Poppy sat close together, hand in hand, quietly waiting. There came the sound of rubber soles squelching over the highly polished floor, followed by the nifty pit-pat of Nan's sensible leather shoes. She and Matron came into the room together. Matron was big and buxom in her navy blue. Her enormous white headdress made her look imposing, like ship in full sail. She fixed Ros with disapproving blue eyes.

'We are sorry to see you go, Rosemary,' she said crisply. 'Ah! Here's Nurse. Take care, Rosemary. Goodbye.'

A nurse wearing a butterfly headdress and a blue-and-white striped dress under her starched apron helped Ros into a wheelchair. The nurse looked efficient but downtrodden and did not wait to say goodbye. She hurried away the moment Daniel came forward and swung Ros up into his arms.

'Lord, Ros!' he teased. 'We'll have to feed you up a bit.'

He carried her to the taxi and lowered her carefully onto the back seat. Nan got in after her and began wrapping one of Flossie's blankets made of knitted squares round her daughter's painfully thin legs. Poppy squeezed in and all but hugged the window in order to give Nan and Ros as much room as possible.

The drive home was made in silence. Ros had her eyes closed most of the time. She was fast asleep when the taxi came to halt outside number two. She woke when Daniel carefully lifted her and carried her inside.

Flossie was waiting. The fire glowed bright orange. A cushion had been set at the back of Nan's chair. There were mugs and a teapot ready and waiting on the tray; the kettle was boiling and spluttering on top of the range. Everything was so warm and homely. Full to overflowing, Poppy took in the scene. The kitchen, no longer a waiting world, was sparkling and alive. The chrysanthemums on the table and the brown dish holding apples and oranges were just right. Nan had thought of everything, had worked wonders, and Flossie had helped finish things off. Even Nan's collection of china on the dresser seemed to glint and twinkle, and the old Toby jugs on the tall mantelpiece over the range seemed to laugh. The cheap wood-encased clock now ticked in a loud and bouncy way. Suddenly Poppy threw off her sense of shock and despair and chuckled out loud.

'You were right, Ros,' she said and knelt down beside the chair to look into her cousin's face. 'Of course you were! How could we have thought different? You're in your own rightful place and from now on, you're going to get well. We're both here with Nan who loves us. Where we're wanted! Oh, dearest Ros, isn't it good to be home?'

Daniel never stopped for the tea Flossie made, and Poppy was sad to see him go. He was so big and strong, he made her feel safe, in the same way Nan made her feel protected and secure. And he had lifted Ros so gently, so full of concern! Tired out, he left them to go to bed.

'Where you ought to be, girly,' he told Ros. 'It's good to have you back.'

Flossie was busy wrapping the large woolly blanket round Ros and fussing and clucking like a nice motherly old hen. Nan jerked her head towards the scullery door and went outside. Poppy followed her.

Aunt Nan must have been up all night, Poppy thought, the place sparkled so. Potatoes had been peeled and were ready in a saucepan of water. Neck end of mutton was simmering with carrots, onions and turnips, not forgetting pearl barley, all flavoured and seasoned with gravy salt and a bay leaf or two. Poppy turned to Nan, wanting to hug her for the wonder she was, but stopped short. Nan had given up all pretence and was now empty-faced. Her eyes held shock, for within just a few days, Ros's appearance had altered so.

'It ain't good, Poppy,' she said very quietly. 'I want you to go in there and hold all of her attention if she doesn't go back to sleep. I didn't realise that getting upstairs'd be too much for her. We'll have to get the bed down in the front. We'll have to ask Daniel to help us move the sofa upstairs. If Ros hears us making a row, explain as how it's to help us! You know, on account it'll make the fetching and carrying more easy, like. You'll have to sleep on the sofa because if you get into bed when you're cold it'll kill her stone dead. Don't let on about her being weak and all that. We've got to make her forget all about weakness and dying. She's got to believe

71

she's going to get well now she's home – and if there's anyone who can convince her, it's you.'

'As God is my witness, I'll make her believe it,' Poppy gasped and fled.

She heard Nan banging fiercely on the scullery wall. Daniel would hear and come back. It was something they all did in Jezebel Street, when they needed help.

Daniel had helped out next door as much as he could, then tried to console dear old Floss, who'd given way to tears once she had returned to number four, and finally fallen into his bed. Now it was late, the day all but done. Daniel had enjoyed a long, deep sleep. Sitting in the top front he rented from Flossie, he thought pensively that it was good to be alive and in full health. Young Ros didn't stand a chance and it showed. Poor old Poppy! She sensed it too, deep down, he could tell by her eyes, though she'd never give in and admit it. Charlie carrying on like that hadn't helped much either. Poor little devil. Poor sparky young Poppy! As he'd watched her standing there facing Charlie, all white and drawn and helpless, she had reminded him of himself all that time ago.

He got up and walked across the room to light the gas. The blue-tipped flames curled round and finally made the mantle glow. Its light showed a comfortable room. The odds and ends of furniture all belonged to him. This was his home, he had got it together himself. He could leave any time he wanted, but chose to stay. He could afford better now, but it wouldn't be the same. Strange how things happened. Life was a rum do all round.

Daniel picked up his library book, which was all about politics. The politicians he admired were Arthur Henderson and above all, Ramsay MacDonald. It was Daniel's desire to see a Labour government, though this was merely a distant dream.

He thought of the national strike of coal miners for higher wages during October of the previous year. For a while back there it had seemed that the railway men would join in and bring about an all-out strike, too. Others, including dockers, were also growling their discontent. But when it all boiled down to it and they should have held fast, the unions fell into

72

disarray. They gave in and the upshot was that the workers felt let down. By Christmas there had been nearly 750,000 men signing on at the labour exchanges.

Daniel frowned, unable to concentrate on his book, finding it impossible to dismiss the memory of Poppy's expression after Charlie had got through with her. Poor little devil, being disowned like that! Charlie was a fool for believing he'd been swizzed. You only had to look at Poppy to know that. But that wouldn't help the poor kid. She'd never be able to forget all those harsh words. He never had. He clearly remembered just how it felt.

The years slipped by and he was standing before a cold, evil old man who lived in a big house.

'Take him away,' the white-bearded, narrow-faced man had snapped, glaring at the woman holding Daniel's small hand. 'Take him to the Home I told you about. Don't bother me with this matter again.'

So he had been taken to the Home, a bewildered seven-year-old who'd just left hospital after a long stay. Something truly terrible had happened to his world: there had been a gas explosion. His parents were gone. His father, John Devere, had died trying to reach his wife. She lay like a broken doll, crushed to death, beside Daniel. He, badly burned on his neck and chest, lay trapped by his legs under the same beam that had killed his mother.

Daniel's mind was racing now. He should be getting ready for night shift, but he'd be going to Temple Mills no more. Not bad for a poor Home kid. Not bad at all!

The Devere Children's Home had taught Daniel to be self-sufficient, neat and tidy. To be obedient, mind his manners and keep out of trouble if he could. Above all, he had learned to stick up for himself in Skelton School. Yah-booed for a rotten orphan most days of his school life, he had become as tough as necessary to survive. The Home was run on strict but caring lines, and owed a great deal to charity. Daniel learned to hate snobs, smug-faced do-gooders and the sanctimonious condescension of the rich. Yet he had to thank those same people, for it was through their generosity that the Home had acquired its library. In spite of his gammy leg, Daniel had been very good at taking up the cudgels on behalf of himself and the timid kids unable to stand up to the bullyboys.

At fourteen he'd gone to Stratford to train as fitter. They were a rough and ready crowd at Temple Mills but they had taken the new young whippersnapper to their hearts. He had rented Flossie's top-front room because of Flossie's warmth and friendliness. Now the stern old man he had hated from the one and only day he had met him, was dead. Perhaps, Daniel thought, he could understand him now, just a little, but he could never forgive.

The solicitor's letter had explained all. The old man had been called Austin J. Devere. The gist of the letter was that Austin J. Devere's brother John had run off with, and then married, the girl Austin was engaged to and loved. The old man's bitterness had lasted him for the rest of his life. His one regret was the casting-off of his only living relative, Daniel. The bulk of the family fortune had gone to various charities, including that of the Devere Children's Home, which the Devere family had themselves founded in 1809. Daniel had been left an annuity of £500, and a place on the board of the Children's Home.

Outside, the temporary peace of Jezebel Street was shattered as Reggie Parker rode his motorbike home. When the engine fell silent, there came the sound of someone opening a front door, then shutting it with a bang. A second later Vic Parker could be heard all down the street.

'You noisy sod! What's the matter with yer?'

The wind whisked the greasy paper that had held fish and chips down the street. It lifted and rustled like a dry white ghost along the kerb. A clouded moon broke through, its beam glancing through the window onto the empty sofa that Daniel had lugged up the stairs of number two.

Downstairs, Poppy, wrapped in a blanket, lay on the floor beside Ros's bed. Both girls were sleeping peacefully, as were their companions, Josh and Jo . . .

Life picked up after that. Ros, now content, began to get better by the day. The doctor came and went, nice-faced, grey-haired old Dr Fox, who really cared for his patients, no matter whether they were rich or poor. After just one week he

74

pronounced a miracle: Ros, no longer stressed, was on an even keel. Though bedridden and not strong, she began to enjoy holding court.

Sandy came often. He was very likable, Poppy thought, quiet and careful where Ros was concerned. Yet he had a waggish humour when he let himself go, and could actually make Ros laugh.

Daniel popped in and brought little presents: a bottle of scent, chocolate, flowers. He would sit with them like a big brother, joining in where he could with the talk. Mostly he would just watch and listen, smiling a little at their foolishness. Jessica made sheep's eyes at him, Ros glowed, and Sandy acted the man and would wink and smile as if to say, 'Girls!'

Poppy knew that she would always adore Daniel. Remembering his threat to marry her one day made her chuckle. Some hopes! Daniel was Daniel and that was all.

Ros did not need her cousin so much now, so Poppy joyfully got on with her own life. She whipped through her usual chores, made a great fuss of crippled Lenny, read heaps, and had fun fending off the Harrys of the world.

Everything was going great guns. Ros was getting truly well and loved being spoiled. Nan's tight expression had relaxed at last.

I can't wait for her to get out of the front room, Poppy thought, glad to be free. A sickroom's a sickroom no matter what, and it gets so stifling in there!

She picked up her library books and all but danced along the road.

Chapter Five

It was April already and Sunday. That morning Charlie had brought bunches of violets out of a tissue-lined box. Delicate perfume had vied with and won against the crisp greengrocery smell. Charlie and Poppy had never mentioned their row and carried on as before, but Poppy's hurt remained and her adoration of Charlie had cooled.

Miracles were happening. Ros appeared to be getting stronger. The girls had been discussing plans for the garden Poppy had made behind the house. It was well dug and sifted, ready for the plants Bill Bannerman was going to supply. Bill had looked at the roses on Ros's chocolate box, recognised them and ordered a bush for Poppy. It would stand alone with alyssum all round it, a mass of pink rising from a sea of white, just as Ros wished.

'Oh, Charlie!' Poppy whispered. 'Don't they smell lovely?'

'Cor blimey, ducks, here we go again! I'll never make a fortune with you under my feet. Go on, take a couple of bunches back to Ros.'

'Ta ever so,' she laughed, mimicking Mrs Peel at her bosomly best. 'You're a real toff!'

Poppy made her way home slowly, holding the violets to her nose, breathing in their delicate perfume. Suddenly she began singing Marie Lloyd's rollicking song 'I'm One of the Ruins that Oliver Cromwell Knocked Abaht a Bit'. Ros liked the song almost as much as her favourite, 'I'll Be Your Sweetheart', and said that she was one of the ruins. But it was only a joke.

Ros was glad whenever Sandy came to see her. She had laughed softly and agreed when he suggested that soon she'd let him carry her outside into the garden Poppy had made. Sandy was certainly big and strong enough, and – Poppy now thought – wonderful all round. His wide, saucy grin showed white, even teeth. He was a good-looker all right, and a friend, loyal not only to Ros, but also to Poppy. He always got her to join in and acted as though she wasn't a gooseberry at all. And he always managed to buy two lots of sweets. Sandy was a regular customer at the sweetshop that dealt in farthings and he could make a halfpenny go far. Then again, Daniel brought chocolate bars and flowers.

Daniel now seemed to be quite rich, for all he never went to Temple Mills these days. Where he went was a bit of a mystery. Flossie said that Daniel was obsessed with politics, that he was a Labourite; some said a Bolshy. Whatever the truth, at home at least, he kept himself to himself. But Poppy knew where to find him: his regular nights at the library never changed. She'd ask him what he was up to, she thought mischievously. Yes, come right out with it if she got the chance. That'd make him screw up his blue, blue eyes. He'd tell her to buzz off, no mistake about that!

Happier than she had been since Ros had been taken ill, Poppy dawdled along. She changed her tune and sang, 'Bluebells I gather, take them and be true . . .' One day, she thought, she'd have enough money to take Ros to the country. They'd see fields and fields of bluebells growing, and smell their scent. In the meantime, the lovely violets would do.

Spring was on the way, and there was hope everywhere. Ros had sensed the coming of spring the previous night, and her cheeks had flushed pink, her eyes had shone bright. 'I've just thought, Poppy,' she said, 'it won't be long before Sandy and me will be officially leaving school. It's a pity you'll have to wait till after Christmas. But it's quite soon for me. Even though I've been able to wangle lots of time off, it's good to know I won't have to sit and keep under Miss' eagle eye ever again.'

They had giggled together just like old times.

Poppy picked up her heels and ran the last few paces to number two. She flung open the street door, then frowned.

77

The front-room door was ajar. Nan usually kept it closed in case Ros got caught in a draft. Poppy went in to Ros, then her mind rose high and wild in a soundless scream.

Nan was sitting by the bed, very upright, quiet and still. There was an unearthly silence in the room. Ros, in the bed, looked like a statue made from wax. Her eyes were closed, her hair was neatly brushed and fanned out against the pillow like burnished gold. Poppy felt the terror inside her well up from her toes and knot under her heart like ice. Her mind was reaching up, up to the sky, begging and crying, 'Ros, Ros, come down from the clouds. Ros, don't leave me here on my own. Ros, I can't bear it. Ros, without you, it ain't worth going on.'

Everything was in slow motion, even Nan turning her head. Nan's face looked skull-like, it was so tightly drawn. Her eyes were large, shadowed, and held such a desperation of soul that Poppy knew Ros wasn't coming back. Not ever.

' I . . . brought her some violets,' Poppy whispered. 'She . . . she likes them.'

'She don't want no violets now,' Nan said in a bleak, empty way. 'She can't see them or smell them. She don't want nothing now.'

Poppy couldn't move. She couldn't tear her eyes away from Ros' waxen, doll-like face.'

'Nan,' she whispered in a small faraway voice, 'Nan – please tell me it isn't true.'

'She's gone,' Nan said bitterly. 'She went to sleep and she never even waited to say goodbye. She's left us. Left us here for ever, d'you hear? They'll take her out of this house and carry her away and stick our beautiful girl in the dark, dirty ground and . . .' Her voice rose high and wild. 'And there ain't no God! I swear there's only a black-hearted devil up there.'

'Don't!' Poppy's hands went over her ears. 'Don't talk about them taking her away. Don't! I think I'll go mad.'

'All I wish –' Nan's eyes were suddenly eagle-bright, awful, her tone so desperate and wretched it was unrecognisable. 'All I wish is that . . . that you didn't look so much like her. I don't think I can stand it. Just seeing you come in was a shock – with your back to the light and all. No, I don't think I can stand anything any more.'

Poppy's legs felt numb. Her mouth had gone dry. There was a tight band closing relentlessly, pressing on everything in her head. She walked stiffly upstairs to the bedroom that she and Ros had shared. Josh and Jo were sprawled out on the old horsehair sofa and Poppy sat beside them. In a daze, she was willing herself to feel something of Ros, sense her, see her, hear her. There was no feeling, no presence in the room, nothing! Ros was not there, she would never have her wish and move back upstairs again. It was suddenly unbearable, and Josh stretching and yawning so unconcerned didn't help to dispel the sense of unreality encasing Poppy now.

Poppy walked out of the room and down the stairs very slowly. Dazed, she went into the kitchen and carefully folded Ros' newly washed and aired woolly jacket that Nan had worked so hard to get. Then she went to the window and stood mutely staring at the tatty little yard. The earth had been dug up all round it, every stone taken away, every weed; the topsoil was sieved and waiting for borders to be made of white, blue and yellow.

But Ros would never see the flowers. Ros had gone, gone, gone. Where? Why? Ros was wicked to leave her so achingly alone. Cruel! A terrible nausea clawed at Poppy's stomach, yet most of her felt numb. She continued to stare at a world that was vast and empty and unreal. As if from a million miles away she heard the splutter and roar of Reggie Parker's motorbike. The departure of the vehicle heralded the return of the awful stillness, and it seemed that Jezebel Street slept.

She turned away from the window. The kitchen around her had altered in some way; it was reflecting herself, motionless, abandoned, cut in half and worn out. Her spirit had gone – gone with Ros. She wanted to run for comfort to Nan, but didn't dare. Nan might look at her in that terrible way again, and hate her for looking like Ros. And . . . and wish it was her, Poppy, who was lying there like wax on the bed. She ought to have died alongside Ros! It was an aching sin to be alive and living in the hell that was Jezebel Street.

Poppy slid to the floor and knelt there. And it was only then that she became conscious of the crushed violets still caught in the steely grip of her tormented hand. Violets? Ros should have had orchids, roses, all the beautiful things Poppy had promised to buy her when she became rich. But Ros would never see that day. She had been born and had died in Jezebel Street, and Poppy wished that she was dead and done for too . . .

Distant relatives and a few friends, including Sandy and Daniel, had departed. Poppy and Nan, drained of emotion now, sat before the fire looking sombrely into the orange glow. Poppy's face was ghostlike, the black of her dress cruelly accentuating her pallor. Her face was now frail-looking, elfin, her skin like parchment. Grief had matured her, had taken away her puppy fat and fined her down. Had she but known it, she was beautiful.

She and Nan remained silent, a gulf between them caused by the unfathomable sadness that had washed everything else away. They had gone about life as it had to be, thinking little, saying nothing, finding it almost impossible to cope. But both had quietly and grimly seen to it that Ros had everything just right. Now the funeral was over. The handsome black horses with their silver harnesses, and tall black ostrich plumes held so proudly on their heads, had gone. And Ros had been lowered into the ground at St Catherine's. All around there had been the flowers that mourners had sent – flowers that Ros would have hated because they were just so many heads imprisoned in wire and moss, not dancing and alive in the breeze. If the mourners had given Ros so much as a single dandelion while she was alive, her eyes would have lit up sun-bright. Now they gave her doomed flowers, and Ros was a prisoner herself – in a long shiny box.

Poppy sat there cocooned in dazed nothingness. She felt old and cold and wiped out.

The door opened and Flossie came in, her black dress and jet beads highlighting her frizzy fair hair. Behind her was Daniel in a black suit, white shirt and black tie. He didn't seem real, he was so smart, but the warm kindness in his expression was just the same. Sandy had gone the moment the priest had finished speaking at the graveside. A strange, reserved Sandy with a tight, empty face.

'I'm going to sit here with you, Nan,' Flossie said. 'And Daniel's going to take Poppy out to get some fresh air and some colour back into her cheeks?'

'Don't bother, Floss,' Nan replied in a quiet, dead voice. 'Clary offered to stay, so did Charlie, but I told them to go. That I wanted to be on my own.'

'Well, me dear ducks, you ain't shifting me!' Flossie was using the tone people used to patients in hospital, like trying to pretend in a bright cheerful way that there was nothing really wrong. 'So just you sit still and shut up.'

'Floss,' Nan sighed tiredly, 'I just want to –'

'Believe that life don't go on? Well, it does, you know it, and so do I. Now me and Daniel have both said as how it's going to be. He's looking after young Poppy, and I'm sticking with you. Tonight you're both coming next door with me for a lovely meal that my mum's going to make.'

'No, Floss, we couldn't,' Poppy stammered. 'I don't think Nan's up to it and . . .' She turned to her aunt, 'Nan?'

Nan continued to stare into the fire. She was hunched up, shrivelled and crushed. She did not look into Poppy's face and never had from the moment Ros had gone. All Nan wanted was to be left alone. That was when she could cry.

Flossie would have none of it.

'Don't be so bloody selfish, Nan.' she said briskly. 'You've got to listen to me and take notice. All right? Mum's wanting to do something just to let you know how she and Dad feel. They remember all the times you've come and seen to them, and helped me out when I've had to finish some work. They specially think of how you were when they both nearly died of flu a couple of years back.'

Nan shrugged and then Flossie lost her patience.

'Gawd, Nan, pull with me, not against! Things can't always go one way. It's nice to give, but gracious to receive. That's what they tell us, right? Besides, you ain't the only one with finer feelings, you know.'

Daniel walked over to Poppy and pulled her out of her chair. 'Come on, matey, up you get. Let's leave them to it, eh?'

She went with him, uncaring, but once in the street, she felt relief.

'Thank you,' she said sombrely. 'I couldn't breathe in there. The whole place smells of wreaths.'

'It's bound to be rotten at first, Poppy,' he told her. 'We all go through hell when we lose someone we love.'

'I didn't think you had anyone to lose, Daniel,' she whispered sadly. 'I thought you were like me, always alone.'

'A long time ago I had a mum and dad. Then they died, but I still remember how it used to be. Then I was left all alone. Now it's all water under the bridge, but just think, Poppy. You're not alone, you've got Nan and Charlie, Clary and Rags, you have your two soppy old cats – and you have me.'

She looked up at him with wide, heart-broken eyes. 'And you're here now when I need you most.' She managed a watery smile. 'Even though I know I'm usually like a thorn in your side. Oh . . . oh, Daniel!'

Poppy's face crumpled and she began to cry as openly and as wildly as a lost child. Then she was in his arms and he was stroking her hair, trying to comfort her.

'It's all right, matey. It'll be fine by and by. Let me take you to the pictures, eh? There's something good showing at the King's Hall.'

'I – couldn't take it in,' she choked out at last. 'Please, Daniel, can I come and sit in your room?'

He put his arm round her waist and led her into number four.

Life after that went on in an automatic way. Nan went off to do her floor-scrubbing at the Home. Her face was still and her eyes empty when she came back early one mid-May evening.

'I hear as how old man Devere popped off a short while ago. He left a lot of money, so the kids are sure of a place to live. There's a new member on the board, whatever that means, but it's reckoned he's got most of the say. He must be a nice sort because all of us have been given a rise in pay.'

'That's good, Nan. Very good indeed.' Poppy was puppy-eager to say the right thing, to please, to get on the right side of Nan. 'Now you'll be able to get new shoes, and –'

'What I'm trying to say is that you don't need to go up Charlie's no more.' Nan's voice was tight, toneless. 'There's no point now I've cleared up the last of what I owed.'

'But I thought the little extra helped!' Poppy argued. 'Nan, I want to help, don't you understand?' The guilt she felt for looking like Ros and, even worse, for not dying instead of Ros, refused to go. 'I don't mind, really! And Charlie's leaned over backwards to be nice to me since . . . Ever since he told me I wasn't his kid.'

'Because he knows he made a fool of his mouth, that's why.' Nan's tone grew edgy. 'Well, do as you like, girl. But I ain't taking your wages from now on. I'll tell him to give it to you direct. The real reason for you working up there's gone.'

She's washing her hands of me, Poppy thought in panicky despair. She stepped forwards, urgent now.

'But I eat, don't I? I live here in your house and –'

'Don't you understand?' Nan's eyes blazed now. 'I need to work harder than ever before. I don't want nothing from anyone, only what I get for myself! Save your money. When you leave school, if you can get a job, save every penny of your wages. Go about your business and get rich. That's what you promised her, wasn't it? And one day,' Nan added bitterly, 'if you're hard-working and careful, you'll get out of Jezebel Street, just like you've always wanted. And don't ever think I'll stand in your way.'

'Nan,' Poppy sobbed, 'I wish I didn't look like –'

'Shut up!' Nan screamed. 'I told you, shut!'

After that, Nan went out of her way to work harder than ever before. Because the house seemed devoid of warmth no matter how much coal went into the range, because it was now just like an empty shell, Poppy also stayed in it as little as possible. She worked far longer than necessary in Charlie's, and he put up with her moping around. When she got under his feet one morning, he jokingly told her to buzz off and help Bill. She looked over to nice, quiet old Bill Bannerman and raised her brows.

'Would that be all right?'

'If you like,' he said in his usual quiet manner. You had to strain yours ears to hear what Bill said. 'Comes from years of talking to hisself,' Charlie had once quipped. 'Come with me now,' Bill went on, then hesitated before adding, 'That's if you want to.'

For the first time since she had known him, Poppy realised how well-spoken Bill was. She thought vaguely that his folks must have been a cut above the sort crowding Jezebel Street. Quite rich they must have been, with their smallholding and all. But their world had died with Mrs Bannerman, and the father and son had closed in on themselves.

It took a long time, it seemed like years, walking beside Bill with his barrow, to get to his old grey house.

Bill Bannerman's place was wide and sprawling on the edge of Leyton Marshes. It was all very run-down and far too much for one man, but the rows of growing things were straight and neat, and clearly received loving care. Poppy saw one big glasshouse with clay pots outside it. To the left was a huge pile of horse manure.

'I pay kids a penny a bucket,' Bill told her. 'It's very good stuff. But none of that need bother you. You really want to help?'

'If I may.'

'I'll give you five shillings if you'll come here through the week and look after the house.'

'I thought you wanted me to plant things and help grow –'

'I'd want you to tidy up inside – if you can.'

'For five bob,' she said gravely, 'I think I'd jump over the moon. Nan wants me to save up, you know.'

He was not listening. His faraway eyes were on long ridges of earth. 'I'll get on with my planting,' he told her.

Poppy would have liked to wander around, but Bill had retreated into his shell. He had said what he had to; now his mind was on other things. He took her up to the door of his house, opened it for her, then turned on his heels. She stood on the step and watched him walk to the end of a row and pick up a handful of plants from a box. As he walked along the row, he stamped the plants in.

'It's a wonder you don't kill them stone dead,' she said huffily to thin air, and entered the house. It smelled stale and stuffy. The walls were solid enough outside, but inside the halfway there was damp. Poppy walked along the hall and found the kitchen. It was in a disgusting muddle, but fairly clean, just as one would expect, knowing Bill. But the Bannerman house had the same feel as number two Jezebel

Street. It was just a shell to cover a naked soul from the world, a hideaway for loneliness.

Poppy rolled up her sleeves and set to. By dusk it all shone, tidy and clean. Every room was swept and dusted, Bill's bed was made, and framed sepia photographs of long-gone relatives looked sternly from behind newly washed glass. There was a fire in the massive kitchen range, now black-leaded and polished. On top there now bubbled a good nourishing stew. Poppy had used vegetables she found in a box under the stone sink, and opened and cubed a tin of corned beef, adding pearl barley, plus two tablespoons of gravy browning.

'This'll warm the cockles of your heart,' she told Bill when he came in. 'Best get it down you.' She cut two doorsteps of bread. 'I'm starving myself, so I'll have just a little if that's all right with you? It is? Good! We'll have what's left tomorrow. After we've eaten, I'll get off back home.'

He nodded, then, having taken off his working boots and set them outside the door, he went upstairs to the bathroom. When he returned she looked at him under her eyelids, amazed at the transformation. Bill had washed and changed and looked like a gentleman. Clearly he had acted this way every night of his life. She felt the colour flooding her cheeks as inspiration burned. She would watch and listen and learn. She was going to be a rich lady one day, and she'd need to know how to speak and act.

He sat down at the newly scrubbed kitchen table. She put his piled-up plate in front of him, anxiously watching his face. She had worked like a dog all day, and it showed, it really did! She had even polished the round, very beautiful table in the next room. Not the large front room, which was clearly used as best, but the one in which Bill stayed most, judging by the books and magazines in there, which were mostly about growing things. Clearly Bill loved his work.

Was he pleased with what she had achieved? No one could ever tell what was going on in Bill's head. She wanted to shake him for not saying a word. He reached for the pepper and salt, then picked up the knife and fork and ate slowly, carefully and in silence. When the plate was empty, he looked across the table and smiled a wide, slow smile.

'Thank you, Poppy. That was very good. Now,' he went on, 'when you're ready, I'll walk you back to the main road where you can catch a tram.'

She crimsoned; trams cost money and she had none with her. 'It's all right, Bill, I've got two strong legs.'

'And a stout heart,' he told her quietly. 'But you must be tired out and you don't need a two-hour walk. Don't worry, I'll pay your fare and at a penny a mile it's cheap at the price. It was nice to come in and find things warm and cheerful. You'll come again?'

'Every night if you want me.'

'I would like that,' he said.

It was a long walk to the main road and dark, with not a gas lamp to be seen. But Bill carried a storm lantern and the time soon went by. He gave her the fare for the ride home and stood at the stop, watching till the tram moved away. She sat there, her body swaying to the jolting of the tram, her mind alive and working things out.

'Five shillings,' she whispered to herself. 'What with that and the half-a-crown I get from Charlie, I'll have seven and six a week. I'll do as Nan says and save it all up. I'll do it for Ros. I'll get rich, and she'll look down from up there in the sky and know I've kept the promises I made.'

Poppy was wide awake and ready for Charlie's at five-thirty the next morning. She fell asleep in class, ignored Miss' sarcastic remarks, and tried to concentrate. But she was thinking of going back to Bill's place that night and determined to work harder than ever before. And from now on, Bill's evening meal would be set on the round table. She now felt instinctively that Bill was not used to eating in the kitchen even though he was alone. No, Bill's mum had taught him to eat in the dining room.

After that a pattern was set. Work and save, save and more work. Bill was pleased with her interest in the growing side of things and even gave her a book he no longer used. Entitled *The Smallholder Encyclopaedia*, it was a mine of information. Poppy liked the section on flower growing the best, but resolved to learn it all by heart. She was not interested in the sections about beekeeping nor livestock of any kind. But vegetable production, fruit and flowers held her interest as greatly as Ros' garden had. Deep down she hoped that Bill would let her work outdoors with him. When she felt she had learned enough, she would ask.

The day came when, wonder of wonders, Bill took her to his bank. Inside the forbidding building, he confidently told the snooty young man behind the grille that Miss Ashton had come to open an account. So it was that Poppy held a book that showed in black and white that she had five whole pounds. This had been made up by a generous Bill, once he had learned of her life's plan.

'Treat it as a small bonus, Poppy,' he had told her. 'Just to give you a start.'

Work stopped her thinking and feeling. Best of all, it kept her out of Nan's sight. Poor Nan still couldn't bear to look at her because she was so like Ros.

Summer came and went unnoticed. Poppy was thinking only of work. In between school and Charlie's and Bill's she still managed to go to the library for old Mr and Mrs Wells. Since she was running Bill's house like clockwork, she was able to leave much earlier. To save the tuppence fare, she walked home. Save, that was now the golden rule. It was important to put every brass farthing by. One day she would be rich. Money made money, Nan said. Well, she had to get the pounds and pennies to start with, and with her every inch of the way was Bill.

She had found coloured covers and curtains, and even gathered wild flowers for vases, since those Bill grew were to be sold. It was getting to feel like home. And Bill, silently looking about him, was clearly pleased. He told Charlie that she was a treasure, but said very little to Poppy herself. Yet he found her extra jobs and paid her accordingly. So she washed and ironed for him, walked miles to the shops, lugging it all back home. She was even allowed to go into the glasshouse and help with the ferns and flowers on one side, as well as the tall, imposing tomato plants on the other bench, and the climbing cucumbers at the far end.

'One day,' he told her, 'I'll get round to getting another house. There's profit in glass, you know. But frankly, I am quite happy with things as they are.'

87

'You can get really rich, Bill,' she said and looked up, her face glowing. 'Wouldn't that be nice?'

He smiled and shrugged. 'I don't know about that. One needs a reason to amass wealth. I have enough money to get by. I think one must work to live, not the other way about.'

Looking round, she realised that what he said was right – for him.

The year dragged on. Poppy left school without a backward glance. Over Friday's 'penn'orth of each', a pennyworth of fish and the same of chips, she read her report: 'Poppy is a clean and decent girl, a hard worker, willing to help others. She has a good community spirit, but needs to control her temper. She is average in studies, but merits A for both reading and writing.'

'Fat lot of good that'll do you,' Nan sniffed when she heard. 'I take it you'll go after a job at Lowerie's come Monday?'

'I tried,' Poppy said humbly. 'They're full up. But they said to keep going back once a week on the off chance. It's up to how many reach sixteen and get sacked.'

'Well, just you hang on with Charlie and Bill. Seven and six ain't bad for a week's donkey-work, and I know you get bits extra where and when you can. You'll only get a couple of bob extra at Lowerie's. Shorter hours, though. And you can't keep on the way you're doing. Next thing, we'll have you in your box.'

It was a shining, golden moment. Nan actually cared! Then Poppy felt heartbroken all over again because Nan added, 'And I don't think I could face having to fork out for another funeral on your account.'

She didn't mean it, not the way it sounded anyway. Nan was still hurt and wanting to lash out at the world. Poppy ached to spoil Nan. The money in her savings account was really growing. When she brought up the matter of wanting to get wool so Flossie could knit Nan a pretty jacket, her aunt's eyes blazed.

'I told you, I want nothing! I can keep myself and this place going on my own. You'll leave one day, oh yes, you will, and I'll have to manage then. Besides, I –' Nan's face flushed up, then went white – 'I'm going to wear Ros's from now on. It'll be like she's cuddling me.'

'Oh, Nan!' Poppy brushed her hand angrily across her eyes. 'Don't you think I feel lost and lonely too? Can't I even help to pay for the coal, the rent, the food?'

'What's up?' Nan was wounded and on the defensive now. 'Fish and chips not good enough for you now?'

'Nan, please, I –'

Nan gave her a single blazing look, and from then on kept up her stiff, distant air.

She wants me to go and leave her, Poppy thought sadly, and one day I will.

Christmas was a miserable affair. It was the unwritten law that presents were bought at Woolworth's where nothing was priced above a sixpenny piece. It was Nan's rule, always had been, in order 'to save others feeling daft because they can't afford more'.

Now, without Ros, there were no chains, no tinsel, no gay paper bells. Nan even spurned the tree that Charlie said they could have. Eventually she turned to Poppy.

'You're to go to Charlie's for your dinner. Got a turkey, Clary has, and fruit and nuts, and all that kind of stuff. I'm going to be with Flossie for a change.'

'Can't I . . . Can't I come too?' Poppy whispered forlornly.

'No!' Nan's tone held panic. 'Not this time. I can't stand the memories and – Poppy, you must understand!'

Try hard though they did, Charlie and Clary couldn't disguise the fact that they felt hurt at Nan's rejection, and since she wasn't there they would have preferred to spend Christmas alone. Poppy was relieved when the whole affair was over. Clearly, she wasn't wanted anywhere.

The only friends Poppy had these days were Sandy Swift, Jessica and Daniel, when he was around. Poppy had little time for reading now, but continued her trips to the library. No longer interested in romance and happy endings, she took out books about gardening and help for the small nurseryman and the commercial producer. She was more than ever determined to help Bill outside when the busy time came. At least she could be of more use now she had left school.

Crippled Lenny was getting ever more wizened than

before. Poppy took to buying him a little something nice every day. She had to be careful, for Lenny had pride. She got round it by saying that the bread, the cake, the cheese sandwich, anything and everything, were all leftovers from Bill's.

The slump was gripping harder than ever. There was no work and to make things worse, during October 1922 Marie Lloyd collapsed on stage at the Edmonton Empire and all of London cried. Thinking back to that fatal morning, when she had been singing about 'One of the Ruins' and holding violets for Ros, made Poppy's grief writhe into new life. To make things worse, Sandy left.

'Gorn, he has,' Jessica told her as they sat together in Nan's kitchen. 'And bloody good luck, I say.'

'Without saying goodbye?' Poppy asked Jessica sadly. 'Why didn't he come and say goodbye?'

'You were working as usual,' Jessica replied sarcastically. 'And where all your hard slog's going to get you, I'll never know.'

'But he could have come before! He must have known, Jess!'

'No. It was a rush. His old man wangled him in, and he had to drop everything and go. He said he'd write.'

'Oh, I hope he does, Jess. He's so strong and nice and I – I like him very much.'

'Cor! Don't you talk posh these days? And my, how you've changed! You liking a mean, rotten, low-down boy?' Jess's sarcasm was tinged with scorn. 'The world's coming to an end. Anyway, I'm off myself, first chance I get, and I ain't sorry that Lowerie's didn't take us on. If you and me had got lucky and been allowed to slave for them, they'd still chuck us out before we reached sixteen. Cunning lot, the rich are. Hate 'em all, I do. Hate 'em to bits!'

Jessica angrily tossed her newly bobbed hair. She was dolled up in lipstick and lisle stockings, and her daring, shorter-length blue dress was beautifully girdled round her hips and finished with a flourishing bow. A necklace of Woolworth's crystals glinted above the round neckline. Jess's shoes looked new too.

'You hardly look poverty-stricken,' Poppy said tartly,

feeling near to tears. Now she knew that Sandy was no longer there, hovering in the background, she was already missing him. 'And I thought you were going to try and catch a nice old rich man? I don't think even you could marry a man you hated.'

'I've got bigger and better fish to fry. I realise Rene's right, there's a great big world out there and I know I couldn't stand the idea of being tied down. My sister Rene's doing all right in a shoe factory up Hackney way. Good pay it is too, because you get piecework. People do murders to get a job there. In spite of the slump they've got contracts and sell to lots of other countries as well as over here. At least, that's what Rene says. You start at basic pay, but with overtime and piecework you can get almost as much as a man. Not to be sniffed at, eh? Why don't you come along?'

'I can't! Anyway, what with one thing and another, I earn quite a decent screw now.'

'You half kill yourself working all the hours God gives, and for what? You wear rotten clothes what you've hung on to for years. Your hands are bloody awful, I swear you'd dig spuds for old Bill if he asked you. Gawd 'elp us! With me and Rene you'd have just one job and less hours for the same money. And don't forget, for overtime up there, you can get double pay. I don't know why you hang on. After all, you said yourself as how Nan can't stand the sight of you. You'd think she'd got over Ros after all this time.'

'I can't let Bill down for a start and –'

'Gertcha! Let Bill down? Keep everyone else out, you mean. You ain't half a greedy little cow. Poor old Beth Hastings would give her eyeteeth to get in there. She even went and asked him, but he said as how he already had you. But that if you ever left, she could step in. Do anything to get in there, she would.'

'What, for five bob?'

'For half-a-crown if she could, anything! She's like you, mad on saving up. Don't know what's happening round you, do you, eh? Beth's set her cap at that bloody awful sod Peel! Made up her mind, she has. Says he's what she wants and that she gets what she wants, fair or foul, and that he don't stand no chance.'

'She's our age! She can't really believe –'

'Probably scare him into it, once she's old enough. What a scream, eh? She's big enough and ugly enough to double for old Ma Peel and her rotten kid's terrified of his mum, for all his lip. Beth's got it all sewn up, eh? Just fancy, Harry and her! One thump from Beth and he'll finish up in the middle of next week!'

For the first time since Ros, Poppy laughed. All the pent-up emotions that had held her in tight bands of tension and pain, now burst in a blaze of near hysteria. The picture rose up in her mind of big, beefy Beth Hastings, who could down three boys at a go. Beth setting her sights on weedy, horrible Harry Peel, who thought he was so tough, really did have its funny side. A picture of the two of them together was so hilarious that she poked Jessica in the ribs and they both rolled about on their chairs, laughing fit to burst.

The kitchen door flew open and Nan stormed in. Her eyes held green fire. Poppy's hand flew over her mouth. Clearly Nan hated her even more now. Laughing was wrong in this house. A terrible, terrible sin!

Both silent and suitably crushed, Poppy and Jessica quickly left number two.

'I'll talk to Bill,' Poppy said. 'If and when you get the word from your Rene that there's a place for me as well as you.'

'And for now?'

'I'll carry on as usual, work like the Dickens and keep out of Nan's way.'

'Stupid old bitch! She's blaming you for looking like poor old Ros. Not that I've ever seen it. Ros was taller and thinner and paler. Ros was –'

'Shut up, Jess.' Poppy's cheeks were drawn in, her emerald eyes now gleaming with unshed tears. 'If you must know, I understand how Nan feels. And as for all that guff about "time heals", it doesn't! But life goes on and we have to go with it. We can't be hating the whole world for what happened to Ros.'

'All I know is, you need your brains tested for putting up with that old girl. I'd have moved out long ago.'

'Where?' Poppy asked fiercely. 'Now, just tell me where? With no job and no roof, just tell me – and I'll go!'

'You could get round Bill. I know Beth would give her eyeteeth to live in. They're stretched at the seems in her house with all them grandparents and kids. You could ask Bill and –'

'No! I'll pay my own way when I finally go. It just about chokes me to live off Nan, but she won't have it no other way. She's too proud and pig-headed and –'

'Just like you,' Jessica said. 'Well, I'll put a word in for you, to Rene. We'll go together,' Jess said feelingly. 'That I bloody well promise you.'

Time went on. Poppy continued to work at Charlie's and at Bill's. She learned a great deal about growing things, and selling them, too. She was always on to Bill to expand his business, seeing the great potential there, but he turned a deaf ear. She could and did fill her days with work at home as well as outside. But when she saw Nan flinch when she came into the room, when she heard Nan gasp when she forgot herself long enough to tell Nan the truth, that she hated going to Ros' grave, her need to escape grew.

One thing was certain, she told herself fiercely, there would be no more weeping and wailing. If life was going to be a battle, then she would go on with all guns blazing. She would work and save for the day when she made her promises to herself come true. And when that was done, she'd aim even higher, go further, and nothing and no one in Jezebel Street would stop her.

Finally, in 1923, after the country had rejoiced at the marriage of Albert, Duke of York, to the beautiful Lady Elizabeth Bowes-Lyon, Jessica heard from Rene.

'I'm off Sunday night, Poppy,' she said jubilantly. 'D'you still want to come?'

'I'll tell Bill to expect someone else,' Poppy replied quietly. 'You tell Beth, since she only lives a few doors away from you. I wish I'd known sooner. I'm flat broke.'

'Pull the other one,' Jessica scoffed. 'I wouldn't mind that stocking of yours.'

'I'm saving for something too special to ever take anything out.' Poppy's tone was quietly determined. 'So if you want me along because you think I'm well off, have another think.'

'Shut up, you silly moo. I wouldn't want your money

93

anyway. I can always earn a bob or two when I want. Besides, I've probably got through more in a week than you've ever earned.' Her tone was so scathing that Poppy flushed.

'Then I don't know why you're so keen to leave,' Poppy snapped. 'Since you seem to have your own little gold mine. Anyway, I know you think I'm mean, but I made myself a promise, one that I mean to keep.'

'Can I know what it's all about, or is this secret like a sacred bloody vow?'

'One day,' Poppy replied, 'I will have a place with a wonderful garden. I'll fill it with flowers, ones that smell nice. There'll be lots of pink roses and it'll be as lovely as the picture in the school book that Ros so loved. See, Jess? I'm saving up to get it all, just as I promised, for Ros.'

'That's crazy. Ros won't know nothing about it.'

'Oh yes.' Poppy smiled in her elfin way. 'Ros will know all right. And what's more, she'll be there.'

'You're daft. Well, I'm off to tell Beth the good news.' Jessica grinned slyly. 'Perhaps she'll have better luck with old Bill than you. I ask you! Five bob with a few perks chucked in here and there? The old boy certainly saw you coming! Beth'll screw a damned sight more out of him than that. Now don't forget. Halfpast nine under the railway arch. Be there.'

'I feel bad about Bill, and if he or Charlie say –'

'Be like me, cut and run and say nothing! Then no one can talk you out of it. Too soft you are, your pride makes you beaver away, but it's your biggest cross. Pride makes it too hard for you to ask for what you deserve. And, if you remember all that rubbish your aunt goes on about, in that Bible and all, pride goes before a fall. Hard and unfeeling, your Nan is. Can't even see that it'd kill you to go to the grave and think of poor old Ros down there in the ground. If you ask me –'

'Half past nine, under the railway arch,' Poppy gasped and fled.

Suddenly excitement thrilled through her. She was actually going to leave all the misery and dowdiness behind. She was going to live life to the full and laugh and sing and not look over her shoulder all the time in case she saw Nan standing there. She was going to be free, like Sandy, who had never written. And Daniel, who was off minding his own business somewhere, though he still kept his room in Flossie's house. She was going to do what she wanted, do as she chose, just like Bill who didn't give a hang about what others said. She was going to live gloriously – for Ros.

Chapter Six

One Sunday afternoon in September, Nan got ready to go and visit Ros' grave. She still could not understand why Poppy refused to visit St Catherine's and believed her to be callous and hard.

'I won't be back till late,' she told Poppy and gave her a cold, dead look. 'I'll be going straight to Flossie, who'll be making tea. You can look after yourself.'

'I always do,' Poppy flashed back at her. 'I don't want to be any trouble, do I? Go on, dash out without taking a breath, and talk to her! And pretend she can hear you! Spend hours up there, talking to the ground, don't you? Yet you never spare a civil word for me! Still can't stand the sight of me, can you? At least when I speak with her I imagine her up in the clouds, not six foot under the dirt.'

'Stop mouthing on and glaring. It don't cut no ice with me. You'd sooner work all hours, and in your spare time read books. That's what you're going to do now, instead of paying your respects, isn't it? Get stuck into that book you borrowed from Bill Bannerman. And don't think I've not heard you reading out loud. Practising at talking posh like him all the time. You've never been satisfied with your lot, have you? This when you're better off than most. You're sixteen on the twenty-seventh and should have a head on your shoulders by now. I don't know why I put up with you sometimes.'

'Well, you won't have to much longer.'

'Remind me to cry,' Nan snapped and stalked out. And even though Poppy knew that her aunt had not meant it, at least not deep down, she felt as though someone had punched her hard. It will be kinder to Nan if I go, Poppy thought, and it's going to be a million times better for me!

By nine o'clock Poppy had finished her packing. She put the letter she had written on the mantelpiece, in front of the clock. Flossie would read it to Nan and understand everything. Flossie was a good sort. In the letter she had asked Flossie to say goodbye to Daniel and explained why it was best she went. The cats, curled up together, blinked up at her with tawny eyes.

'I'm going to miss you two,' she said then. 'But you'll be all right. Nan loves you as much as I do. In fact, she loves you more than she's ever loved me.'

She almost ran out of the house. Once she had turned the corner, hurried along Skelton Street and into the High Road, she was palpitating with delighted fear and excitement.

Night lay uneasily over all. A clouded moon shed a dimmed light over soot-begrimed roofs and glittered in pinpoints on rain-washed roads. The fierce yowling of a cat momentarily drowned the distant rumbling of an approaching train. Glass-fronted shops glinted like eyes, filled with shadowy hats, vegetables, groceries or shoes. The cobbler's held a red-jacketed clockwork boy. During the daytimes, when he was wound up, with black face beaming and eyes rolling, he brushed back and forth, back and forth, polishing a shoe. 'Goodbye, shoeshine boy,' Poppy whispered and imagined that his wide, beautiful smile was just for her.

The railway arch made a dark tower overhead. There was no sign of Jessica. Now Poppy had made up her mind, she knew that she would never go back, never! As the minutes went by, her unease grew. Where was Jess? Jess must come! Feeling frightened, Poppy wandered down to where the railway walls gloomed, indented and shadowed like bricked-up black holes. Suddenly Poppy heard Jessica swearing, and hurried forwards. She found her friend huddled against the brickwork. Jessica's nose was bleeding and her mouth was split.

'Jess,' Poppy gasped, 'what happened?'

'My dad, that's what happened. Bashed me up rotten, he did.'

'For running away?'

Jessica grinned, then swore because it hurt her bruised lip. 'Caught me at it, he did. Half-a-crown I got from this bloke and when he went, my dad appeared. "Hand it over," he says and I said, "Sod off," so he bashed me until I handed it over. He'll have the time of his life in the Coach and Horses and when he's had a skinful, he'll go home and beat up Mum. Black and blue she'll be by morning.'

'Then shouldn't we go back and warn her?'

'Don't worry, she's used to it. We all are. That's why Rene buzzed off. It was either go, or swing for the old man. Come on, don't dawdle. I'll tidy myself up in the waiting room.'

'Are we going by train?'

'No, we're taking trams. The hostel we're going to is too far away from the station. Oh, Gawd, our luck's in, no one's around. Come on!'

They bent double, creeping under the office window, past the unmanned barrier and onto the station platform. One or two passengers stood about, gawping. The railways staff were fussing round a fat, pompous, very bad-tempered old man who seemed to have enough luggage to sink a battleship. He was obviously very important, and no one took notice of the two girls.

'I felt as if the eyes of the world were on me,' Poppy gasped as she and Jessica stood side by side, staring into the waiting-room mirror. 'I wonder who that man was? He must be very rich. Did you see the leather cases he had? And I've never seen a bigger watch hanging from a chain so thick. It was all solid gold! The train's not late, like he says, I know it's not. Don't the rich carry on?'

'That was old Tilsby,' Jessica said through a cloud of face powder. 'Him what Reggie Parker drives for. Know something? The only one I'm going to miss is Grant. I really like him. He never had to pay me like –'

'Don't tell me, Jess,' Poppy said quickly. 'I don't want to know!'

Jessica's eyes stared out of the mirror into Poppy's face. 'My Gawd,' she said softly, 'you're going to have to change, you know. This job Rene's got us is only a sort of stepping stone. I thought that was understood.'

'I – I don't know what you mean. I –'

'Oh, come on, it don't matter. You'll learn! Let's go.'

They left the station, pushing through with the travellers who left the train Mr Tilsby had been moaning about. Jessica gave the still mouthing man a sour look.

'Old sod, acting like he owns the world! In with all the old tarts, he is. He knows what goes on in his taxis, gets quite a good screw out of it all. Knows his way around, he does, and he helps girls to find places, know what I mean? Helped Rene, he did, and she's grateful. But he's a right'un and no mistake. Threatened to have Rene's face cut, he did, if she opened her mouth about his business – For Gawd's sake, shut your gob. You look like a fish!'

'Jess, I don't think I –'

'Going to run back home, are we?' Jess jeered. 'Scared the world's a bit more than little Miss marm-stink can chew?'

'Jess,' Poppy whispered desperately as they walked to the tram stop. 'There is a job in the shoe place, isn't there? Really and truly? A job?'

'If Rene says so, yes.'

The tram came along and with a single backward glance at the High Road, Poppy followed Jess on. She stared numbly out of the window for a long time, following Jessica in silence when they had to alight and cross over a wide main road to catch yet another tram. The journey seemed to go on for ever.

'We get off here.' Jessica broke into Poppy's uncertainty. 'Come on!'

After a short walk they arrived at a bleak-looking building with a notice outside reading, 'St Martin's Lodge for Young Ladies'. They walked in and found themselves in a hallway with closed doors on either side. The floor was covered with shiny brown lino which also covered the staircase on the right. The walls were washed a dingy beige which on one side held a large, green, baize-covered notice board, headed 'Rules of the House'.

Jessica knocked on the door marked 'Office' and went in straight away. Poppy followed her, feeling sick with nerves. A stern-looking woman with dark hair parted in the middle, pince-nez resting on a sharp nose which pointed accusingly above thin lips, was sitting at a desk. She was dressed in black, and a gold crucifix hanging from a chain round her neck gleamed in the gaslight. Her hands were folded together and resting on a pile of forms before her.

'Evening,' Jessica said brightly. 'We've come to stay. Our room's been paid for by a Miss Rene Davies.'

'Miss Davies has left us,' the woman said crisply. Her eyes behind her pince-nez were so cold and hard that Poppy guiltily looked down to the points of her shoes. The woman rummaged through the lists, then handed Jessica a slip of paper that had been set to one side. 'You are the sister? You are to go to her at this address, and –' she looked down at the form she had taken from the pile – 'Miss Ashton is to stay here. Miss Davies has paid Miss Ashton's rent for a full seven days.'

'Good old Rene,' Jessica exploded, delighted with the turn of events. 'She must be in the money to go the full whack and pay for your room! Well, I'm off.'

'No!' Poppy gasped and felt faint because her inside was churning so. She reached out and clung desperately to Jessica's arm. 'You can't do it, Jess.'

'Do what?' Jessica's brows were raised above suddenly very aggressive eyes. 'What's up with you?'

'You can't leave me here, in a strange place, all on my own.' Poppy's panic grew. 'You promised me!'

'But things are changed. You heard this lady. I'm to go with Rene and you're to stay here – all paid for!' She swung round towards the front door, snapping, 'What d'yer want, jam on it?'

'Jess! Jess, wait! What will I do?'

'Oh, Gawd, and they all think you're the toughest kid down Jezebel Street! Look, Rene's told Mr Carson about us and it's all been settled. You've got to be at Farringdon's at eight o'clock sharp. He's the big cheese up there and what he says goes. The workshop's not two minutes' walk from here. Don't be late, else they'll have your guts for garters. Ta-ta.'

She twisted free from Poppy's grasp and almost ran out of the door. Poppy stood there, terrified, holding the battered suitcase that Ros had used when she went to hospital.

'You are in number fourteen,' the woman said crisply. 'I

will come up with you and turn out the light once you have settled in. One of our most stringent rules is lights out at nine thirty. We have been very lenient, allowing your entrance at this hour. Follow me.'

The woman got up and walked towards the door with a crisp, businesslike air. Poppy followed her like a sleepwalker, shocked at Jessica's betrayal, and already hating the hostel she found herself in. She went upstairs and along the passage to number fourteen. The woman opened the door and went in. Poppy's heart sank even further. The pale gaslight glowed on green distempered walls, and two plain wooden beds, each with a small bedside cabinet. On the beds were a pair of clean, unbleached sheets, a pillow and two folded grey blankets. The floor was covered with dark-green lino patterned with dull brown squares.

'Make your bed. Hurry, please, and get into it as quickly as you can,' the woman ordered spitefully. 'It's cold up here.'

Suddenly Poppy's cheeks flamed. Though her eyes held misery, her tone was quiet and crystal clear.

'Since this room is paid for, it belongs to me for a week. I will make my bed while you wait, but then you will go. No one on God's earth may stand over me and watch me undress.'

'I am Miss Henderson.' The woman's face went white with anger. 'And I am the supervisor of this place. You will do as you are told, Miss Ashton. Otherwise –'

'You can't throw me out. You've taken the money. Please go now, Miss Henderson. I will manage very well, and I will turn out the gas as soon as I'm ready.' Because the woman was now gasping like a fish, Poppy lifted her chin and glared as she added politely but firmly, 'Thank you.'

'Please leave everything tidy before you leave in the morning.' Miss Henderson gave glare for glare. 'You may buy breakfast – porridge or one thick slice of bread – for a penny. You may buy slices of bread and dripping to take away. Any other meals are up to you. I shall give you ten minutes and then I will return to make sure you've turned off the gas.'

Once Poppy heard the woman's crisp footsteps walking away, she made the bed. Her cheeks were scarlet and her eyes bright with unshed tears. She was shaking from head to toe as she undressed, padded over the cold floor, turned out the gas which was set on the far wall, and felt her way back over to the bed. She climbed between sheets that felt damp, and curled herself up in a tight, tense ball.

The room was pitch-black, windowless. It was terrifying, like being shut up in a coffin ready to be buried alive. She might just as well be! No one gave a tuppenny cuss about her, and the final, most soul-cutting desertion of all had been delivered by Jess. Poppy put her head under the bedclothes and cried herself to sleep.

Farringdon's was easy to find, but all the way along the road Poppy looked in vain for a sign of Jess. Surely she wasn't going to pass up the chance of a job? A stroke of luck that many unemployed would give their eyeteeth to have?

Poppy's heart was beating too quickly as she entered the gates of a stark-looking building. On the right side of a cobbled yard stood a door marked 'Office'. Poppy went to it and knocked.

'Enter,' called a voice, then, when Poppy, openly quaking, went in, 'Yes?'

'Please, I have an appointment with Mr Carson.'

The plain-looking, bespectacled secretary sitting at a table looked her over. With her flowing hair sporting a ribbon as green as her eyes, and in her best, though sensible, dark-brown Sunday clothes, Poppy looked lovely. The secretary's lips curled as she snapped, 'Name?'

'Poppy Ashton.'

'Just a moment, please.'

The secretary made a great play at sorting through forms, plainly getting some satisfaction out of keeping Poppy standing there. Feeling small, Poppy looked round her, her pulses racing with fear and dread. She hated Judas Jess in that moment. She wanted to cry, turn tail and run back to the safety and familiarity of Jezebel Street. Instead, she tried to concentrate on the scene before her. The office was clean and smelled of polish, paper, ink and files. There was another girl, sitting at a small table almost hidden behind a screen. She had bobbed hair, was wearing navy blue and was slowly and painfully tapping on the keys of her large typewriter. Poppy started as the secretary handed her a form.

'Please fill this in and then sit down and wait.'

Feeling she was back at school and up before the headmistress, Poppy filled in the form, then sat down on one of the chairs against the wall and waited. The form was taken by the girl with bobbed hair, out of the office. Clasping her hands firmly in her lap to stop them shaking, Poppy sat there, all squeezed up inside, wondering wildly what was to come next. She jumped when a buzzer sounded, just like the one in Doc Fox's waiting room, and the secretary said, 'Mr Carson will see you now. Through that door.'

She waved vaguely and Poppy walked to the door marked 'Private', feeling as though she was going to her own execution. She knocked timidly and entered as instructed. Directly facing her, sitting at a huge, carved oak desk, was a large, well-dressed, florid man. He had receding, sandy hair, rather nice blue eyes fringed with all but white eyelashes, and a kind mouth with full lips. He was clean-shaven and she could smell the tang of the pomade he wore, fresh, manly and with a hint of apples. His hands were folded together before him and resting on a new white blotter pad. In one swift glance Poppy took in his wonderfully clean fingernails, the gold watch chain looping from his tweed waistcoat, and she knew she was facing a gentleman.

He smiled and pointed to a chair in front of his desk. 'Ah! Good morning, Miss Ashton.'

'Good morning, sir,' she whispered.

'You have come here highly recommended by a Miss Irene Davies, is that correct?'

'Yes, sir,' she replied and gulped.

His expression was friendly as he looked her over, and she stared back at him, her eyes large in her face. Her apprehension made her look deer-nervous and infinitely lovely. Her innocence shone through, also her panic and desperation.

'Tell me, Miss Ashton,' he asked in meaningful tones. 'just what is it that you feel you can do?'

She crimsoned, feeling she was losing ground. He was tapping the blotter pad with one thoughtful finger and

103

watching her closely. She lifted her chin and replied, 'I am sure I can do anything that Miss Davies can do, sir.'

'Ah!' There was a knowing twinkle in his eyes. 'I rather doubt that, at least, not yet, Miss Ashton. Well, now, could you manage hard work and long hours, do you suppose?'

'I have come here for a job, sir. I – I have never been afraid of hard work or long hours.'

Poppy blinked sharply and her heart fell like a stone. Mr Carson had risen to his feet in a firm, purposeful way. He was much taller than she, and powerful. A toff in his fine clothes and superior manner. Yet he was kind because he was smiling in a nice way, even though he was going to show her the door.

He walked to her and put his arm round her in a friendly, fatherly way. She could smell the faint tang of tobacco mingled with his pomade, and she could feel the warm power of the man through her clothes.

'We will find you something, Miss Ashton,' he told her. 'Give you a little try just to see what you can do, eh? Come along.'

Miss Ashton! Give you a little try? Poppy felt giddy with relief and delight. This rich and powerful man seemed to like her and respect her, even. He was going to give her the chance of a job.

'We make shoes for the rich, and for rather special people, Miss Ashton,' Mr Carson said. 'Many of them in the theatre, some in the moving pictures, and we are famous far and wide for design. You have head of Farringdon's footwear, of course?'

She hadn't, and thought fleetingly of Ginny's Old Clothes, where you could get a decent pair of boots or shoes for tuppence if you had enough patience to sort through the piles. But this was a new and wonderful world. She was going to have a job and get rich!

She followed Mr Carson into a large, long room. The air was thick with the sounds of tapping and banging, and with glue, oil and steam. Poppy saw racks of shoes in all stages of completion, bins full of buckles, bows, leather plaits, laces and fancy leather designs. There were mountains of white shoe boxes and swathes of shiny tissue. There were women at long benches, working quickly, gluing, pulling leather over shapes, swiftly and neatly, never looking up. Mr Carson walked on to a long room separated from the rest. Here men in aprons stood at benches, cutting leather.

'This is called the Clickers' Department,' Mr Carson told her, 'where you will work.' He nodded recognition as a small, bald, chubby man bustled up. 'Ah, Mr Banes, I have decided that this young woman will take over the studding machine to replace Miss Davies.'

'Yes, sir, very good, sir. Training as before?'

Mr Carson looked down and smiled at Poppy, then turned back to Mr Banes.

'Of course,' he said, and left.

'Come with me,' Mr Banes ordered. 'and listen hard because I don't have all that much time. You will receive seven and six a week, and have one hour off for dinner. A second late and it'll cost you a quarter of an hour's pay. Here we are. Here's your machine.'

Unnerved, Poppy looked at a small black machine fixed on a bench, its pedal on the floor.

'Sit down, girl,' Mr Banes said crisply and picked up a toe-shape of navy-blue leather. He placed a templet that had been punched with a sun-ray design of small holes, then rubbed a chalk bag over the surface, making sure that chalk powder had gone through all the holes. 'Now,' he went on, 'you put your piece in the machine, place the pattern directly in the centre and press the pedal with your foot. Get a stud in the centre of each chalk mark, see? Gotta be neat, gotta be quick, gotta be right! Oh, and this is how you load the machine with these small gold studs. Simple, eh? Get on with it, and no messing about. I'll come back later and see how you're getting on.'

She sat down bemused. She saw the stacks of toe-shapes, different sizes and colours. Tentatively she did as Mr Banes had shown her and sighed with relief. It was as easy as pie and she would manage very well.

It wasn't until later that she realised that she was going to earn about the same amount as she had at home. She had no idea of how much rent she would have to find for the hostel, where to get food for dinner, or what the rules and regulations of this new life would be – and it didn't look as if riches were about to fall in her lap as Jess had said. Jessica! 'Just wait till I get my hands on her!' Poppy muttered and pursed her lips. 'I'll strangle her!'

She was intent on her gold studs when Mr Banes returned. He examined her work while she held her breath.

'You've got the hang of it,' he told her and handed her a mug of tea, 'Here, take this, it's on me for today. Oh, and keep working, we don't have no breaks before or after the dinner hour. If you're a bit short of money, you're to go to Mr Carson and ask for a sub. Act like you think he's your fairy godfather and you'll do well. Got an eye for a pretty girl, he has, and he's taken to you fair and square. Never known him to bring a new employee in himself, not even Miss Davies. Mr Carson likes to play the waiting game.'

Poppy was not listening, too anxious to be sure of her work. 'Is the studding really all right, Mr Banes?' she said uncertainly after she had thanked him for the tea and taken a sip. 'You think I'll keep this job?'

'Don't see why not. We'll all breathe easier now you're here. Quite a shenanigans it was, when Rene upped and left. Real nimble-fingered, she was. Made black-studded stars come out like they'd been made in heaven. Above all, Mr Carson liked her a lot. Now he seems to have taken a shine to you.' He picked up one of the pieces of leather and nodded slowly. 'These bits are special, for a big show somewhere. We're lucky on account of this firm having connections. We'll survive the slump if our luck holds out, but we'll all breathe easier with Mr Carson in a good mood, believe me. String him along, girl. You just string him along!'

That night Poppy walked back to the hostel feeling unsure of the change she had made. She had left home to earn money and found herself earning less in a way. And Nan had refused to take a penny. Here, every penny would count, and the awful thing was that Farringdon's kept a week in hand. But she had her past week's wage from Bill and Charlie, and would make it do as best she could. She would not touch a single farthing of her savings. Rather than do that she would go home. Her eyes sparkled like emeralds, but she refused to let the tears fall. She could see Nan's kitchen in her mind's eye, with its wall covered with chrysanthemums, its shining black-leaded range, to which Josh and Jo could never get near enough. And Nan, so tough, so prim and proper – so empty and lost without Ros. Poppy brushed her hand across her eyes. Of course she would have to stick it out, no matter how hard things turned out to be. She would never go back like a dog with its tail between its legs. If and when she went back to Jezebel Street, it would be as a success – and rich enough to buy Nan's house for her. Her spirits lifted at the thought. Yes! Nan should own the house she loved, and there would be another house with a garden, for Ros.

Poppy arrived back at St Martin's and went to the office. 'Miss Henderson,' she said politely to the supervisor, 'may I please know how much I must pay for rent, and –'

'I am busy,' Miss Henderson replied icily and pointed at a yellow poster. 'You will find all you need to know there.'

Clearly she was not to be forgiven for so imperiously dismissing the woman the night before. Poppy's heart sank and she remembered Nan saying bitingly on more than one occasion, 'Life ain't a bed of roses, my girl, and you'll learn that for yourself one day.'

She went up to her room and found that the bed Jessica should have had was now occupied by a surly-looking girl who had mousy hair, a button nose and pimples. Poppy disliked her on sight. The feeling was mutual.

The following days went by in a blurred pattern of desperation, loneliness and need. Poppy stayed in the Clicker room during the first dinner hour and ate nothing, too scared to move away from her bench. When she realised that Mr Banes stayed in too, eating his bread and cheese, and seeming not to mind her presence, she made a habit of buying a slice of bread and dripping from the Lodge and taking it to work. The men rushed off about their own affairs and left her to it.

On the first night in St Martin's, when she found herself cold shouldered when entering the large, draughty communal room, Poppy went out. She found a fish-and-chip shop, bought a pennyworth of chips and ate them from the newspaper as she walked along a long main road. All the shops were shut, but an eating place named Tony's was well lit and doing a roaring trade. Having loitered outside for as long as she could, Poppy returned to the hostel before nine and went straight to her room.

She soon came to realise that the waspish supervisor hated her – so openly, indeed, that the others took their cue from her. The upshot was that Poppy was left severely alone. Life followed a dreary pattern after that, but doggedly determined to make her way in the world, Poppy refused to give in. As soon as she was settled she wrote to Flossie, giving the St Martin's address and saying she had a good job and would write more later on. She sent everyone her love. She received no reply.

At Farringdon's she was the only girl in the male-dominated Clicker room. The females in the other departments knew nothing of her, nor she of them. Sad, missing Nan, Charlie and Clary, and all her friends in Jezebel Street, Poppy wanted to run back home more than once. But Beth Hastings had taken over her job with Bill, and Charlie didn't really need her help in the shop anyway. What was a million times worse, Nan couldn't stand the sight of her face.

For the first time, Poppy understood how good, generous and full her life had been in Jezebel Street. The money that Bill had paid her, and Charlie too, had been more than enough. She had in fact been wealthy if she considered the poor wretches trying to exist on the dole. Even the little houses at Nan's end of the street had been like living in a different world to the Peels, the Kings and the Lambs at Charlie's end, where whole families existed in one awful room.

Her resolution to stay where she was strengthened, even though she hated the Lodge and loathed the mere thought of Jessica Davies. Deep down she was homesick, but she had her pride and somehow she would do what she had set out to do: get rich for Ros.

She wrote another letter to Flossie, telling her a lot of lies about the splendid life she was living. Sending the letter seemed to bring them closer somehow.

Surprisingly, Mr Carson seemed to take a fatherly interest in her. Aware of the dawning admiration she saw in his eyes every time he walked the shop floor, Poppy began weaving romantic dreams about him. Filled with gratitude, not really needing financial help since her own money had given her a start and she lived cheaply on bread and chips, she went to Mr Banes and asked whether he thought Mr Carson might advance her a sub.

'You're really stony-broke?' he asked and winked. 'Or are you just playing games?'

She flushed pink, not wanting to admit, even to herself, that she thought she had fallen in love with Mr Carson. He seemed to have so many occasions to walk through to the Clicker room, and made her heart skip a beat every time he smiled down at her in his warm, kind way. She now daydreamed about him to an almost absurd degree.

'I don't think I'll have enough to get me through, at least not this week, Mr Banes,' she whispered. 'Sometimes I find it very difficult to pay my way.'

'Didn't think you wanted to splash out for a birthday,' he said but joking did not sit well on Mr Banes.

Even so, his words touched a sore point. Her birthday had come and gone, and never had there been a colder or more desolate one. She had hoped for a card with Nan's cross on it, or at least a message from Charlie. There had been nothing. It had been a day like any other, except she had treated herself to a bit of cod with her nightly pennyworth of chips. But it hadn't mattered, not really. She was sixteen, and if it hadn't been for the slump, she would have been working in Lowerie's for the past two years. And be getting ready for the push, no doubt! Lowerie's always did use beggar-labour for the nastiest, most menial jobs. Still, she was now adult and starting all over again, even though it was only for seven shillings and sixpence a week. This was not a step back, she told herself fiercely, but one in the right direction.

'I'm not sure as how you're being very wise, Miss Ashton,' Mr Banes said stiffly. 'I'll have to think about it and let you know.'

He walked away and she watched him, feeling humiliated and angry. 'All for the sake of a measly sub,' she fumed under her breath. 'Why is money so hard to come by? The rich just love seeing the working class down on their knees.

Well, I won't be done. I won't! I have plenty of spare time in the mornings before coming to this place, as well as long lonely evenings. I'll look round for something to do. As Nan says, everyone's got a doorstep that needs scrubbing, or washing to do, not forgetting that we all have to eat!'

She had no friends to waste time with, but it didn't matter. She would earn extra money somehow. Find jobs somewhere, anywhere, and remember what Mr Banes said, 'Gotta be neat, gotta be quick, gotta be right!'

Those words hold all the sound common sense in the world, she thought to herself. As he approached she smiled at Mr Banes, all wide and melting, thinking that his fat little figure held the soul of a sage. He would put in a word at the office for her, too, he needed to keep on Mr Carson's right side. She would give herself a treat and once again bask in Mr Carson's lovely smile. She would ask if she might please be forwarded a half-crown.

She had an idea forming at the back of her mind. With the extra money in her pocket she'd buy herself a hot dinner at midday instead of subsisting on a doorstep of bread and dripping. This she had bought each morning from a kitchen woman as hard-eyed and bitchy as the rest of the St Martin's crowd.

'I reckon as how it'll be all right. You're like a lamb going to slaughter,' Mr Banes said and shook his head. 'It's nearly one o'clock. Best go to his nibs's office now. Tell him I sent you. Good luck.'

Poppy made her way to Mr Carson's office. He called out 'Enter', so she went in, flushed, bright-eyed and nervously excited. He was leaning back in his desk chair, smiling. She stood before him, shy, hardly able to raise her voice above a whisper, she was so besotted.

'Please, sir, Mr Banes said that you might see your way clear to – I mean, I'd like a sub, please, if –'

'Don't be frightened of me,' he told her blandly while his blue eyes looked her over and seemed to like what they saw. 'I will help you, of course. Mr Banes tells me that you are doing very well. Will an advance of two-and-sixpence do?'

'Thank you, sir.'

She stood there, adoring him with her eyes. He was tall and

110

noble, and as different from the Vic Parkers of the world as chalk was from cheese. And he liked her, she could tell. What magic might happen in her life? If she was lucky, the story of Cinderella could come true, with Mr Carson as the handsome prince! She stood there, blushing and bemused. He was putting his hand in his waistcoat pocket and bringing out a shiny new half-crown piece.

'There is no time for you to go to the office and get the loan before they close for dinner,' he told her. 'So we will make this little transaction something between ourselves, eh, Miss Ashton? Will that help?'

She nodded, glowing, her eyes like brilliant green stars. She could sense his dawning awareness and little squiggles of delight were running through her and curling her toes. He cleared his throat noisily.

'And please don't hesitate to come and see me if you have any further problems, Miss Ashton. We like to be of use, you know.'

She went out of the office almost reeling under the weight of his understanding. As she reached her workbench the bell rang. Workers were throwing on their hats and coats, getting out as fast as they could. Poppy, leaving her paper-wrapped bread under her bench, put on her own outer clothes and followed them.

A fat, frumpish girl with a pasty face caught up with her, grinned, then walked alongside as they left the building. Poppy noted the nitty-looking hair held back by blue slides, and the tide mark round the girl's neck, and could almost hear the scathing remarks Nan would make about carbolic soap.

She could always get a good hot soak at the communal bathhouse just off St Martin's Road. Poppy had discovered the place and all but wept with joy. A bath in hot water, tuppence if you took your own soap. Blissful Saturday mornings, indeed!

'Bloody marvellous, init?' the girl said in a friendly way. 'They all half kill themselves, but they have to take their turn just the same. Me? I take me time and get there when the crowd's gone. I'm Edna Ames, by the way.'

'I'm Poppy Ashton.'

'Poppy?' Edna sniggered. 'Some bleeding fine flower you are, working up Farringdon's! We're all slave labour, that's what we are. Though I do hear as how you're one of God's chosen few.'

'I don't know what –'

'And watch him is all I can say. He's a slimy bleeder. Cross him and you're out on your ear. Don't let his smile charm you. He can change into a right bastard in the twinkling of an eye. You going home for dinner?'

'Not really. I'm staying at St Martin's.'

'Gawd help you then. Stricter than a lot of nuns, they are. Who sent you to that dump?'

'Rene Davies' sister and I came up together, but – Jessica dropped me and I haven't seen her since.'

'I'm not surprised. Rene was all right till she got uppity. Used to put in a good word for the girls at first, since her and old Carson was thick as thieves. But in the end, the rotten moo told tales out of school. Got two women the sack for nicking a measly bit of ribbon, and herself a raise. She even let old Carson down, and she's now living in this posh place. She works for this bloke. Know what I mean?'

'I think so,' Poppy said carefully. 'So she left poor Mr Carson high and dry, just as her sister left me?'

'Gawd! Are you wet behind the ears or just plain daft? Poor Mr Carson? He's about as poor as my arse! Here we are, Tony's. Coming?'

Tony's was much larger than it appeared outside. It was a long, low building bursting at the seams with customers. A double row of wooden tables ran down its full length, the tables seating four to a side. It was a steam-filled, homely place with a smell of cooking food. At the long counter men and women stood before enormous metal containers of cooked eels and liquor, tuppenny meat-and-potato pies, mashed potato, peas, saveloys, pease pudding and a vat of thick vegetable soup.

Edna leaned against the counter, screwed up her eyes in thought, then ordered, 'Pie and a penn'orth with liquor.'

'And I'll have the same, please,' Poppy said and watched as a meat-and-potato pie was slid onto a white china plate, quickly followed by a good helping of mashed potato all covered with a scoopful of tasty pea-green liquor.

'Threepence each, hurry along there,' the plump, good-looking man who'd served them said.

'Ta, Tone,' Edna replied and when Poppy looked up at him, startled, he gave her a roguish wink and made her blush.

They grabbed up knives and forks and rushed to get to two empty seats, then sat down to eat. Edna plastered everything on her plate with salt, pepper and vinegar, then concentrated on her food. She ate fiercely, wolfishly, saying between mouthfuls, 'Hurry up, for Gawd's sake! If you're a minute late they stop you a quarter of an hour. If you're late more than three times in one week, it's the sack. I've worked there for donkey's years and held on by the skin of my teeth, but I hate it! Dogsbody I am. Just a dogsbody and nothing more.'

'Do they take on people to do odd jobs here?' Poppy asked. 'I mean, could I go up to that man and –'

'If you don't hurry and get that grub down you, you'll be out of Farringdon's, let alone –'

'You know him! Tell him I'll work any hours, morning or nights.'

'Cor blimey, you're mad!' Edna leaned across Poppy and bawled out, 'Oi, Tone, wanna a casual? My friend needs the work.'

Large dark eyes twinkled as they looked into Poppy's embarrassed face. He shook his head and shrugged in an exaggerated way.

'Satisfied now, you silly moo?' Edna said impatiently. 'Come on!'

Poppy, who had been thoroughly enjoying her meal, relishing every lovely mouthful, now had to rush. They had to run all the way back to work.

'See yer!' Edna said and grinned. 'Tomorrow dinnertime, all right?'

Feeling happier than she had been since she'd left home, because at last she had found a friend, Poppy sat at her bench and worked with a will. That night, in her hostel room, she wrote yet again to Flossie. She gave a glowing account of her new friend Edna, and described the hostel a little more. 'It's

113

cheap and cheerful,' she wrote, 'but all I need. Please give Nan and everyone my love.'

She walked out of the hostel and along to the postbox, having already bought the stamp the day before, and posted her letter. Seeing Miss Henderson's beady look when she returned, she felt too angry to take all the cold-shouldering lying down. She tossed her head and with quick, determined steps walked along to the communal room. The women already sitting at the long table looked up as she entered, but said nothing. Poppy smiled brightly.

'Hello,' she said with polite confidence. 'Any room for a little'un?' She sat down without waiting for a reply, then turned to her neighbour. The young woman seemed to be about twenty years old, a case-hardened sort with knowing, near-black eyes.

'Please, can you tell me how long we can stay here? And do they ever change their rates? I mean, make it a bit cheaper for us regulars?'

'Jesus! Where've you been all your life. Under a goose-gog bush?'

'Not really. It's just that I don't want to have to beard Miss Henderson in her den again. She might bite my head off.'

'She can be a moo at times.' The older girl's lined face creased in a swift but cold smile. 'And you always pay the sixpence a night. A bloody fortune for what we get, but this place is like a luxury hotel against the doss-houses round here.'

'Three and six a week is all very well if you've got it,' Poppy replied feelingly. She knew the score very well. Having paid her rent she was left with the princely sum of four shillings to do everything with. She could manage, but she wanted to save up. She needed to earn more, much more! One day she would have the house and the masses of flowers. She would prove to Nan, and to all those who laughed, that she had meant what she said. And when it happened, she'd look up at the sky and smile and say:

'Hello, Ros! What do you think of all this, eh? Kept my promise, didn't I? Well, you just come down from the pearly gates for a little while, and walk with me among the roses. Hold my hand and tell me how you have always believed in

114

me. Because, my sweet Ros, you were the only one that ever did! And oh, my dearest dear, without you this old world is so lonely . . .'

'Ain't so bad,' the young woman was saying with rough sympathy. 'You'll live. We all do. So you don't have to blub. Has that bitch Henders been bawling you out?'

'No.' Poppy wavered. 'I'm not really crying. It's just . . . just that I was missing someone, that's all.'

'A fella?'

'No.' Poppy was smiling as she brushed her hand across her eyes. 'But I can live in hopes.'

'Can't we all?' a slight, ginger-haired, freckle-faced girl said pertly. 'I'm Cyn, by the way, and her next to you's called Kath. Cheer up. At least you're in work. We all just hold on by the skin of our teeth.'

'Do they throw you out if you can't pay the sixpence?'

'They let you have it on tick sometimes, if you show willing. And you can always go to the good old Sally Army for help. This place is a bit dear, but it's a step up from most. It's run by a sort of charity, and they've all got kind hearts.'

'Even Miss Henderson?' Poppy had pulled herself together now and the group of women joined in with her and laughed.

'Bloody hell, you're actually human,' Kath quipped. 'And here we were believing what Henderson said, that you were a high-hat and too good to be true.'

'No one can be grand when they were born in a place called Jezebel Street,' Poppy admitted wryly. 'Still, I try my best.'

'Don't we all?' Cyn pulled such a face that they had a fit of giggles.

By the end of the year Poppy had found her feet. She was now used to living in St Martin's and she and Miss Henderson shared a guarded truce. Cyn drifted off somewhere, without saying a word, and tall, dark Kath was arrested for stealing. Edna and Poppy were now firm friends and spent as many free moments as possible together. Not that there were many, because Poppy had kept on and on at Tony, a big, fat, lovely man, until he gave her work. He gave her one and six every early morning for peeling potatoes, carrots, onions, turnips and any other vegetable necessary for the day. She also washed up, and even stood at the counter at six when Tony's served up early-morning breakfasts for men on the road. She relished work and adored all the workers, Burney and Tony in particular, but kept well away from the man who cut up the eels.

Poppy was always smiling and acting on Mr Banes' words: she was neat and quick and right.

The customers came to know her and call her by name. Seeing she was a favourite, Tony said she could work evenings, too. She did, until just before nine when she had to leave to get back to the hostel on time. This added another one and six to her money and her savings slowly grew.

Poppy took readily to Burney Bellini, who lived over the shop. He, a thin, dark-haired young man, took a fancy to her and made her blush with his teasing and merry ways. He was Tony's nephew, he said, and the general dogsbody, doing all the fetching and carrying in the large basket fixed on the front of his bike. His mother lived and worked in a plush hotel and was a wonderful cook. One day Barney wanted to have his own place, cook wonderful meals, and have things all posh and just so. Not rough and ready like Tone's.

'Then we both have dreams,' Poppy told him one factory dinnertime when he came to stand by the table where she was eating with other Farringdon people. 'It's good to have something to work towards, Burney. One day we'll both be rich.'

'That leaves me out,' Edna said and sniffed.

'Where I go, you'll go. You're my friend,' Poppy said stoutly.

'And she ain't the only friend you've got, is she?' a fat, coarse woman worker from Farringdons jeered across the table. 'Right little bloody pussyfoot, ain't yer? Gawd, your sort make me sick! All eyes an' teeth, getting round men.'

'Take no notice,' Edna said, though her face went mottled grey. 'They're all up you somethink rotten at work.' She jutted her chin out belligerently and snapped, 'Got nothing better to do than listen in, Fanny Adams? Sod off!'

'But why do they feel like that about me?' Poppy asked as they went back to work.

116

'Because it's as plain as day that old Carson's only waiting his chance. I don't know what you've got, Poppy Ashton, but it's what all the men round here want. They don't give a shit about the blokes in Tone's, but when you've got old man Carson sniffing round, oh, my Gawd!' Edna wagged her finger warningly. 'You make sure you don't take one step out of line.'

'If . . . if Mr Carson ever looked at me – in that way,' Poppy said quietly, 'I think I would die with joy.'

'Garn!' Edna jeered, quite unimpressed.

After ten weeks there came a letter from Flossie. Not before time Poppy thought, but wanted to sing as she ripped open the envelope. So they hadn't disowned her after all, she still belonged! Then her heart lurched. The page had a thick black line round the edges. What Flossie had to say was stark and to the point.

Everyone was as well as could be expected, but she was barely able to bear her own grief. Her two dear old ducks were dead and buried. There had been something wrong with the oil stove and they had died in their sleep of fumes. Daniel had gone away. He had a live-in job at Devere's, Flossie thought, but wasn't sure because he kept his business to himself. But he had put a word to the authorities and pulled a string or two, and now crippled Lenny was in the Home. The Jacobs crew were threatening to kill Daniel because of it, and Mrs Jacobs had sported a black eye and cut mouth, and had had some teeth knocked out. It had been hell all round and Poppy was well out of it. If it hadn't been for Nan and Sandy Swift, who had been home at the time and helped, she would have gone mad. Charlie and everyone sent their good wishes and regards.

'Wishes and regards,' Poppy whispered out loud, 'not love!' Then she remembered once having almost hated the poor old Wellses because they had an oil stove when Ros went without. And she had not given a second thought to who'd change the dear old ducks' library books. She remembered Vic and Liz and the Peels, Kings and Lambs, how they went shouting and fighting on Saturday nights. Flossie was right! She was far better off here, working and saving for better things. And there was always her friends,

Edna and Burney – not forgetting her wonderful dreams and fantasies about Mr Carson.

She shivered as she realised just what Mr Carson would think if he ever set foot in Jezebel Street. Then her hurt returned. No one had remembered her birthday all those weeks ago. No one had tried to come and see her even though they knew where she was.

All her half-formed dreams and plans now went by the board. It didn't matter that the shop windows were getting tinselled and had lots of holly and bright paper chains. It didn't matter that there was a mechanical Santa laughing his head off in the shop selling toys. She wouldn't go home for Christmas after all. She would stay where she was and bluff it all out. The hostel could do with cheering up. She'd go to Miss Henderson and see if the woman would be halfway decent for a change.

Poppy drew in a deep, shuddering breath, screwed up the letter and threw it away.

Chapter Seven

Poppy sat at table in Tony's, eating a bacon sandwich. She felt a little tired, having been up since five thirty, but rather pleased with herself. The job at Tony's was a great help all round. As well as the money she earned, there were free meals, making it easier to save. She had to pay for her midday dinner, of course, but the counter hands saw to it that she and Edna were served very well, and with a slice of bread thrown in.

Tony came over to her. He was a large, dark, very Italian man, swarthy-faced, white teeth gleaming, with merrily dancing eyes.

'You ar-er a gooda girl,' he told her. 'You worka long hours for Tony, eh? You ar-er happy here?'

'Yes, sir,' she replied and blushed because he had leaned over and stroked her hair.

'I am glad. You make the place looka nice. You always looka nice. You ar-er a beautiful child, and Burney, he thinks a lot of you, eh?'

'We are friends, sir, yes.'

'You talk to him, eh? Make hima beautiful like you.'

'He is already beautiful,' she replied gravely. 'He is nice inside.'

Tony threw back his head and laughed. 'You ar-er blind, bambina, but never mind. We will see you tonight, eh?'

'Yes, sir.' She smiled and finished her sandwich, then left for Farringdon's feeling as though she was walking on air.

The world was a workplace, long, hard hours, time-consuming, but all was well. She had Edna and she had

119

Burney, and she was in love. Mr Carson was now in the centre of all her dreams. He had begun smiling into her eyes whenever they came face to face, and passing friendly, sometimes even faintly jocular remarks. He seemed to go out of his way to speak to Mr Banes, but he would look over the foreman's head, and once had even gone so far as to give her the merest wink. It was almost as though he and she were sharing a secret, and she revelled in it all. Her days were filled with counting the minutes before he appeared, and when he did, she stared up at him with adulation in her eyes.

Mr Banes wore a sprig of holly in his overall top pocket and that afternoon Mr Carson, standing near Poppy's bench, remarked on the fact.

'You are looking forward to the festive season, Mr Banes?'

'Indeed I am, sir.'

'You have a large family, Mr Banes?'

'A fine wife and six whippersnappers, sir. Five at home, the sixth now lives and works at Rowston Stables, sir, but he'll be home for Christmas, which will gladden Mrs Banes' heart.'

'That is very good.' Mr Carson turned enquiringly to Poppy. 'And you, Miss Ashton? Will you be going home for the yuletide?'

'No, sir. I – I shall be staying at St Martin's Lodge.'

'Oh, and have you no friends?'

'They will be with their families, sir, and I do not care to impose.'

'I see,' he said slowly and looked grave. He nodded politely and walked away.

Before Edna and Poppy parted for the evening, Poppy told her about the conversation.

'I'm really worried, Edna. I suppose he looks down on me now, knowing that I haven't a real home.'

Edna pulled a face. 'Nosy old sod! I hope as how you let him see that you had places to go. I mean, you're welcome to come with me. My old ma would squeeze you in. There's thousands of us, as you well know, but Ma –'

'Is a wonderful lady,' Poppy said genuinely. 'And how she copes in two rooms, and having to walk all that way for

120

water, I'll never know. I'll not forget how welcome she made me feel the first time I went home with you.'

'I can't see why you won't come with me for Christmas.'

'Because Miss Henderson has become human enough to say we can have a small celebration at the hostel. We're all putting something towards the food and are determined to have a jolly nice time.' She squeezed Edna's arm in a warm, loving way. 'You're lucky to have your ma and da, Edna. I could have stood anything, anything at all, even Jezebel Street, if I could have kept Ros, but . . . she's gone.'

'And you've been bleeding inside ever since! You ain't living, Poppy. You're killing yourself with all that hard work. It's not as if you spend any money. In fact, I'd go to say you're downright, bloody mean!'

'I'm working towards making a dream come true, that's all.'

'Garn! Just as long as old Carson's not in your dreams! If I thought he was, I swear I'd ask God to strike you down.'

'Mr Carson is my knight in shining armour,' Poppy tried to joke, but her eyes were wistful. 'He gave me my job, and I'm so grateful I could cry. I earn money, I met you and, through you, Burney. I have a good life, Edna, and I now know more people than I ever did before. I like work! It . . . it makes my life worthwhile. When I think of all the queues at the labour exchange, and the starving millions all around, I realise how lucky I am.'

'Oh, my Gawd!' Edna was suddenly very angry. 'I think you're bloody mad. And don't count on your job. Every so often they sack people. Old Carson don't care. He just walks along and waves an arm and says, 'From here to there.' And all them in the gap go. They're out, just like that! Now there's talk of getting rid of some of the women to make way for men. Thank Gawd, men ain't got my nimble fingers. No one's quicker than me at my job. Earn 'em a fortune, I do, but that don't matter. We're like slaves, and I hate Carson and all his lot for the pig shit they are!'

'I'm sorry, Edna,' Poppy whispered, crestfallen, but Edna stormed off.

Later that night, while working at Tony's, Poppy thought of all that Edna had said. But one thing stood out a mile.

121

Edna thought that she, Poppy, was downright, bloody mean. Well, yes, that was the truth in a way. But she was mean with herself, too. Penny-pinching, scrimping and saving and every so often sneaking into the bank to put in her savings. The bank! No one in Jezebel Street had a bank account. No one in Jezebel Street put money in the Post Office either. There was never anything left over. Bill Bannerman used a bank, his family always had. If he'd use his noddle, old Bill could be as rich as Mr Carson, she was sure of it. But Bill with his kind, faraway eyes merely worked to live. Unlike Poppy, who was just living to work.

Poppy decided that the money she made from then on till Christmas should be spent on presents and cards. The Saturday before Christmas she made her way to Market Street, and drank in the sights and sounds: a street accident, a stubborn horse, a drunken man. Women were clutching their purses, frowning, and carrying shopping baskets. There were children of all ages, some quiet and pale-faced, being grasped firmly by mothers; street urchins laughing, yelling, racing past stalls, stealing as they ran. Men stood on corners, downtrodden, defeat in their eyes, or else, pinch-faced and furtive, sneaked through the door under the three brass balls to get money for the only decent things they had left to pawn.

It was bright, sunny and bitterly cold. Exhilarated, Poppy pulled her coat round her tightly and walked on. She found her way blocked by a crowd hanging about the toy-shop window. Though she had seen it all before, Poppy wormed her way through to watch the jolly clockwork Father Christmas, who drew from his sack a gaily tied red parcel, held it aloft for a second or two, then put it back, over and over again. Further along there was plum pudding at ninepence halfpenny a pound. The meat shop was hung with rosetted carcasses. The butcher in his striped apron was noisily sharpening his knife in the doorway. He was beaming and shouting at the top of his voice, 'Buy! Buy! Buy! Buy!'

Poppy went with the ebb and flow of crowds. What with the stream entering and issuing from shops, the wedges of loiterers glued to shop windows, and the two main currents of saunterers, progress was difficult. But she turned into her favourite at last: the large, lively Woolworth's store with its gleaming counters filled to the brim with tin drums, toys, balloons, china, jewellery, perfume, biscuits and sweets, temptingly displayed. Poppy felt safe from embarrassment in Woolworth's. Everything was plainly priced and nothing cost more than sixpence. The shop was filled with colour and scents, its gramophone music rising above the busy pinging of the tills.

It was wonderful to spend money, blissful to work out just what to buy. The jewellery attracted her first, it sparkled and glittered so. Poppy bought a brooch for Edna. It was shaped like a daisy, with a false diamond in the centre of the pink flower; its curved stem and single leaf were of yellow metal. She thought it was beautiful in its little box. She bought Burney a gift-packed razor and blades. For Edna's brothers and sisters she chose a packet of twelve balloons and two huge sixpenny bags of mixed sweets.

She bought Christmas cards, choosing each one with great care. A picture of red roses and holly all twinkling with silver dust for Nan. Robins and a squirrel on branches laden with snow for Charlie and Clary. For Flossie a snowy country scene. Poppy hesitated, then chose two more cards, plain white with a scarlet-edged gold 'Happy Christmas' emblazoned on each, one for Daniel and one for Sandy. She would send Daniel's to Flossie's house and Sandy's to his home, hoping that they would get passed on. She bought herself a notepad and envelopes, a packet of pen nibs and a bottle of ink. At the wrapping and decoration counter she bought two sheets of red paper covered with a mistletoe design.

She left Woolworth's and began to make her way back. On the way she bought halfpenny stamps. She stopped in at Tony's for a well-earned pie and mash, and since Tone was nowhere around, she didn't have to pay. Burney saw to that! She hugged herself with delight. Once it was wrapped, she'd give Burney his present. How surprised he would be! How he would wink and smile!

As she ate her pie she began daydreaming of Mr Carson, making believe that he had married her and said that she could have anything she wished. So, because he was rich enough for her to spend money like water, she made her choice. To wander round Woolworth's and buy and buy. Buy anything and everything. Just because she liked what she saw, and not just because of need.

'Oi there, Poppy,' Burney said and sat down at the table with her. 'Why don't you wipe that soppy grin off your face?'

'I was imagining spending a fortune in Woolworth's.'

'If I had a fortune,' he said perkily, 'Woolworth's would be the last place I'd spend it in. Are you working tonight?'

'Of course. I can't do without my one and six. I've just spent a lot of money on Christmas presents.'

'Got anything for me?'

'Wouldn't you like to know?' She laughed.

That night she gave Burney the razor and blades that looked so fine in the presentation box.

'Blimey,' he said, 'I didn't think – I mean, ta, Poppy!'

On the Monday Poppy gave Edna the wrapped-up presents.

'Not to be opened till Christmas morning,' she warned. 'There's balloons and sweets for the kids.'

'Lumme, you ain't 'alf a silly moo,' Edna said feelingly. 'Fancy wasting your money like that! I thought you had to save up every brass farthing. I ain't got you nothing. I give every ha'penny I earn to Ma.'

'You're my friend,' Poppy replied, 'and that's the biggest present of the lot. As for these things, it's only Christmas once a year and a very special time.'

'Not in St Martin's Lodge, it ain't!'

'Oh, I don't know,' Poppy replied and still politely refused to spend the holiday with Mrs Ames. An extra mouth to feed would be too much for the woman whose husband had lost an arm in the war and had been out of work ever since.

On Christmas Eve, the residents of St Martin's began to make merry. Some of the girls had clubbed together and sneaked in some bottles of gin. Poppy had paid the extra shilling asked for towards the food, and helped the large kitchen woman to make mince pies. Then a message came.

'You're wanted in the office. Better go now. You know how old Henders is.'

What had she done wrong now? Poppy hurried to face the supervisor. Burney was there, looking sheepish, and Miss

Henderson was glaring and glassy-eyed. The moment Burney saw Poppy, he stepped towards her, smiling, and shoved a brown-paper-wrapped parcel into her hand.

'Have a good time, Poppy. Ta-ta.'

He was gone before she had breath to thank him.

'We do not allow male visitors here,' Miss Henderson snapped. 'Please remember that in future, Miss Ashton.'

'I'm sorry,' Poppy said gravely, but her eyes were dancing with pleasure. A present! Someone had given her a present. It really was Christmas Eve after all. She turned round and was about to leave the office when the supervisor said, 'Oh! Before I forget.' She held out some cards.

'Thank you, oh, thank you!' Poppy gasped tearfully and ran up to the privacy of her room. Two of the cards were written by Flossie and had 'Merry Christmas. We are all thinking of you. From Nan and me.' Beside Flossie's name there had been printed in pencil Nan's firm signature cross. The second card held the message, 'Merry Christmas. Behave yourself. From Charlie and Clary.' This also held two crosses. The third card showed a laughing Santa Claus with 'Ho! Ho! Ho!' written underneath. It was signed simply, Daniel. Openly crying now and hugging the cards against her pounding heart, Poppy thought with love and joy of those in Jezebel Street. It was a long time before she became composed enough to open Burney's present, and then the tears started all over again. He had given her chocolates and there were pink roses on the box.

'Have a lovely heavenly Christmas, Ros,' Poppy whispered to the ceiling. 'You seem to be so far away now. Don't forget us. I'll never forget you.'

Christmas was not the washout that Poppy expected. The St Martin's residents tried to make it merry. Miss Henderson had even helped to put up crepe-paper chains and lots of red balloons. Everyone gathered in the communal room and sang all the rousing carols that Poppy and Ros had so enjoyed. The Christmas dinner of turkey and plum pudding went down a treat, as did the apple and orange each, and the handful of raisins and nuts.

When the holiday was over and Poppy went back to work, she was more confident now she had heard from home. With

125

a twinkle every so often in her lustrous eyes, she became the pet of the Clicker room. The men smiled and winked at her, teasing her and joking – when Mr Carson was not around. And Mr Carson himself began to show an open admiration for her, which made her glow. Poppy could hardly believe it, but he seemed as besotted with her as she was with him. She ached and longed to tell Mr Carson how she felt.

One day Poppy was reading a newspaper that someone had left on the table at Tony's. She was not interested in politics, taking Nan's view that all the loudmouths in Parliament only tried to line their own pockets. But on reading that the first Labour government in British history had taken office under Ramsay MacDonald, Poppy's mind flew to Daniel. So, his hero had reached the pinnacle at last!

Dear Daniel, what was he doing now? Memories flooded back and Poppy thought of his direct gaze, the way he walked and held his head high, the shine of his hair and beard. Then a picture of Sandy flashed into her mind, handsome, white-toothed Swifty, who had such a roguish smile and devil-may-care air. He was a merchant sailor now, a man of the world.

That night, when she was sitting in bed, having worked her nightly chores in Tony's, she waited. At last she heard Miss Henderson's rubbery footsteps returning down the stairs. Risking the fine should she be caught, Poppy jumped out of bed and defiantly lit the gas. The room, not so bare now it had the Christmas cards on show, and Burney's chocolate box as well as Ros', was still far from homely. The opposite bed was empty once again and for this Poppy was grateful. She sat down and wrote a letter to Daniel, just a short one, to say that she was pleased that he was at last seeing his dreams of a Labour Party leading the country come true. She wrote another letter, this time to Sandy, telling him of her job, her friends, her part-time efforts at Tony's. She said she would love to get some postcards from him, sent from all parts of the world.

Two days later Mr Carson sent for her. Terrified that she was about to get the sack, Poppy knocked on his door, her heart beating fast. At his invitation, she went in and stood before his desk, her hands clasped behind her. He was leaning back in his chair and remained silent for so long that she crimsoned and looked down at her toes. He cleared his throat and she jumped, looking up, startled and afraid.

'What would you say,' he asked silkily, 'if I told you that I know of a large, very nice two-room flat near here? One that is available for your use right now?'

She was watching his face, hypnotised. her emotions beat in a heavy, painful way. Slowly and carefully she replied, 'I think, sir, that I'd wish I lived in it – on my own. There is not much privacy to be had in St Martin's. Not even in one's room, for it has two beds, and strangers come and go.'

He began stroking his chin, his eyes very direct now; his lips were moist and little beads of sweat could be seen.

'What if I told you that the place is mine? That I sometimes hold private business meetings there? I hold a great many responsibilities over and above those at Farringdon's. Because of this, things need to be kept in apple-pie order, Miss Ashton. It suits me to have certain visitors in a place other than my own home. It is my mother, you see. She is well intentioned, of course, but – The bedroom would be yours and sacrosanct. And I would need the use of the living room only on rare occasions.'

Mother, she was thinking rapidly, he had spoken of his mother. Not wife! Because she remained so still and silent, he continued.

'I don't go there very often, as I have just said. Usually the place remains empty and uncared-for. I would not offer it to anyone else, but you are such a nice little thing, and ever since I realised that you were staying at St Martin's, I have had this idea at the back of my mind.'

Poppy began silently weighing up the pros and cons. To live in a flatlet owned by Mr Carson, the big boss of Farringdon's? What a rise up in the world! To be near the man she adored, to walk across his living room – the mere idea made her go weak at the knees. Suddenly she saw a picture of Nan floating before her eyes. She could almost read what would be on the older woman's mind, almost hear her sarcastic remarks.

'Flattered, Poppy? How stupid can you be? I'll swing for you if you bring shame on my house.'

'Look at me, Poppy,' Mr Carson said quietly. 'I am making you a genuine offer. In return for your keeping the place fit to live in, I am prepared to pay you ten shillings a week. This will be from my own private account, and nothing to do with what you earn at Farringdon's. Incidentally, you have been in the Clicker room long enough to be paid more. I shall see to it that you get the full rate of pay from now on.'

'Mr Carson,' she said uncertainly, 'I – I work at Tony's early mornings.'

'That will be entirely up to you. Well, Poppy, I take it that you will accept?'

'Yes, sir,' she whispered, going weak at the knees with her own daring. 'You . . . you are very kind.'

He brushed this away and was now briskly efficient. He pulled a notepad forward, wrote with a gold pen, then handed a torn-off sheet of paper to her.

'Here's the address. Collect your things from St Martin's and go to my place just as soon as you like. Oh, and –' He took a ten-shilling note from his waistcoat pocket and held it out to her. 'Take this as a token of good faith. I'm sure that we will both manage very well.'

She stared at him, her hands still clasped firmly behind her back. Now there was naked suspicion in her eyes, and fear. Mr Carson mustn't shatter her dreams, he must not! She loved him in a pure and beautiful way. If he were to look on her as some kind of bought woman, she would break her heart and die.

He smiled and raised his brows.

'Come along, Miss Ashton, Poppy! I should think that by now you and I can trust each other? I merely wish to make sure that if necessary you can pay someone to help move your things.' He took out his watch and, fascinated, she watched the light playing on the thick gold of its chain.

He was looking at the large round watch and frowning. 'Please make up your mind. Time really is getting on.'

Her hand trembled as she accepted the ten-shilling note. She was in Mr Carson's power now, for fair or foul. It didn't seem real that such a wonderful, rich and important man should even bother to give her the time of day, let alone offer her a place to live. Life was getting to be quite an adventure, one more exciting than even Jessica could find. If only Ros could be here!

'Thank you, sir,' she whispered and, giving Mr Carson one final searching look, turned on her heels and fled.

Having changed into her best clothes and packed her few belongings, Poppy walked out of St Martin's Lodge for the last time. She hurried along the street, past Farringdon's, and turned into Coopersale Place. It was a cul-de-sac of tall Victorian houses with an air of shabby grandeur. Poppy was quick to appreciate that the stone steps leading up to doorways were swept clean. Nan would have approved.

Thinking of home made Poppy's brave smile a little watery as she marched up the steps to the front door of number sixteen. The brass door knocker and letter box were polished bright, some poor skivvy had been up at the crack of dawn, no doubt. Poppy's heart was pounding as she knocked. A large-bosomed lady with a round face and unfriendly look confronted her. Noting the woman's scrupulously clean pinafore, the neatly pinned-back hair, her hoity-toity air, Poppy pulled herself together. It was really and truly going to be grand, a huge step up to live in such a place.

'Please,' she said quietly, 'I have come to live in flat number nine.'

The woman looked contemptuously at the shabby suitcase Poppy held. She stepped to one side, saying, 'Upstairs, to the left.'

Poppy smiled brightly and said in her poshest tone, 'Thank you so much. The rest of my luggage will be along later.' She swept by the woman with her nose in the air.

The flat was a surprise. The key was already in the lock and she turned it and went in, finding herself in a diminutive lobby. She took off her coat and set down her suitcase. The living room held a large fireplace that was carved oak and had cream and beige tiles. It had already been laid with paper, wood and coal. There were tongs and coal scuttle, poker and shovel all in shining bronze on the hearth. On the mantelpiece above there were gorgeous vases and ornaments of Oriental design. The wallpaper was velvety, patterned in red and gold. The carpet was red and had a Chinese look. There were red-upholstered armchairs and an oak dining table and high-backed, beautifully carved dark oak chairs. At one end of the room there stood a tall, black-lacquered screen, patterned with birds and flowers in red and gold.

Poppy walked behind the screen and found a tiny kitchen, with cupboards and dresser as well as a small gas stove. Here everything was white and blue. The bedroom held a double bed with thick woolly blankets and pure white linen sheets and pillowcases; the bedcover was of heavy silk cream brocade patterned in a fern design of old gold, the fern leaves a shade or two deeper than the warmly glowing walls. Here all the furniture was of light walnut wood: a tall chest of drawers, a dressing table and a double wardrobe. Off the bedroom was a white-tiled bathroom with lavatory and sink in dark blue.

It was like being in Paradise. Poppy, looking at everything, loved everything. It was all so clean and beautiful and luxurious. And the knowledge that she was to stay here, was being actually paid to keep things nice, made her want to fall on her knees and bless dear, wonderful Mr Carson. Almost in a dream, she went into the kitchen and found the matches. She lit the fire and sat in one of the red armchairs and waited for it to blaze into life.

She was sitting, reading a book about smallholdings that Bill had given her, when the door opened. Startled, she looked up and watched speechless as Mr Carson came into the room. he was carrying several brown-paper carrier bags; out of the top of one there glowed the butter-bright heads of chrysanthemums. He walked with purposeful strides towards the table, put the bags on it, then turned to smile at her.

'Well, well,' he said. 'You have made the place come alive already.'

She stared up at him, getting slowly to her feet. Her eyes were wide in her face and she was afraid, suspicious and sad all at one go. Mr Carson sensed none of this. He walked towards the fire, holding his beautifully clean hands towards the flames. 'He's never done a day's wok in his life,' a little voice whispered inside her. 'He's used to getting his own way. Better watch out!'

130

'Forgive my intrusion,' he said. 'On future occasions you will know well beforehand if I'm going to come here. However, I was on my way home when I realised that the cupboard was bare. So I've brought you some provisions.'

'I see, sir,' she said, feeling confused.

'Actually, we must always make certain that there are things on hand – for my visitors. On the rare occasions they come during the evening, you will wait on us, then make yourself scarce. It will help if you make sure you have something to do in your room, such as sewing or whatever young ladies do in their spare time.'

'I understand, sir,' she replied primly, though she felt perplexed.

'My business meetings are private and confidential; they will usually occur while you're at Farringdon's and therefore will cause you no concern. Either way, my guests never stay long. I shall provide things for you to keep on hand for my people, such as wine and spirits, which you will not touch. But since your position here is one of importance, you shall have housekeeping money for yourself, quite apart from your wages. Make no mistake about this, Miss Ashton – er, Poppy – you are my part-time housekeeper, one that I need to trust, and you will be treated as such. Do I make myself clear?'

'Yes, sir!' She realised that everything was above board and was glowing now.

This must be where Mr Carson had meetings with famous show people, and worked out what they needed of the famous Farringdon designs. How exciting! What a wonderland she was now in!

'Good!' His tone changed and became jocular. 'Now, since it is rather late, I am hoping that you will at least offer me a cup of tea? You will find all that you need in those bags and more besides. Please take everything into the kitchen, my dear. And don't worry. I'm sure that you will get used to all this in no time at all.'

'Yes, sir.' She gathered up the things and saw that he had walked to the lobby area. He was undoing the buttons on his coat.

As she unpacked the carrier bags, she was remembering all the romantic novels she had read. She began putting the things away: bread, butter, eggs, cheese, tinned evaporated milk, a packet of tea, and sugar in a blue paper cone. There was jam and marmalade, and a tin of cocoa, chocolate biscuits and a tin of corned beef. There were six large rashers of bacon wrapped in white paper, and a small round tin holding cherry cake. Looking at all this abundance Poppy realised that her life had changed for ever. She was Mr Carson's housekeeper – for now! But who knew what the future might bring? Surely he must think something of her, to have chosen her for this situation? She was convinced there were millions of women out there who would leap at the chance of standing in her shoes. But Mr Carson had given her, Miss Poppy Ashton, the opportunity of a lifetime. She would work her fingers to the bone for him, and never betray his trust.

She made a pot of tea and took it in on a tray, noting the willow pattern on the china teapot and cup and saucer. She thought of the blue enamelware back home and knew that she was now truly living in another world.

'Fetch another cup and plate,' Mr Carson told her in a smiling, friendly way. 'There's no need to stand on ceremony with me here. Come along, join me and have a biscuit.'

Poppy had never felt less hungry in her life, but the chocolate digestives were something she had never previously tasted. A pound of broken biscuits was a luxury in number two Jezebel Street. She tried to sip the tea in a ladylike way and eat the biscuits he had put on a plate before her. He was trying to be friendly, she knew, but she was in love and needed to impress him. Now self-conscious and feeling his eyes fixed on her, she felt she was being weighed up from head to toe. He cleared his throat and the noise startled her and made her jump. The teaspoon leaped from the saucer and fell to the floor.

She felt foolishly embarrassed over this small incident and worse still because Mr Carson had left his chair and was scrabbling beneath the table. His hand brushed against her ankle and she felt liquid fire at his touch. Her cheeks were burning as she thanked him and took the spoon from his outstretched hand. With great care she replaced the spoon in

132

the saucer and sat back, silently signifying that she would eat and drink no more.

The silence was unbearable. She could feel him watching her, and she wondered wildly whether he knew how she had felt at his touch. She tried to converse lightly, pretending that she was quite at ease in her new surroundings.

'Where do I get the coal from, Mr Carson? And do they have washing facilities here?'

'There's a wash-house in the basement and individual coal cellars. Mine is of course number nine. You can't get lost, but if you do I'm sure that Mrs Flanty will be on hand to help. Now, Poppy, please remember that to all intents and purposes this is your home. I am merely your guest for this evening. You must do as you choose.'

'Thank you, sir,' she replied quietly.

He laughed at that. 'Poppy,' he said, 'at work I am sir. At work I am Mr Carson. But here, in this room, I hope that we can be friends.'

She felt the colour rising to her cheeks again, her pulses were leaping and she could not forget the feeling that had rushed through her at his touch. He was standing up and her mouth went dry. His eyes, fringed so thickly with near-white lashes, were wise and kind, and she felt her legs turning to water as she too stood up. For one wild moment she thought he was going to walk round the table to her, but he turned away. He was heading for the door and the lobby. 'No!' her heart cried out. 'Don't go. I want you to stay!'

Composing herself, she followed him and politely helped him on with his coat, then stood back and bobbed slightly as he took his leave. She returned to the beautiful room, cleared away the tea things and carefully replaced the uneaten biscuits in the barrel.

That night, in a bed that felt as though she was lying on a cloud, Poppy made a vow. She would make Mr Carson love her. She would work and scheme and do everything she could to make him look at her and see her as someone desirable. He was her sun and moon and stars. He was a god.

Chapter Eight

Life had become rosy, Poppy thought a couple of months later. Burney and she were good mates now, and Edna and she were firm friends. She had notified everyone at home of her change of address and, surprisingly, had her first reply from abroad. It was a card from Sandy, postmarked Calais, and read, 'Dear Poppy, this one's from France.'

A few days later there was a letter from Daniel wishing her good luck at her new address and saying that he had taken over the caretaker's cottage at the Devere Children's Home some time ago and was becoming very involved in the care of orphans. He asked if she still read a lot, and Poppy looked lovingly at the book old Bill Bannerman had given her. The *Smallholder Encyclopeadia* with its wealth of advice and knowledge held a strange fascination for her.

Flossie wrote to tell that she was now letting out rooms to gentlemen and that Nan had refused to do the same. Nan had been quite fierce about it, saying that no stranger, man or woman, was going to set foot in her place.

'No,' Poppy said to herself. 'Nan loves that house too much to have strangers in. I'll buy it for her one day. So help me, I will!'

Over and above everything else, Poppy hugged the knowledge to her heart that she had become necessary to Mr Carson. She kept the flat spic-and-span, polishing and burnishing. Every time he arrived he looked round the place, but he was looking more at her. And the expression in his blue eyes, the way he blinked those white eyelashes of his, always made her go weak at the knees. She had to make him

134

declare himself, had to! He was her lord and master and she loved him with all her heart and soul. She must make him love her. She must! She ached for his smile, the touch of his hand, the sight and sound and apple-tobacco smell of him. He filled her dreams and every waking thought, and now that she was living in his flat, the trusted caretaker, she felt that romance could only progress. She imagined being in his arms and wanted to swoon.

The only faint cloud on the horizon was that she had never met any of her employer's business associates. She wanted to be taken into his confidence. Once, when she returned home earlier than usual, she could have sworn that she had seen none other than the fat Mr Tilsby hurrying down the steps of the house. She thought she recognised the irascible man who had been making such a fuss on Leyton station. Mr Tilsby, the rich man who owned taxis – who gained extra money from whores!

Furious with herself, she brushed the thought away. There were other flats in the building that had nothing to do with Mr Carson. Her governor would not be seen dead with someone like that. He was a gentleman through and through. That was why she loved him so.

Mr Carson was wonderful to her. He appreciated the work she did and praised the way she set out the drinks and snack trays on the days she knew that he was to have visitors.

At Farringdon's he ignored her. Gone were the winks, the occasional jocular remarks. At Farringdon's she was just another worker, to earn her money or else. She got over her first hurt at his changed attitude, and quite understood once he explained that it was advisable that her being in his direct employ would make things very difficult for her so far as the other employees were concerned.

Not certain about all the secret meetings in spite of what he said, Poppy nevertheless obeyed. It was easy to hide where she lived from Edna, simply because Edna never asked. So far as Edna was concerned, St Martin's Lodge was like a prison, to be given a wide berth. So even though Poppy had been to Mrs Ames' small, crowded, scruffy rooms, Edna had never once visited Poppy's place. Burney was always too busy on business of his own to worry too much where Poppy lived. He spent every spare moment practising his mother's recipes in the café kitchens. He told her proudly that he already had one or two people who asked him to prepare and deliver hot meals. Burney was as determined as Poppy to become rich and successful one day. Apart from the time he went to St Martin's to give Poppy chocolates, he too gave the Lodge a miss. The three friends' meeting place was always Tony's.

If Mr Carson had told Poppy that black was white she would have wanted to believe him. He always stayed on to spend a few moments with her on the days he had received his business associates. He treated her politely and took his leave shortly after she had told him how she had got on at work that day. It was merely a small courtesy on his part. Just to let her know, he said, that he had had a conference in the flat that day. She smiled and nodded and did not say that his explanations were unnecessary. Poppy loved every little thing about the flat, nothing was allowed to stray out of place. She knew to within half an inch just where everything should be. She would have known at once if people had been there.

As time went on she began to feel that the unknown visitors were violating her own personal sanctuary. It was worse because, make goo-goo eyes though she did, and try to act the vamp, Mr Carson always treated her the same. He oozed sex appeal and the torch she was carrying for him burned ever more brightly. But he visited the flat only for his conferences. She found herself loathing the idea of these business people who were far more important to him than she was. What went on while she was away? What were the secret deals that Mr Carson arranged? Certainly they had nothing to do with Farringdon's. Perhaps Mrs Flanty might know?

These days Poppy and the caretaker were on a more or less friendly footing. Feeling treacherous but determined, Poppy climbed the stairs to Mrs Flanty's attic room. She rapped on the door with her knuckles and waited.

'Hello,' she said breathlessly and smiled at the woman who opened the door. 'I'm getting very lonely down there on my own. I wondered if we could have a chat?'

'My goodness, this is a surprise,' Mrs Flanty said and

ushered her in in her usual brisk way. 'The girl before you wasn't the friendly sort at all. A proper little madam was our Rene Davies, and what Mr Carson saw in her I'll never know. He took her on, like you, to look after his flat particular like. But she was a hard case. I'm not at all surprised that he let her go. Made a good move, she did, though. And earns more for herself – though Mr Carson can be very generous when the mood takes him.'

'I know,' Poppy said and smiled, remembering how Mr Carson had refused point-blank to take back the half-crown she had borrowed.

Poppy looked about her while Mrs Flanty busied herself at a small black two-ringed stove. Tea things were set on the table beside it. Everything was neat and clean. The oddments of furniture shone. The brass bedstead gleamed and reflected the red cover. The dull red floor covering was polished like glass.

'You wouldn't half get on with my aunt Nan,' she observed. 'Like two peas I reckon you are. Always scrubbing and polishing and using the old elbow grease.'

'And you take after her,' Mrs Flanty replied. 'I've seen the way you keep that flat. Don't look so surprised. I do have the other key, you know, and I let them business folk in when you're not here. Everything is kept like a new pin and I hope as how he treats you right.'

'He treats me very well. And thank you for being so kind.' Poppy was now flushed with pleasure. 'Mrs Flanty, about the people who visit? Are they rich and famous theatre people?'

'I don't know and I don't care.' Mrs Flanty put a screw of tea wrapped in muslin into a small brown earthenware teapot. 'They seem very taken up with themselves, not that they ought to. Jumped-ups most of them are. Just jumped-ups pretending to be high class. Though, like toffs, they all seem to be rolling in money – and why they meet in that flat and what they get up to, God only knows.'

'Mr Carson wouldn't have anything to do with something dishonest!' Poppy said quickly. 'Mr Carson –'

'Could do murders and get away with them as far as I'm concerned,' Mrs Flanty cut in. 'He kept me on here when my Berty got killed in the war. What's more, he paid me the same

137

money. He's always treated me right, even when Farringdon's started to slide.'

'Never!' Poppy was shocked. 'I thought the shoe place was always filled to the brim with orders.'

'No. They often have to sack people. So it's a good job that Mr Carson has other interests.' Mrs Flanty sighed. 'Though there'll always be the rich and always be the poor. I reckon what some people pay for a pair of shoes would keep some families for a month. How do you like it at the shoe place?'

'Very much. Even though –'

'You're not daft?'

Poppy crimsoned, but her voice was steady as she accepted and thanked Mrs Flanty for the tea she had made.

'I . . . I don't know what you mean, Mrs Flanty.'

'If they didn't need you out of the way, you could be his nibs's housekeeper full time, couldn't you?' Mrs Flanty said bluntly. 'It's clear as day that you enjoy keeping his flat like a little palace.'

'I enjoy working in the early hours for Tony's café, as well as my job at the factory.' Poppy's cheeks had crimsoned because Mrs Flanty had voiced her own treacherous thoughts. 'The flat belongs to Mr Carson, but it is also my home and I treat it as such.'

'The whole house belongs to Mr Carson. The other three flats are rented by people who keep themselves very much to themselves. Actresses they say they are, and right hoity-toity. I do their fetching and carrying and keep my place, and my thoughts to myself. Come and go like shadows, they do.'

'The whole house?' Poppy was taken back. 'He must be very rich, because he has another home. The one where his mother lives and – I have never seen hide nor hair of the other people here.' Poppy laughed then, in a shy, depreciating way. 'But then I wouldn't, would I? I'm always off out working somewhere. I go out early and come back late. And here at home I stay put just concentrating on my chores. I never knew that Mr Carson owned everything. It might be an idea to try to get to know some of the actresses living under this roof. Are they very lovely?' she asked wistfully. 'And so rich and beautiful that they would look down on me? Oh, dear! Mrs Flanty, what do you think?'

'Drink your tea. It's getting cold.' Mrs Flanty was looking ill at ease. 'And forget what I said. It strikes me that I've been telling tales out of school.'

Poppy drank her tea and took her leave as quickly as she could. The truth hurt. It made her miserable to have to admit to herself that Mr Carson wanted her out of the way. The wonder was that he needed her at all while Mrs Flanty was around. But thank God he did! She knew that her life would end if Mr Carson sent her away. And he might send her packing because instinct told her that Mrs Flanty would let him know about her visit.

The following Saturday evening, after she had returned from Tony's, she poked the smouldering fire into new life. This was her favourite time of all. She did not have to get up for Tony's on Sunday mornings. The whole of the next day was her own to indulge herself. She sat in her chair and began to read the book Bill Bannerman had given her after she had been plaguing him with questions one day.

'Anemone,' she read, 'the cormose anemones, so called because their leaves spring from corms, or swollen stem bases, are among the most brilliant late-spring and early-summer flowers. Prominent among them is the –'

She looked up, startled. The outer door had opened. Someone was coming in. She hurried out to the hall. Her heart lurched and her face lit up when she saw Mr Carson. There was no disguising the expression in her eyes. He smiled, seeming warm and relaxed as he took off his outer clothes.

'Good evening, Poppy,' he said. 'I know that this is your home, but I hope very much that you will invite me to be your guest for the evening. If you'd rather not –?'

'I ... Thank you, I would enjoy your company, Mr Carson,' she replied, outwardly with quiet dignity, but inside she was swooning.

He laughed teasingly and put his arm round her shoulder as they walked into the main room. His touch made her shiver with delight.

'Poppy,' he said, 'at work I am Mr Carson. But here, in this place, you may call me Nigel.'

139

She watched him as he made himself comfortable in one of the red chairs. Firelight glinted on his face and hair. Her heart was pounding and she felt completely unnerved. She didn't think she would ever have the nerve to call him Nigel. Nigel! She cradled the name in her mind.

'Would you like a drink?' she asked breathlessly. 'I – I never touch the drinks cabinet, as you ordered, but I'm sure there must be –'

'I am about to enjoy this evening,' he told her, 'and hopefully, so are you. You are to be a lady of leisure for once in your life, Poppy. So please, set the table for two and then come and join me by the fire.'

He was speaking in riddles, but, anxious to obey him, she hurried into the kitchen and gathered the tablecloth, cutlery and crystal condiment set. When she returned she saw that Mr Carson had his eyes closed and seemed to be asleep. Not sure what to do once she had set the table, she sat in her chair opposite Mr Carson and again picked up her book. But the words were dancing before her eyes and her hands were trembling. She knew how she felt about this wonderful man, and deep down a dawning hope began to glow. Was there to be a step forward in their relationship? Was he at long last coming to feel a little for her? In the beginning he had been aware of her, but now perhaps being aware wasn't enough. Oh, she did hope so! Now if things were indeed changing, it was up to her! She must go out of her way to charm him, to make herself interesting. To act like a lady of leisure – well, lady, at least – more than an ignorant girl from the working class.

A knock made her jump and Mr Carson, now fully alert, smiled at her.

'Open the door, please, Poppy.'

She hastily did as she was told, and there and then wanted to die. Burney was standing there. He was dressed in a long, clean, white coat and balancing a large wooden tray on his head. It was covered with a white cloth. His eyes opened wide at the sight of her, then his gaze cut through her like ice. It hurt. It hurt a lot, and she gulped, feeling the scarlet winging to her cheeks.

'Usual place, miss?' he asked.

Poppy looked over her shoulder at Mr Carson, who was now standing up beside the table.

'Yes, Burney,' he said easily. 'And thank you for being so prompt.'

Poppy stood aside while Burney walked in and set the tray down. She had known all about the order Burney had received that morning from one of his private customers. Someone who insisted on nothing but the best, and who gave generous tips. Oh yes, Burney had boasted about his growing clientele and she had been delighted for him. Never had she guessed that she was about to taste Burney's culinary arts.

Money changed hands and Burney left, still acting as though Poppy was not there. And she stood there, dazed, cut in half with nervous excitement, and sadness too, because quite clearly Burney did not like her any more.

Then everything was forgotten because, as instructed, she began setting hot covered dishes on the table. Mr Carson had gone to the drinks cabinet and taken out two tall bottles of wine.

Later, as she sat opposite Mr Carson, eating a chicken dish that was as delicious as it looked, she could not dismiss her sense of unreality. There was a fruit tart to follow, with pastry that melted in the mouth, lashings of cream, cheese and biscuits and, of course, the wine, sweet and potent. She loved it and nodded happily every time Mr Carson offered to refill her glass. And all the time he was gently teasing her, calling her beautiful, and asking her about herself, her home, the people she knew, her relations, her lifelong ambitions.

By the time the leisurely meal was completed, Poppy was lost in a warm, rosy glow and Mr Carson had learned all about Jezebel Street, Ros, Nan and Charlie. Even about old Rags and Josh and Jo, and above all, her ambition to get rich.

'I am lucky, Mr Carson,' she told him and heard herself chuckling in a merry way. 'I like work and I have my plans. I have learned a lot of things since I've been here.'

'Oh?' He leaned nearer, his eyes intent.

'Yes. I have noticed – noticed how far chefs can make vegeta–' she was having difficulty with the word and changed it – 'make food go. And I've also seen just how far Bill can make bags and packets of seed go. So, if you can

141

grow things, and then also cook them, you can make the kind of profits you only read of in books. And on top of that there will be flowers. Hundreds of millions of flowers for the shops, mostly scented ones – for Ros.'

'Tell me more,' he said in a rich, warm way and refilled her glass.

'I often think,' she told him owlishly, 'how lucky I was not to get a job at the jam factory. They're slave drivers there, and in summertime the place gets alive with wasps. They have a school-leaver there specially to dig out the dead wasps from the tops of jars. Most of the workers get stung to bits in the season. Horrible, really horrible it must be. In the winter the women still have to go down on their hands and knees to scrub concrete floors. The owners aren't sticklers for cleanliness or anything like that. It's just that the workers would skid and break their necks else. My aunt Nan scrubs floors, but she works in Daniel's Home, and when we had Ros to worry about, she'd go and do doorsteps, too. I love my aunt, but she doesn't care for me. Even so, know what? One day I'm going to get her really secure.' She blinked at him, her face wreathed in smiles. 'Talking too much, eh, Mr Carson? I can hear myself carrying on and on . . .'

She heard herself giggling, which was not her way. It didn't seem to matter, though. Mr Carson was interested in all that she had to say.

'You have set your sights very high, Poppy,' he said easily. 'I admire you because you are prepared to put one hundred per cent effort into everything you do. I have noticed this at work.'

'And you don't think I'm a ra– raving idiot?'

'Far from it.'

'Edna thinks so. She said if I keep on like I am, I'll cave in.' She leaned forward in a confidential, very earnest way. 'But I won't, Mr Carson. I swear I won't.'

'I know,' he replied, 'and I am going to help you. Shall we turn off the light and drink our wine by the firelight?'

'I don't think there's any wine left, Mr Carson?'

'I shall fetch another bottle, while you get the bedcover and set it before the fire. Then we can make ourselves comfortable while we talk.'

142

'All friendly like?'

'Exactly.'

She raised her brows, befuddled, momentarily unsure. But he had got up from the table and walked round to cup her chin in his hand.

'I have never enjoyed a meal more, Poppy,' he told her. 'And you are such a lovely, intriguing little thing. Please don't make me leave yet. I don't want this evening to end.'

'Go on,' she chuckled. 'That's a lot of old toffee for a start.'

'Ah!' he teased. 'Getting brave, are we?'

She screwed up her eyes to stare at him, smiling all the while. 'Am I getting very tipsy, Mr Carson?'

'Are you in a good mood?'

'Ever shuch a good mood, Mr Carson.'

'Then I suspect you are, but who minds that? Go and get the bedcover, while I fetch us something else to drink.'

As she stood up she felt giddy and laughed. Mr Carson's eyes were looking her up and down; there was sweat on his upper lip. He laughed too. This couldn't be happening, Poppy thought in a vague, rosy way, it was all too wonderful to be true. She was having a marvellous time and Mr Carson was actually happy to stay with her. Yes, he actually liked Poppy Ashton from Jezebel Street. How miraculous! Let the world go hang. She didn't care any more.

It was Mr Carson who spread the bedcover on the floor. Mr Carson who turned off the light and told her to sit on it, by the fire, while he refilled her glass. Mr Carson who looked more human because inexplicably he now wore only a dark-blue dressing gown. Feeling dizzy and happy, Poppy did as she was told. In a faraway realm a little voice was telling her that she was dicing with danger. She ignored it and was filled only with her love for this huge, wonderful man.

'Drink up,' he told her in a deep caressing voice,' then I can fill your glass once more before we both settle down.'

She did as she was told.

'Now,' his voice was deep, coaxing. 'Lie back. Come on, beside me, close. Relax and we'll talk.'

It was a dark, cosy world, lit by the flickering blue-yellow flames of the fire. She felt languorous and wanted to melt against the reclining figure at her side.

'You are a dear, sweet little thing,' he told her. 'You make me feel . . . at home.'

'You are at home, Mr Carson,' she said dreamily. 'And I can't thank you enough for letting me come here to stay.'

'You can thank me, Poppy.' He took her in his arms. 'You can give me a kiss.'

'No!' She was suddenly wary and frightened, but also excited. A wildly daring part of her was shouting, 'Why not?'

'Yes!' Mr Carson said huskily.

He lowered his lips to hers and kissed her, gently at first, then passionately. She knew she should struggle, but she was wanting him to go on. The kiss was making her feel wild and wanton, as she had never felt in her life before. She wanted the kissing to go on for ever. She found herself responding even more as he kissed her again and again.

He was leaning over her now. She saw him above her, strong, fierce, a man of riches and power. A strange sensation creeping through her body was making her feel helpless, not in control, because deep down she knew that she should not be enjoying this. A man kissing her, taking advantage. Nan would hate her. This was wrong!

She began to fight him, beating his chest with her small fists until he caught them both and pulled them above her head, holding them there with one large, firm hand.

'Poppy,' he was saying harshly, 'I must see if your body matches your lovely little face. Don't you understand?'

He began fumbling with the buttons of her dress. She kicked him, but he threw a leg over her and with one rending movement tore her dress apart. Poppy screamed, only to find his mouth covering hers again, and in spite of herself, the feel of him was making her head spin and her heart race in a madly excited way. His lips moved down to her neck. With his free hand he began caressing her neat little breasts. She felt a trail of fire leaping through her veins. She began to struggle again.

'Don't!' he told her, his voice deep in his throat. 'Let me show you just what I can do to make you really come alive.'

'This is wrong, Mr Carson,' she whispered frantically, fighting to retain her senses. 'All wrong!'

'Behave,' he murmured with his mouth against her face, 'and I will let you go.'

He freed her hands and all she was able to do was whisper, 'Please leave me alone, Mr Carson. Please?'

Then she was gasping because he was fondling her breasts and pulling away at her undergarments. She began struggling in earnest then, but she was tiny, he large and strong. They were both panting by the time she lay on the floor, helpless at the end of it all. And she was as naked as the day she'd been born. He was looking her all over, his face stern.

'If you let yourself go,' he told her, 'I will show you what I can do for you. You are certainly doing a great deal for me.'

'Do you love me, Mr Carson?' she whispered, her eyes large and wistful. 'Really and truly love me?'

'Why else am I here?' he asked her. 'Poppy, would I be with you else?'

She was staring up at him, hypnotised. He loved her! That meant he would marry her one day. It really had happened. Mr Carson loved her! He began stroking her body slowly his hands like velvet, tantalising and smooth. She began to shiver and tingle, then gasped as his lips closed about her breasts one at a time, while his hand was stroking, caressing, travelling down past her navel, lower. She heard herself moan, and him whispering, 'I've only just started, my dear. Let yourself go.'

He pushed his knee against her legs to open them. He was stroking her, teasing her, and she felt on fire. She didn't want him to stop. Something wild and scary was happening to her. He was rolling on top of her. She could feel his hardness. her mind cried out for him to stop, but her newly wakened body was screaming out, demanding that he go on. Gradually the world changed into a spinning wheel that whirled so quickly it finally flung her high, so that she hung in heaven for a single ecstatic moment.

She was weeping for joy when it all ended, and Mr Carson had slumped over her, satiated at last.

After a while she was composed enough to whisper in youthful honesty, 'Mr Carson, that was nice!'

'Yes, it was,' he agreed and smiled. 'Keep it up and I won't be able to let you go. What do you say about that?'

145

'I always want to stay with you,' she whispered passionately. 'I love you, Mr Carson, love you with all my heart and soul. All my life I've dreamed dreams, but I never knew how it would really be. I will love you until the day I die.'

'There's my good girl,' he told her. 'Now let's get to bed and sleep.'

In a distant dream Poppy heard the bells of St Martin's Church peeling. She smiled and snuggled down, realising it was Sunday, her lazy day. The best day of the week. Gradually, memory made little golden lights in her brain. She turned round, smiling, her heart singing.

She was alone. Mr Carson had gone.

Fear came then, a terrible, gnawing terror that Mr Carson now felt only contempt for her. That he hadn't meant it when he said he loved her. That the wonderful time they had had together would never happen again. If she had lost Mr Carson because she had been a scarlet woman, she would want to die. Love was terrible, it was worse than chains. It strangled the heart and mind and soul – made girls do what they knew was wrong.

For the first time in her life she consciously thought about her mother. Her whore of a mother! She could hear Aunt Nan spitting out the words. What would Nan say if she ever found out? Nan must never find out, nor Charlie. What of Sandy and Daniel? Sandy's lips would curl in utter contempt. And Daniel? He'd not want to be in the same room with her. He would tell her to buzz off and mean it, and she would want to sink through the floor in her shame. But none of that would matter if Mr Carson loved her. If he hadn't left out of disgust. She should never have taken all that wine. If she could turn the clock back she would just sip at the glass in a genteel way and be certain of staying stone-cold sober. But instead, she had shown herself up in front of Mr Carson. Thrown herself at him. And, being human, he had accepted all that she had to give and . . . and then made his escape.

Tears came then, floods of tears which made her headache even worse. She heard herself praying out loud.

'Dear God, let Mr Carson still love me. You say in the Holy

146

Book, "Ask and ye shall receive." I ask you, God, no, I beg of you, please let Mr Carson still love me.'

All that day she worked and worried. She scrubbed and polished and took the bed linen down to the wash-house to clean. She changed the bedclothes and made tea. She carefully cleared the evidence of last night's meal away and washed and polished the silver containers it had been in.

She heard a merry tattoo on the door and ran to open it. It was Burney standing there. His eyes were wry, but his lips smiled as he said, 'Gorn and caused it now, haven't you? Never thought I'd see the day.'

'Won't you come in, Burney?' she whispered and felt sick and faint. 'It's all right. He's gone.'

''Course he has. Never stops, does old Carson. But he'll treat you right, Poppy, make no mistake about that.'

'He loves me.'

''Course he does,' Burney replied and, at her gesture towards one of the red chairs, sat down. 'How long you been here, then?'

'A little while.'

He grinned. 'I bet a pound to a penny Edna don't know.'

'No!'

'Thank Gawd for that! You know what she's like where old Carson's concerned.' His expression was now the same as always, warm and friendly. 'You'd better not tell her. Don't worry, I won't say a word. Here, how was it with his nibs?'

Her face blossomed like a rose, but her eyes were shy. 'I told you, Burney, I love him, and what happened last night is between me and him.'

'Last night? Was that the first time –'

'Yes! Don't go on, Burney, please? I'd ask you to stay for a cup of tea but I'm scared he might come back and –'

'You won't see him here till next Saturday night, Poppy. I can promise you that. It's always the same.'

'You've delivered meals here before.'

''Course! A hard bitch named Rene lived here before you. All over him like a rash, she was. She had to keep house, just like you. And wait in for Carson on Saturday nights. Real possessive old sod he is, and he'll want to know where you are every minute of the day when you're not in Farringdon's.

147

That's why Rene got fed up. Gone on to bigger and better things, she has. Men are Rene's business – unlike you. Fancy you loving that old fart!'

'Burney!' she choked. 'He told me he loves me. He's going to marry me one day, I'm sure of it. Rene Davies was someone very different to me. Mr Carson loves me and I love him. One day –'

'He'll never marry you, Poppy, you can bet on it. He lives in a great big posh house where they've got a cook and maids and treat the tweeny like shit. The rumour is that he's something to do with Farringdon's granddaughter, and that's how he got his nose in the firm.'

There was panic in her heart and she was shrivelling and dying inside. He looked into her face and saw her agony, shame and despair.

'You're wrong,' she whispered through frozen lips. 'He has nothing to do with people's granddaughters. He would have told me. Your story must be about somebody else.'

'Whether that's the case or not,' Burney said stoutly, 'my mate Fabian hears talk. He knows lots of easy ladies, some of them very high class. The story goes that in the old days, the founder of the place where you work was a real crook. Dabbling in all kinds of shenanigans, he was. Receiving, thieving, forging, anything to swindle the rich. Got to be a sort of gang boss. In them days his cobbler's shop was a front – just like the factory is now. Anyway, that's how the story goes. Farringdon's has always been involved with arty-farty people, and Carson's cousin, Fatty Tilsby, has made good use of the fact. Everyone knows about him!'

'Are . . . are you telling me that Mr Carson –'

Poppy was unable to go on. Taken back by the stricken look on her face, Burney hastened to reassure her.

'I don't know nothing about him!' He took a quick look over his shoulder, disturbed. 'And I haven't said anything. Right?'

'Of course, Burney! I didn't mean –'

'I can tell you about old Tilsby, though.' He grinned, now on safer ground. 'He deals with women, all kinds. But the ones he likes most is them that'll do anything to get on. There's a scheme worked where rich respectable men get caught with their trousers down. What a surprise! Of course, from then on they have to pay through the nose. Do anything, them girls would, and most of them are met because Farringdon's deal in fancy show-business shoes. That's one of the reasons old Tilsby toadies up to Mr Carson. And all kinds of crooked business deals are hatched here and –'

'You're making it all up,' she whispered, horrified. 'You've been reading too many of them American paperbacks. For a start, Mr Carson would never ever allow that sort of thing to go on here. And he would never –'

''Course not, Princess.' Burney let her off the hook. 'What a girl you are! I was only telling you stuff that Fabian gossips about. Yes! I was having you on, wasn't I?'

'Are you sure, Burney?' Her eyes beseeched him. 'Really?'

'Even if it were true, Carson probably don't even know what's going on. Anyway, I think he cuts off and leaves them to it once they've been settled down and had a drink. Then he makes sure the business is over and done with before he comes back – if he comes back. Anyway, who cares?'

'I care!' She was suddenly angry where before she had been so afraid. 'And I think you've just made all of this up because you hate me for falling in love and staying here! Burney, how could you?'

'I'm only telling you what Fabian says. He's my mate who's an actor. A nice bloke, he is. He goes round everywhere, on try-outs, plays all kinds of roles. It must be rotten, standing there on an empty stage, acting your guts out for some lousy unseen git who just says, "Thank you, we'll let you know." That means "get lost", of course.'

'Is he famous?'

'Don't be daft! Fabian's a bit, well – a bit like me, but more so. Know what I mean?'

'Burney, I –'

'Come on, Poppy, weren't born yesterday, were you?'

'No, but –'

'They call him a nancy and they treat him like dirt. This makes him cry like a baby, because his feelings are hurt and he wants to be liked. He's a thin-skinned sort, and only too grateful to the lousy devils that throw him a kind word. I tell

149

you, Poppy, no one's ever going to treat me like that – or use me! I've got better things to put my mind on. Like rising above it all, and getting to be successful and filthy rich.'

'I suspect that your friend bitches about people and tells lies just to get back at the world, Burney,' Poppy told him fiercely. 'Yes, that's it! Your Fabian dreams up horrible things just because inside he feels horrible himself. I don't believe a word you've told me. How could I? I'll just put the kettle on.'

Poppy tearfully fled into the kitchen. He followed her, his face anxious now.

'Do you want to spit at me, Poppy?'

She swung round to face him, her heart aching, her eyes emerald-bright.

'I could never even think of such a thing, Burney. You're my dearest friend, just as special to me as Edna is. I want things to stay the same between us as always. That is, if you don't hate me too much.'

'You're the nearest I'll ever get to – to loving a woman, Poppy. Are you going to stay on here?'

'If Mr Carson says I can. Burney, my aunt Nan says that you should treat people as they treat you. Mr Carson has always been more than fair with me, and kindness itself.' She crimsoned, remembering what had happened during the night, and added, 'I really and truly love him and he loves me. And in spite of what your Fabian says, I know he is going to marry me. All right?'

'Fair enough, Poppy.' He was grinning now. 'And in spite of your being about as green as grass, I'd rather be your friend than your enemy. Your eyes were flashing just then. Fair give me a turn, you did. Old Carson's lucky all right. I hope as how he knows when he's well off.'

'Oh, be quiet and let me get on with making tea.'

'Don't want no tea, Poppy. I only stayed to have a talk. And yes, I'll go along with you. I agree that Fabian could have got things wrong, seeing how bitter and twisted he is. You catch your bloke if you can. Hook him fair and square, and, Poppy –'

'Yes?'

'You know I've got a job for life at Tone's, if I want, that is. And I have my own room up top?'

150

'Yes, I do know that, Burney.'

'Well, if you ever – I mean, if things ever get rough, you come and see me, all right? The back door of Tone's and the stairs leading up to my room is in Berry Street.' He gathered up the tray on which had been placed the scrupulously cleaned casseroles. 'Ta for cleaning everything, Poppy. You didn't have to, you know. The washing-up afterwards is all part of the service.'

'Get away with you.' She was smiling mistily now and pretending to box his ears. 'I'll see you tomorrow, first thing.'

'Cheerio.' He was back to his handsome, roguish self. 'Be good.'

Once alone, Poppy looked round at the flat she had come to think of as her own. She wandered into the bedroom and felt her heart beginning to beat at the remembrance of the feel of Mr Carson at her side. She ran her hand tentatively over the pillows and felt the fluffy blankets under the cover. She thought of Mr Carson's lovemaking and her knees went weak. She loved and adored Mr Carson and she would never give up until he married her. He would put that plain gold ring on her finger, whether he had another house with servants or not. It would all happen just as in the romantic novels. She, Poppy Ashton, would one day have her own deliriously happy ending – if only she hadn't blotted her copybook where he was concerned.

At Farringdon's the next day, Mr Carson came into the Clicker room. Behind Mr Banes's back he gave her the most wonderful smile and the merest wink. Later he came back and, under the pretence of looking at her work, said quietly, 'I can't wait till next Saturday. I will see you soon. I'll let you know.'

Suddenly, blazingly, all was right with her world.

Two days later he came to her, frowning. 'Where were you last night?'

'Last night?' she replied, perplexed. 'Only doing my job at Tony's, Mr Carson.'

'I want you in the flat every evening.'

'Mr Carson, I –'

151

'I will see you on Saturday, Poppy, and we'll talk about it then.'

Poppy wafted through the rest of the week with a singing heart.

Chapter Nine

It was Saturday, so there were many people in Market Street. Happy and excited, Poppy looked around her, loving the sights and sounds, the smell and the feel of the market. Women from the maze of back streets beyond wore aprons, slippers and scruffy coats and caps that probably belonged to their men. They pushed doggedly through the crowds, with language that could put a navvy's to shame. Then there were the other women, the darkly clothed, dour, tight-lipped, doggedly determined type. The poor but proud kind, who kept their hats firmly on, anchored by many hatpins, and had polished their shoes and wore threadbare cotton gloves. Women who set out to make a farthing do the work of a halfpenny, a halfpenny to do the work of a penny and a penny to do the work of two. Women like Nan, Poppy thought, who did their best and would never give in. They were stronger, perhaps, than the poor devils who had fought the war like heroes, returned to find themselves on the scrap heap, and now felt all semblance of their manhood gone.

A chestnut mare, which had been pulling a load of pots and pans, clattered its hooves on the cobbled street and blew through its nose. 'Whoa!' shouted the van man and thumped a gnarled fist against the horse's rump, which made it snort and toss its head. Then it made a rude sound before depositing its dung. It had hardly landed before an urchin rushed forward, shovel and bucket in hand. Good for the garden, Poppy thought and smiled, thinking of Bill Bannerman and his faraway eyes.

Poppy hurried on, eyes bright, lips smiling, excitement in

her heart. Tonight she would see Mr Carson again and it would be wonderful. She softly joined in with a street singer who in a high, glorious voice was singing, 'O Danny boy, the pipes, the pipes are calling . . .'

As always, Woolworth's was warm and jolly, counter after counter set out with lovely things. There was always a buzz in Woolworth's, Poppy thought, of conversation, scratchy music from the record stand, the crackling of paper bags or toffees being unwrapped. And every so often, children bawling for things they couldn't have.

The toiletry counter was a dream. Perfumed oils, shampoo, bath salts in lovely colours, scented soap, lily-of-the-valley talc, tins of tooth powder, brushes for teeth and hair. One could smell like a flower garden, she thought, and added to that, a little spot of Ashes of Roses dabbed tastefully behind the ears! Mr Carson would fall in love with her all over again.

After buying toiletries Poppy wandered over to the jewellery counter, which was an Aladdin's cave of crystal beads, brooches, bracelets, rhinestone-decorated tiepins with cuff links to match, and rings. Wonderful rings that blazed and flashed and winked and blinked under the lights. Engagement rings at sixpence a time. No matter that they would turn the finger black after a week or so, Poppy would have given her soul to own one if Mr Carson saw fit. Oh, how lucky she was! Remembering Edna and feeling guilty, not quite knowing why, Poppy bought a pretty blue scarf with a yellow daisy pattern for her friend. Then she left the store and made her way back to the bathhouse.

Back in the flat she was eating bread and cheese and reading a story in *Women's Weekly* about a little angel child named Bundle Dawn, when she heard Burney's knock on the door. Delighted, she ran to open it, grateful that the silence and loneliness could be broken for a while. the waiting and uncertainty was almost too awful to bear.

'Wotcher, cock,' he said. 'Looking all bright-eyed and bushy-tailed, ain't we?'

'I'm so glad you've come to see me, Burney. Come on in. Know something? I was just wishing that I didn't have Saturdays free. I was beginning to wonder whether Tony could do with an extra pair of hands and –'

154

'Cor! You ain't half a glutton for punishment, Poppy,' Burney teased as he followed her into the sitting room and sat down on one of the red chairs. 'Don't think you'll be in luck, though, seeing as how we have regular Sat'day people. Still, cheer up. I've got presents for you. Wait till you see them.' He handed her a large brown paper bag. 'His nibs dropped this round to my room all secret like, know what I mean? Got him where you want him, I see.'

She took the bag and pulled out the contents. Two nightdresses, one pale blue, one pink. Both shimmered like silk and were lace-trimmed, frothy and beautiful. She flushed scarlet and could barely look Burney in the face, but he was chortling, his eyes mischievous as he teased.

'Bet the old bugger can't wait to see you in them, Poppy. You'll look a regular princess. Princess Poppy, how's that?'

'Don't!' she gasped painfully. 'Don't poke fun at me, Burney. Am I like a – I mean, do you look down on me for what has happened? Am I a fallen woman in your eyes? Dear heaven, Burney, don't turn against me. You're my friend!'

'And I'll always be, Poppy, no matter what. I hope as how you'll remember that if the day ever comes when you need someone.' He looked at the clock and raised his hands in horror. 'Oh, sod it, I'm off! It's all right for some, Sat'days to yourself must be heaven. Ta-ta!'

Once alone, Poppy looked at the nightdresses again and glowed. Mr Carson must have been remembering their night of love. And tonight would be a beginning. One day she would be married and perhaps she and Mr Carson would have a little girl nicknamed Bundle. She hugged herself and began to sing the romantic song, 'Bluebells I gather, take them and be true. When I'm a man, my plan will be to marry you . . .'

By eight thirty she was frantic. He wasn't coming! She had been stupid to believe otherwise. Mr Carson must think her cheap, and he was probably laughing up his sleeve at her. She would die if he didn't come, she would want to weep and wither and fade away. Life would mean nothing without him.

She began to feel as she had on the day she had lost Ros. Her hands were trembling and she felt cold, her stomach was

155

beating like a drum and shaking her insides. Her mouth had gone dry.

Then, magically, she heard him open the door. And she was running, laughing and crying and all but throwing herself into his arms. He held her close and kissed her eyes, her forehead, her shining auburn hair. And she had no more doubts, because the way he felt was plain to see. He wanted and needed her as greatly as she wanted and needed him. Together they were in Paradise.

'You're wonderful,' he told her. 'Sweet and lovely, and innocence itself. I'll never let you go.' He laughed deep in his throat, his eyes were dancing. 'And how such a tiny young thing could so capture me, I'll never know. But I was hooked from the moment you walked into my office asking for a job. Ye gods, Poppy, you're important to me!'

They made love and she was as passionate as he. Afterwards they spoke together and smiled into each other's eyes, and felt content. By the time Burney delivered their delicious meal, in the same cheerful but distant manner as he had the week before, Poppy was happily blooming and more confident than she had ever felt in her life. But there was one thing she could not make herself do: call her man Nigel. He was Mr Carson to her, her beloved lord and master. He made her feel small and feminine, cherished! She gloried in the sight and sound and smell of him, and was in awe of his masculinity.

Later, looking like a love-in-the-mist flower in her blue nightie and sitting at his feet in the firelight, she tried to explain. He laughed softly and ran his hand through her long, flowing hair.

'You make me feel wonderful,' he told her quietly, 'as I have never felt before. I set out to charm you, but you have charmed me instead. I shall be calling here at every available opportunity, Poppy, and I must know that you will always be waiting for me. I must be able to imagine you here, safe and warm and wonderful, just resting and indulging yourself, and dreaming only of me.'

'I – I can't!' she stammered in quick dismay at the picture he'd drawn. 'I – couldn't, honestly!'

'What?' he teased gently. 'Do I come second to your evening job, Poppy? You don't mean that, surely?'

'No, oh no! It's just that I'm not the kind of person who can sit and twiddle her thumbs, Mr Carson.' She looked earnestly into his face. 'I'd go mad doing nothing, really I would. It was like burning in hell waiting for you today. Besides, I like my early-morning job. I like walking to Tony's when the streets are empty and clear. I enjoy evening times when I meet up with all the new friends I've made and ...' Her voice faded and she was drowning in his eyes, surrounded by such beautiful, thick, near-white lashes. 'I mean, I have made friends and –'

'Later,' he muttered and his hands began sliding down to her breasts, his lips were against her hair. 'We'll talk later, but not now.'

He carefully and skilfully took her to heaven again.

Mr Carson stayed all that night and joined her for Sunday breakfast. His hair was tousled, his face was full of light and he looked younger by far.

'You do things to me,' he told her across the table. 'You're mine now and don't you forget it. From now on, you're to have eyes only for me.'

'And you for me?' she asked and smiled shyly. 'We will marry one day, Mr Carson?'

'Mr Carson still? How Victorian! My love, when the time is right everything shall be just as you want. In the meantime we will keep our secret, eh? Just remember you are mine to indulge in and spoil.' He laughed softly. 'In fact I'm getting to loathe our fleeting meetings in Farringdon's. Do you know that I'm rather like you? When I was young I was a salesman and staying in the office irks me at times. When that happens I decide to become a salesman again and they put up with it, providing my efforts pay off. That's how I'm able to be here now. They believe I'm busy working. I think I shall put forward a rather more expansive sales scheme. Yes, and get away from this area rather more often.'

'Oh no! That means I won't see you and –'

'And do most of the travelling myself. I will need a young lady assistant, of course, one who will point her pretty little

157

toes and show our clients the new designs of shoes. Yes, yes! That is a capital idea.' He looked sombre then and added, 'Poppy, the senior shareholders will take this all very seriously indeed. They are not the kind of people to trifle with. They will pay good money, but expect results. I will arrange it that you will get commission on sales, and believe me, you will earn every penny you get.'

'I don't think I want that kind of job, Mr Carson,' she told him and looked apprehensive. 'In fact, the thought of your share-people glaring and weighing up what we do or don't do, frightens me.'

'Does the thought of us travelling around together put you off?' he asked her and the awareness in his eyes made her heart dance again. 'Even if we get held up on Friday nights? That would mean us having to stay in grand hotels, of course. That's where I'm believed to be now, Poppy, in a hotel, having been held up on a business deal.'

'Wouldn't telling the truth be easier?' she asked gravely. 'Why do we have to be so secret about our love? I can face the people at Farringdon's, and Tony's is no trouble at all. Why can't —'

'It's my mother, Poppy.'

'Oh?' She went as red as fire, on the defensive at once, 'I — I'm just a lowly working-class girl, is that it, Mr Carson?'

'Stop that! Poppy, you could be the Queen of Sheba and it would make no difference. My mother is like me, rather dominating and very possessive. At this time she needs to feel that I am her only concern. She is old now, and she has been very ill. And she meets many of the Farringdon notables. Any hint of what is happening between us would kill her. Poppy, sweetheart, you must understand and believe me.'

The great man was actually pleading with her, Poppy Ashton! Feeling sick with love and, above all, relief now that she had been told the reason for the secrecy, Poppy smiled and nodded, her eyes twin wistful green stars.

'Thank you for telling me,' she said quietly. 'I hope that your mother gets better very soon. In the meantime I take it that I may work at Tony's and —'

'Keep your other job going, if you really must. And you

will continue at Farringdon's the same as usual. At least until I have put my suggestion forward to the board. Incidentally, there will be no more meetings here during the day, or any other time, come to that. My outside interests, which are separate from Farringdon's, will be considered and assessed elsewhere. This flat is yours, Poppy. Yours and mine. Our secret place.'

'I can hardly believe all this is happening,' she whispered unsteadily. 'Mr Carson, I think I must be the happiest person in the world.'

'Even though you won't give up your evenings at the café?'

'Couldn't I wait till –'

'All right.' He capitulated unwillingly. 'On second thoughts, there wouldn't be much point at this stage. But the moment you become a Farringdon representative you won't have the time.' He smiled ruefully. 'I have never given way to a young lady in my life before, miss, and don't you forget it.' He took his watch from his waistcoat pocket and looked at it. 'And now I must go. I'll use the telephone downstairs and get a taxi. I don't suppose you have ever ridden in such a fine vehicle, my Poppy? I intend to change all that!'

'You spoil me,' she murmured. Then, because by loving Mr Carson she had shamed Nan, she had to lean on pride which made her add haughtily. 'But I have been for long drives and, yes, even in a taxi.'

'Oh?' There was a hint of amusement twinkling in the back of his eyes.

'We hired one to bring my cousin Ros home from hospital,' she said flatly.

'Ah! The youngster who died.'

'It was one of Mr Tilsby's taxis.' She suddenly went cold in the pit of her stomach and held her breath, remembering what Burney had said. Then she added uncertainly. 'But since that's Leyton way, I don't suppose you'd know anything about that particular firm.'

'Really?' he teased. 'My sweetheart, it's a small world! I do know of Tilsby's. Rather well, in fact. He is my cousin and I have a share in his business. I have shares in several moneymaking concerns, Poppy. This merely means that I put

159

money into them. I know nothing of the running of these affairs and don't want to. I'm only interested in the profits they make.'

'Oh, I'm so glad!' She coloured furiously. 'I mean –'

He smiled ruefully, rose from his chair and walked round to her. She stood and looked up at him, adoration in her eyes. He gave a little groan and took her in his arms to hold her close.

'My sweet, I don't want to go, but I must.'

He kissed her and left quickly. She stood there, dazed and helpless with love.

Monday found Poppy busily putting in gold studs, working with a will. Mr Banes was being nice, too nice. He's guessed, she thought, and he wants to keep in with me in case I tell tales to Mr Carson. He's desperate to keep his job. Poor old devil.

At dinnertime she stood outside and waited for Edna, who seemed offhand and out of sorts.

'Cheer up.' Poppy smiled and held out the little parcel she had made. 'This is for you.'

Edna took it, looked at it suspiciously and opened it, her face set.

'I thought it would match your hair slides,' Poppy said uncertainly. 'I . . . I hoped that you'd like it.'

'Thought you were always broke?' Edna's tone was belligerent. 'I thought you shoved every brass farthing in that long pocket of yours? What did you do, eh? Swipe this?'

'I'd never steal, Edna, and you know it! I saw it and bought it because I thought you'd like it, that's all.'

'How come you're in clover all of a sudden, eh?' Edna sneered. 'Got friends in high places, have we? Gawd, you make me sick!'

'Edna, please don't look at me like that. Why are you so cross? I haven't done anything that can harm you, and I –'

'No?' Edna's tone became louder and harsher, her eyes were glinting with spite. 'Been down that road before, ain't we? Went along with one of Carson's tarts before, didn't we? And she turned into bloody lady la-di-da. Got people what needed their jobs the sack, didn't she? Well, let me tell you

160

something, I'll drop dead before I'll touch your tainted scarf.'

Before Poppy could reply, Edna threw down the scarf. It fluttered forlornly in the kerb. Then Edna was hurrying away to Tony's, leaving Poppy alone.

When Poppy reached Tony's she asked for pie, mash and some of the delicious green liquor purely out of defiance. She had never felt less hungry in her life. Edna was sitting with some of the Farringdon women, who all looked at Poppy and sniggered as she walked to a table.

Maisy, a fat woman with a squint, called out to no one in particular, 'Watch it everyone. We have Carson's new trollop among us. I must say as how the old fart's got real rotten bad taste.'

They all had a go after that.

'Somethink stinks round 'ere.'

'Jumped-up moo!'

'Bloody little whore.'

A chorus of whistles and howls rose up and all eyes in Tony's were on Poppy. Only Edna, surprisingly, remained silent and was looking down at her plate.

The colour rose to Poppy's forehead. No one catcalled a girl from Jezebel Street and got away with it. No one!

With calm deliberation Poppy sat down her knife and fork. She left her table and walked up to the troublemakers. She stood there, watching them, her face so still and quiet, so cold, that one by one they stopped their mouthing. Clearly, if anyone could cause trouble at Farringdon's, this one could and would. She might be small and young, but the expression in her green eyes could be read by one and all.

When she had their full attention, Poppy said clearly, 'I can out-swear and out-yell everyone here if necessary. What's more, I can out-fight everyone here. Believe me, back home in Jezebel Street, I've never lost a barney. So, I'm warning you, the next person that opens her mouth about me is going to get the hiding of her life. All right?'

'You stupid little cow,' Maisy began, then gasped because Edna had leaned across the table and shoved her fist in the squinting face.

'Shut it!' Edna snapped. 'You're mouthing on about my mate.'

'Mine, too.' Tony had appeared from somewhere out back. 'Put a sock in it, ladies, or else get banned from here.'

Poppy gave him one heartfelt, grateful glance, then turned back to her tormentors.

'I meant what I said,' she told them. 'And I swear I'll knock you into the middle of next week if you start backbiting at me again. All right?'

There were filthy looks and Maisy opened and shut her mouth, but said nothing. Poppy left them all to it and returned to her table. Tony went back to the kitchens. Poppy heard rather than saw Edna gathering up her meal and following. Edna plonked herself down opposite and grinned.

'Got that little lot off your chest, didn't you? Come on, hurry it up. I've got to find my scarf.'

'Who spread the word around, Edna?' Poppy's cheeks were still burning. 'Was it Burney?'

'Lord love you, no! He'd top himself first. But they've got eyes and ears in the Clickers.'

'Oh no! It's got to be kept a secret from Mr Carson's mother.'

Edna opened her eyes wide and raised her brows in a sardonic way. 'Workshop gossip don't go that high, Poppy. The nobs don't know us sort are alive. No, you don't have to worry there! Old Banes and his Clickers are different. Putting two and two together ain't no hardship where they're concerned.' She sniggered then. 'Right now I bet they're painting haloes all round your head.'

'They – they are?'

''Course. They need old Carson to be in a good mood. When he ain't, he gives them the chop at the least excuse. One day he'll send you packing too, Poppy. Then where will you be, eh? I think Maisy and her crowd are right about one thing. You are a silly moo!'

'I don't want to hear that kind of talk! Edna, it's important that you believe this. I truly love Mr Carson and he loves me.'

'All right, if that's what you're determined to believe. It's no skin off my nose, and I know you mean what you say. I also realise that you ain't got a treacherous bone in your body, so the girls can let go of their sleepless nights.' Edna leaned over the table and said earnestly, 'I wish I'd kept my trap shut back there, but it's all over and done with now, eh? But make no mistake, Carson's a – a real blee–'

'Edna! Please?'

'Oh, all right! But when the bubble bursts, don't think I won't say I told you so. Now let's bloody well hurry up!'

The scarf was gone.

Search though they did, and with Edna moaning about thieves at the top of her voice, and swearing like a trooper all the time, it was nowhere to be found. In the end they had to run full pelt back to work. Even so they were late and had fifteen minutes docked off their pay.

Poppy continued to work diligently, both at Farringdon's and at Tony's, trying at all times to live up to Mr Banes' creed, 'Gotta be neat, gotta be quick, gotta be right.'

Unasked, because she wanted to stay out of the flat as late as possible at night, she stayed behind one night when the café doors shut.

'Cor!' Tony remarked. 'Put a sock in it, Poppy. Ain't you got no home to go to? Talk about showing the rest of us up.'

'I can't help it if I enjoy scrubbing and washing up and preparing vegetables.'

'You're talking through the back of your neck. Are you frightened of going home? Scared of walking the streets alone? I'll take you back if you like.'

She shook her head, smiling and appreciative, liking him more and more for the genuine soul he was. But his question made her stop and wonder why she stayed behind as long as she did, and why she so determinedly kept herself to herself inside number sixteen Coopersale Place. Then she bit her lip and felt hot tears start to her eyes. Oh, she was afraid all right, but not of street marauders.

She was remembering other snatches of gossip she had heard – about the occupants of the flats. She dreaded bumping into any one of them. The very idea made her palms go damp and her mouth feel dry. If the rumours were true, Mr Carson did not belong on the pedestal where she had put him. He would be the owner of a house of ill repute. The house in which she lived, beholden to him, and, even though unmarried, slept with him.

She didn't want to learn anything awful about Mr Carson. She had to hold on to the golden wonder of her dream. Had to know him as her hero, or shrivel and die with a broken heart. She didn't want to know a thing about the other occupants of the house either, because if the whispers were true –

Dear God! She could almost hear Aunt Nan's caustic remarks and see the utter contempt in her eyes. She shivered and remembered Charlie's taunts about the mother and wife who had run off and left him, having two-timed him all along. His lips would draw in, if he knew how it was with the 'whore's daughter' now. He'd swear and say awful things about mother and daughter being as alike as two peas. He'd carry on about tainted blood!

The thought made her shake and feel physically ill. Deep down she felt guilt and self-loathing, because what they'd think of her was all painfully true.

'Stop it!' she whispered fiercely to herself. 'I love him and where there's love, there must be faith and trust. I do trust him, and will with my life!'

Because she continued to work all hours both early and late, Tony gave her a raise in pay. Adept at penny-pinching, excitedly watching her savings grow, Poppy added it to the cash already in Ros' chocolate box. Once a month she went to the bank, religiously determined to fulfil her ambition on behalf of Ros and Nan. She was not certain how she could bring it about, but knew that lots of money was the key. Bright-eyed, ambitious, dismissing her doubts, she was happier than ever before. The row with Maisy and company had strengthened her friendship with Edna and Burney rather than the reverse.

Mr Carson's regular Saturday-night visits were longed for with passion and Poppy's most beautiful dreams all centred on him. Clearly he was as besotted with her as she was with him. No two people in the history of the world had loved each other as much as they did. And when his mother was strong enough to stand on her own two feet, they would marry. Little squiggles of joy made her wriggle her toes as she thought of the time when she, Poppy Ashton, would become Mr Carson's wife.

With her conscience now clear, Poppy wrote endless letters to Nan, Charlie and Clary, via Flossie, and to Sandy and Daniel. Daniel liked writing so his replies were full of interesting things – when they weren't going on and on about politics, of course. Poppy usually skipped those parts.

Daniel was furious when the general election resulted in the return of an overwhelmingly Conservative House of Commons.

Baldwin's out of touch with the people. Who would have thought that after only eight months in office, the Labour government would fall? Especially when they were brilliant. But I don't suppose you want to hear about that, Poppy. Nan comes to work every day and is as sprightly as ever. I think she misses you but would drop dead before admitting it. Charlie is the same cheerful chap as always, and Clary's a dear. One little bit of spice. Flossie's getting very keen on one of her lodgers. It's good to see her perking up a bit. Losing her parents like that made her quite ill. We nearly lost Lenny with fever, but he's getting stronger now. There's talk of the Devere Trust acquiring the old pickle factory next to us. If you remember, it's been empty for years. A Home for orphaned girls is the latest idea. Here's hoping.

Goodbye for now,
Daniel.

Sandy sent postcards from many Eastern places. His scribbled words were few and to the point. 'This is Hong Kong, Poppy. Love from yours truly, Sandy.'

All the picture postcards read exactly the same, apart from the different names of places. And with every one that arrived, a picture of tall, handsome Sandy rose up before her eyes. She thought of his kindness and loyalty to Ros, of how quiet and steady he had been at the funeral, how he had brought that one pure rose. He had looked across the abyss holding the coffin and understood her agony. He had been aware of the grief that had taken over her heart and soul and every fibre of her being, and she could feel his concern

165

reaching out to her. He never had to say a word. He was her dearest friend and now always so very far away.

Postcards from Sandy always made the wistful tears start to her eyes. She had known him all the days of her life. Even Nan had accepted him and spoken of him as a 'real nice boy'. She liked him more than she liked Daniel, in fact.

Remembering Ros and the funeral brought back the old sense of loss. 'Time heals,' Daniel had said. It never would. Poppy knew that she would never forget Ros nor cease to mourn her passing. Nor would she ever cease to be part of Jezebel Street, not really. Her own folk lived there. Her earliest memories were there. And one day she would take her husband, Mr Carson, back and show him –'

Her mind rejected the thought almost before it was born. Somehow she could never see him there, neither could she make herself write about him in her letters. She and Mr Carson were in a world of their own, private, confidential, and their golden moments were too precious and wonderful to be shared.

He showered her with gifts: a gold heart on a chain, bracelets, a watch-brooch, many pairs of silk stockings. On the first Saturday in October, the nearest to her birthday, he bought her a gorgeously skimpy tubular dress in apple green. To go with it, a pair of the most expensive Farringdon ladies kidskin shoes. Golden-brown they were, with a thin strap across the instep and faintly pointed toes. There were kid gloves to match.

'Now go and put your glad rags on, sweet,' he told her. 'I'm taking you out. You are going to have a ride in a car and eat in a hotel, and be fussed and spoiled as you never have been before.'

Chuckling with delight and excitement, she ran to do his bidding. She brushed her long hair and held it back with large tortoiseshell combs just as Mr Carson liked. He refused to let her follow the latest fashion and have it cut. 'It's your crowning glory, my sweet,' he said. 'And if you turn into a shorn lamb, things will never be the same.'

When she stood before him in her finery, he whistled long and low. 'You are beautiful and should be in pictures,' he told her. 'Now, close your eyes and wait there.'

She did as she was told, standing still with a smile on her lips and a rapturously beating heart. She heart him go into the hall, then return, and she could sense his own excited pleasure as he commanded, 'Now open your eyes.'

He was holding a coat out, waiting for her to step into it. A coat such as she had seen worn only in magazines. Green velvet, dark and rich, a wrap-over with a high fur collar and fur round the hem. With it came a small, matching pillbox hat. She marvelled at his knowledge. He might so easily have bought a cloche that could only be worn with short hair.

Mr Carson stepped back, watching her, his eyes alight with pleasure.

'My very own sweet,' he said softly. 'You will be the centre of all eyes.'

'Do you think we make a handsome couple?' she asked him shyly, admiring his good looks, his beautifully cut dark suit and his white shirt with its shining stiff collar. His tie was tastefully striped and his handmade shoes sharply pointed.

'I do indeed!' With his hand under her elbow, he led her to the door.

'Do you realise,' she asked him breathlessly, 'that this is the very first time we have been out together?'

'It won't be the last,' he promised. 'And since that's the case, I'm going to give you a monthly dress allowance. You can wear to work those dull, sensible, excruciatingly boring things you cling on to.'

'I don't want a dress allowance,' she told him fiercely, hurt beyond reason at his criticism. 'And I'm sorry that I am not a fashion plate, but working girls have very few occasions to dress up and –'

'You may be a working girl. That's your own choice, miss, and don't you forget it. You are also my own very special young lady. As such, you will dress the part, if only to please me. You shall have an allowance for lovely things of your own choice. Anything left over must go into your savings. Come along, you are glaring! Very unlike my sweet, smiling Poppy.'

She could not argue, she was too stunned. At the kerb, she saw the ultimate luxury: a Rolls-Royce sedan. Beside it,

167

waiting, stood a uniformed, peak-capped chauffeur, who leaped to open the doors for them.

Poppy found herself being driven through the City of London. She gazed dreamily at the traffic: open-topped double-decker buses, taxi cabs, horse-drawn vans, three-wheeled carts, and men and boys pedalling bicycles. The helmeted policemen looked to her like navy-blue oak trees, staunch and steady, standing for security and upholding the law.

'That's the Bank of England, you should be interested in that.' Mr Carson teased. 'That's right, to your left. The pillared portico just ahead is the Royal Exchange.'

'I like the statue of the man on horseback.' Poppy was all but whispering, she was so awed. 'Mr Carson, stop laughing at me!'

'Nigel!' he told her firmly. 'When will you cease to have a little part of you for ever keeping me at bay?'

He was speaking rubbish, but it didn't matter.

They enjoyed a delicious meal at a secluded hotel. The white linen, crystal and soft lights gave it an almost holy atmosphere, accentuated by the quiet, airy music coming from a palm-tree-decorated dais. The shadowy quartet, three men and a woman, played rapturously, lost in their haunting melodies. Poppy felt embarrassed at being waited on, uncertain of the order in which to use the knives and forks, but she managed to pull if off by surreptitiously copying Mr Carson. Then, because she was suddenly aware that she was being watched by people at other tables, she felt a distinct unease.

'What is it?' Mr Carson asked her, smiling across a centrepiece of exotic flowers and ferns. 'There's something troubling you, Poppy?'

'I was wondering if there was something wrong. Has my dress pulled up? I'm not used to such a short skirt and – oh dear, people are looking at me!'

'You honestly don't know how very beautiful you are, do you?' he asked her softly. 'Or how greatly I adore you. My sweet, you are the centre of attention because you look winsome and fascinating, and I am the envy of every man in the room.'

168

'Thank you.' She glowed at his compliment, but still felt uneasy. 'But I was wondering what would happen if your mother ever found out about this.'

'Is that all?' He laughed. 'Relax, my sweet. She is away. Her health has improved sufficiently for her to take the flight to Paris. She has old friends there.'

'To Paris, France?' She was awed all over again, thinking that Mr Carson must be a millionaire.

'Yes. If the weather is with them, the flight time will be a mere two and a half hours. I shall take you on an aeroplane one day. What do you think of that?'

'I think that if I was meant to fly up in the sky, I would have been born with wings,' she said, adding excitedly, 'driving in your car was adventure enough. I haven't written to my aunt about you yet, but I will say that I have been in a real posh motor when I go home at Christmas. I have so much to tell Nan and . . . I can't thank you enough.'

'It isn't over yet, sweetheart,' he teased.

She rushed on regardless. 'I think this has been the most wonderful birthday of my life. And on top of it all, I had cards from everyone. Not like last year, when they found everything so sad.' She brightened again. 'But I heard from home last Christmas, though, and this year I'll handle things much better. I can't wait to see them all. I write heaps, but letters aren't really the same, are they?'

'You eyes are like jewels,' he told her softly. 'Like shining emeralds and, forgive me, but I can't wait to get you back home. I want to make love to you, Poppy. I can't bear the thought of leaving you even for a few hours. Don't talk about going home for Christmas. I need you there, in our flat.'

Poppy did not go home for Christmas after all; Mr Carson insisted that she stay. He gave her an absurdly generous allowance, for all she told him that she did not want it. It was almost as though he had to beat down her will, make her do as he said; he acted as though bribery was the only way he could keep her. It hurt, but she glorified in his open desire to please. She sensed that he needed her to be beholden to him, believing that it gave him a sense of power over their destiny.

During the time that followed she was getting to feel like a confident young woman of the world. She tried very hard to be one, in dress and manner, likes and dislikes. For all that, she clung to down-to-earth Edna and rascally Burney, whom she adored. They were her true friends, and her own sort. Mr Carson, lovely, wonderful, dearly beloved Mr Carson, was in a class of his own.

She went to clothes shops at his insistence and bought new things with the crisp five-pound notes he pressed on her, getting furiously angry if she even tried to refuse. When she attempted to return any unspent money, he dismissed it with an impatient wave of his hand.

'Put it in your bank, sweetheart. Yes, you must! I can and will see that you do.'

As the months passed he became even more possessive and arrived at the flat at every opportunity he could. Sneaking away while his mother slept, he said. Or staying for weekends while officially he was on business trips. And every time he brought her gifts of flowers and chocolates, jewellery and wickedly expensive perfume. Poppy obediently sprayed it on, secretly preferring her Woolworth's Ashes of Roses. Alive to her moods, he asked her what was wrong.

'Nothing, really,' she admitted, shamefaced, 'but you're so generous, too much so, and . . .'

'Yes?'

'I saw some lovely rings in Woolworth's. Engagement rings! If you bought me one, it would make things seem more definite somehow.'

'When I buy you rings, my sweet,' he said with a laugh, 'I assure you that they won't come from Woolworth's. Ye gods, I swear I've never set foot in the place. but next week I'm going to take you to the picture palace to see Rudolph Valentino. That is, if you promise me not to swoon.'

Poppy fell in love with the handsome film star almost as much as she loved Mr Carson. She left the picture palace starry-eyed.

Another year slipped by. Another Christmas came, with presents and red roses from Mr Carson, and cards from home and from people in Tony's. Suddenly, heart-wrenchingly, Poppy found herself actually missing Jezebel Street,

170

especially since, after vowing that he would be visiting her during the festive season, Mr Carson failed to show up.

Then, on New Year's Eve, Mr Carson brought her a diamond ring. Weeping with joy, Poppy looked up into his face.

'We are engaged?'

'Only if you'll call me Nigel.'

'Nigel, Nigel, Nigel!' She was beaming, wide-eyed and wondering.

'Are you happy?' he asked, his voice deep, his eyes hot. 'Sweetheart, I'd do anything to make you smile up at me as you are now.'

'I think I'm the happiest person in the world.' She gulped. 'And I believe I'm dreaming.' She looked at the three small stones set in gold through a blur of tears. 'Oh, it's beautiful! Beautiful! Please, please put it on for me.'

He slipped it on the third finger of her left hand and she stared down at it, almost too happy to think straight. Then he was kissing her fiercely and she melted against him, wanting him, needing him and, as his passion grew, aching for him in return. They made love fiercely, joyously, abandoned as never before. And at the end of it all, flushed and rosy, she finally had the courage to ask him in a shy, sweet way, 'Does . . . does your mother know?'

'Not yet, sweet,' he told her, 'but soon. One day soon.' He laughed softly. 'And when I take you to see her you must look like the princess you are. You shall have the very best of everything. A whole new wardrobe, jewellery, a fur coat. You will take her breath away just as you do mine. I want to buy you –'

'You are generous to a fault,' she breathed. 'You give me lots of money to buy the kind of clothes you like to see me in, and I never spend even half of it, so –'

'All the better,' he teased. 'You must always salt something away in that bank account of yours. I need to know that you're financially secure no matter what. Have you looked at your account lately? It must be mounting up quite decently now.'

'I'm getting rich!'

'By your standards, perhaps. Such an earnest, honest little

171

thing! Poppy, I don't need you to itemise every farthing you've spent, and then offer me back what you haven't used. You do it every time and it hurts like hell. Can't you get it into your pretty little head that it gives me great pleasure to indulge you? I have money to burn and I have never felt so happy about it before.'

'I'm sorry.' Her cheeks flamed with distress. 'But don't you see? Making me take money in that way feels like you're turning me into a kept woman. It is humiliating. I need to work for what I have.'

He began kissing her passionately and saying against her lips, 'Never that, sweetheart! The only humiliating thing about all this is the fact that I can't get you out of my mind. That and the knowledge that there's a part of you always distancing yourself from me.'

'I never do! You are the love of my life,' she crooned, starry-eyed.

'Then let me be part of your dream. Flowers for Ros and buying that little house for your aunt is now part of my dream too. I want to be part of everything about you. You belong to me, and I belong only to you and –'

Suddenly she felt cold. He did not belong wholly to her. He did here and now, in the privacy of Coopersale Place. But there was a great big outside world where they lived separate lives.

'You're not being strictly truthful,' she whispered sadly. 'I have still not met your mother. In fact, I'm not part of everything about you at all.' She continued in a small shaky voice, 'We're engaged now, but I still know very little about you. You know all about Jezebel Street, my life there, my relations and friends, but I know nothing about your family, except that you have a sick mother and a cousin named Mr Tilsby.'

'Sweetheart,' he promised, frowning, 'that will all be corrected very soon.'

'And I'm still waiting to earn heaps of money in the correct way, by being a saleswoman for Farringdon's,' she told him quietly. 'Oh, I'm happy doing what I do, very happy indeed! But the sales thing was your idea – to give us more time together. I would give up both my regular jobs to achieve that!

Yet everything along those lines seems to have been forgotten. It's almost as if we live in separate worlds, Mr Carson. And what's more –'

'Say it,' he ordered roughly. 'Call me Nigel!' He was all but glaring at her. 'And for what it's worth, I can hardly introduce you to anyone, least of all my mother, when you insist on calling me Mr Carson!'

He was blustering. Knowing him as well as she did now, she knew that she had pushed him too far. He was unable to commit himself further, at least not yet. Anguished, she looked down at the lovely ring sparkling on her finger. It must have cost the earth. She was ungrateful. It was all her fault!

He left soon after, saying that he had to be with his mother before midnight.

Poppy saw the New Year in alone.

January brought bad weather and trouble with it. Dizzy, depressed and worried, Poppy began to add up the weeks. A little warning light began blinking on and off in her mind. Part of her soul began to scream in horror.

By the Friday evening she was beside herself and sobbed with relief when she heard Mr Carson's key turning the lock in the door. She ran to him and fell into his arms weeping.

'Nigel! Thank goodness you're here,' she sobbed. 'I – I tried to let you know before, but Mr Banes' eyes seem to be on me all the time these days. I – Oh, thank God you're here!'

'What is it, my dear?' He was holding her gently and kissing her eyes, her lips, her hair. 'Sweetheart, what is it?'

'I think I'm going to have a – a baby.'

She heard his sharp intake of breath, felt him stiffen and clung to him, knowing for a fact that things had gone terribly, terribly wrong.

'Are you sure, Poppy?' he asked roughly. 'Quite sure?'

Feeling guilty and ashamed, she nodded and gulped. 'Almost. I – yes, I think I'm sure.'

'Then we'll have to get you to someone who deals with this sort of thing straight away. Damn! It couldn't have come at a worse time. I've all but set up our sales promotion.' He brightened. 'No matter, we'll get this business over and done

173

with, and then we'll be on our way. You will enjoy travelling, Poppy, and – What is it, my dear?'

She had pulled away from him and was staring up at him with wildly hurt eyes. Her face was white and her lips trembled.

'What do you mean, Mr – Nigel? What do you mean when you say you'll get me to someone who deals with this kind of thing?'

'Oh, you won't have any worries, Poppy,' he told her masterfully. 'I can get you to someone who will be very discreet. In a week or so you'll be like a new person. Then we can get on with our plans.'

She felt sick, then shattered as the truth dawned. 'You . . . you mean that we won't be getting married?'

'How can we – yet?'

'But your mother will understand, surely? I mean, my baby will be her grandchild and –'

'No!'

'But – Look, it's a terrible shock, I know, but we can get over it.' Her cheeks were scarlet and she tossed her head defiantly. 'And I don't want to be taken to someone very discreet! Wouldn't you like us to have a baby? Our very own little child? Can't you imagine –'

'No!'

'Please?' she begged frantically. 'I could stay at home, just as you're always asking me to. I would give up all thoughts of the past and –'

'I've never had a child,' he told her evenly. 'And, yes, the idea has a certain appeal, but it cannot be, Poppy. Don't you understand? It just cannot be! You will have to do as I tell you and get rid of it.'

Heartsick and more hurt than she could have believed possible, she pulled away from him and replied in a tight, shocked little voice. 'I don't think I've ever actually been forced to do anything in my life. I usually manage things as I want to, Mr Carson, and in my own time and way. I rarely knuckled down, even at school. And I don't think I can make a five-minute decision about something as important as our child. Please go away and leave me alone.'

174

'You have no choice in the matter, Poppy,' he said, then added bleakly, 'And neither have I.'

Her heart leaped then. She could tell by the expression in his eyes that the thought of having a child had come as a shock to him, but now, in spite of himself, he was letting the idea of their baby grow and take hold. Mr Carson would tell his mother, he must! She began to hope then, to feel an inrush of joy. It was going to be all right and Nan would not have to swing for her after all. Liz Parker wouldn't curl her lips and call her names, and Charlie's mouth wouldn't go thin as he looked at her and saw the whore of a wife who had left her dirty linen on his doorstep.

He was letting her go! Turning away from her and looking distressed, he was walking towards the door. She covered her face with her hands and sobbed when she heard Mr Carson firmly close it behind him.

Chapter Ten

It was unbelievable how grey the whole world became after that. Her whole body shook with fear. Her hands trembled and she felt sick, sick, sick! Mr Carson was going to let her down, she knew it. She could not go back to Nan and Jezebel Street, she knew that too.

At work Mr Carson was nowhere to be seen and she found the sense of loss intolerable. She loved him with all her heart and soul, but her treacherous body had let her down. The trouble she was in was all but driving her mad.

By the middle of the week, when he still had not put in an appearance, she began to feel angry and betrayed. His mother? She thought. The man in my life, whom I have idolised and put on a pedestal, is afraid of his mother? She tried to feel contempt, but the tears still scalded her eyes and that night she fell on her knees and prayed to the God she couldn't stand, 'Please, send him back to me, God. Ros is there with you, so listen to Ros, if you won't listen to me. Ros knows how I feel. She'd want you to send Mr Carson back to me. Tell Him, Ros. Tell Him from me!'

Only God and Ros and Poppy herself knew how things were. To the outside world Poppy tried to show her usual happy, perky self. But Edna remarked she looked peaky one dinnertime, and Burney put his arm round her waist the following evening and asked, 'You all right, Princess? Ain't with it, are you? Been in with your thoughts all day. Penny for 'em?'

She had laughed and tossed her hair out of her eyes in a defiant way. 'My thoughts are not worth a brass farthing,

Burney. Stop gawping and let's get on with the spuds. We gotta be neat –'

'I know,' he groaned. 'And gotta be quick and right. I ain't never met that bloke Banes, but sometimes, after hearing you carry on, I feel like strangling the bloody sod.'

On Friday night she dressed in the blue dress Mr Carson – no, Nigel! – liked best. She put on her kid shoes and wore her gold heart and chain, her bracelets and her beautiful engagement ring. He would be there soon – if his mother would let him escape. Hateful, grasping old crone! Why did all the wicked people survive in the world and the dearest of dears die?

That night she cried herself to sleep.

He came the next evening, bearing flowers and gifts. She felt her heart doing somersaults just looking at him. Then she was laughing and crying and being held tightly in his arms. She had been so scared that when they came face to face it would be like looking at a stranger. But everything was wonderful!

'She knows,' he told her. 'Don't you understand, sweetheart? She knows and I've told her that I am going to leave her to be with you.'

'Oh!' She felt delirious with joy. 'Oh, Nigel!'

Their lovemaking was fiery and more passionate than ever. Yet he was tender and the expression in his eyes left no doubt at all.

'You're adorable,' he told her. 'And you're having my child. Poppy, I never thought things could happen this way. You make me feel as I never have before. I love you.'

'And I love you – Nigel.'

'Why is it so hard for you to call me by my Christian name?'

She nuzzled against him and looked adoringly up into his eyes. 'I think because I've been brought up to believe that people in position, people with money are . . . are above me. I am working class and you, you're a gentleman, rich and high class, a toff. Nan was strict and taught us to keep neat and tidy and know our position. So calling you Nigel is rather like . . . taking liberties.' She smiled and there were happy tears in her eyes. 'And I think I would die before I'd have you believe I was doing that.'

He clasped her tightly against him and laughed softly, warmly. 'Poppy, if only you knew! Some of the people you'd believe to be high above you are less than the dregs beneath your feet. And I myself am nothing. My parents were comfortably off, but nowhere near high class. In fact even middle class would be stretching it a bit. I had a good education, that's all, and I became a salesman for Farringdon's. Then . . .'

'Yes?' she whispered lovingly, caring only that he was trying to put her at her ease.

He frowned and hesitated, then said, 'Then I found Mother had connections, close connections with Farringdon's, that's all. My life changed from then on. I became part and parcel of it all, sweet, and what with shares in their very lucrative sidelines as well as a finger in several pies of my own, I am a well-to-do man. I thought my life was well set and thought nothing would change. Then you came into my life.'

'And you really and truly fell for me the moment you set eyes on me?' She laughed softly and felt delicious little thrills running through her. 'Oh, Nigel, it was the same for me!'

'Now things are to be different. I'm making arrangements for us even now, you know. Whatever happens, I shall see to it that your future and the future of our son – yes, you're carrying a boy, I'm sure of it – is assured.'

'We're to get married?'

'As soon as it can be arranged. In the meantime, first thing Monday morning we'll go to your bank. You will deposit one thousand pounds and that will be just the start.'

She sat up straight and pulled away from him, shocked. That much money would buy Nan's house three times over. It would – it would make her like a bought woman!

'No!' she gasped. 'No, that isn't the way.'

'Oh but yes, sweetheart!' he said insistently. 'You could continue to stand on that ridiculous dignity of yours if it only entailed yourself. But things are different now. You're to be the mother of our child. Ours, Poppy! So you must be comfortably off in your own right. In that way I'll at least have some semblance of peace of mind. I need to know that you'll be fine, no matter what. Don't you understand? And a thousand pounds is a mere drop in the ocean to me.'

'Out of shoes?' she whispered disbelievingly. 'You make fortunes out of shoes?'

'I've told you, Farringdon Fashions deals in many things outside shoes, and so do I. But that's nothing to do with you, sweet. You don't need to know anything about that side. Just accept that what I'm offering you is very little in real terms.'

'No!' She was feeling sick again. There was something about his tone now that made her afraid. There was an urgency about him that was hard to fathom.

'Poppy,' he went on, 'you must do this for me!'

'A fortune?' she whispered. 'You are speaking about a fortune! I won't even think of such a thing. What is it that you're not telling me?'

'To hell with what I'm not telling you!' He was getting angry, his tone imperative. 'Just concentrate on what I'm saying now! First thing Monday the money goes into your account and stays there. It's for you to use how and when you see fit. Now come here, give me a kiss and stop looking like a little fish stranded on dry land.'

It was no use arguing with him. He stayed with her, adoring and now very human, not the lordly Mr Carson at all. Her love for him knew no bounds. And when he stayed the whole weekend, leaving for work just before she did on Monday morning, her cup of joy was full.

'Soon we'll be together the whole time,' he told her as he kissed her goodbye. 'But for the present, we'll keep up normal appearances for the sake of a peaceful life at work.' His tone became boyish and teasing. 'Of course, you realise that the time's going to come when you'll have to slow down? How terrible! My Poppy will have to give up slaving away at two jobs and actually settle down and twiddle her thumbs!' His tone changed and became deadly serious. 'Now don't forget what you have to do. Tell me again.'

'I have to ask Mr Banes to let me off for half an hour at eleven. You will meet me outside my bank.'

'Exactly. Don't be late. I want this settled and done with before I start sorting out the rest of my affairs.'

'Is you mother very angry?' she asked wistfully. 'It would have been nice if she had wanted to meet me. My own mother couldn't wait to run away, and it would have been wonderful if Mrs Carson –'

'Be there by ten past eleven at the latest. Now I really must go.'

He left the flat then, and she stood there, dewy-eyed and smiling, hardly knowing whether she was on her head or her heels.

By the time she walked to Tony's with Edna at dinnertime she was a very rich young woman and it didn't seem real. Nigel said that the thousand pounds would give her and the baby security for life, and it would, it would! It could make all her dreams for Ros come true as well – once she could work out how to get flowers to grow in Jezebel Street. But she would do Nigel proud and use the money wisely and well. Nigel, her saviour and her dearest love!

It was hard to carry on as usual after that, but she worked with a will, longing for the moments she could spend with Nigel. During the week she caught occasional glimpses of him and he smiled and winked. Then on Thursday morning he never came into the office at all. She knew this because Mr Banes let it slip.

I expect Nigel's making even more of his absurd plans. Even perhaps for us to begin sales trips together, she told herself.

Poppy spent the weekend alone, huddled before a blazing fire. It was still January and bitter outside, but even inside she felt cold and afraid and hardly knew why.

The next seven days she was in purgatory, wishing that she could ask someone where Nigel was. Something had gone very wrong, she felt it. Fear grew and began to gnaw at her insides. Then, on the Friday evening, as she walked home from work feeling tired and dispirited, she looked ahead and saw the Rolls-Royce.

Poppy picked up her heels and ran.

Her heart was singing as she entered the flat. Nigel was there, waiting for her. She had been a fool to have fears. Her happy ending was about to be fulfilled. Nigel would name the day and all would be right with her world.

She entered the sitting room, smiling and rosy-cheeked, then froze. She saw a thin string of smoke curling up from a cigarette in a long holder. The air was heavy with the perfume that Mr Carson always bought Poppy, but now it exuded from a mature woman sitting in one of the red chairs. Someone older than Poppy, but certainly not old enough to be Nigel's mother.

Her long, silk-clad legs were crossed under a fir-trimmed blue coat shorter than Nan would have thought decent even in this day and age. A slim woman with strong features, thin lips and stylishly short-cropped brown hair, darting Poppy a malicious look out of a pair of darkly outlined, near-black eyes. Poppy felt she had been weighed up and found wanting, and worse. Much worse! She knew instinctively who the woman was. And her whole world was crashing round her ears. But she did not let it show. She smiled brightly and cocked her head to one side.

'How do you do?' she said in her best genteel Bill Bannerman voice. 'You have come to visit Nigel, I presume?'

Twin patches of colour burned high on the woman's cheekbones. 'What makes you think I have come to see Mr Carson?' she asked in a cold, metallic voice. 'My dear, I rather think you presume too much. But then, your kind always does.'

Poppy smiled politely and with cool deliberation sat down in the chair opposite the visitor. 'Forgive me, do!' she replied in an ultrapolite tone. 'I naturally thought it was something to do with Nigel, since it is his car standing outside.'

'*My* car!'

'Oh! Oh, dear, I'm so sorry.' Poppy's stomach was churning. It was even worse than she thought. Nigel was in trouble, by the look on the woman's face, and so was Poppy. The awful suspicion was killing her by inches, but she had to be sure. 'May I ask who you are?'

'Mrs Carson.'

The words were like bullets piercing Poppy's heart. There was a cruel half-smile curling the woman's lips now. She was

181

triumphant and waiting for Poppy to curl up and die. Poppy smiled back, outwardly cool and assured. Even though the person so openly sneering at her had right on her side, Poppy simply had to make a stab at fighting back.

'Oh,' she said sweetly, 'Nigel's mother! I've heard so much about you. How lovely that we are meeting at last!' She jumped up. 'Please do allow me to make tea for us. It's about time that we had a get-together.'

She had hit where it hurt and was rewarded by the patches of colour burning even brighter on Mrs Carson's face. Then the near-black eyes were distending as they fell on the ring dangling from the chain round Poppy's neck. The ring that Poppy had deliberately pulled into view, saying, 'After all, Mrs Carson, I am to be your daughter-in-law one day, aren't I? Would you like to see the engagement ring?'

'You little bitch!' Mrs Carson snapped. 'You common little tart! How dare you!'

'Excuse me?' Poppy opened her eyes wide. 'I don't think I understand you, Mrs Carson.'

'I am his wife and well you know it.'

'His – wife?'

'And don't think you're the first bit of trash he's had here.' The woman's tone was silky with venom. 'Oh, I've known all about this hideaway of his right from the start. And to my shame I've kept quiet about it, rather than be humiliated before my friends, but not now! He has gone too far. As for the fleeting fantasy of wanting to leave me to marry you? My dear, you have as much chance as a snowflake in hell.' She stood up, taller than Poppy, and stringy and hard. 'Believe me, he's going to be put in his place for this. I know enough about him and his sidelines to have him put behind bars for life. You too, since you're so clearly up to your neck in what's going on here.'

'No!' Poppy felt her blood seeping away from her body. Having the woman standing over her made her feel shivery cold and sick. 'No!'

Mrs Carson had the whip hand now and she knew it. Poppy was not like Rene Davies, she could tell. She shrugged, but her tone was thick with contempt.

'You're not really part and parcel of any of this, are you?

You're simply not in the same class. We run on different lines, girl, and he's stepped off the tracks, intrigued by your honest milksop looks. Face him with the truth, why don't you? Tell him I know everything. Say that you'll take him on regardless, but that he'll have to face me and the family first. Then wait and see what happens.'

The sneer looked like the scarlet mouth lines painted on by a child. Crooked, uneven, stretching across a chalk-white, staring-eyed face. Poppy was hypnotised by that moving mouth.

'Yes, that's the best way,' the woman continued. 'I will leave it up to you.'

'He loves me,' Poppy insisted defiantly, even though she was trembling from head to toe. 'He wants to marry me. I'm going to have –'

'His child? I believe they breed like rabbits where you've come from. Even so, your kind know very well how to lie.'

'It's the truth,' Poppy insisted. Her cheeks were flaming now. 'There's no need for it to be otherwise. And if you must know, I love him as much as you do. In fact –'

'Love?' Mrs Carson laughed in a harsh and bitter way. 'How naive! This is merely a question of face-saving. I will never lose my husband and most certainly not to someone like you. Why don't you go back where you came from? He's a rat, but mine. I could kill you with my own bare hands simply because his play-acting has never gone this far before.'

'Not play-acting. Never that!' Poppy replied fiercely. 'He loves me!' She stood up slowly and carefully, not taking her eyes away from Mrs Carson's face.

'He loves himself more,' Mrs Carson flared. 'He'll finish up by letting you down, just as he lets everyone down eventually. The girl Davies did not leave here of her own free will, did you know that? She was brought here as most tramps are, by that fat pig Tilsby. She was used while it suited him and then passed on.' Mrs Carson's eyes dilated like a cat about to kill. 'Do you understand me? She was passed on! The other girl was turned down simply because the idea of a redhead was more intriguing than taking on a younger sister.

183

The plan was to get you here right from the start. A game, my dear, that's what you are. That and nothing more.'

'You knew all this?' Poppy said white-faced and with quiet dignity. 'Are you saying that you knew all about this, about a string of other girls, Jessica and . . . and me, all along?'

'I'm not stupid, even though he thinks I am. Of course I knew!'

'Then,' Poppy said quietly, 'I think that you must be a very sad and sick person. I would never sit back and allow that sort of thing. How – how nasty you are!'

'Perhaps, but that's another matter.' The woman smiled coldly, for she knew she had won. Poppy was no fool and could recognise the truth. Mrs Carson pressed home her point in a hard and malicious tone. 'Make no mistake, he'll tire of you when the fantasy of youth and impending fatherhood palls and he realises that the family is breathing down his neck. You have no idea of the strength and power of my people, you slut. So why don't you just pack your bags and get out of here?'

'Knowing all that you do –' Poppy no longer hid the revulsion she felt – 'why have you lowered yourself to come here to look me over?' She gave a harsh little laugh that held all the pain in the world. 'My, my! You're making me feel very important indeed, Mrs Carson.'

'You are a nuisance and that is all.'

'And,' Poppy persisted, 'since this sort of thing has been going on for years, how is it that you haven't packed your own bags long ago?'

'You little bitch!' Mrs Carson raised her hand, but Poppy was standing tall now, green eyes flashing, ready and willing to match blow for blow. The twitching fingers fell harmlessly to the woman's side. With a final impatient shrug, Mrs Carson swung on her heels and slammed out of the flat, leaving a pall of cigarette smoke and perfume behind her.

Sobbing, Poppy ran to the bathroom and was very sick.

Later, drained and dazed, she all but crawled to the bedroom and lay there wide-eyed, bereft. She knew that Mrs Carson had spoken no less than the truth. And the real villainess of the piece? No less than her own pride-filled, arrogant self! She had become Nigel's willing puppet,

184

anxious, adoring, a slave with wide-open legs waiting to be taken to Paradise. He had made her feel voluptuous, immodest and in a passion of love. In his arms she had forgotten the stress and strain of always being neat and quick and right during the long working hours. She had dismissed the loneliness of national holidays spent with Edna or extra duties working alongside Burney in the café.

Now, when all the self-excuses were in so many shards, she faced herself naked and ashamed. She had joyfully fallen in love with Nigel and hadn't given a hang about the consequences. He had opened up a new way of existence, one where there was fancy food, warmth, lovely things to wear and plenty of money to hand. The kind of living that showed Jezebel Street to be the mean little hellhole it was, with its dirt, its drunks, its hordes of kids, and the working-class snobbery of Nan and other folk.

Poppy hated Jezebel Street and always had. So why was it that she now found herself weeping and wishing she could turn back the clock? To be in the little brass bed that she had once shared with Ros? Feel Nan's rough hand ruffling her hair and scolding that she had never seen such an unruly mane? That if she didn't watch out, the nit-nurse would be in for a job?

She could never go back, never! Nan would kill her if she brought shame to her house. But she couldn't stay here in the flat either. Nigel would bluster and try to bluff his way through. He would lie and evade, make believe that there was no wife. He would expect Poppy to play the part of a low, very dull-witted working-class girl, to accept all he said and with no questions asked. But it had been true, every word, she knew it. The cold maliciousness in Mrs Carson's eyes had not wholly hidden the anguish and the pain.

Amid all her heartbreak was Poppy's self-hatred. Mrs Carson loved her husband in spite of all his lies. Loved him and was prepared to fight for him, no matter what. That was a love far greater than Poppy's own, she knew that now. Because accepting the fact that Nigel was married brought all Nan's lessons about right living to the fore. She loved Nigel, and she probably always would, but faced with the truth, all she wanted to do was run away and hide from her shame.

Poppy washed in cold water, trying to banish the swelling round her eyes. Her tear-sodden reflection stared back at her and she could see the despair, the uncertainty, the wistful longing for the once beautiful bubble that her life had been. Now the bubble had burst and she saw what the outside world would see: an ill-fated, very tarnished affair. Quietly, miserably, she began to put her things together. Ros' old cardboard suitcase would no longer hold her possessions, so she filled the pillowslips too, taking as much as she could carry. She would come back for the rest. She had earned it, she thought bitterly, earned it in full. And to think she had once looked down on Jessica for the way she earned the odd half-a-crown!

'A hypocrite, that's what I am,' she whispered out loud and was startled at the hollowness of her own long drawn-out groan.

Before she left the flat she looked at her reflection in the mirror again. She was agonisingly aware of the change in herself: energy and eagerness drained away, the excitement and dreams of youth dried up and dead, leaving behind someone hard and bitter, and distrustful of love. Loving meant losing either through death or desertion. Falling for handsome strangers was out from now on. She would trust only those she was sure of. The dreams of romance were as withered as the roses on Ros' grave.

Suddenly a terrible fear of loneliness overcame her. She would be an outcast, a fallen woman, looked down on by everyone. She would, must, grasp at any straw to get through this. Take any help she could get. Thank God for two wonderful friends.

The roads were empty, still. Street lamps made pallid circles of light like cold soulless eyes staring into her guilty heart. Shadows were blackest at the openings of alleyways, reminding her of the dark secrecy of the one running alongside the Coach and Horses. How far away it all seemed now. Night-time in the East End, and Nan's tales of whiteslavers, dark-skinned Arabs who stole girls and took them off to the deserts. Not forgetting the Chinese who owned evil opium dens Limehouse way. There the yellow men prayed to strange gods and used women solely to

186

indulge in their wicked games. How scary Nan had made it all sound, and exciting in a strange kind of way. But it had taken neither Arab nor Chinaman to get her off the straight and narrow, oh no! It had been Mr Carson with his white eyelashes, lordly ways and pure silk shirts. Poppy Ashton hadn't put up a fight. She'd gone running to her fate, with neither dignity nor pride, and oh, dear Heaven, she was paying for it now.

She was sobbing like a baby by the time she reached Berry Street. She made for the side entrance of Tony's and knocked on the door. There was no reply. She rapped again, the noise cutting staccato slices out of the silence around. Surely she must wake up the world? What if Burney was out?

Suddenly the thought that perhaps Mrs Carson's family might come after her sprang to mind. How strangely the woman had stressed the word 'family', as if they were a powerful clan who could tame a hundred Nigels if that's what they chose. Mrs Carson said that they'd believe she was in on all the goings-on in Coopersale Place. They might come and beat her up, or worse.

Tears were streaming as she banged on the door again and again. At last, it opened and Burney was there. She fell into his arms.

'Princess!' he said quickly. 'What's up? Come on in. There, there, it's all right now. You're safe with me. There's no need to cry.'

For the rest of that night, Poppy lay close to Burney in his lumpy bed. He stroked her hair, talked to her as if she were a child, telling her over and over that she was not alone. That Carson was a swine, and that it should be good riddance to bad rubbish so far as she was concerned.

'He – he said he loved me,' she sobbed. 'He ... We were engaged. I have his engagement ring here, see? But, Burney, that's not the half of it. I'm going to have his baby.'

'Do you want it?'

'No!'

'Are you going to do anything about it?'

She had a swift memory of all the whisperings about horrible old Mother Mangel, a filthy old crone who did unmentionable things to desperate women with a crochet

187

hook. Everyone knew of Mother Mangel and thought her
either devil or saviour according to the situation they found
themselves in. Being pregnant had no true meaning to Poppy
yet, but the idea of such a person touching her made her feel
ill. She shook her head.

'No, Burney. I'm not.'

'Have you made any plans, Princess?'

'Not really. Up until tonight I thought – I thought
everything was to be plain sailing. Then ... then ... Oh,
Burney, why didn't I believe you when you said all those
things? And –'

'You didn't want to, that's why. Still, there's no need to cry
over spilt milk. Have you got any friends, I mean real friends,
apart from Edna and me?'

'There's Daniel, but he's not a friend like Edna and you,
Burney. He's more like a big brother. I thought I was madly
in love with him once.' She smiled a watery smile. 'I think
because apart from Nan and Liz Parker he's the only one that
ever dared to tell me to buzz off. I wouldn't dare tell him
about what's happened to me. He'd give me one of them
looks and stare down his nose and – no, I could never tell
him!'

'Anyone else?'

'Sandy, but he's far away at sea. He's a merchant seaman
and his ship deals mainly in cargoing tea or rice, things like
that. He loved my cousin who died, and I like to think that a
little part of him loves me. He knows nothing of ... of how
I've lived since I left home. He wanted to come and see me
once. I wrote and said visitors weren't allowed.' She gave a
shaky laugh. 'I – I was too ashamed, so I suppose that even
though I adore Nigel, I've known all along I was doing
wrong. Even by going to the flat in the first place!'

'And that's all?'

'I can't go to my aunt, and it'd be like heaping coals of fire
on my poor old dad's head.' Poppy drew in a long shuddering
breath. 'So I think it's the workhouse or the Sally Army for
me.'

'Or you could stay here.'

'Oh,' she whispered, overwhelmed. 'You don't know how
desperate I was to hear you say that! I want to stay here with

you. You make me feel safe, you're so down to earth and –'
She stopped, suddenly panicky. 'Oh! Won't Tony mind?'

''Course not.' Burney fluttered his long lashes at her in a
mock innocent way. 'And it'd bloody well restore his faith in
miracles if you could make out I'm the father of your kid.'

'Oh, Burney!'

'Shut up, Princess, and do us a favour, eh? Go to sleep!'

He closed his eyes and she lay there, her head in the crook
of his arm, wide awake, giddy, unsure of herself and
everything else. Burney's question had shaken her to the
core. Friends? Of course she had! Four wonderful friends and
she would never underestimate their importance again. She
had allowed them to be there in the background but Nigel
Carson had blotted everything else from her mind. She had
been obsessed and deep down still was. He would only have
to lift a little finger and – no! She would never be taken in by
a man again. She had Edna and Burney, Daniel and Sandy.
She fell asleep wondering where Sandy was.

Chapter Eleven

His world, Sandy Swift realised, as he walked slowly towards the drab buildings of Victoria Dock, had crashed in fragments around him on that first foreign leave. Then he had seen his father's idea of having a good time on foreign shores. His dad, Freddy Swift, his admired hero! The all-action man.

There had been nothing admirable about the drunken old fart slobbering all over the port pros. And his father couldn't get enough! Crude, lusty, disgusting, he was either on a rollicking high or a grizzling, self-pitying low. Freddy Swift on rice wine was a despicable sight. Even then, there could be some excuses made. Life at sea was tough, you worked hard and played hard. Freddy had every right to spend shore leave as he chose.

Sandy was no prude and also enjoyed himself with a drink, chatting up rather more decent girls. But his father sank to the lowest of the low, revelling in filthy bars, sprawling in gutters, singing bawdy songs, peeing, spitting and spewing up no matter where. That was bad enough. And among the sewage that spilled from his mouth there was one regular theme. Freddy Swift was for ever foul-mouthing his wife for being a wishy-washy, pathetic old cow.

The first time he'd heard his father's opinion of Meg Swift, the frail nervous little woman that Sandy adored, he thought he must be dreaming. The second time, for all he was still young and immature, he had grabbed hold of his railing father and shaken him hard, threatening to punch him on the nose. His father had beaten him up savagely, and Sandy's

190

mate, Les Pickles, known as Onions, had to carry him, bruised and bleeding, back on board.

Because under the terms of his signing-on Sandy had to stay with the *Stockton* to serve out an apprenticeship of sorts, he had to stand by and watch and wait and put up with it. Every time they hit foreign ports, the drunken bad-mouthing went on, now with added jeers about an ungrateful, wet-behind-the-ears son. A bloody whippersnapper that wouldn't have got a job if it hadn't been for him, Swifty, man among men.

When his old man sobered up it was a different yarn. Then there'd be apologies and oaths of affection for a fine boy, and unyielding love for sweet little Meg who waited so patiently back home.

'He's a wicked bastard,' Sandy told Onions. 'I hate the old sod. I'm going to jack it all in. I'm fed up with all the shit he lays on when we go home. My mother dotes on him. If she knew the half of it, she'd curl up and die. I can't stand the sight of him and I'm leaving ship.'

'Here, hold your horses,' Onions, shaggy, craggy and a little older, warned. 'Wait till you've done your stint. Get your papers, then try and sign on for another ship. The *Stockton*'s not the be-all and end-all, you know.'

So Sandy had waited out the three years. Nothing had changed. Freddy Swift's lifestyle on foreign shores was long set. He was a very different fellow to the good old Swifty downing a pint in the Coach and Horses back home.

One night when the moon looked like a plate of cold porridge in a sky of gun-metal grey, Swifty was at it again. Sitting at a table in the Inn of One Thousand Delights, with a girl on either side, he stared mouthing off.

Sandy, now broad-shouldered and a fine, tough young man, strode over and jutted out his chin.

'Shut up!' Sandy said. 'I'm warning you, stow it!'

'Who d'yer think you are?' Freddy roared. 'All mouth and trousers, you are. Getting to be too much like that mother of yours. Sod off.'

Freddy took a swing at Sandy and caught him on the jaw. Sandy socked him one back. So they fought it out, fiercely and with all flags flying. No one had ever grappled with a

191

drunken Swifty before, he was mouthy, mean and tough as teak. Everyone's money was on Swifty. They lost. Sandy won hands down. Onions never ceased to crow about it on the long voyage home.

They docked and Sandy signed off and that was the end of Sandy's career on the *Stockton*. Onions decided to leave, too.

Finding new berths had been far from easy, but they had plugged away. Now experienced and self-assured, Sandy strode on. Onions and he were between ships again and for a while things were slack. But old salts heard rumours and one had tipped Onions the wink. Sandy began to hurry. He reached the office and found Onions waiting inside.

'What kept you?' Onions asked and grinned a lopsided grin. 'We're in luck, I think. Nothing doing yet, but the *Vanessa*'s in for repairs and I hear as how we do stand a chance. Bit of a rusty bucket, they say, but anything's better than nothing.'

They were in luck. They were to join the *Vanessa*, a cargo steamer of 10,000 tons, as deck hands in five weeks' time.

'I'll see you then, mate,' Onions said and grinned. 'I'm off home. Gotta see my Annie and tell her the good news.'

'I've got to find my girl!' Sandy replied. 'See you.'

Sandy made his way home. Leyton was grey and unlovely, but it was his place. He missed it when he was away. Strangely, the moment he was back in Gran's stifling little house he needed to be off again.

He could understand his father in some ways. After all, his dad was the same as himself where mothers were concerned – and the elder Mrs Violet Swift was the matriarch to end them all.

At last he reached the small terraced house at the far end of Beaumont Road. The best and uppity end, Ros used to say and smile that sweet smile of hers. With all his boyish heart and soul he had loved her. Her pale loveliness, her frailty, with the same gentle expression his own mother had to this day, had made him catch his breath. He had thought of Ros as an angel. When she died, dear God, how it had screwed him up. Had done for Poppy, too. They had stared across the grave at each other, in that moment twin souls, each knowing and understanding the other's pain.

These days Sandy thanked God for Poppy. She wrote in such a lively way and so regularly, and was such a brave little thing. A go-getter if there ever was one. And she was his! All his mates knew of Poppy Ashton, Sandy's girl! The one who loved and adored him and sent him long, newsy letters that were the envy of all. Those letters had followed him everywhere. When he left the *Stockton* he sent a card, saying simply, 'Write home!' Well, she had. From them on, each ship's mail, no matter where it happened to be, held a letter from Poppy. Now he'd received a card at Christmas, but then nothing. She knew he'd be back in Beaumont Road. If there were no letters waiting for him, he'd go to the Home and see if Daniel had heard.

Devere was a good sort, friendly chap and wholeheartedly on the side of the kids. Moved up in the world, had Daniel. He was well off and important now. Daniel spent most of his cash on the welfare of the kids and still lived in the caretaker's cottage. More importantly, he still wrote to Poppy. And because they had known each other for many years, and had Poppy as a link, Sandy and Daniel were quite matey. They had often drunk a pint together in the Coach and Horses – when Freddy wasn't around, of course. Daniel and Sandy always talked of Poppy, Daniel acting as though he was her big brother, Sandy going on about his one and only girl.

He walked through the front gate and opened the door. The smell of lavender furniture polish almost choked him. Since being at sea Sandy was always struck by how small his home was. As a child he had believed it to be far larger, but now, with his new-grown great bulk, he felt himself absurdly out of scale. Inside it was flimsy – that was the only word he could think of to describe it. There was a bamboo plant stand in the passage that led to a gimcrack little parlour. Here a small round table was draped in white muslin, there were muslin covers everywhere, bits and pieces tied up with pink ribbon, even on the back of the slippery mock-leather couch that all but covered one rose- and forget-me-not-covered wall. Gran's choice of wallpaper always amazed him. Sweet and feminine she was not! The front room was the best room and treated accordingly. As a boy he had never been allowed inside it. But these days it was where his mother escaped to, even though there was no fire. He knew he would find her there.

Meg Swift, dressed in powder blue and with silvery strands in her light-brown hair, sat by the muslin-curtained window, knitting. She looked up and her pale face glowed with love. Her voice was soft, warm and kind.

'My dear, how good of you to come straight home. Was it a worthwhile trip?'

'The *Vanessa*, Mother. She's about 10,000 tons and carries general cargo. In about five weeks her holds will be full and she'll be down to her marks. Then we'll sail. Are there any letters?'

'Where to, dear?' Meg's honey-gold eyes were alight with pleasure for her son. 'Oh, I am so pleased for you. You've been so unsettled since you lost your place with your father, and —'

'Cape Town and Sydney, New South Wales,' he cut in hurriedly. 'Quite a different run. Mother, are there any letters for me?'

At that moment the door opened and Vi Swift entered. She was a fat, dumpy woman of sixty. Her eyes were hard and light and seemed to lack true colour. Her straight hair had gone salt-and-pepper grey. Her face was fleshy and sallow and set in discontented lines.

'Letters, Cyril?' she snapped. 'Are you still mooning over that girl from Jezebel Street? I'll never cease to blame your father for letting you go to Skelton School. Nothing but riffraff! You should have gone to Ruckholt, boys only.'

'Freddy was sure Skelton was the best,' Meg put in gently. 'After all, it's so near and —'

'And mixed.' Vi's eyes glinted with impatience and dislike as she glanced at her daughter-in-law. Meg flushed and looked down at her trembling hands.

'Gran,' Sandy put in bluntly, 'why don't you change your tune? Everyone round here knows that Skelton School is divided into two sections. Even the playgrounds are divided by a ten-foot-high wall! But all us kids played outside the school together. Would you like them to wall off whole damned roads?'

194

'If only they could. To my mind, the –'

'And as for Poppy, she's my girl. And if you must know, her aunt's house is as clean and decent as ours. You know it and I know it. But you just like any excuse to tear other people down.'

'Jezebel Street holds the dregs, and it lives up to its name in more ways than one.' Vi had the old familiar hateful glint in her eyes. 'And if you intend living in my house –'

'Gran,' Sandy said in a cold level tone, 'I've had it drummed into me all the days of my life that this is your house. That Grandad bought and paid for everything we see. I can imagine him in his grave all smug and superior because of it.'

'How dare you?' Vi spluttered, shocked because she had never been talked back to before in quite the same way. And no one, no one at all had ever dared criticise the long-gone Cyril. 'Your grandfather was –'

'As evil and as spiteful-tongued as you, I remember. You've never forgiven Mum for getting pregnant with me and so catching your darling son because of it, have you? You both made it clear right from the start that Mum and me are little more than lodgers while my father's away. How Mum's put up with you all these years, I'll never know. I'd take her out of it, given half the chance.' He snorted contemptuously. 'But she's too loyal to your shining, wonderful son.'

His handsome face was now white with fury. He wanted to spill the beans, tell the bossy old woman just what darling Freddy got up to in his tea half-hour, but it would break his mother's heart. His tiny nerve-wracked mum sitting there so humbly, staring down at the knitting in her lap. He stepped forwards, glaring at the old woman who for years had cruelly enjoyed twisting the knife in his mother's bosom. 'In the meantime, you can keep your kitchen sofa. I'll happily lay my head down elsewhere.'

'No, son!' Meg gasped and let her knitting fall.

'I'm sorry,' he told her gruffly. 'I think you're a saint to put up with all that you do. But I've got to go, Mum. I'll strangle her else.'

He ignored Vi's outraged gasp and smiled into his mother's tear-filled eyes.

195

'I . . . You'll come and see me sometimes, son?'

'Wild horses won't stop me. Well, since there's no letters, I'm off.'

He went to her and gave her a gentle hug.

'I meant what I said all that time ago, Mum. I'll rent us a place and get you away from Gran's spiteful tongue. Why don't you let me, eh?'

'Your father likes to know I'm safe under this roof, dear,' she whispered, a pleading look in her eyes. 'He wouldn't hear of me living anywhere else.'

'Have it your way, then. But remember, I'll always come back to see if you're all right. And there's folk round here who'll soon let me know how things are. Do you understand what I'm saying? Got a name for herself, has dear old Vi, and the neighbours are all on your side!' He gave his gran a final contemptuous glare, kissed his mother, then left.

As he turned the corner, Sandy saw that Charlie's was empty and neither he nor Clary was to be seen. Old Rags was on the step, head on paws, so Charlie couldn't be far away. Poppy's dad, eh? Everyone knew how old Charlie had sent Poppy down to Nan. Some father-in-law, Sandy thought and grinned. It'll be easy to handle him!

Jezebel Street was grey and grumpy in the January gloom. The kids were either inside their homes or at school. The women were not on their steps for a change. It was freezing, too cold for rain. He strode on, a fine figure, his face tanned by salt winds. At last he felt free – free of his father and of his detestable old gran.

Now he must find Poppy and set the date. The sooner the better as far as he was concerned. They had not been together for years, but her letters had kept what they had alive. He had looked forward to and cherished those letters. He still had that first Christmas card she'd sent, with its greeting in gold on red. It had come like a shaft of light, the first message after such a long time.

He frowned, wondering for the millionth time why Poppy had always been so dead set on his not visiting during times ashore. First it had been the rules of the women's hostel. Then she had written to say that her new place also put men out of bounds. She hadn't been able to meet him anywhere, since she had no free time. She worked all the hours God gave and was just too tired.

He had been happy to let things ride. Shore leave with Onions had been roistering and fun-filled. They'd met some jolly nice Stratford girls and had a good time. Had drunk many a pint together in the Stratford Arms, and shacked up in Onions's place afterwards, conveniently near the pub. But this state of affairs couldn't go on. Poppy was his girl! She always signed her letters 'With Love' and that was good enough for him. He'd find her and ask her outright to name the day. Tell her it was time to settle down. Yes, make a home together as Onions was going to do with his Annie. Dear old Annie had set her cap at Onions, who'd been a dead duck from that day.

Sandy was whistling by the time he reached Nan's place. Number two Jezebel Street looked empty and after he had knocked several times, Flossie came out from next door. Her fair hair was in curlers and her round face wreathed in smiles.

'Sandy! Nice to see you. How's tricks?'

'Fair enough. And with you?'

'Now I take in lodgers.' Flossie gave a meaningful wink and giggled. 'Just fine and dandy, Sand. You looking for Nan? She won't be home for a while yet, but you could try at the Home.'

'Right! Take care, Floss.'

'And you, Sand. Hope to see you again soon.'

He grinned and waved and in a moment or two had turned into Skelton Street and made his way to Devere's Children's Home. He saw that the rambling old ruin of the pickle factory was already spruced up. For girls, they said, poor orphaned kids. Well, they'd be a darned sight better off under Daniel's wing than huddling in shop doorways with hardly a stitch on their backs or a crust to eat. The poor and homeless looked the same the world over, he thought. Sad and wan and with no hope in their eyes. No life, no zest, no will to get up and fight back, unlike his little red-haired Poppy. Sandy pictured her with her long shiny tresses and green eyes flashing, and wanted to shout aloud his pride and joy. He'd been mad to wait so long before putting his foot down. If she wanted to

197

keep in work, it would be up to her. But not all the time, oh no!

Sandy couldn't find Nan, but Daniel was where Matron said he would be, in the caretaker's cottage, mucking about putting coat hangers on a long wooden board. He looked up and grinned when he saw who it was.

'Home again?'

'For five weeks or so.'

'Your dad was back a while ago. Before Christmas. Though you'd be with him.'

'He likes crewing regularly for the *Stockton*. I like a change. I've signed on with the *Vanessa* this time round. She's in for repairs but is bound for Cape Town and New South Wales, all in good time.'

'A great life, eh, mate?'

'Not half! Heard from Poppy lately?'

'Not recently, no.'

'Has Nan?'

'She hasn't said, she usually does.'

'Damn! Well, the only thing for it is to take the bull by the horns.' He stared at Daniel hard. 'Have you ever been to see her?'

'No reason to, never had time. In any case, reading between the lines, I don't think Poppy wants visitors. Not from this place, anyway.'

'Are you saying she's ashamed of us?' Sandy asked, suddenly beligerent.

Daniel grinned and his very blue eyes danced. 'Come off it, mate,' he said easily. 'But knowing young Poppy as I do, she has very good reasons for not writing – to either of us. If I were you, I'd wait for an invite before I called.'

'Well, I'm not you,' Sandy said flatly. 'Cheerio.'

'Good luck,' Daniel said, hiding his feelings.

Poppy's leaving had come as a shock to Daniel. Then her letters began to arrive. Gradually their tone had changed and, reading between the lines, he guessed that she had fallen in love. Poppy was an all-or-nothing kind of person. He knew then that he stood no chance, now or ever. To make things worse, she kept on stressing how dear he, Daniel, was, like a big brother and close to her heart.

'And there goes another poor devil,' Daniel said out loud as he watched Sandy's lithe figure turning the corner. 'I know just how he'll feel . . .'

Poppy winced as she got out of Burney's bed and pulled a face at the state of the blanket, which smelled as bad as it looked. Burney woke, blinked his eyes, smiled, yawned and sat up. He slept in his shirt and long pants.

'Bloody hell, Poppy, don't you never have a lie-in?' He groaned. 'No one will be round for at least another three quarters of an hour. Relax!'

She gave a shaky laugh. 'I wish I could, Burney. Oh, dear!'

'Now, no more of that. Only kids blub. Stiff upper lip is the order of the day, Princess. Come on!'

'I'm sorry.' She faltered. 'I don't want to be a nuisance. I've always got up at the crack of dawn and . . . Now I've made you wake up when you could have –'

He chuckled. 'It's not like you to look down in the mouth and keep saying you're sorry. Where's the old sparkle, eh?'

'I don't feel like sparkling, Burney. I've made a terrible mistake and –' She hesitated, then added mournfully, 'I wish one could turn love on and off at will, like you can a tap. I'm in a state. I'm scared and I'm sad, and I don't know what I'm going to do.'

'Stay here with me, that's what.' He rolled over and jumped, shivering, out of bed. 'Later on we'll tell Edna together, and we'll have a go at sorting everything out. Cheer up! Gawd, it's taters and my feet are freezing. Where are my things?' He grabbed his trousers from where they'd fallen under the bed, pulled on woolly socks and shoes and smiled in his long-lashed, mischievous way. 'It's a good job Tone sees to it me washing's done. He's even treated me to chef's whites for when I do my special thing. I'd be done for else. A good egg is old Tone. I've got to go. Slip back into bed, Princess. You look done in.'

He went out of the room, whistling shrilly. Poppy looked round at the dirty clothes flung here and there, the fly-specked mirror, the chest of drawers leaning drunkenly against the wall, grey and peeling plaster. The small fireplace had a grate red with rust and was filled with ashes. Blue floor covering stretched its weary plainness over the greasy planking that showed here and there where the lino had worn away. Poor Burney! So this was the place he was so proud of?

Poppy took a deep breath and said out loud, 'You'll have everything nice here by the time I've finished, Burney. Just you wait and see?' She began gathering the dirty washing-up and putting it in a pile in the corner. She would have to find out about water and cleaning materials, and sort out some pillowcases. The pillows, once white and blue-striped, now yellow and horrible with age, had never seen a white pillowslip, she was sure.

Trying to drown out her heartbreak and fear, Poppy began planning how she could make this room into a nice little home.

The door burst open and Burney came in, looking fresh and washed and wearing a clean white jacket. He was carrying a tray holding tea, bread and butter and kippers.

'Here we are, Princess. Get stuck in.'

'I – I can't,' she said faintly. 'Burney, I feel sick!'

'Oh, my Gawd! What are we going to do with you, eh? Shall I eat mine downstairs?'

'Where's the lav?' she gasped and fled.

By the time the nausea had passed and she was washed and tidy, glad to leave the stinking bathroom on the middle landing, she found that Burney had gone. Saturdays were busy and he'd be working all through. The day stretched before her. With all her dreams dashed, she wanted to sit down and howl. But, as Nan said, crying over split milk was a waste of time. The best way to get out of the doldrums was to work through them. Moods weren't good for man or beast. An hour of hard scrubbing, using plenty of the old elbow grease, was enough to put anyone straight.

Poppy had never met anyone as wise as Nan. She knew she would give her soul to be able to run home to her now. But it was out of the question and she had to get on. She searched round and found the few cleaning things Burney had, then made a hasty list. She unpacked her belongings, placing them where she could, and used the pillowcases for Burney's bed. Then, leaving via the back entrance, she went out and began making her plans. Today, she decided, she would shop first and then go to the bathhouse. There were lots of things to get and plenty to do. She would not think! She would lift up her chin and get on with it, just as Nan said.

All that weekend she scrubbed and polished and put on the new sheets she had bought, made do and mended as if her life depended on it. Burney came up, saw the transformation and whistled.

'Cor, Poppy, you ain't half a one! This is a miracle.'

'No matter what happens,' she told him gravely, 'I'll never forget what you've done for me, Burney. Has – has Edna been in?'

'She don't often come Sat'days, Princess. Helps her mum, don't she? You'll have to leave it till Monday. We'll have a pow-wow then.'

Monday morning, after her duties for Tony, Poppy made her way to Farringdon's. She went to clock on, and was standing there perplexed, when Mr Banes showed up. His expression was blank and he acted as though she were a stranger.

'Mr Banes,' she said quickly, 'my card's not here. I've got to clock on soon, else I'll lose a quarter of an hour.'

'I'm sorry,' Mr Banes said coldly. 'You are to go to the office, collect your cards and any money that's due.'

'No!' She was shocked and outraged. 'Oh no you don't! I wish to see Mr Carson.'

'Mr Carson is away and will be for some weeks. Now do as you're told, miss, and collect what's due.'

'Mr Banes, I don't –'

'At once!' he said crisply. 'Your job here is already filled.'

The mortification was unbearable, and at that moment Edna came in and clocked on. She gave Poppy a look and went inside. Poppy, head held high, marched to the office, where her cards and pay packet were already waiting.

Before she left the yard she heard someone running after her. 'Poppy, wait!'

Poppy turned, her humiliation and heartbreak hard to fight. 'Looks as though you were right, Edna,' she gulped.

'Told you about the old sod, didn't I? You lasted a bloody sight longer than most. Look, I've gotta go, they'll sack me if they find me missing. Will you be up Tone's dinnertime?'

'Yes.'

'Good. I'll see you there.'

Edna ran back and disappeared inside the factory door. Poppy made her way back to Berry Street and was just going in when she bumped into Tony himself.

'Ah!' he said. 'You 'ave come to-er stay with Burney, eh? You will make-er the man of him?' He threw back his head and laughed in a merry way. 'Somehow, I don't-er think so, eh? But, bambino, you are welcome to try.'

He ruffled her hair in a rough, friendly manner and went on his way.

Would he feel the same when he learned the truth? she thought as she ran up the stairs and flung herself down on Burney's bed. Nigel, who had sworn he loved and adored her, had cast her off like an old shoe. And she had so loved him! Her whole body had ached for him. Her soul had shone at all the promises he had made. Even so, she would never have let things go so far, had she known. Oh, he had set out to make him love her, right from the start, but she hadn't dreamed he was married. And he had lied all the way along the line. He didn't have a bossy mother, he had a strong-willed, no-nonsense wife!

And the truth of the matter was that it was all Poppy's fault. Wives belonged with husbands, and husbands belonged with wives. She had sinned, coming between a married couple. Just as the man who had come between her mother and Charlie had sinned. And the sins of the fathers were suffered on the child. 'No!' she screamed in her mind. 'No, no, no!'

Chapter Twelve

Poppy was in a daze. She spent her time between café duties scrubbing, cleaning and polishing. She black-polished the grate, whitened the hearth and bought a 28-pound bag of coal. The fire made all the difference in the world. Then she searched the market and second-hand stalls, and bought bits and pieces: a cushion here, a length of cloth there, candy-striped sheets and pillowslips with faults, but usable. Even a pair of heavy red curtains with bobbles hanging from each side. She scraped the rickety furniture and painted it shining new red-brown as Aunt Nan had showed her how to do. The bed was covered with a surplus army blanket; Poppy paid three and six to Edna's mum, who dyed it dull red. Edna's mum also supplied two large, home-made rag rugs. The price Poppy paid for them would keep the Ames kids in food for two weeks. They hid most of the awful blue lino, while Mrs Ames managed from then on with creosoted bare boards. Everyone was pleased. At last Burney's room looked like home.

Poppy's resolve deepened. She was rich beyond her wildest dreams, but the thousand pounds was not hers. It had not been earned by the sweat of her brow. Nigel had told her that it was for her to use the best way she saw fit. He needed to know that his baby's future was assured. She remembered him telling her how he put money into businesses. He bought shares, he said, and left those responsible to do the work. She could do the same, she thought. Let others do the worrying; she'd only be interested in the profits they made. She would try to give her child the kind of living the offspring of a rich father should have. But all that would be in the future, when she was more composed and knew what to do.

Nigel would have explained financial affairs to her, had she asked. Clearly he knew the secret of how to get rich. Like marrying a rich wife was was part and parcel of – of a family! Why had the woman so emphasised such an ordinary word? No, not ordinary. It was the most wonderful word in the world and Poppy was away from her own, Nan and Charlie and dear Clary who made such wonderful toast. Nigel Carson could never have been part of her clan, she saw that now. Still, no matter how he had lied and cheated, she believed that he did love her, and that he would have stayed with her, had he dared to defy his wife. Her lip curled with contempt for herself, and for Mr Carson too, as she realised that she still loved him. The awful thing was, she no longer respected him.

Burney came in. He was smiling and holding out a huge bunch of crepe-paper roses.

'Bought them off a Gipsy' he said. 'They'll match in with the colour scheme you've got here. I must say as how you've made things cosy Princess. I won't never let you go.'

'You know very well that I'll have to leave one day,' she told him gravely. 'In any case your bed's too small – and what will Tony's neighbours say?'

'He'll never know, since he don't live here. As for the local nosy parkers, I reckon they'll think as how we're living in sin and reaping the harvest.' He chuckled. 'Princess, you know I'll marry you and make things right in the eyes of the law, don't you? What do you say?'

His offer stunned her. She smiled through her tears, but shook her head.

'I think that's the kindest and most genuine offer of help I've ever had in my life,' she told him and walked over to kiss him full on the lips. 'Burney, you are my dearest friend. Without you and Edna, I think I really would have gone mad.'

'Then, when shall we get spliced?'

'We won't. The neighbours would see us leading our separate lives and make things a million times worse. You see, Burney, if we were married I wouldn't let you see your – your friends, at least not under any roof we shared with a

little one. And I would feel guilty because of it. What's more
_'
'You're ashamed of me, Princess?'
'How can you say that?' she exploded, amazed. 'But – but I wouldn't feel right, that's all. No more than you would if Nigel Carson wanted to come here!'
'That reminds me,' he told her brusquely, 'this is for you. I'm to give him your reply when I take the meal he's ordered for Mrs Flanty. He has always looked after the old girl. In some ways he's not a bad sort.' Burney shoved a letter into her hand and walked out.

Heartsick because she had offended the one person she never should have, she looked down at the envelope in her hands.

It was from Nigel. He wrote to say that he loved and adored her. That it was impossible for them to meet at this stage, but he would come to her somehow. They would run away together, hide somewhere abroad, probably France. That she and their son were the main stem of his life, and he couldn't get her out of his mind.

Weeping, she went to the chest of drawers, on top of which there now stood a prettily decorated earthenware bowl. She took from it the gold chain on which hung her lovely diamond engagement ring. This was placed in an envelope, addressed simply to Mr Nigel Carson and sealed. No words could have made her answer as clear.

The following evening she looked up from the counter where she had been serving twopenny meat-and-potato pies, and went dizzy with delight – and fear.

'Sandy! Oh, Sandy!' she gasped and promptly burst into floods of tears.

Later, in Burney's room, with the fire now poked into a cheerful blaze and the curtains drawn, she and Sandy sat side by side on the bed. His arm felt like a steel band round her waist. He was smoking a Nosegay cigarette and the smell made her feel sick.

'Why did you leave the other place?' he asked. 'The posh flat you were always on about?'

'If you put your cigarette out,' she said in a faint, wobbly voice, 'I will tell you the truth, the whole truth and nothing but the truth.'

'That sounds grim,' he told her, his blue eyes dancing, his bulk making the bedsprings scream as he moved. 'Wish you had a decent armchair in here.' He raised his brows, looking handsome and charming, tanned and devil-may-care. 'My fag's really bothering you, Poppy? All right, here goes.' He stubbed it out and put it behind his ear. 'Now what gives?'

'Before I say anything else,' she told him quietly, 'I must explain that this room, where I'm living now, and sleeping, belongs to my friend Burney.'

His face went very still. 'Oh?'

'Burney is a wonderful person. He ... he's not like other men. I mean, he doesn't like girls, at least, not in that way. But he's stood by me through thick and thin. He has even offered to marry me. A name-only thing, of course, but the offer was genuine and ... and splendid and –'

Suddenly she couldn't bear the look on Sandy's face. Her cheeks flamed, her green eyes flashed. She tossed her head and lifted her chin in a defiant way.

'All right! Here's the story of Poppy Ashton who was going to find a fortune and be a lady. You want the truth and you shall have it, Sandy. And then you can go back to sea and forget all about me and never bother with me again.'

She told him everything that had occurred and finished wryly, 'So you see, Sandy, I was not so worldly-wise after all. I fell for the oldest trick going and believed every word a married man told me. At first he suggested that I get rid of the baby. Then, when I refused, he became intrigued and delighted with the idea. He ... he still loves me and ...' She got up from the bed and walked over to the bowl where she had deposited Nigel's letter, and took it back to the huge, quiet man sitting so still on Burney's bed.

'Read this, Sandy. In answer, I have just returned the diamond ring he put on my finger.' She smiled and shrugged. 'Another of his empty promises, wouldn't you say?'

He read it carefully, word for word, then handed it back. 'What are you going to do?'

'Stay here with Burney until I can sort myself out. I have another friend, Edna, who's as loyal as they come. Between them they'll help me in every way they can. No one on God's earth could have two more wonderful friends.'

'I'm glad about that, Poppy,' Sandy said and stood up, dwarfing the room. 'Well, I'll be off. Take care.'

'Goodbye, Sandy,' she whispered. 'And thank you.'

'For what?'

'For not calling me names.'

He ruffled her hair. 'I'd never do that,' he said.

When he had gone she lay on the bed, wide-eyed and heartbroken. Sandy, who she had always thought loved her a little bit, couldn't wait to leave. He couldn't bear to look at her and probably thought she was lower than the low. She couldn't blame him. She had been shaken to the core at the sight of Sandy, who had grown so large and attractive: bigger than his father now, and better-looking by far. He would have been the ideal person to have married and looked after Ros, had she lived. With Sandy on your side you couldn't go wrong.

'Goodbye, Sandy,' she whispered to the empty room, and felt very lost and lonely.

It was late and Burney did not return. Feeling rejected by just about the whole world, Poppy sat up eagerly when the door opened with a bang. Sandy strode in. He looked stern and purposeful as he walked to the bed and towered over her. He reached down and pulled her to her feet, then, holding her close, he kissed her.

Shocked and dismayed, thinking Sandy was taking her for a whore, she remained limp and unresponsive. He held her away from him, his eyes teasing now.

'Is that the best you can do? Having read that letter, Poppy, I'd have thought you at least knew how to give a bloke a decent kiss.'

'I'm sorry,' she whispered sadly. 'Sandy, I'm . . . I'm not a scarlet woman and —'

'You've loved and lost the person you wanted, just as I loved and lost an angel,' he told her roughly. 'And since in that way we're both in the same boat, I reckon I can make an offer as good as your chum Burney.'

'I don't know what you mean, Sandy. I —'

'Be quiet and listen. I'll make all the arrangements. You'll have to sign the papers and there'll be witnesses needed and other things like that, but I'll handle it all. We'll get married.' He stared at her hard. 'But my proposal has a difference, Poppy. Unlike your Burney, this won't be a name-only thing. I'll expect my rights, understand?'

She was staring up at him, taken aback, too confused to be either happy or sad that he had so completely taken hold of the reins.

'Do you understand, Poppy?' he asked and now there was naked awareness in his eyes. 'I shall want to not only wed but bed you. If I take a wife it's got to be in the fullest sense of the word. Agreed?'

'No! I've sworn never to be used by a man again. I'll never –'

'Shut up! You're talking like one of them books you always had your nose stuck into.' He grinned wickedly. 'Don't you think it might be fun if we used each other, Poppy? And with me you'd at least have a plain gold band on your finger.'

'You're poking fun, and if – if I did as you suggested you'd hate me by the end of a year. I'm going to get fat and ugly. My temper's as bad as Nan's. I'd –'

'Every ship I've been on, every bloke I've met has heard of Poppy Ashton, who is my girl!' He hugged her, his eyes twinkling. 'Oh, come on Poppy, you've never backed away from a challenge in your life. Can't you see that I'm trying to make sure that I get at least a dozen letters waiting for me at every port? It was your letters that kept me going when things got rough. You'll be doing me a favour!'

He meant it! He was serious! He was prepared to take her on! And even though she knew she shouldn't grasp at straws, that she wasn't being fair to him, she heard herself responding.

'At least kiss me again,' she quavered. 'And let's see!'

His kiss was rough and tough. She could feel his strength and his hardness. He needed her and, dear God, she needed him.

'Well?' he asked roughly. 'What do you say?'

'Yes. Yes please,' she said quietly. 'That's if you're sure.'

'I am. I'll sort it out and we'll marry from here. I met your

Burney and we talked. He's put me straight about a number of things. He's a nice bloke and he doesn't want you to go.' He grinned then. 'And I can't say I blame him, but I'd like it to be back home for us. After the three necessary weeks here.'

'Your parents, they'll hate me. They'll call me –'

'Mrs Swift, that's what they'll call you. And don't worry. I've not been at sea for a while, between ships, but I've signed on now. I've spent a lot of time with my mate Onions in Stratford. You'll like him and he'll be dotty about you.'

'But – but when my tummy swells, they'll –'

'Think I'm a bit of a dark horse, but no one can call us liars, Poppy! I've spent my time going backwards and forwards from Leyton to Stratford. No set times, just coming and going as the mood took me. No one will ever be sure.' He suddenly looked deadly serious. 'But you've got to swear one thing.'

'What is it?' She was breathless. He was going to fast for her to take it all in, and over and above all, she was palpitating with relief.

'Anything, Sandy. Anything!'

'To the world at large, and to you and me, the baby is mine. If you'll agree to that we can go ahead. The baby is mine! All right?'

'He will have a father to be proud of, Sandy,' she stammered.

'I'll make sure to at least be a damned sight better dad than mine. And boy or girl, I don't give a damn, just so long as it's all in one piece. Come here, give us another kiss. This could be something I really get to like. Grown into a little beauty, you have.'

They sealed their bargain with another kiss and a long while after they were still talking and planning. Because Sandy seemed so happy at the idea of becoming a dad, Poppy became truly aware of the human being growing inside her. It was awe-inspiring rather than terrifying now she had Sandy on her side. He would make a wonderful father. But then Sandy was wonderful all round. She decided to tell him one last thing.

'Please don't hate me all over again,' she said quietly, 'and

209

above all, don't say that I should give it back, because I'm not going to. In fact, I'm going to use it as instructed: to make sure of the future.'

'Now what are you going on about?' he groaned.

'I'm a very rich person, Sandy. He ... he gave me a thousand pounds.'

'To buy you off,' he said harshly.

'No. He gave it to me when I found out about the baby and he had accepted the idea. It happened before the balloon went up and his wife stepped in. He described her all right – but said she was his mother! She's not that old, but past having children, perhaps. I wouldn't be certain, but what I do know –' she tossed her head and glared – 'is that you'd better mind your words. I'd never be bought off, Sandy. Make no mistake about that! I accepted the money because he insisted. And I shall use it as intended.'

'To bring up his child?'

'No,' she replied with quiet deliberation. '*Our* child, Sandy. And know what? If we work things out right, once this one is born we might go in for another. Then we'll have a family and they'll be wanted, not like me who was given away. They'll be loved and wanted, and between us we'll fight for them tooth and nail. What do you say?'

'Atta girl!' he told her and nodded. 'Trust you to get it right.'

In a daze after that, hardly knowing whether she was on her head or heels, Poppy let go. She allowed Sandy to take everything over and was grateful not to have to care. Burney, Edna and Tony entered into the spirit of things. Tony was arranging a reception in the café, his present, he said. Burney was making and decorating a cake.

'Three tiers,' he said importantly. 'Fit for a princess.'

The regular customers all joined in. It was going to be a 'fair old do'.

The time passed and Poppy hardly saw Sandy. He had turned into a brisk, efficient stranger, going here and there, making arrangements, seeing to things and making plans that she herself had no heart in, for all she tried. For his sake, she attempted to play along.

She took Edna shopping and went back to Burney's

pleased with the buys. Edna was broke, but Poppy insisted on getting her a new dress for the wedding, one that she could wear afterwards as well. Edna picked a blue one. For herself Poppy chose an ankle-length pale-pink crepe dress, and a headdress of rosy pearls and silver leaves. Pale-pink satin shoes set everything off. Sandy was to buy flowers.

'I want pictures to take back and show my mates,' he told her. 'So, Poppy, I'd take it as a favour if you look like a proper bride. The photo's won't be ready for when we get back home, and since all this supposedly happened a few weeks back, we can say we forgot them. Then Edna will send them on.'

'As you like,' she said carefully, and deep down felt that she resented him for being so efficient and for rushing her so.

It seemed cold in the registrar's waiting room where they had all crowded. The place had the atmosphere of an office or institution. A business deal, Poppy thought miserably, and wanted to cry. Surely this is all a bad dream and soon I'll wake up and Nigel will be here –

'Do you feel all right, Princess?' Burney asked, his face anxious. 'You look beautiful, but . . .'

She smiled and nodded and prayed not to cry. Not to break down and blub like any spoilt brat crying for the moon. And as the door opened and the previous couple came out, and she and Sandy, plus party, were ushered in, all Poppy could think about was that she mustn't let go and sob.

There was a large polished table at which the registrar sat, flanked by another man and a stern-faced woman. Three rows of chairs were set before the table. Sandy and the witnesses, Onions, Tony and Burney, stood in front of the table, like kids up before the head. The registrar began, and all the while he was joining hers and Sandy's lives together for ever, Poppy was fighting for self-control. Two tears fell like slivers of crystal to the brown linoleum-covered floor.

Outside for the confetti and the photographer, they began laughing as they ran hand in hand to the posh car with white ribbon on it, which Sandy had hired. Driving to Tony's they were alone together and Sandy said quietly, 'You're doing fine, just fine!'

She caught her breath and looked at him, seeing him as no distant stranger at last. By the time the cake had been cut and toasts had been drunk, Poppy was herself again. Now Sandy sprang his last surprise.

'Get changed,' he told her. 'Edna has already packed your overnight things.'

'Oh, but –' She laughed up at him, her cheeks going as rosy as her pearls. 'We're having so much fun and the party will go on for hours yet.'

'Come on,' he told her, 'I think I've waited long enough. We have to walk to the next street. It's a nice little family hotel. Everything's booked. Are you game?'

'Of course,' she agreed, then hesitated. 'Sandy, I –'

'I know,' he told her. 'Go on, Poppy. Get changed.'

He held her hand all the way. She glanced up at him and saw how strong his profile was. A bronzed sailor who had seen the world. Who had probably had many women. Who, in effect, knew how many beans made five. She bit her lip, wondering just what was to come.

The room was small, neat and clean. The bed was large and comfortable. Sandy and Poppy stood side by side, just looking at it, then Sandy told her firmly, 'You're not to close your eyes, Poppy. I want you to be very clear that it's me, Sandy, your husband, who's making love.'

'Sandy, I –'

'No pretending I'm someone else, understand?'

Her heart was beating like a drum. Her mouth felt dry. Yet she smiled and looked him directly in his eyes.

'Very well, Sandy,' she replied, praying that he couldn't see into her heart. 'Providing you do the same. I'm not and never can be Ros, you know.'

'Then we'll just have to forget everything except you and me, Poppy. Try and think and feel and learn about each other. It's just us, eh?'

'Just us,' she whispered and allowed him to take her into his arms.

His kiss was long and strong, his arms a tight band about her. He lifted her and carried her to the bed, and began to undress her. Then his lovemaking began. His strong, expert fingers began to explore, to squeeze and press in a fiery, prickly but gentle way. She felt herself stiffen.

'Don't think about it,' he told her. 'Let yourself go and just feel.'

'I – I am.' Her whisper was a soft breath in the night. She gasped as his mouth found her nipple, his tongue licked, his lips closed. He began to draw at her and his hand went down, gently pushing her legs apart. Then his fingers searched round for and found the area he needed, and began its teasing until at last she moaned.

He was very big, his movements strong. He knew exactly what to do, what she must also do.

'I am your husband,' he told her firmly. 'Let yourself go!'

She let herself go . . .

The next morning, feeling warm and at home with her husband, Poppy walked with him back to Tony's. They said tearful goodbyes and began the journey to Jezebel Street.

'Talk about back to square one,' Poppy said and smiled up at him in a half rueful way. 'Are you sure we're doing the right thing? Are you quite certain that Nan wants it this way? I really hate the way we've lied to her and –'

'You didn't lie, I did, and all in a good cause. I need to know you're being looked after while I'm away. Knowing you, you'll carry on till you drop, but you're going to need Nan when the nipper arrives. And though she never said much more than, "You bring her back home where she belongs," her face was all beams. She's missed you, Poppy, make no mistake about that.'

'Let's go through it again, then. Oh, Sandy, you don't know how greatly I've missed her and needed her and dreamed of going home. But I was too scared and you've made it all happen for me. I . . .I don't know if I'll ever me able to thank you enough.'

'You've trusted me to handle the rest of your life. You've trusted me to be the father of our kids. I reckon that's thanks enough. Now, here's what I told her. That you and me were married from Tony's some weeks ago. We didn't tell anyone because I've had some hassle from home. Since I didn't want my family present I thought it would be too hurtful for my mother if you asked your people and I didn't. Ye gods, Poppy, I can just imagine your aunt and my gran shut in a room together! It'd be the battle of Waterloo all over again. Anyway, I told Nan that we found you were pregnant and you wanted to come home. I said that we wondered if we might rent a room off her. She didn't want rent, but I've insisted – and the old dear don't argue with me. Anyay, she's pretty chuffed that she's the first one to know. She'll queen it over Gran, of course, and everyone else. But Poppy, there's one thing I'd like you to do.'

'Anything!'

'Be a mate to my mum. She's not very strong, and my gran's a bitch. She makes her life a misery at times.'

'If she wants me once she knows I've taken you off her hands, I'll be the best friend she's ever had in her life!'

'She . . . she has a faint look of Ros about her, Poppy. It scares me sometimes.'

'Then I shall love her dearly,' Poppy promised and felt the pink of emotion flushing her cheeks.

By evening they were walking along the passage of number two. Tears fell as the warm familiarity closed round her. She entered the kitchen and it was as if she had never been away. Nan was glaring at her.

'Why didn't you knock and give me fair warning? D'you want me to drop dead with shock?'

'Sorry, Nan!' Weeping uncontrollably, Poppy dropped Ros's suitcase and ran to her, arms outstretched. For a fraction of a second the older woman returned the embrace, her eyes soft. Then she pushed Poppy away, embarrassed, for Sandy strode in, weighed down with suitcases and carrier bags. He dropped them on the floor, grinning broadly and saying, 'What about me? I'm family now.' He gave Nan a bear hug and she was like wax in his hands – for two seconds flat. Then:

'Go and pick up all your things and take them up to the back room. Go on, pick everything up! Do you want me to trip over them and break my neck?'

Poppy was smiling through her tears. 'Nan,' she spluttered, 'nothing changes. Have you missed me?'

'Like I'd miss jaw-ache.' Nan's face crinkled up like a

214

walnut as she smiled. 'And I can't wait to see Charlie's face.' She gave Sandy a wicked wink and watched him gathering up the luggage.

'Hang on,' Poppy said. She opened Ros' case and took from it a china crinoline lady, and handed it to Nan. 'This might look nice among your other things. When I saw it in the shop I thought it was so pretty, I had to get it for you. Do you like it?'

Nan carefully examined the delicate face, the yellow curls caught up with lavender ribbons, the full pink skirt, the fan, the salmon slippers, the china violets at the dainty feet. She beamed.

'It must have cost a fortune,' she said. 'Fancy wasting your money! She'll be in pride of place and God help them cats if they as much as put a whisker near. Now help your husband up with all that stuff while I make us a nice cup of tea.'

After tea Sandy took his leave. 'I'm off to break the news to Mum,' he said. 'Are you coming, Poppy?'

She shook her head. 'If we gave Nan a surprise – and she knew we were coming – just think what it would do to your mother. You can't go there with me tagging along. No, you warn them first, and we'll go there together tomorrow. Just as we'll see Charlie and Clary tomorrow. Agreed?'

'You're the missus,' he replied and winked. 'Well, I'm away.'

When he'd gone Poppy turned to Nan, loving her with her eyes. 'So now tell me all the goings-on. I seems I've been away for ever.'

'Well, it's been years,' Nan sniffed, 'so I'd say all the goings-on have been up to you. Things round here are about the same as always. As you know, Daniel's moved and taken over the cottage in the Home. He always visits, though, and treats Flossie like his mother. Oh, Flossie's taken in a lodger – one she's after!' Nan's mouth curled disparagingly. 'Little baldheaded bloke, he is, wears horn-rimmed specs and flutters round the coal office like a tit in a trance. Flossie's changed since her poor old mum and dad got killed by fumes. Took it terrible, she did, blamed herself. Then something came over her and she went wild. She's had more blokes than

I've had hot dinners, but then Bert Chalmers came on the scene. Talk about chain herself down!'

'How's Daniel?'

'He'll be happy to see you back. Thought it was a bit of a lark, you putting gold studs in women's shoes, I mean. He reckoned you'd have done better to go in for Parliament, seeing as how you can argue the hind leg off a donkey. He also reckons you could wither the opposition with just one of your glares. Daniel's fond of you.' Nan gave another wicked, green-eyed smile. 'Shows he don't know you, I'd say. He gets on well with Sandy, too. I think you've done well for yourself, Poppy. I'm glad you're safely married and back home.'

'I wonder how he's getting on.' Poppy's face became rueful. 'I bet he has to stop in the Coach on the way home and down a pint or two. His mum's all right, he reckons, but old granny Vi's going to be trouble. Poor old Sandy! I'd sooner him than me.'

'I tell you what I heard,' Nan began and Poppy was all ears, waiting for the next juicy bit of scandal. Within a few moments she and Nan were giggling like a couple of kids. And Poppy's heart soared, because it had been years since she had seen her aunt as happy as this. Oh, she thought, it's so good to be home . . .

Sandy stood at the bar, a pint in his hand. He felt lonely, restless and unhappy. Just as he had many times, on shore leave abroad. Sometimes he had felt sick and tired of flirtatious women. Luscious creatures they were, and he'd been able to pick and choose. But in one way or another, they all had a price. He'd always been very particular, of course. Not like his randy dad, who'd take a whore from any filthy gutter in the world and not give a damn.

Then a letter would come from Poppy and – bingo! All his good resolutions about girls would go overboard, and he'd begin to think about red hair. Worse, have stupid ideas. Serious thoughts!

Marriage, he had always known, wasn't just having a crush on a girl and sharing the same bed. There was a sight more to it than that. A man wanted someone who'd sympathise with him, and not preach and try to make him do what she thought he ought to do. That was the way Onion's Annie looked at things. And above all, she should never be the sort to worry him out of his mind, by making him remember some other man she used to know. There was the rub, the heart of it! His idea of marriage had been a high and mighty thing.

He was about to leave when a group of mates he remembered from schooldays came roistering in.

'Bloody hell, it's Sand! Here, mate, what'll you have?'

'How are yer, chum? Strewth, it's been years. You don't half look brown.'

'Bli, Sand, you didn't get to look like that on a saucer of cockles and a day out at Southend.'

'How's that bleeding ol' father of your'n? Last time he came 'ome, he had us rocking in the aisles.'

Sandy grinned, accepting their pints and their friendship. He bought beers back and shared a yarn or two, but at the back of his mind he'd begun to wonder. What if he returned to the house only to find that Poppy had changed her mind?

The bell for the last drinks gave a shrill warning. Sandy waved goodbye to the blokes and went out, momentarily blinded by the dark. He stumbled over rough cobbles and swore.

He cursed himself for his stupidity in leaving Poppy behind. He should have gone back and insisted she came with him. But he'd needed a breather. His mother had been gentle and wonderful as always, it was his gran's wicked glare that had left the nasty taste in his mouth. That and her remarks about the den of iniquity that was Jezebel Street, all its inhabitants tarred with the same brush. Common as muck they were, every blessed one!

'My wife is a lady,' he had replied and meant what he said. 'And to be honest, Gran, she's a cut above you. She has class and good looks and has held down a very good and important job.'

He'd left the old girl gasping, and was grinning as he'd swung along to enjoy a pint. Then his mind had gone back to the previous night. Just as it was doing now.

His mind pictured Poppy and the small hotel room in the early dawn. He remembered her nakedness beside him, the

217

softness of her skin and the deep shadows of her eyes. And then she had said those bloody words. Put him in his place! Told him not to expect too much.

Sandy swore again, his pace slowing as he turned the dismal corner, chokingly aware of nothing but the drumming of his heart. He was still remembering every moment. Couldn't get it out of his mind.

Only when a woman slept did one realise fully the beauty of her face, the skin tinted like a blush buried within ivory, the relaxed symmetry of soft lips. He had not wanted to wake her, but he had kissed her lightly on the mouth and breasts, and she had smiled in her sleep, and somehow that smile had just about cut out his heart. Whom was she dreaming about?

He loved her. He knew it now with a sharp, anguished clarity. She was part of him and he wanted her. It was not only a physical want, it was a new kind of craving. His body wanted her, his bones and every sinew, his nerves and his mind. It was not just lust, he wanted her for her colour, form and beauty. His eyes ached for the sight of her, his brain needed the stimulation of her presence. He wanted to hear her, touch her, smell her; wanted her and himself to be like a pair of shoes, one useless without the other. Yes, he loved her, and he knew that this love was no passing thing. But it would never be the same for Poppy. Ye gods! Would he never forget that dawn? The whispered words? The agony in her eyes?

Sandy began to hurry, spurred on by the bitterness of his thoughts. Perhaps she had changed her mind even now. What if she had gone – back to Burney and Tony, and the all-important work in that bloody café?

Then he looked ahead and wanted to shout out loud. He strode towards the open door. She was standing there in a patch of light. In a moment his arms were around her and her head was nuzzling against his chest. He lifted her face and saw that she was crying and heard himself saying, 'What's the matter, Poppy? What's up?'

'Nothing.' She faltered. 'It's just that you . . . you've made everything so right!' She swallowed and smiled up at him in a misty way. 'And I was waiting here. You were so late, and . . .'

She stopped speaking and they went inside. It smelled of

lavender polish and warmth, and there was privacy, for Nan had gone to bed. They went upstairs together and sat side by side on the bed. Their shadows were cast hugely upwards by the flickering candlelight.

They sat for a long time. Sandy held still, making no move to caress her or to speak, aware that Poppy was happy in the silence and the relaxation of their companionship. Then he felt her watching him; her eyes were serious.

'Sandy,' she told him softly, 'you saved me. I don't think you'll ever know how afraid I was. I think I might have gone mad. Mostly I think it was the awful sense of betrayal and loneliness I had.'

'You don't ever need to be lonely again,' he told her. 'Not if you don't want to.'

'I know. Thanks to you.'

'Don't keep on about it, Poppy. After all, we're an old married couple now, and that's all we need to know.'

She lay back, then turned on her side to face him. 'Sandy, I . . . I'll be sorry when you have to go.'

He looked across at her quickly. Her frock was dappled with candlelight and shadows, and tiny touches of coppery brilliance flecked her hair. Her body was half turned and her small firm breasts thrust roundly against the thin cotton. Suddenly his aching hunger returned, and the yearning of his body and mind, and he knew that he did not want to go. He accepted with complete sincerity that he would never want to go.

'I'll be sorry too,' he told her carefully. 'Still, we have a little while yet.'

'But not all that long, Sandy,' she said plaintively.

'I know, Poppy.'

'Well, then?' She was smiling in a shyly teasing way. 'After all, I am your wife!'

'And you'll keep your eyes wide open,' he insisted, heart pounding. 'You'll look at me and not try to pretend –'

'Sandy!' she was leaning over, reaching out. Her fingers were busily undoing his shirt buttons, he could feel her nails against his skin. He began undressing her and fumbling because they were looking into each other's eyes.

He gloried in her and after that it was all the exotic

219

sensations in the world. And Poppy was wild and wanton, rewarding him in the only way she knew how. And deep down, he also knew.

Poppy lay, eyes open, listening to his regular breathing, finding that she quite liked belonging to this strong, very positive man. He was a new experience. Just as lying in Aunt Nan's double bed was an experience.

She wondered whether Nan had moved into Ros' bed for her and Sandy's sake. Or had she been in the small brass bed long before? Now, for the first time ever, Poppy was remembering Ros without tears, but rather with a deep affectionate love. It had seemed that this old house in Jezebel Street, with all its joys and sorrows, its memories, had welcomed her back with open arms.

Determinedly pushing the memory of Nigel Carson away, she snuggled up against Sandy's back. Then she smiled in the darkness as two soft thuds announced the presence of Josh and Jo. Clearly they were used to sharing the bed with Nan. They crept up, purring and rubbing against her cheek with their soft furry heads.

She went to sleep and not even the Parkers having their usual slanging match disturbed her. She slept dreamlessly and woke to a cold, clear morning that was moist and misty and pierced with gold. She heard the clattering of crates and the milkman's merry whistle, then Sandy saying good morning to the man. She smiled a little. So Sandy was not going to suffer tea made with condensed? He liked sugar and cow's milk, and manlike expected things to go his way.

Poppy stayed where she was, realising that although Sandy would always love Ros and she, Poppy, would always be second best, she could live with it. He made her feel secure and she knew that she could and would adapt. Her trip into the outside world had been little more than a few tramrides away; her experiences had been those of a lifetime. Some folks lived and struggled, fought and died in and around the street where they'd been born, knowing nothing and caring less about anything else. She had seen how the other half lived. And she had learned one thing: people were people no matter how rich or poor they were. They could be liars or cheats, good or bad, nice or nasty the world over. The thing was to be honest and remain true to oneself.

Poppy was a child of Jezebel Street and would remain so for as long as it took. But one day, she vowed, one fine and glorious day she would leave the shabby little street in triumph. She would make something of herself, just as she had promised Ros. She would have that house with its flowers and fine things, but she would do it on her own. She had her savings. Nigel's money did not feel like her own. And one deep purple evening she would take a moonlit walk in a garden filled with the scent of roses. Then she would wait until she sensed her presence. Yes, Ros would float down like a wisp of pearly mist. They would dream together, just she and Ros.

Poppy heard Sandy's heavy footsteps coming up the stairs. He was smiling as he came in, holding a mug in his hand.

'Morning, missus,' he said. 'I thought you deserved a cup of tea. How's tricks?'

'I'm very well, thank you,' she replied and smiled into his face. 'How did things go?'

'Like a ton of coals as regards Gran. I tell you, I was glad to make my escape. But Mum's longing to see you. I told her round about ten. All right?'

'We'll take her some flowers, Sandy. Don't worry! Your mother and me will stand shoulder to shoulder from now on. Even better, we'll have Nan on our side.'

'Poppy, you make it sound like there's going to be all-out war.'

'If there is,' she chuckled, 'I know who'll win.'

'Women!' he groaned in mock horror. 'I think you enjoy a scuffle far more than men.'

'Really?' Suddenly, inexplicably, she was laughing out loud. 'Just let's say that life's going to be a bit of a challenge from now on.'

'Too right,' he agreed and groaned again.

Chapter Thirteen

Poppy and Sandy entered Charlie's arm in arm. Her father and Clary were stacking cauliflowers and turned simultaneously. Charlie's mouth seemed to stretch from ear to ear as he grinned.

'My Gawd, ducky, you're a little cracker! And you're all grown-up! Not too much of a lady to give your old man a smacker, I hope?'

'Dad!' She let go of Sandy and ran to him, stars in her eyes. She felt his rough chin against her face, and his bear hug. 'Dad!'

'Oh, Poppy!' Clary wept and gave her a big slobbery kiss. 'My little precious, you've come back home.'

'Well, I just had to,' Poppy chuckled. 'I couldn't wait any longer for a slice or two of your toast.'

Charlie, who was pumping Sandy's hand up and down and seeming unable to let go, turned and laughed.

'Cor blimey, old girl, what are you waiting for? We'll all have a cuppa and hot toast and a good old jaw.' He turned his head over his shoulder and shouted, 'Oi, Rags, come here. Rags, look who's come home. Rags!' He turned back to Poppy. 'He's getting past it, Poppy, like we all are. He sleeps a lot and I think he's going deaf.'

'Well, he looks very young and spritely from where I'm standing,' Sandy said and laughed. 'He's been out on the razzmatazz if you ask me. See?'

They looked out of the window and saw Rags bounding along the street towards the shop. His tail was held high, his tongue was lolling.

'I dunno,' Charlie said and shook his head, 'talk about life in the old dog yet. He's been after that bitch at number fifty again. Gawd help us! You'd think he'd get fed up with having Mother Mason's toe up his arse.'

They had tea and toast in the kitchen and Poppy saw its muddle and mess, how small it all seemed now, and dark, and didn't mind. This was Clary's place, hers and her father's, and if it was right for them, it was right for her. He had come out with it, called himself her old man! All was right with her world.

Before they left, Charlie looked at her, admiration in his eyes. 'Well, ducky,' he said, 'I'm proud of you. You look bloody beautiful, you smell nice, you talk posh, and yet you ain't acted no different to Clary and me.'

'You don't know how often I longed to be back here,' she said, choking. 'I got to be very homesick, and –'

'Now you're here having a cuppa and a bit of grub just like the old times,' he said, chuffed. 'Yet, by all them letters what Flossie read out to us, you've done well for yourself. You could have swanned in here looking down your nose.'

'Now you're being daft!' She beamed. 'And as for doing well for myself, I have! Just look at my wonderful husband.'

'Dunno about that,' Charlie quipped. 'And as for that whippersnapper you're going to have, I hope as how you learn him not to be the tealeaf his father was.' He grinned at Sandy. 'There's many an apple gone missing after you and your mates come here on errands. And to think you little perishers thought I didn't know!'

Everyone was laughing and joshing each other as Poppy and Sandy left.

'Now for the hard bit,' Sandy said. 'Are you ready to face my gran?'

'I want to meet your mum,' she replied. 'Funny, isn't it? We've known each other all these years, yet I've never laid eyes on her.'

'She doesn't go out too much, Poppy. It's her nerves mostly, and she gets palpitations bad. Gran doesn't help. Just the opposite, in fact. She never forgave Mum for getting pregnant and trapping Dad. Of course it was all Mum's fault in her book.'

'Oh!' Poppy smiled wryly. 'Then she'll just about crucify me if the truth ever came out.'

'Let's get this straight, girl,' he told her earnestly, 'I want you. I will always want you, and nothing's going to make me let you go. Fate couldn't play the same game twice on me – and sometimes, when you're quiet and thinking, you're so much like my Ros it hurts.'

'Don't,' she whispered. 'Please don't, Sandy.'

'That being the case, I personally wouldn't care if the truth about the baby came out. My back's broader than you think. I'm only too proud you're capable. I don't think Ros would have ever been strong enough to have a child. So, from where I'm standing, I would have stood by you no matter what. The reason for all the pretence and that the baby's got to be mine, is Gran! If she found out, her and her cronies would hound you down, and Gran would bring up old scores to Mum again. I've seen Gran wither my mother with her hateful sneers and mean, catty barbs. We mustn't allow that to happen, Poppy. Agreed?'

'Trust me,' Poppy said. 'The old girls round here will never change, and I can handle anything they dish out. But for both our sakes I'll keep as quite as a mouse.'

They smiled at each other, conspirators, and in that moment very close.

It was grand to walk down the full length of Beamont Road holding on to her husband's arm. Poppy was immensely proud of her Sandy. He was good to look at, reliable and a wonderful catch. Above all, the plain gold ring on her finger proclaimed to the world that she belonged to him. He was as open and as honest as the day, not a dirty, devious swine like Mr Carson. She resolutely pushed the thought of Nigel away.

Vi Swift was waiting for them in the front room. Big-bosomed and belligerent, her arms folded, she was ready for war and it showed.

'Took your time,' she observed nastily. 'We've been ready and waiting for the past hour.'

'Sorry, Mum,' Sandy said, looking over her shoulder to smile at his mother. She was sitting in her usual place by the window, knitting in her lap, plainly near to tears. The old harridan had probably been having a go at her, Poppy thought. 'We were talking to Poppy's dad,' Sandy went on, 'and didn't realise the time.'

Before the defenceless little woman could reply, Poppy was moving across the room, a beaming smile on her face. She bent down to kiss Meg.

'I'm so pleased to meet you at last,' she said and chuckled. 'May I call you Meg? I love your son very much and always have since schooldays, but I'll never get used to calling him Cyril. Indeed, I never even realised that was his name until I saw the form he filled for the registrar.'

'There's nothing wrong with having your grandfather's name,' Vi snapped from behind them. 'Anyone would think you had reasons to rush out and get married so underhand. Why all the secrecy up till now? That's what I'd like to know.'

Her discourtesy was astounding. Nan had always taught her girls to be polite. Yet this fat ugly woman considered herself to be a cut above a mere peasant from Jezebel Street. Poppy smiled to herself, thinking about the beanfeast of scandal Vi would enjoy from now on.

On top of her list would be her granddaughter-in-law's father, Charlie Ashton, whose wife cut and run, and who'd lived in sin with his Clary for donkey's years. Then Nan Eden would get a turn, the aunt who scrubbed floors, and whose old man had perished in jail. Dear heaven, there'd be fur flying if even a whisper of that sort of talk reached Nan! Nan and Vi, who practically lived on top of each other, were in reality worlds apart. The snobbery of the working class was the worst snobbery of all, Poppy thought. But who cared? Not her?

Poppy ignored Sandy's ignorant grandmother and continued to smile steadily into Meg's quivering face.

'It would have been nice if you had been well enough to have been with us,' she said in her quiet, well-modulated voice. 'Sandy bought me flowers, and everything was beautiful. We had a three-tiered cake, wasn't that marvellous? My friend Burney, who's quite brilliant, made it for us. I have brought you a piece, here it is, in this little fancy white box. The other is for Sandy's grandmother.'

'I would have liked to have been there,' Meg whispered. 'But –'

'Sandy explained that the journey would be too much for you, so we didn't ask my family either. Still, Sandy had his friend Onions. There's another nickname! Also Annie, his girl. My friends were there, too, and we have had some pictures taken specially. I forgot to put them in my bag in the rush of packing. I'll write to my friend Edna and ask her to send them on. When she does, I'll bring them round.'

'You're as lovely as Sandy said,' Meg told her quietly. 'I'm very happy for you both.'

'Which still don't explain why it all had to be kept so quiet,' Vi kept on, her eyes squinting with suspicion.

Poppy laughed, but her green eyes were glinting dangerously. She had to hold back for Sandy's sake, yet she was dying to give the woman the tongue-lashing she deserved.

'Oh, Lord, Mrs Swift,' she teased, 'you're like a dog with a bone! We kept our marriage quiet simply because I would have been given the sack else. Married women may not work at Farringdons. They are a very famous firm, you know.'

'Then why change all that now?'

Poppy opened her eyes very wide and was innocence itself. 'My goodness! Didn't Sandy tell you?' She turned back to Meg. 'We're going to have a baby. Some time in August, I should think. And then you'll be a grandma. Will you mind very much?'

'My dear!' Meg was smiling tearfully and absolutely delighted. 'I can't wait! So you won't be going back to Hackney now? You'll be staying here and –'

'There's no room in this house, if that's what you're thinking,' Vi cut in firmly. 'And we're too set in our ways to put up with –'

'There's no need to worry on our account,' Poppy beamed. 'We'll be living with my aunt in Jezebel Street until our baby is born. Then I believe we will think again. We'll probably buy our own house, all in good time.'

'I've never heard such boasting,' Vi was determined to put in her twopennyworth, no matter what. 'And it'll take Sandy years to save up enough to get a deposit.'

226

'But we have enough already,' Poppy put in blithely. 'Sandy has been saving like mad for a very long time and so have I. You'd be amazed how well putting gold studs on special shoes gets paid.'

'Ha!' Vi's sniff held all the contempt in the world. 'Fancy rubbish, more like. You'd have done better to work on decent low-heeled shoes with strong straps across the instep like we all wear. Seems to me you're too uppity for your own good. After all, you've only been killing time since you've been away from home. Just waiting to get our Cyril.'

'Which shows how wise I am, don't you agree?' Poppy's tone was all sweetness and light, but she was glaring directly into Vi's eyes, silently warning the woman that she was no slouch if it came to a battle of words. She went on in a cool, matter-of-fact way, 'On the other hand, I think you are being very rude.' Vi Swift opened her mouth to reply, but Poppy continued, 'Rude about my work, I mean. I was very lucky, and extremely proud to hold a position in Farringdon's. After all, I had a job, which is surely unusual in this day and age? I think that my husband has always been pleased with me?' She turned to him questioningly.

Sandy's great roar of laughter rang out, making everything all right.

'Pleased and proud!' he affirmed. 'About you and the way you're giving as good as you get. Why, girl, I'm like a dog with two tails!' He kissed her soundly in front of the two older women, then went to Meg and gave her a hug. 'We mean it, Mum. We'll be getting our own place and when we do, there'll always be a room waiting for you.'

'I know,' she whispered and adored him with her eyes. 'But my place is with Gran. We're content to wait here at home for your dad.'

'You know best,' he told her easily. 'Now me and Poppy are off. Got to make the most of the rest of my leave. I shall be away six to nine months, perhaps even longer, if things don't go smooth. I hope everything gets to be plain sailing because I'd like to get back for when the baby's born.'

'You said – six months!' Meg was distressed.

'Didn't want to upset you too much, but everything's

227

changed now. You've got a brand new daughter-in-law who'll keep an eye on things.'

'You should have stayed with your father,' Vi cut in, determined to have the last word. 'He would never have let you –'

'Stop it, Gran!' Sandy's tone was sharp. 'That's enough! You won't let anyone be nice, will you? If you must know, I've had to make my own way since my first voyage as a youngster of fifteen. Dad was a full-blown engineer, and I was green and scared. He had other things to do, rather than wet-nurse me! But I learned and learned jolly fast.' He was unable to stop himself from adding, 'No thanks to my dear old dad.'

'Cyril, I won't have none of that,' Vi snapped.

His smile was cold, his gaze direct as he replied. 'My life is my own affair, Gran, make no mistake. And don't forget either that it now also includes my wife. We'll manage very well, believe me. Now we've got to go. Ta-ta.' He was hustling Poppy out, his hand under her elbow. He turned to look back at his mother and smiled fondly. 'Don't worry, we'll be back to see you before I have to leave.'

Then they were outside the muslin-bedecked home and chuckled together like naughty children.

'I'm glad that's over,' Poppy admitted and then laughed out loud. 'I think it must be dinner time. Shall we have fish and chips?'

They headed for the chippy's hand in hand.

For the rest of his leave Sandy stayed close to Poppy's side. At night he made love and, though it was nothing like Nigel's smoothly practised approach, Poppy was warm and relaxed in her husband's arms.

During the day he went everywhere with her. To the shops, to visit Flossie, to eat toast in Clary's kitchen, to share a joke or two with Charlie. Going to Hackney was a must, so that Poppy could meet Annie again, who was a whippet-thin joker and liked by all. And they often saw Meg. But Vi was always there, like a fat devil of spite. Sandy was riddled with guilt.

'I can't stand leaving Mum,' he said flatly. 'She's like a

228

moth caught in a web, hypnotised by Gran. But I can't budge her. She really believes she's fulfilling her duty.'

'Then she must be happy in her way,' Poppy told him. 'But don't you worry too much. I promise to keep my eyes and ears open. Let's go and see how Daniel's getting on.'

They went to see Daniel several times and it was warm and good to have such a close friendship.

Daniel was smaller than she remembered, but then Sandy had grown bigger all round. Daniel's limp seemed a little more pronounced, but he was more handsome than ever. Like a film star, she thought, with his dark hair and beard, and brilliant hyacinth-blue eyes.

'Hello, matey,' he always said on greeting. 'You're all grown-up, I see, and a little beauty at that. It's a good job that Sandy here saw you first. He's a very lucky bloke.'

'No.' Her reply was always the same. 'I'm the lucky one, Daniel. I feel I'm the luckiest person in the world.'

She meant every word. It was a standing joke and the two men would look at each other and grin and wink in a matey, companionable way. Yes, things were easier all round, being the wife of Sandy.

Suddenly she realised that she was dreading the time when he had to go. Although he did not love her in the way he had loved Ros, and in spite of the fact that nothing and no one would register with her as Nigel had, she felt that Sandy was very special. A warm, understanding man who was fiercely masculine, who could be tough as old boots if it came to a reckoning. Even so, he was carefully masterful with her, increasingly so as the nights went by.

As the end of his leave approached he became more possessive. In bed he was strong and fierce and all-demanding. He filled her whole body with his wanting and needing, and she responded every time. Soon she too became caught up in the fierce rhythm, pushing back at him, her arms raised to clasp him tightly round his neck. Desiring him to go on, feeling agony and ecstasy and needing more. And with Sandy it was legal and binding! It was no sin and all right! It made her feel abandoned and wanton, being his wife, he could do to her what he wished. And the marvel was that he needed her over and over again.

229

Sandy had nothing of Nigel's velvet smoothness. Nigel's foreplay had been a ritual, almost an art form in itself. Nigel had made her feel like a flower, slowly and inevitably opening up the radiant brilliance of the sun. But Sandy made her feel that she was caught up in thick orange flames and being devoured. And there was no guilt afterwards, no secrecy during the days, no hiding, no lies! It was all above board with Sandy. With him she felt a person, a proud, whole person hanging on to his arm. She didn't want him to go back to sea. Didn't want to face the future without him. One evening, she looked down at her toes to hide the blush that was flooding her cheeks and told him so.

Sandy sat opposite her in Nan's kitchen chair, his expression watchful and still.

'I mean it,' she told him quietly, now looking directly into his handsomely chiselled face. 'You make me feel safe. I really and truly don't want you to go.'

'That's nice,' he said at last and leaned across to ruffle her hair. 'Very nice. After the next leave, I'll see what I can do.'

'You mean, you really mean that you can?'

'Yes,' he told her firmly, 'if that's what you'd really like. I've already signed on for this particular stint, but after that, there can be far shorter runs. Perhaps Onions will think that way too, once he's married young Annie. I'll see what he thinks.' He smiled then, twin devils dancing in his eyes. 'Lord, Poppy, this is all turning out to be a really rum do!'

She smiled across at him, rosy-faced, green eyes like gems.

'The thing is,' she pointed out, 'that we like each other. That things . . . things between us come naturally. We have always been friends and now we have taken a great step forwards, together. You've made me very happy, Sandy, and yes, I mean it, I don't want you to go.'

He was grinning and pleased. He stretched out his long legs so that he could nudge at her with his toe.

'You don't do so bad yourself, wife,' he told her. 'Not bad at all.'

On the day she waved Sandy goodbye, it seemed natural to go to see Daniel and weep a tear or two.

'I quite like Jezebel Street when Sandy's there,' she said, sniffing. 'But I know he'll never give up the sea.'

'Well, you've got a family, and me of course,' he told her. 'Poor Meg only has that old battle-axe Vi.'

'And she has me,' Poppy said swiftly. 'I'm going to make sure I visit her at least once a week.'

'Good for you,' he replied. 'Now buzz off, matey, I've got work to do.'

'I'm sorry for wasting your time,' she said, humiliated at his tone. Then his white teeth flashed through his beard as he grinned.

'Come on, Poppy! Haven't you learned yet how pretty you are? But you belong to Sandy now and I'm bloody damned sure if you stay here much longer I might forget the fact.'

'What a lot of old toffee!' She was smiling wickedly now. 'All right, I'll let you get on with those bookshelves you're making. Oh yes, I know all about it, and about the extra books you've collected over the years for the kids. There's not much that goes on around here that Nan doesn't know.'

It was getting near teatime when Poppy left. She was missing Sandy already, as well as the warm friendliness of Edna and Burney. In Leyton she had no close friends and with Sandy gone, the spice seemed to have gone out of her life. She was beginning to see the grime and poverty all over again.

As she turned into Jezebel Street she saw the fiery-looking, gipsyish Maud Ewebank, who with her husband and son had moved into the Jacobses' place. The Jacobs crew had done the moonlight flit, leaving Lenny high and dry, a long time ago. Now, as Maud and Poppy came face to face, Poppy smiled warmly, and Maud raised one finely arched brow and nodded.

'Not so good today, is it?' Poppy asked, referring to the weather.

'Could be worse,' Maud said in an offhand, half angry way.

Poppy had seen Maud about ever since she and Sandy had moved in with Nan. She had liked the look of her and wanted to be friends. Clearly she was after Nan's heart since Nan kept going on about 'them lovely white net curtains across the road'. Curtains were luxury in Jezebel Street, at least at most of the top end. Poppy tried again.

'Better than last week, eh? When it's dark and grey it affects you and makes you feel really down. What d'you think?'

'That it don't take no bloody weather to depress me,' Maud replied, and her near-black eyes flashed. 'It takes only one rotten kid.'

'Your boy? I've seen him coming and going. He's a little charmer with all that dark hair and such large, beautifully dark eyes! I hope that my baby looks a little like that.'

The praise lightened Maud's mood. Her expression cleared as she smiled.

'Really? What, take after someone like my Arty? Not like you, nor his dad?' Maud nudged Poppy with her elbow and winked. 'Don't tell me that it's someone else's bun you've got in the oven!'

'Fat chance of that!' Poppy laughed and found herself praying that the baby would look like her and nothing like Nigel. 'Where are you off to, or shouldn't I ask?'

'I'm about to knock on old mother Lacey's door. She's been up the school about my Arty again. Her kid's twice as big as my Arty by all accounts and a bully with it. I'm just off to tell that woman what's what. Every night it's the same. Arty comes in black and blue, and I'm going to put a stop to it.'

'Want some company? She's bound to be surrounded with cronies. All of us from Jezebel Street seem to be tarred with the same brush so far as the Beaumont and Skelton Street lot are concerned. You might need someone on your side.'

'Can do my own dirty work, thanks, but –' Maud Ewebank's Egyptian-looking eyes were now really warm and friendly. 'Why don't you come along and watch my back? Afterwards come back to my place and we can have a cuppa and a bit of a chat. What do you say?'

'I'd like that. Thanks. I'm at a loose end and don't know what to do with myself now my husband's back at sea. My aunt's at work, so I could do with a bit of excitement.'

'All right then. Don't blame me if you get your eyes scratched out.'

It was all a bit of a letdown because Mrs Lacey was either out or refused to open the door. A few women, standing on doorsteps, eyed them up and down, folded their arms and got on with their bitching and scandalising, but giving quick looks over their shoulders all the time.

'Glad you're with me,' Maud said. 'Some of them look like they could take on the world's greatest boxer and win every round.'

'We're wasting our time here,' Poppy said. 'Let's go back to your place. I'm gasping for a cup of tea.'

They walked back to Jezebel Street, chatting easily, getting to know each other, sizing each other up. Taking to each other.

Maud was someone after Nan's heart. The house was clean and tidy. The furniture was clearly second-hand, but it had been polished till it shone. The netting at the windows was snow white and the kitchen grate had been black-leaded, the hearth stoned and pristine.

'You've made this place really homely and cheerful,' Poppy told her. 'It's warm and nice.'

'I'm happy with it myself – now.' Maud looked rueful. 'They must have been a filthy lot that lived here before. I nearly lost my kneecaps, I was scrubbing so hard and so long, but we like it now, Arthur and me. We want to do lots more to the place, but money don't grow on trees. We could do with a lodger, but they don't seem to grow on trees either. Ones I could live with, I mean.'

Arty pulled the string to open the front door, and came clumping in. His black hair was tousled, his face dirty and beaming, his bootlaces were undone. In spite of the cold, he was carrying his coat, and his mud-stained shirt was hanging out. Clearly he had been scrapping again. Maud's expression changed in an instant.

'Oh, my Gawd!' she said. 'I'll kill you, our Arty. I'll just about choke the living daylights out of you!'

She swung her hand up and clumped him one. He glared up at her. His ear was red but he was defiant. Maud glared back at him and in that moment Poppy saw how alike they were, both dark-haired, brown-eyed and quick-tempered.

'I don't know what I've done yet except bash a kid twice my size and – ' Arty began, but Maud cut him short.

'You know what you've done all right, little swine! You just wait till your dad gets in, that's all!'

'I don't know what –'

'You've been fighting Johnny Lacey again. I warned you not to last week, didn't I? After his mum went up the school.'

'Ya! And did dear Johnny-wonny go and see Miss too?'

'No and why should he? From all accounts you half killed him!'

'You ain't seem him.' Arty was indignant. 'And if you 'ad you'd 'ave clumped old mother Lacey instead of me. 'Er kids –'

'If I have to tell you again about using your H's I'll – It's *h*im and *h*ave! You'll get the whole damn street saying you've been dragged up next. Just like what they say about the Kings and the Lambs. What's –' Maud stopped, gave her Arty a quick look then. 'Are you telling me God's truth? Is her kid really bigger than you?'

'Twice as big as me and twice as ugly, and if I'd 'ave had twice the time I would have gone for him twice as 'ard. No one's going ter call me a lice-head from grungy old Jezebel Street.'

'Oh, shut up!' Maud looked at Poppy, who looked back, both indignant at the slur. Arty was in full flow now.

'And even if I 'ave only lived 'ere for a few rotten months, it's our street now and – anyway Lacey's twice as big as me.'

'Here – remember H E R E!'

'And his mum's twice as big as you. So there!'

'Will you shut up?' Maud was jutting out her chin while Poppy pushed her red hair away from her face with an impatient gesture. Grungy, she thought, that's a new one, grungy! Maud took in a deep, furious breath and went on, 'Twice as big as you, is he? Are you sure?'

'Big as an 'ouse!' Arty insisted, his voice rising even higher. Maud made up her mind then. 'You'd better be telling me the truth,' she warned. 'You go making a fool out of me and I'll – keep your coat on!'

'Why? It's 'o– hot in 'ere.'

'When I say keep your coat on,' Maud said dangerously, 'I

234

mean keep your coat on. We're going to see that woman, oh yes, we are! I'm not having no mouthy bitch coming round here threatening to go up the school again when it's not your fault.' She swung round to face Poppy. 'And to think I let her go on because I know what a young devil he is. Wasn't his fault! I don't put up with no name-calling myself. Oh, Gawd, I'm going to give her the length of my tongue.'

While she was speaking, Maud Ewebank was pulling on her coat and turning the gas off under the kettle. Arty was smirking.

'Blow me, Mum, you're mad as 'ell, ain't you? Now let the whole of rotten Skelton Street watch out.'

Maud grabbed Arty firmly by the arm and marched him outside into the raw evening air. She turned to Poppy. 'Coming? I want a witness to this. I want someone with me in case this barney's leaked out to the school.'

'I'm with you,' Poppy said, wanting to hug herself. At long last, she was feeling really at home. At one with all her neighbours. This was all as she remembered, rough and ready, tough and touchy, lively down-to-earth Jezebel Street. She had felt like a square peg in a round hole when Sandy brought her back, but now everything was falling into place.

They turned into Skelton Street. Maud marched onto the step of the Lacey house and knocked on the door hard. Within seconds a tall rangy woman with a big nose and small dark eyes confronted them.

'Here's my kid,' Maud said sharply. 'Now I want to see your kid.'

Several of the Skelton street women were beginning to gather in a menacing way, so Poppy took up position, curled her lip and glared. She recognised most of them, and they knew her as the kid they'd seen for many years, helping in Charlie's shop. Unlike Maud Ewebank, she was one of them. This being the case, her fierce stance was enough. They kept back, all listening, watching, enjoying it. A good barney was like a bit of mustard livening up yesterday's beef. High expectancy was in the air.

Mrs Lacey towered over Maud. Her face flushed darkly, but her eyes, after one swift look at Arty's small, wiry frame, were uneasy.

235

'Get orf my step!' she said and folded her arms over her chest. 'Go on, clear orf.'

'I'm not budging till I've had a good look at your kid!'

'He ain't here and what's more –'

'Wot's up, Mum?' Johnny Lacey asked as he came out. He was eating a slice of bread and jam. There was jam on his nose.

'So!' Maud snapped. 'Here's the poor little weakling my boy's half killed! I've seen all I want to see.' She stepped nearer to the woman and poked her hard on the chest. 'Now let me tell you this! If I get any more trouble from you, I'll be up the school tomorrow. And, my Gawd, I'll spin them a tale that'll make their ears drop off.'

'You're as bloody mad as your kid!' Mrs Lacey was rearing up like a turkey cock. 'For two pins I'll have you orf my step and in the gutter where all your sort belong.'

'Try it! Go on, try it and just see what happens. No one's going to talk to me like I'm dirt. Just you lay your hands on me and see what happens.'

The audience were getting their money's worth now. The two women were going at it hammer and tongs. Their voices grew higher and faster, and inside seconds the windows were opening all down Skelton Street. Poppy, intrigued, saw Arty take a ball out of his pocket and begin kicking it backwards and forwards against the front garden wall. Johnny Lacey slithered out of the house, still eating his bread and jam. Since he did actually tower over Arty, Poppy moved close enough to watch and also to overhear.

'They'll be at it all night,' Johnny Lacey observed and grinned a grin that spread each side of his long nose. Arty nodded and kicked the ball to him. Johnny lobbed it back.

'They'll be at each other's throats for weeks after this lot,' Arty said and groaned. 'Women can't 'alf 'ang on to things, can't they?'

' 'Course. They're like that. Oi, Art, I didn't mean ter say that about your street. I'm mates with Bill King, and we 'ate the Lambs. We thought you was mates with the Lambs.'

'I daren't play with any of that lot. My mum says they've got nits, and anyway, she'd skin me alive.'

236

'Mums!' Johnny groaned. The two boys sniggered. The voices became shriller behind them.

'Look at that!' Mrs Lacey yelled. 'The little swine! They're playing!'

The two boys froze.

'Crikey,' Arty breathed. 'Now it's our turn. Sock me one, Johnny, for Gawd's sake, sock me!'

Poppy watched and wanted to laugh out loud at the little devils. They began to scuffle, enjoying themselves no end until they were torn apart by irate parents.

'The little sods!' Maud said to Poppy as they all walked home. 'Gawd help you when yours arrives.'

'I think I've learned not to take sides in a boys' fight,' Poppy said and laughed, 'but you didn't do half bad. The woman towered over you. I can see where Arty gets his courage from.'

'But he shouldn't fight! I keep telling him.' She turned to her son. 'I keep telling you not to fight, don't I? You should – should turn the other cheek!'

Arty gave his mum a wicked grin. 'Like what you do? I've gotta fight back, Mum. I've gotta! If I don't, my mates would call me sissy.'

'Bloody hell, Arty, what am I going to do with you?'

'Let me have me bread and jam, that's what. I'm starving to death.'

'See?' Maud groaned. 'Talking to him is a waste of bloody time. He's going to be a real Bill Bash'em, just like his dad.'

'No, Mum!' Arty said quickly, and now the mischief had gone from his eyes and his face looked drained. 'I'm like you, ain't I? Just like you!'

' 'Course you are!' Maud said quickly and smiled down into his grubby face. 'And I'm proud of you, Arty. That Johnny Lacey is twice, no, three times as big as you!'

'And his mum made you look like a tiddler.'

'I think you've both won with honour,' Poppy chipped in. And they were all chuckling and teasing and going over it all again as they went back to Maud's house.

Meeting Maud was special, Poppy thought after that. She was good company, warm and friendly, but she could fly off

237

the handle at the drop of a hat. She and Liz Parker eyed each other like wary opponents when they met, but, for the time being, left it at that. Liz seemed to preoccupied with the sudden, very regular visits she was receiving from Julie Peel. Julie had grown up amazingly fast and had a knowing look in her eyes. It was said that Julie had set her cap at Graham, which was a laugh for a start. Even so, there was something very pushy about Julie and in that direction, at least, poor old Liz seemed to have met her match.

It became quite a habit for Poppy to go across the road to Maud's for a cuppa. She and Poppy got on well. Arthur Ewebank was a big lumbering man of few words and had a mean look about his mouth. Maud always rushed to do his bidding, 'for the sake of a quiet life,' she told Poppy brightly. 'You know how it is with men.'

And Poppy did know about men. Two completely opposite men. She yearned for Nigel and hated herself for doing so. She missed Sandy and needed his support at times. She wanted to have a son, perhaps just a little bit like that scallywag Arty. In the meantime, she had idle hands and hated it.

Poppy had to find something to do. She cleaned and polished for Nan, and offered to help Charlie, but there were no paying jobs to hand. People seemed depressed, unemployment increased and newspapers held little happy news. Poppy found herself wondering how Bill Bannerman was getting on. He had had a bad winter, Charlie told her, and, after a bout of flu, had found it all a bit too much on his own. He had stopped clinging to the past so much, and had at last dispensed with his barrow. He now owned a horse to pull a rather fine van. The idea of motors were abhorrent to him.

'I reckon he's settling down to live on his means,' Charlie said. 'Dunno how good they are. You can never guess with old Bill. But he don't make many calls these days. And I don't think he'll be up to all that hard work, planting and sowing and stuff, come spring.'

'That will break his heart,' Poppy observed, remembering the look in Bill's eyes when he planted and tended growing things.

'Just a shadow of himself, he is,' Charlie said. 'Proper

bloody shame. But you know Bill! He's proud and pig-headed, and tough as old boots about giving away his privacy. Young Beth Hastings all but mothers him, but Bill won't dream of having help from outside.'

'I think I'll go and see Bill tomorrow,' Poppy said one early morning while they were sitting in Clary's kitchen.

'Good heavens, what's that?'

She jumped up, narrowly missing Rags who was sprawling near her feet. She heard angry, high-pitched cries and screams and it sounded as though someone was getting murdered. Charlie stood up, furious.

'The little perishers, I'll bloody kill 'em. This is what I get for closing my eyes to what goes on in me own back yard.'

He stormed outside, yelling and waving his arms at two scruffy urchins who were trying to kill each other. Rags joined in, jumping up and barking loudly, thoroughly enjoying the fun. Poppy and Clary watched the proceedings from the back door.

'Sodding hell,' Clary moaned, 'now I'm for it. Charlie's bound to see them decent spuds, and the couple of cabbages that I should have stripped off and sold. I feel sorry for them kids, I really do. They can't help who their parents are. Oh, shit! Nothing gets better in this ugly old world, does it?'

'Blow the world.' Poppy's joy at homecoming was fast fading. 'Don't you mean, nothing gets better in Jezebel Street?'

She watched the two boys running out of the yard as fast as their legs could carry them. Charlie was about to come in when he saw the two cabbages – cow cabbages, he called them. Their outer leaves were curling and brown, but when stripped the hearts would be seen to be full, round and white, like large shiny balls. Poor Clary had been found out. Clary liked kids and would have given her soul to have had a brood of her own. The gods weren't that kind. There were no bread-snappers for Clary and there never would be. She had been told that by a doctor a long time ago.

'D'yer want to see me in the poor house?' Charlie bawled. 'Am I in this business just for a lark? Cor blimey, Clary, fancy you putting stuff out there, just asking for them to come in and pinch it.'

239

'Why are you such a tight-fisted old fart?' Clary yelled back. 'It won't kill you to let them poor little devils rummage round to see what they can get. All they're after is a bellyful of grub.'

'And you're after getting the back of me hand!'

Clary folded her arms and at that moment looked big and motherly and rather beautiful. She smiled and cocked her head to one side. 'Do you mean that, Charlie?'

He went red and looked shamefaced, but still held on to the cabbages as he walked back into the kitchen. Poppy grabbed up her coat and left them to it.

As she walked through the yard gate, she looked about her. Everything seemed a little greyer, poorer and uglier than before. Even number two was matchbox-small against the flat in Coopersale Place. Suddenly a picture of Nigel's flat weaved in her mind. She had loved it as dearly as though it were her own. Nigel had said that it was. That it was their home, that he loved and adored her. Doubt set in and she shivered. It was all too clear now that in the first place Rene Davies had been sent to him by his cousin Mr Tilsby. It stood to reason, then, that Nigel had known her, Poppy, for exactly what she was: a nothing and nobody from Jezebel Street. And the cream of it was, she had honestly believed she could change all that. Speak well, act well, mind her manners and be and do all that he wanted her to. The man had probably been laughing up his sleeve all along.

A very real terror filled her then, and it all but outweighed her grief at losing Nigel. Of all people, Charlie must never find out. At long last, he was proud of her, called her his girl, and that had made a lifelong dream come true. If he learned how it had been, that Sandy had married her to save her face because she'd become pregnant by her boss, he would disown her again. He had hated her mother enough to want to kill her. With his daughter it would be even worse.

Feeling sick, she reached the home of the King clan. There was sacking at the windows, and the peeling front door hung drunkenly on its hinges. Many people shared the squalid dwelling, sleeping, squabbling, boozing, swearing at the hordes of scruffy children. Family and in-laws, liking, loving, hating, managing to exist, determined to survive.

Next door were the Lambs: like the Kings, overcrowded, filthy and running alive. Lambs and Kings were deadly enemies and they fought it out regularly on Saturday nights. The children were no better and no worse than their parents and it was their pleasure to battle over the unsaleable items in Charlie's back yard.

A couple of doors along, the Peels' place. Still overcrowded, but you could approach them without feeling you'd get your throat slit given half a chance. Aggie and Clem prided themselves as being the salt of the earth. 'Some salt!' Nan was heard to say. Still, big Mrs Peel and her wretched little Clem were close, for all the outside world might think otherwise. As she walked by, Harry came out, saw Poppy and whistled. She smiled, accepting the compliment.

'Wotcher, Poppy,' he said. 'You back again?'

'I think so,' she replied easily and smiled into his black eyes. Harry grown up didn't look so bad, but he was a tricky customer. His only saving grace so far as she could tell, was that he loved his mum and stuck up for his dad.

'He'll do anything for his own,' Nan said. 'Even for young Julie, and that's a laugh for a start! Like oil and water, they are. But she stands up for her brother, does Julie. Says you can't blame him for his ways because he's scared we'll all think he's an obedient little weed like his dad.'

'How's tricks, Poppy?' Harry asked.

'Not all that special, now Sandy's gone back to sea,' she replied. 'I miss going to work a bit, but Sandy insists I stay with Nan, so –'

'They want a waitress at the Blue Diamond, now Nellie Dukes is up the duff. Why don't you try there?'

'Because I know what the Blue Diamond waitresses get up to after they've finished waitressing. That's why.'

'That's only lies and scandal, Poppy. Anyway, it looks like Mother Dukes might leave, too. She works in the kitchen.' He grinned knowingly. 'I'll give the old girl another couple of weeks on the outside. Mouthy she is, too mouthy by half. Jay'll get to hear about it and out she'll go.'

'Well, from all I've heard about Jay Wray, he'll enjoy giving an old girl the boot. He treats women like dirt, and eats

241

them up like hot dinners by all accounts. My goodness, Harry, the company you keep!'

'What about you?' he asked silkily. 'Daniel Devere's the same lucky sod as always. Girls seem to see him as some kind of Valentino. Run after him, they do. Mind you, I don't do so bad myself.'

'Lucky old you!' Poppy laughed and walked on.

Aunt Nan was black-leading the range when Poppy got in. There was hearthstone to hand and emery paper to make the fender gleam. She looked up and smiled.

'So there you are. Are you feeling all right? Not sick?'

'Not too bad. I asked Charlie about a job as you suggested, but he can't afford to give me work. This lolling about doing nothing is killing me, but since customers are few and far between these days, I'd just get in the way. Oh, I've just bumped into Harry Peel.'

'Then you'd best wash yourself all over with carbolic. Always hanging round Jay Wray's place, and, I'd swear, up to no good. Little stinker, he is. Aggie's all right, and Clem, and young Julie's turning out real nice. Not like them Davies girls. I hear that young Jessica's as bad as her sister these days. If I was Mrs Davies, I couldn't bear to walk down the street.

'Nan.' Poppy hastily changed the subject. 'I feel fidgety and I don't now what to do with myself. Do you think it would be all right if I went along to see Daniel again?'

'If he's not busy, he'll welcome you with open arms. Why are you asking me?'

'You know what they are round here, and that Vi Smith is gunning for me already. So –'

'And you can't handle that sort?' Nan gave a wicked little laugh, 'Don't tell me you ain't my kid, Poppy Swift! Go on, walk down to see him. Cheer yourself up!'

Poppy walked through the huge wrought-iron gates of Devere's Children's Home and along the gravelled pathway to the caretaker's cottage. When she knocked on the door, Daniel opened it almost at once and beamed when he saw her.

'Good Lord,' he joked, 'you again! How are things, young'un?'

242

'I feel a bit older and wiser these days,' she told him as she followed him to his kitchen and sat down. 'But it's good to be home.'

Blue imps danced in his eyes. 'Really? Changed, haven't you? As I remember, you couldn't wait to get out of Jezebel Street.'

'Now you're laughing at me,' she flared. 'I'm still a child to you, aren't I?'

'Not a bit of it,' he teased. 'I can tell that now you're a real woman of the world, and married as well, and a really lovely little thing.' He reached out and ruffled her hair as he always did. 'I bet the blokes Hackney way told you that too. I'm glad Sandy won out.'

To change the subject, she looked round at the neat cleanliness of the room. 'Do you manage this place by yourself, or does Nan give you a hand?'

'Nan's got enough on her plate, matey, and well you know it. This place taught me to keep neat and tidy when I was no bigger than a matchstick. And also –' he winked – 'various friends who visit have been known to give a helping hand. Know what I mean?'

She went as red as fire. 'What I really came to ask,' she said, 'is whether Lenny is well enough to have visitors these days? Nan tells me he's been very poorly again.'

'We'll go and see,' he told her and held her under the arm when they left the cottage and walked to the main building.

It was cheerful-looking inside and quiet too, since most of the children were at school. Lenny was stretched out on a full-length wickerwork wheelchair. It was a marvellous contraption and clearly Daniel's doing. He did have his good side!

Lenny's face was pink rather than the putty-grey it had been before, but he was very small for his age. Now he was looked after properly his hair shone and was quite fair. His eyes were empty and vague.

'Hello, Lenny,' Poppy said softly. 'Remember me?'

Lenny's wide-eyed emptiness continued.

'He's been like this off and on ever since his people left,' Daniel said quietly. 'Poor little devil. We're doing all we can.'

The matron, Miss Finn, who was well liked and well known locally bore down on them. 'Time for Lenny's medicine and then he must have a little nap,' she said firmly.

'That means we'd best shove off,' Daniel laughed. 'Matron is boss round here.'

Back in the cottage, Poppy said quietly, 'You're very special, Daniel, looking after the children and seeing that they get a better deal in life. I admire you, and I've learned one thing. I could never do it. Never be a sort of Florence Nightingale, I mean. It would just about break my heart. But I'd like to help in any other way. I'm not capable of –'

'You'll learn to be all things rolled into one once your nipper's born,' he said, chuckling. 'Our little Poppy a mum, eh? Have you been round to see Dr Fox?'

'There's no need. When it's time, Nan will take over. She'll get the midwife and – oh, be quiet, Daniel! I don't want to talk about all that!'

'All right, let's talk about much more important things,' he teased. 'How are things with Charlie?'

'He's having a job to make ends meet, just like everyone else.'

'I tell you, matey, it's dog eat dog in this world. I reckon if it keeps up, the fur will fly.'

'And you'd like to be in the thick of it?'

'No,' he told her. 'These days, my first duty is to the children here. The poor little perishers, boys and girls, who've known nothing but the hard knocks of life. Thank God your young'un will always have love and care.' His teeth flashed through his beard as he grinned and added, 'And a nice old uncle Daniel as well.'

A short time after that Poppy hurried away and found herself praying. 'Please God, don't let the baby have white eyelashes. Let them be dark like mine. Then no one will start questioning Sandy and me.'

She felt too sick and worried to go and see Bill.

Sandy's first letter came. The *Vanessa* was an old rust-bucket, he said, but she would do. He and Onions were chuffed because the skipper was a real fair-minded bloke. Onions and Annie were going to get married next leave. And yes, he and his mate were seriously thinking about going on shorter runs. Was Mother all right? Was Poppy keeping well? It was signed 'With love from Sandy your husband'.

At a full seven lines, it was a masterpiece, Poppy thought and smiled. Dear Sandy, she missed him a lot.

Right out of the blue, Edna showed up.

'Got the sodding sack!' Her words shot out like bitter bullets. 'Nothing was said open like, but it was found out I was mates with you. There's a rumour going round that Slimey-guts's wife is gunning for Burney too. She's going to forbid the workers to go to Tony's at dinnertimes. Mark my words, Burney's going to up sticks to save ol' Tone.'

'She can't forbid –'

'No? You just watch the old cow! They need their jobs, so they'll do as they're told. I would have hung on, given the chance. You know how it is with my ma, she needs every brass farthing. But that woman's like a ferret, in for the kill. You mustn't half have got under Carson's skin. I bloody well hate her!'

'If you must know,' Poppy said quietly, 'I hate myself. I'll ask Nan if you can stay here with me. If it isn't all right, we'll move somewhere else. Oh, and there might be a job in a club called the Blue Diamond. Only kitchen work, but better than nothing, eh? I'll go and see Harry Peel later on.'

'A job?' Edna's mouth was open. 'Well, why ain't you snapping it up?'

'Because the Blue Diamond has a bad reputation, because the job's probably horrible and –'

'I'll take anything, anything! Don't try and put me off.'

'I'm being honest with you, Edna. The club's a dive. And I have other plans.'

'Like what?'

'Like going to a nice old man I know, and begging him to let me dig up a field or two.' She laughed, then threw her arms round Edna. 'Oh, I'm so happy to have you here!'

'That's all right then,' Edna replied and grinned.

The door swung open and Nan came in. Her knees were aching, so she was not her usual bustling self. Nice worldly-wise old Edna took over.

'Mrs Eden,' she said and hurried to her, 'let me take your

shopping basket. I'm Edna. I'm sure Poppy has told you about me? She's told me all about you!' Her smile stretched from ear to ear. 'Funny? I can't see your halo.'

'Blow me,' Nan groaned, 'you don't half lay it on.'

'No, I'm telling the truth as I see it. I hope as how you take to me as much as my mum took to Poppy. 'Ere, Poppy, don't sit there gawping, get your aunt a nice cup of tea. While you're doing that I'll take Nan's coat, see her comfy, then get out the wedding pictures.' She turned back to Nan, having been well schooled by Poppy's letters. 'I know the wedding's old news, but Poppy here forgot to bring them along. Ain't that daft? Now I've done it for her!'

Poppy made tea, hugging herself. Edna had a way with her. She knew how to make friends – look how she had approached Poppy. Poppy knew then that Edna would be staying at number two Jezebel Street. Edna had shown sheer genius by talking about her mum.

The next day Edna went off to the Blue Diamond, which was situated in a part of the High Road called the Blue Row. Poppy caught a tram to the Town Hall. From there she would take the walk to Leyton Marshes and Bill's place.

She found him bending over one-inch drills.

'Globes ready for summer pulling, Bill?' she asked as though she had never been away, and, before he could reply, hugged him.

He seemed thinner, but well enough. He had always been quiet and shy.

'Poppy, my dear,' he said in his calm, gentle way, 'how very nice to see you. Let us to go the house so you can meet Beth.'

She linked her hand through his arm as they began walking to the house.

'Next month I'd like to be helping to sow the long-type beetroots, that's if you'll have me, of course. I need a job, Bill, and I can start right away. Oh, please say yes. I've been reading and studying all the time I've been away. I fell in love with this place the very first time I set my feet on it. Say something, Bill!'

'We will talk about it, my dear,' he said.

Sandy lay on his bunk, remembering. His thoughts went back to that small hotel. Everything had been so good that night, so wonderful when he and Poppy made love. He could see their room now. There had been a filtered greyness of early dawn when he opened his eyes. Poppy was asleep next to him. He remembered the ethereal silver of her body half turned towards him, almost luminous. She looked fragile, a bit too much like Ros, and he felt the need to grab hold of her and hang on.

He had watched her for a long time. And in the waiting silence there was only their breathing, soft and tremulous, and he could smell the heady sweetness of the jasmine perfume she wore. It was a perfume he had brought back for her, a scent that reminded him of the places he had wandered through abroad.

He had been unable to look away from his wife. Her lids had fluttered open, and she had stared at him. Her eyes were deep black shadows and as he cupped her face in his hands, he could see no expression in them.

He wanted her with an angry, aching want that he had never experienced before, although he had enjoyed some gorgeous creatures in his time. He had reached out and put his arms round her possessively. It was remarkable how cool her body felt – cool and firm and fragrant.

Her fingers had lightly fluttered against his cheek, then her arms closed tightly about him. He could feel beneath him the ripe, warm firmness of her breasts and thighs, and he had kissed her as a lover should. He could see her eyes now, wide and imploring, and she had whispered, 'You . . . you're not sorry, Sandy?'

'Quite, quite sure,' he had told her and meant it.

'Say that again.'

He had said it again, then felt the almost imperceptible yielding of her body to his.

'I want you so much,' he had said hoarsely, but she had not answered.

It had been a long time before she spoke next, then she had whispered, 'Do you think this will be for always?'

'If that's what you want,' he had promised, deep down determined never to let her go.

'Then it will be for always. But, Sandy, you won't expect – I mean, you won't ask for what I can never give, will you?' Her tone became more anxious. 'You understand that –'

'That you and I have made a bargain,' he had replied, feeling as if cold water had been dashed in his face. 'I'll never forget that, Poppy. It doesn't matter, girl. Really! Now come here.'

But it did matter, he thought. It mattered, and it hurt like the devil. Ye gods! he thought. She had reckoned on his agreeing to a kind of workmanlike attitude to their relationship. She was prepared to accept what she had to, but that was about it.

And knowing her so well, he understood that from then on, he would have to keep up a pretence, of going along with it all. Act as though taking her was due payment for the bargain they had made. It was that or lose her. He knew that he would never want that.

Right then and there he cursed Carson to hell and back. He was still cursing when Onions woke up.

Chapter Fourteen

It was a dreadful disappointment to sit there and learn that there was no job with Bill. He was merely allowing things to 'tick over' these days. Besides –

Poppy sat with Bill digesting all that he told her. Suddenly she was beginning to feel excitement, a tinge of daring, a sense of an adventure more wonderful than her wildest dreams. She listened very carefully as he went on.

'As it stands, Poppy, imagine Jack Hayhurst's land as T-shaped, the top length stretching along my borders and going to the banks of the River Lea. That's no problem. But the stem of the T cuts right through the middle of my land. Mr Hayhurst senior has always allowed me to rent it at a nominal price, but now he's gone, and his son Jack wants to sell up. When he does, my land will be cut in half. It won't seem the same, and frankly, my dear Poppy, I don't see the need to carry on.'

'But why, Bill? You can buy the strip that splits yours in two and it will all belong to you.'

'It is to be sold en block. My dear, I ask myself, to what purpose do I wish to own not only the strip, but all that extra ground? I was seriously thinking of letting some of my own acreage go, and just using a plot or so to potter round.'

'You can't do that,' she said fiercely. 'You really can't! It would be a terrible shame.'

'Why not? I was rather ill a while ago and it made me think. What is the point of it all? I have no heir, so no one will care very much about Bannerman's, and it will all go back to nature when I'm gone.'

'I care! Oh, Bill. I'm so sorry you feel that down! You've got years ahead of you yet. Charlie told me that you were under the weather, and now I know why. It must feel as if Jack Hayhurst is cutting your soul in half. Well, we won't let it happen, will we? We can get round it.' Her heart began thumping as she asked him, 'Bill, how long have you known me?'

'For as long as I've been supplying Charlie, my dear.' He smiled. 'And I was tremendously sad when you left me to spread your wings elsewhere. Still, you never let me down even then, and sent Beth to me. She is a treasure and, young as she is, she mothers me. She has her own living quarters upstairs, you know. Small but adequate, and I pray that she never leaves me. I trust her implicitly.'

'Do you trust me?'

'Of course I do. Why?'

'You know you showed me how to open an account at the bank? How I've always been on and on about saving up? I'm rich, Bill. I've saved up nearly four hundred and sixty pounds all by my own efforts. Would it be enough to save the piece in the middle? Perhaps even buy me a little part of it? You can have every penny. I mean it, I really do. I love this place and I've always longed to try out the things I've learned from the book you gave me. Will it be enough to save the day?'

He was staring at her, his faraway eyes holding little silver stars, but he shook his head.

'Poppy, you're too sweet and generous by half. Don't you understand? It isn't the money. I have enough for that. It's just that – well, there seems no point.'

'But I'd be here every day Bill, we could work and plan together. And – and you may not have an heir, but some time in August, I will! You shall be my baby's godfather, how about that? In fact, you could be my baby's second granddad if you like.' She drew in a deep breath and added, 'You see, Baby won't have a grandfather on Sandy's side simply because his dad is always at sea. You've got to let it happen, Bill. Don't you see? I love to work, but going up and down like a monkey on a stick has no point for me either. I could learn from you! Progress!'

'You would really hand over every penny of your savings

to help me and be part of this place?' he asked softly. 'My dear!'

'I'm game if you are, Bill. We can go to the bank together and you can sort everything out from there.'

'Your faith in me is outstanding,' he told her, 'and that in itself has worked miracles. I will take your life savings, Poppy, on one condition. And that is that you will become my partner, not in the one central strip, but of the whole.'

'But that would be too much, Bill! I didn't want, I mean, I –'

'You shall be my partner, and I will have an heir to work for. I would like that very much. We'll see just what we can make of things together, eh? You have given me incentive, Poppy, something I have been lacking for a very long time.'

'Oh, Bill!' She wept and could think of nothing further to say.

Bill was a new man. He had taken over the reins, accepted Poppy's money with dignity and Bannerman & Swift's Smallholding was born. Poppy was brimming over with enthusiasm. Her days were full. She loved helping with the hardest of chores, labouring from dawn to dusk. But as April made ready to bluster itself out of the year, Poppy found herself wanting to slow down.

Bill, who had taken on four men and was spending money freely on the project, began talking about getting more glass.

'We're going to need more customers, the rate we're going,' Poppy said, pleased. 'Especially for flowers.'

'I was thinking of tomatoes, cucumbers and things like that,' he teased in his gentle, old-world way. 'However, if you insist, we could become specialists in carnations and pinks. They're scented and beautiful, just the kind of thing you like. We have good rose-growing soil, but we'll make more out of the others. At this stage it's profits we need.'

'May we have some pink roses in a little patch somewhere?' she asked wistfully. 'For Ros?'

'Leave it to me, my dear,' he told her. 'Off you go and talk to Beth. You really are doing too much.'

So Poppy was pleased to go and find big, bosomy, bonny Beth, who had not yet been able to pin down her Harry Peel.

251

Poppy whiled away the time telling Beth the latest news. Vi Swift and Nan had met in Charlie's once and pointedly ignored each other. Charlie had made Vi go red by calling her his 'new-found relation' at the top of his voice when the shop was full.

'He kissed her full on the lips.' Poppy chuckled at the memory. 'Deliberately daring her to disown him, he was. She almost fell over Rags in her haste to leave the shop, and she's never been back since.'

'How do you get on with your mother-in-law?'

'She's a dear. Under Vi's thumb, of course, and scared of her own shadow, but I'll bring her out of herself one day, I know I will. Perhaps the baby will help; Sandy reckons it might. He writes me postcards every chance he gets.' Poppy laughed richly and added, 'And I can all but tell word for word what they'll say.'

'But you're in his thoughts and that's what matters, Poppy.' Beth sighed. 'It's a pound to a penny, Harry forgets all about me most of the time.'

Her words pulled Poppy up short. She felt treacherous as she recognised that most of the time she didn't think about Sandy. He was there in the background of her mind, comforting and reliable. With Nigel, she had mooned about the man, dreamed and romanced about him every minute of the night and day. Been on fire for him, longed for him – and sometimes she did even now, in spite of realising what he was like. Sandy had more character in his little finger than Nigel had in the whole of his form. Sandy was stability incarnate. In his absence, Poppy could focus on her job. She had another idea for expansion.

'I'd best be going,' she told Beth, and jumped up. 'Are we going to have meat pie this evening? I only want a couple of hours off.'

'Liver and bacon because it's good for you,' Beth told her firmly, then relented. 'But there's your favourite apple dumplings and custard for afters. It's a good job you enjoy your journey back home at night. You need to work of all the food you're packing away these days.'

'I'm eating for two, didn't you know?' Poppy laughed.

252

'It shows,' Beth teased. 'Slow down! Where are you off to in such a hurry?'

'To the Blue Diamond. I want to see Edna and find out who supplies the kitchen with veg. I understand they serve meals as well as drinks, so there might be a chance for us to get a toe in the door. Bill's only supplied greengrocers up to now, but there's cafés galore and clubs, and if we get Jay Wray's place it will be as good as an open sesame to the whole area.'

'You should be keeping quiet these days, not get het up about future plans. Besides, there's certain expert people trained to go round knocking on doors and that. You've never done that sort of thing.'

'Someone once told me that I'd make a good saleslady, so now's the time to try it out. Oh, Beth, that's how I can really help things along. I'm getting a bit past being much help with the heavy work, but I can go the rounds.'

'You don't half go on!' Beth laughed. 'I thought you were just wanting to have a little heart-to-heart with your mate.'

'Edna's very busy these days,' Poppy replied light-heartedly. 'A chap named Gus, I understand. She's even taken him home to see Nan, which says it all. I never dreamed it was possible, but Nan and Edna get on like a house on fire.'

'Gus? Oh, he's a great big brute. The chucker-out!'

'I wouldn't care if he was a chimpanzee so long as he makes Edna happy. Well, I really must go, Beth. I can't wait for those apple dumplings of yours. I'll see you when I get back.'

Poppy, sitting at a small table opposite Harry Peel, felt let down. This place had a reputation, but there was certainly nothing wild and wanton going on. Suddenly a thrill of unease went through her. Reggie Parker was sitting alone at a table by the door. Of all people, Poppy thought, Reggie Parker! I can't bear the way he stares. He's always watching me. The taxi driver's face was as expressionless as ever, but his eyes glittered in a strange way. Poor Reggie, it was said that he'd been a bit off beam ever since the war. Driving for horrible old Mr Tilsby couldn't help much either. Tilsby!

Nigel's cousin! Oh, dear heaven, was there, could there be a reason for all this?

'What's up, Poppy?' Harry asked. 'You look a proper misery-guts. Don't you like it in here?'

She pulled herself together with an effort, dismissing her fears as silly, and looked around. The Blue Diamond was dimly lit, with shadowy people sitting at tables. The men looked quiet and secretive, the women preening and self-conscious, as if hoping to be seen despite the gloom. Poppy found herself thinking that the Peels, Lambs and Kings had the best of it. Right now they would be roistering in the Coach and Horses, determined to drown their sorrows and kick up their heels, shout vulgar jokes, have a singsong, then a row and, to top the lot off, watch someone having a barney at chucking-out time. Rowdily cheering on the loser, betting on the winner, they would go hell for leather down the road when the local bobby showed his nose. Oh yes, they'd be having fun all right. But this lot? Even the painted-up waitresses were unfriendly, at least at the tables where women sat. The men were greaseballs, she thought, in their black suits and bow ties, and enough to put anyone off.

Harry had ordered a Scotch and a sweet white wine for Poppy. He was proud to be with her and showed it. She mellowed towards him. She had asked to come here simply because Edna had said that only people Jay Wray met personally could get any ins. Well, it had occurred to her that as well as vegetables, the owner might be persuaded to buy ferns and flowers to decorate the club, so she was hoping to meet him and get a fabulous standing order for Bill. The moment she had stepped inside she had hated the whole atmosphere, but that was beside the point. She must at least be courteous. She lifted her glass and smiled across the table at Harry.

She hadn't tasted sweet white wine since she and Nigel – She hastily brushed the memory away and bit her lip to stop it trembling. There was no room for broken hearts in the scheme of things, she told herself fiercely. She would continue as she always had, look to the future and to the devil with the past.

Harry was leaning back in his chair trying to catch

everyone's eye. Not many who passed even glanced in his direction. He lit a Players Weight with a flourish and winked at her.

'You've done me proud, Poppy. Every bloke here must be jealous of me. Wait till Jay sets his mince pies on you. You're just his type.'

'You're very irritating when you speak like that,' she told him. 'I know from Edna what the kitchen needs are. I merely wanted to see the interior of this club. It needs brightening up a great deal. Each table should at least have a few flowers. As it is, the whole place looks furtive.'

'Must you think of business all the time and talk so posh?' he complained, then grinned. 'How's about forgetting Sandy and being my bit of fluff for a change? The whole street reckons as how you could do with a man.'

'Harry!' she spluttered, outraged. 'Don't you dare –'

' 'Course,' he continued regardless, 'everyone knows how it is with Daniel. He's so dead set on helping them kids that he's keeping you at arm's length. Mustn't do anything to get the officials questioning his morals, must he? Lose his position of trust else. Poor old you! The whole bleeding world knows as how you see him once a week, also your scared rabbit of a ma-in-law once a week, and the rest of your time you're slaving over Bannerman's. I reckon Nan thinks you're some sort of stranger seeing as how you must see her about five minutes a day.'

'Have you finished?' Poppy asked him in a quietly dangerous tone. 'I want very much to fly at you and teach you a lesson you'll never forget, but you're not worth me showing myself up for. Especially here. What Beth sees in you I'll never know. She's a fine and lovely person whereas you are one of the nastiest little worms I know. And since I find you and this place distasteful to a degree, you may take me home – now!'

'Well, well,' a velvet-smooth masculine voice drawled from behind her. 'I'm sorry we're such a letdown, Mrs Swift.'

'Wotcher, Jay.' Harry was leering at the man who had approached so silently.

Poppy looked up at the man who was, so it was said, into every crooked deal possible. He was handsome in a

255

Mediterranean way. His straight black hair was well greased and brushed firmly away from his forehead. His eyes were dark and compelling. His thin moustache served to accentuate his strong, even, white teeth. He had an aura of power about him, and a kind of malignant charm. He was arrogantly eyeing her over and undressing her with his eyes. He smiled, nodding with approval. 'You are the beautiful doll Harry described,' he told her. 'I understand you wish to do business with me?'

'Forgive me, Mr Wray,' she said, and stood up. 'Harry made a mistake. I don't wish to do business with you, now or ever.' She turned to Harry, eyes flashing. 'My coat, please, Harry.'

'Stay where you are,' Jay Wray told Harry smoothly, then he smiled and laid his hand on Poppy's shoulder. 'Not so fast, Mrs Swift. You misunderstood. We would be delighted to do business with Bannerman & Swift. Will you come to my office and discuss the matter in a purely professional way?'

His expression was such that she knew what he had in mind. Certainly not vegetables and flowers!

People were looking in their direction now. With cool deliberation Jay Wray put his other hand on her shoulder. He was smiling and confident, and looking her over in a very proprietorial manner. 'If you play ball with me, I'll play ball with you.'

She wanted none of it. He was rumoured to be a kind of ruler over this territory and of all the local crooks and criminals. No one had been able to pin any proof on him, of course. He had been getting away with it for years because all his henchmen were too ignorant and scared. According to his reasoning she should by now be either falling at his feet in sheer gratitude, or else shivering in her shoes. Some hopes! she thought. Staring him directly in the eye, she said quietly, 'Let go of me. I said, let go!'

He did so and as she stood up to face him he suddenly pulled her close against him. He put his mouth close against her ear and whispered sibilantly, 'My dear Mrs Swift, I know what you really want. Why else would you bother to come here? After making Carson jealous, are we? Pussycat, you've come exactly to the right place!'

256

Shocked and distressed, she went rigid. The people at the nearest table were smirking, believing that Jay Wray was kissing her ear. He wasn't. He went on, quietly confident, 'I can make bells ring for you, doll, and I'm going to.'

'No!' she gasped. 'Never!' and tried to pull away.

To give him credit, Harry growled, 'Leave it, Jay. She ain't like that!'

The man ignored her and hissed even closer to her ear, so that she winced as his hot breath tickled her cheek.

'Believe me, doll, you'll do as I say because you wouldn't want your sailor to know about Carson, would you? Or your neighbours to learn whose kid you've got tucked away in there.'

Shocked to the core, she wondered wildly how he knew her secrets. He was leering confidently now, knowing he had her in his power. Well, he damned well knew wrong!

She smacked him hard across the face and, ignoring Harry, stormed out. As she slammed the door behind her she caught a glimpse of the stone-faced Reggie Parker still sitting by the exit. He must have seen everything, she thought bitterly, and would in all probability tell his loud-mouthed mum. Nan would get to know and then the cat would be among the pigeons. Nan wouldn't give twopence for her explanation that getting the Blue Diamond's custom would be a boost for Bannerman & Swift's Smallholdings. Not Aunt Nan! She'll probably threaten to box my ears for coming to such a dive, and I wouldn't blame her for that! Poppy smiled angrily through her tears.

She ran all the way home, but the terror stayed with her and the questions spun round in her mind. How did Jay Wray know all about her? Was he in cahoots with Nigel? No! Not by the tone of his voice. He hadn't seemed to like Nigel much. So, was he trying to get one over him? Of course Mr Tilsby was the connection there. Horrible, fat, foul Mr Tilsby who liked easy girls, who used them and passed them on, either to Jay Wray or – Nigel? No! her heart screamed. He loves me. Not Nigel, no, no, no!

The lights were out when she reached home and flew upstairs to her bedroom. I've got to take hold of myself, she thought wildly, I must. Oh, God, what am I going to do?

Charlie must never know the truth, nor Nan. It will kill them if they ever found out. It would kill me. As if seeking comfort, she lay her head on Sandy's pillow, but she was still feeling sick with fear. She hadn't heard the last of Jay Wray, she knew that. Especially because he fancied her, she knew that too.

She heard Edna come in, calling 'Night' to Gus and clattering into the downstairs front room. Then the springs of the sofa that had been a bed for them all in its time groaned. As a menial in the Blue Diamond Edna was sure to hear of the scene in the club.

'Please, God, help me,' Poppy whispered. 'I'll die with shame if Charlie ever finds out. He'll never call himself my old man again. Please, God, don't let Charlie ever find out.'

Since she couldn't sleep, she wrote to Sandy, telling him everything. She finished with:

> Honestly, it seems harder and harder to get rich. I only wanted to help Bill sell lots more things. With my own savings, Sandy, not that £1,000! I'm never going to use that for anything to do with the baby either. It's our baby, yours and mine. The money Nigel gave me will go to a good cause one day. Something that will have very little to do with you or me. But I'm determined, and I'll work like a horse until I can match that £1,000 through my own efforts. That's the reason and the only reason I was at that club. Now it looks like I'm in it up to my neck. I wish you were here . . .

When morning came, local tittle-tattle was out of everyone's mind. The Trades Union Congress had called for a national strike. Now it was on, full blast. The government met the situation head on.

'The bastards called out the troops!' Vic Parker was heard yelling down Jezebel Street soon afterwards. 'Bleeding soldiers with guns on guard at the railway, everywhere. The wicked sods are treating us worse than Germans. I hope as how they all rot in hell!'

It all went over Poppy's head. She was too worried about the hornets' nest she might have stirred up. But everything seemed to have gone quiet.

Then out of the blue a parcel was delivered by post. It had a local postmark and she tore it open. A present? From whom? It was her coat and a letter. Red-faced, she read:

We were seen, doll, by witnesses who are prepared to swear that you and me are close. Come to your senses and to me. I'll be waiting impatiently.
Jay.

She did no more than put the letter in an envelope with a scribbled, 'See what I mean?' and posted it off to Sandy. Let Jay Wray tell his lies to the whole world, she thought defiantly, I'll never knuckle under to a slug like that, not even for Nan or Charlie.

After that she filled her days working with Bill. She felt secure with her old friend and Beth, in the cold, bracing air. She worked round the clock, and when not working she wandered down the rough track that led to the river with its rushes and overhanging trees newly covered in green. Here she would sit on a lichen-covered stump and take in slow, deep breaths until the fear of Jay Wray and the rest of the world receded, and past and future were cut off.

Existence in the present moment gave everything an extreme vividness and purity. She felt clean and wholesome, all sins absolved. Content to sit and watch the swans gliding by like the shadowy figments of dreams, she would dream dreams of when she had been happy and in love and the whole universe had seemed to be singing with joy. Then Bill would come and find her and, without a word, sit at her side. They would stay together, like islands, self-contained, whole and serene, respecting each others solitude, yet joined in a friendship hard to express.

At the end of the day, Poppy would return to Jezebel Street, to laugh and sing and act as though she had not a care in the world. But the fear of being found out remained, together with the fear of Jay Wray trying to press home his point. She became consumed with the desire to see Nigel and ask him how he could have told secrets to someone like Jay Wray. And it was all mixed up with the need for Sandy to stand beside her.

Before she slept, each night she would put pen to paper and

259

pour out her heart to Sandy. She would also tell him of the digging, the planting, the lovely sense she had while holding handfuls of damp earth; of the sheer exhaustion at the end of a hard-working day, the excitement of getting up each dawn to make the journey back to Bannerman's; pointing out that a mere half-ounce of Brussels sprouts seed would give seven or eight hundred plants. All it needed was hard work and care and fish netting to stop the birds from taking the seedlings. And while she wrote she thought tenderly of Sandy, and wondered what he was doing and where he was at . . .

Sandy and Onions, off duty, stood side by side, gazing out to sea. From time to time the full moon showed through the gaps in the racing storm clouds, casting silvery light on the white-topped waves. The old rust-bucket rolled steadily on her course.

'What's up?' Onions asked. 'What did she write about? You ain't been yourself since we got mail.'

'Wasn't thinking about home at all,' Sandy lied. 'Just about it's going to be a dirty night.'

'Usually is in this old crate. Come off it, Sand.'

'God's truth, mate. The wind was north-east, now it's east. We've been shipping some pretty heavy seas –'

'Oh, shut up! The wind's on the port quarter, where it should be.'

'But rising and it's getting on for eight bells and Third Mate will be taking over the watch. So –'

'Come off it,' Onions argued. 'You're like a bear with a sore arse. And it ain't nothing to do with the weather. That's Cap's business, not ours. So what is it with you?'

'It's personal,' Sandy growled. 'I've got to sort it. All right?'

'Want a fag? Come on, bloody well cheer up! There ain't nothing we can do about home right now. All right?'

Sandy grunted and shook his head. Onions knew when to hold his tongue. He lit a cigarette and inhaled. Something was up with old Sand and he took a guess that it had to do with that wife of his, Poppy, who always took pains to talk as if she had a plum in her mouth. The lovely redhead who smiled like an angel and had a will of steel. Sandy had taken

260

on a right'un when he'd married his Poppy. But if it was true what Annie thought, then Sand had got the end of the stick what stank.

'She's real nice, Les,' Annie had said after the wedding. 'But she don't love him, not really. Not all wholehearted like I love you.'

The last part of his girl's speech had been the bit that really counted. He'd dismissed the rest as idle speculation. Now, he wasn't so sure. If Annie had hit it spot on, it was a bloody shame. They didn't come better than Sand. Onions counted himself lucky to have Sandy as a mate. He not only liked him, he admired him, and if he were in trouble he'd rather confide in Sandy Swift than in any other man. Sand's standards were high.

These days foreign shore leaves meant a good old booze-up, but not very much else. Sand was old-fashioned and believed in being faithful to a wife. Onions often slipped, but he wasn't married – yet! When he was it wouldn't make no difference because Sandy'd drop dead before he preached. He understood human nature and its weaknesses. He was a good-natured, peace-loving man, but God help anyone who upset him. Like the bloke that had been ill-treating a horse, last shore leave. A foreign sod with a horse that was all but knackered anyhow. Sandy had knocked the living daylights out of the cruel bastard, and paid good money to have the nag put out to grass. Soft old Sandy, a real gent.

Nan was in her chair, the cats snoozing at her feet. Nan was looking tired these days and Poppy went and put an arm round her shoulders.

'Nan, you're always telling me to ease up, but what about you?'

'I can't read books and write like you. All them letters to Sand and then saucy cards you post to that Burney bloke are fun to you. I can't do nothing like that, nor knitting and stuff like Floss. I have me house an' me job.'

'But it's too much, Nan!'

'Working's in my blood. Put an old horse out to grass and it dies of boredom. That sort of thing's not going to happen to me. 'Sides, I have bills to pay and –'

'Why won't you let me buy you this house?' she asked quickly, thinking of the profits Bill had insisted on sharing. 'I could do it easily in a few payments. I wanted to do that the moment I came back home, and all I got was a flea in my ear. I would have preferred to see you set, much more than buy a piece of Bill's land.'

Nan looked at her very directly. 'I don't know how you've come to be such a Miss Moneybags,' she said sharply. 'And all I hope is that you come by it in an open and honest way.'

'Is that why you wouldn't let me help you?' Poppy felt the hurt cutting into her heart. 'Why you'll only take Sandy's money for rent and coal and so on? Do you distrust me that much?'

'Don't be daft! I was merely making a remark. As for you buying this house, over my dead body! This place is mine. I pay my rent, so it's mine, d'you hear? If you bought it, it wouldn't be mine. Nothing doing, girl. If you're so set on spending money, buy something for yourself. Next door to one from Flossie's will be empty soon.'

'What? Me buy something in Jezebel Street?'

'Home is what you make it, my lady. Never forget that!'

'Nan!' Poppy flounced out of the house.

In the street she bumped into Maud. Her friend had a black eye.

'Goodness!' Poppy said in quick concern. 'What happened to you?'

'I was a silly moo and walked straight into the door.'

'At the gin again, I suppose?' Poppy said flippantly but felt suspicious. 'And you talk about me not looking after myself!'

'That'll larn me to,' Maud quipped. 'You off to work? When are you going to ease up? You're looking dead harassed these days.'

'No more than you. Is your Arthur still carrying on about that new eiderdown you got off the tallyman?'

' 'Course not. He knows I only buy things for our nice home.' Maud was going pink and looking shifty, so Poppy knew it was best to leave well alone. 'They've got House-Housey at the church hall tonight,' Maud went on. 'First prize a fiver. Coming?'

262

'I might if I get back in time. Now I'm off. Musn't miss my bus.'

As she walked away, Poppy was seething. The pig! she was thinking, The mingy, cowardly pig, he's been bashing her. No wonder young Arty don't go much on his dad! I wouldn't let any man hit me! In fact I – She bit her lip and frowned, realising that in a way she was letting someone hit her – below the belt! Jay Wray was as good as torturing her with his threat. And she had been skulking about in fear and trembling, waiting for the axe to fall. Well, she'd simply have to do something about that!

As she turned the corner she came face to face with Reggie Parker. Apart from a slight dilation of his eyes, his expression remained the same. He made as though to walk on, but she put her hand on his arm.

'Reggie,' she said brightly. 'What a surprise! And there was I thinking that you were all but glued to that motorbike of yours.'

'Went for a packet of fags, mate.' His voice was low, as if rusty from disuse. 'You all right?'

'Very well, thank you. Oh! Just in case you're going to see your friend Jay Wray, you might tell him from me that I'll be along to see him one of these bright fine nights. I shall sit at one of his tables and expect a jolly good meal before he and I have a talk.' She laughed in an easy, breezy way. 'Not a threat, tell him, a promise!'

She let go of Reggie's arm, waved merrily and continued towards the bus stop. Her heart was pounding, but now she had thrown down her challenge, she was feeling her old self once more. Nothing like a good barney to cheer you up, she thought, but not tonight. Tonight I think old Maud could do with a bit of company. Pity Edna won't come along too. Edna was in love and living in a different world: the only person who saw much of her these days was Gus. Poppy smiled reminiscently to herself.

'Wotcher, Poppy. Poppy!' Poppy swung round, still smiling.

'Julie! My, what a stranger you are.'

'No, I ain't. Am only across the way most of the time. With my future in-laws, you know.'

263

'Oh? Gone that far, has it?'

'Of course.' Julie grinned. 'He's a dead duck, Poppy, and for your info, I intend to ignore his common family and stand up to him, but she's a tough nut and no mistake.'

'Takes one to know one, Julie.'

'Too right!' Julie laughed and waved goodbye as Poppy came to a halt at the bus stop. 'Ta-ta!'

'See you,' Poppy breathed and thought that just about everyone was falling in love. Still, no matter, tonight she'd be with Maud and perhaps Nan and Flossie might come along to. She would leave Jay Wray until she had decided the best way to handle him. Witnesses. Oh, yes, witnesses, he'd said. Well, she would have to see about that!

Chapter Fifteen

That evening Poppy washed and changed and made ready to go out. From her outline, seen reflected in a shop window, she still looked in shape. She had filled out all over, but there was no huge bump. She was pleased about that. She would face up to the baby, really accept it later on. Right now there were other things on her mind.

She ran downstairs and went across the road to get Maud. Arty was outside, scuffling around with Johnny Lacey. They were great mates these days. He looked up and called cheekily, 'Wotcher, Hauntie Poppy!'

'Hello, yourself,' she replied, smiling. Clearly Maud had been on to him about his H's again.

Maud was trying to cover her bruises with cream and powder and Poppy's mind flew back in time to when she had stood beside Jessica in the railway waiting room, watching her fair-weather friend doing the same thing. Jessica! What was she doing now? Clearly she and Rene had gone one step up from Mr Tilsby and Nigel. Probably they were both quite rich by now. Better to be dirt poor! she thought indignantly, and tried to dismiss her hurt and pain.

'Hurry up, Maud, we won't get places together else.'

'Oh? Who else is coming?'

'Nan and Floss – who's left her Burt for a change. And for once in their lives, Edna and Gus have an evening off together. Oh, and take no notice if Edna's on her best behaviour.'

'Best behaviour? For Gawd's sake, why?'

'She always is when Nan's around. She's far from scared

of my aunt, but she adores her and wants to be thought well of. She can really let go, though, I promise you. She sticks up for herself in no uncertain manner if the occasion demands. She's the salt of the earth, Maud, truly! But what with me working all day and Edna working nearly all night, we don't see very much of each other. Still, Edna's my greatest mate. She and a chap named Burney stuck by me in some really awful times.' Poppy stared directly into Maud's eyes, then added meaningfully, 'Just as I'd stick by you if you ever needed me. You know that, don't you?'

' 'Course I do,' Maud replied and went pink, but closed her lips like a clam.

They all met up outside Nan's.

'Blow me down,' Maud teased Gus. 'You're even bigger than my Arthur!'

And Gus, bullish, massive and slow, with the strength of ten men, but like a lamb with Edna his love, gave Maud his huge all-embracing smile. Edna, with a slick new hairstyle and done up to the nines, hung on to his arm, looking proud.

'Gawd help us!' Flossie chirped. 'What are we hanging about for? Half of Leyton will be up there by now.'

'Rubbish!' Nan replied and sniffed. 'They'll be queuing up at the King's Hall no doubt. They've got Charlie Chaplin up there.'

They turned into Skelton Street and walked up to the High Road and across, and into St Catherine's Road. Church Hall was beyond the church itself and the graveyard. Poppy's heart began beating too quickly and she averted her eyes from where Ros lay in her last sleep on earth.

It was good to get into the hall, inhaling oil-stove-warmed air, surrounded by women all clacking away nineteen to the dozen. It was all so bright and alive, raffish and rowdy. To Poppy it was light-hearted fun, being among her own kind. Gus looked out of place, too big for the seat, but aware only of the gleam in Edna's eyes. Poppy looked over at Edna, who grinned and winked. Nan was now talking to Flossie, about the price of coal of all things, and Maud? Maud was thinking about something and was best left to herself.

Maud sat quietly next to Poppy. The woman in front of her was very fat and wheezing painfully every time she inhaled.

Even so, Maud could see that she was cramming her mouth full of salted peanuts. Silly cow, she thought, nothing's worse than nuts. She'll choke herself in a minute. The woman did cough, violently, a few seconds later and Maud felt smug.

Her mind drifted back to Morry Bloomfield, the tallyman. She felt a flush tinging her cheeks. She was terrified of Morry calling again, moaning and whining about her not bringing her payments up to date. She had paid him little bits and pieces, of course, just to keep him quiet. But Morry, nice though he was, was getting into trouble with his boss, and now he'd been threatening to let Arthur know how it was. Arthur! Dear Lord, not him!

And to think, she pondered bitterly, that I've put up with Arthur all these years. She thought of her husband, of his swarthy good looks, his quick temper, his way of riding over her rough-shod, treating her like a downtrodden slave. One that had to be punished whether in the wrong or not.

She had loved Arthur dearly once – long ago. Before they were married and he had become her lord and master in the fullest sense of the word. In the beginning she had fought back, given as good as she got – till Arty was born. Since then she had given in, kept everything quiet, determined at all times to protect her son. The way Arthur had looked at the boy sometimes had filled her with dread. Still, he was on the two-to-ten shift this week. She would be home well before then.

'Here he comes!' someone yelled, then a roar from the crowd. 'Wotcher, Wally!'

Wally stepped onto the platform, a thin, wiry man with sandy hair and ruddy cheeks. Wally was a wag, everyone said so. Wally was all right! A few minutes of joking, and catcalls and joshing from the crowd, then the game began.

'Clickety-click, sixty-six; two fat ladies, eighty-eight; Downing Street, number ten; house next door, eleven it is . . .'

A good time was had by all, though no one from Jezebel Street won. Poppy was tired and ready for bed. Maud didn't seem to want to go home. Edna and Gus were willing everyone to vanish and leave them alone. Nan went next door to have a cuppa with Floss.

'By the way, Poppy,' Edna said, just before Poppy went in, 'have you heard from ol' Burn lately?'

'Not really,' Poppy replied. 'But he doesn't write all that much, does he? The hours he works for Tony and all. Besides, there's nothing much for him to answer. I just send him lots of cards.' She smiled in the street gaslight. 'Some of them are quite vulgar, I'll have you know. Still, it's my way of keeping in touch.'

'Well, I spent a whole morning writing him a long letter about me and Gus last week,' Edna said indignantly. 'And the little shit hasn't even bothered to answer. All right for some, innit?'

'Give him time,' Poppy said and yawned. 'Goodnight, you two. Goodnight, Maud.'

' 'Night,' they all said, and she went in and closed the door.

Maud walked unwillingly across the road.

Arty was freezing cold. He rubbed his feet together and buried his head under the bedclothes. He tried to pretend he couldn't hear those voices raised so harshly in the kitchen downstairs. Arty put his hands over his ears, but still had to listen. He bit his lips hard to stop himself from blubbing. I wish they wouldn't keep on and on, he thought.

Arthur Ewebank threw half-a-crown on the table. His face was mean, his eyes glinting.

'That's what I've got to last me, and you can bleeding well stand up to that bloke and tell him to sod off! And if you get anything else on the tally, I swear I'll do for you.'

'It's only because I want a lovely home for us, Arthur!' Maud's tone was defiant, but she looked trapped. It was going to happen, it always did. She could never please him. He liked to give her a good bashing. Then afterwards he'd hold her down and commit nothing less than rape. Then the tears would come, the protestations of love. 'I wish I hadn't asked you for a few extra bob,' she panted, 'but it's your fault as much as mine. You warned me never to have a pigsty, and I work my fingers to the bone on this place and –'

'Don't defy me, you saucy bloody cow. If I've told you once, I've told you a dozen times –'

She didn't wait for him to finish, but fiercely stepped

268

forwards. She was throwing her cap over the mill, caution gone. 'Yes, to the bone, Arthur! Till you can eat off my bloody floors. But that ain't good enough, is it? Is it, eh? You rotten bastard! You just need a sodding excuse, don't you?' She was verging on the hysterical now, face flushed, tears in her eyes. 'I don't get nothing for myself. It wouldn't be so bad if I did. But you keep telling me you like nice things and –'

'I slog my guts out for a bloody whore,' he snarled, 'and you as good as chuck me wages down the drain and make up to that sodding Bloomfield.'

'If you really believed that, why don't you have a go at him instead of me?' she asked fiercely. 'You rotten devil, I hate you! D'yer hear me? Hate you to hell!'

'Now we have it, cow!' There came the sound of a sharp slap and Arty heard his mother's pained shriek. 'I'm going to teach you a lesson.' Arthur was yelling at the top of his voice. 'And you won't forget it in a hurry. That I promise you, bitch!'

The noises of a beating came again.

Arty wanted to be deaf. He wanted to run down and help his beloved mum, even to kill his dad. But he had to stay put. His mum had made him promise, on her own life, that he would always keep out of the way. Had told him that Dad couldn't help himself when the booze got to his brain.

Arty winced and shivered again. In spite of trying not to, he began to blub. Tomorrow Mum would be acting as if nothing had happened, but he knew, oh yes. It would happen again and again. He stiffened, fear growing into terror. His Mum had had enough. She was standing up for herself, fighting back! And by his ferocious roar and awful-sounding thuds, Dad was really going to kill her this time.

Wild with fear, Arty jumped out of bed, ran down the stairs, along the passage and out into the street, then across the road to pound on the door of number two.

Edna opened it, staring owlishly at the boy.

'Come quick,' he panted, tears streaming down his face. 'Tell Poppy and come quick. It's Dad – Dad and Mum!'

'Do what?' Edna was standing there befuddled, not sure what to do. Then Poppy came pounding down the stairs.

'It's Mum,' Arty stammered. 'Dad – Dad's killing her!'

'Is he now?' Poppy snapped. She ran into the kitchen and grabbed up Nan's heaviest stewpan. As she ran past Edna, she cried, 'Get Gus! Get him quick, Edna. D'you hear me? Run like the devil and get Gus!'

She streaked across the road and into Maud's house. Arty had spoken the truth: Arthur had gone berserk. He was shouting and raving and punching with all his might. Maud was screaming, trying to defend herself and still fighting back when she had the chance. Her nose was streaming with blood, her eyes were closing, but she was a game'un and now had nothing to lose. But it was all too unequal and her back was against the wall. Exhausted, terrified because she had seen murder in his eyes, she was unable to stop herself from slipping down. She was growing too weak, and there was nothing more she could do.

Arthur was leaning over her, mouthing obscenities, fist raised, his back to Poppy. Without thinking, Poppy leaped up and brought Nan's stewpan down hard on Arthur's head. He roared and staggered round to face her. She stood in front of him, pan raised in readiness.

'You bully!' she panted. 'You filthy, wicked bully, Arthur Ewebank!'

'You nosy stuck-up moo!' he roared. 'Who d'you think you are?' His eyes were red and glinting as he lunged towards her. She stood her ground, green eyes flashing cold fire. As he neared, she hit him full on the face with all the force she could muster. He stopped in his tracks. Oh, dear God, she was thinking frantically, I've broken his nose.

Her heart was beating too quickly, her mouth went dry. She felt the room swaying round her and Arthur Ewebank looked as though he was going to mow her down. But he took only one step more, faltered and fell. Then Maud, Arty and Poppy were all clinging to each other and bawling their eyes out. And feeling utter relief because of the sudden presence of Nan.

'Stop that caterwauling,' Nan said briskly. 'Arty, go outside and get the clothesline. Hurry up before you dad comes to.'

Arty gave Nan one startled look and went outside like a whippet. He returned, breathless and triumphant, all but

270

tripping over the length of rope he'd cut down with a carving knife.

'Give it here,' Nan ordered. 'Then go and put the kettle on. She began tying Arthur up until he looked quite helpless. He groaned and opened his already puffed-up eyes. One of his front teeth had gone. Looking dazed, he tried to sit up, couldn't make it and collapsed, groaning, again.

'Got a headache?' Nan asked sourly. 'I hope as how you have. An' I'll tell you something else, you ain't done my saucepan no good!'

Poppy hardly knew why, but she laughed. The saucepan, the dear old thing that had faithfully cooked pearl-barley stew for years, had given up the ghost. It was hanging down, all cold, blue and defeated, hinged to its handle only by one last bent screw.

'Nan,' Poppy choked, 'if we pull it right off I'll fill it with earth and put a plant in it.'

'Nothing but a geranium,' Nan said, still sour-faced. 'A big red bushy one. Nothing less will do. It'll serve to remind me of this spiteful pig's nose. That'll learn him!'

Poppy looked at poor Arthur's bloody nose, and though it shouldn't, her little laugh grew large and out of hand. She wanted to stop, needed to, but couldn't. Then Maud started, then Nan. They stood in a circle, facing each other, shrieking and laughing and holding their sides. And in spite of the hilarity there were tears in their eyes.

For Arty, the tears had stopped. It was he who made the tea, hot, strong and sweetened with sugar as well as condensed milk. As they all sat at Maud's table and drank the tea, they gradually became calm.

Maud said quietly, 'We can't leave him like that, can we?'

'Why not?' Nan asked crisply. 'At least he's out of harm's way. You still hankering after him?'

Maud looked at Arty, whose water-streaked face and big frightened eyes told their own tale. She shook her head slowly.

'No, I'm not. I ain't mad! I've done my best for all these years. We moved from our old place, near his people up Walthamstow way, because the neighbours got to know how ... how things were. I couldn't stand that! They all used to

271

look at me knowing like, but never held out a comforting hand.'

'P'raps they were scared of the cowardly toe rag,' Nan said, and her lips went all grim and thin. 'He's a nasty piece of work. But p'raps his mother would understand? Be of some help?'

'She'd be on his side, always has been. Cow! Besides –' Maud was all seriousness now – 'I'm not budging. I love this street and I ain't moving, not ever. Not leaving my friends!'

'It'll be hard without a man's wages,' Nan told her bluntly. 'I know, girl. I've been there.'

'He's not sodding worth the effort,' Maud said quickly, then stopped and looked at Arty. 'Or am I speaking out of turn, luv?'

Arty was silently weeping again as he slowly shook his head. 'No, we don't want 'im, Mum. I don't want 'im to ever lay 'ands on you again.'

Maud turned to Poppy, smiling and defeated, her bruises, red and purple, standing out like flags. 'The little devil will never remember his H's,' she said wearily. 'I dunno what to do.' She suddenly hid her face in her hands and sobbed. 'Oh God, I just dunno what to do!'

'Have another cuppa,' Nan told her bluntly. 'And thank the good lord that young Poppy here's got the heart of a lion. Not that she should be beating up madmen in her state of health. Yes, we'll all have another drink and wait for Edna. She'll bring Gus back and he'll know what to do. It takes a man to sort out this kind of thing.'

'I don't want him hurt no more,' Maud said faintly. 'It ain't all his fault. I do keep getting nice things off the tallyman and –'

'A man what hits a woman is a coward and a bully, and has no excuses,' Nan cut in briskly. 'And as for Gus, he'll just sort of help your old man out of the house, and explain to him very clear just what'll happen if he ever tries to come back. All right?'

Maud nodded and then Poppy whispered, 'Can I go home now, Nan? I . . . feel a bit sick. I don't think I should have drunk the tea.'

'You cut off, girl, and get straight to bed,' Nan told her, and reached out to pat her cheek. 'You done good, almost as good as me in the old days, eh? There'll be no Bannerman's for you tomorrow, mind. You'll have to have a lie-in for your baby's sake. Go on! Skedaddle.'

Poppy's legs felt like jelly as she made her way back home. She crawled into the bed she had shared with Sandy and found herself needing to cry all over again. It wasn't at all ladylike to hit drunken men over the head with Nan's stewpot, she thought dejectedly. She tried to picture the snooty Mrs Carson doing such a low and common thing. Then she brushed her hand fiercely across her eyes. Whom was she trying to fool? Not herself, not anyone! All the world knew that she was Poppy Swift, born and bred in Jezebel Street. Try to better herself though she did, nothing could alter that. To think Maud actually loved the place! She closed her eyes and wished that her husband was beside her. Suddenly she badly needed the comfort of his arms.

Dawn came moist and misty and pierced with gold. Poppy awoke and lay still, wondering why she felt so drained. Then remembrance came and she jumped out of bed too quickly, became giddy, steadied herself, then dressed and went downstairs. Nan was at her usual chore, kneeling at the hearth, sifting cinders. She looked up and stared into Poppy's face.

'You all right, girl?'

'Fine. What – what happened, Nan? Did Gus –'

'It's all sorted. Arthur was shown the door.' Nan smiled grimly. 'Taken all the way to Walthamstow where his people live, he was. He won't come back here in a hurry, believe me. Gus ain't the sort of bloke you argue with when his blood's up. Good riddance to bad rubbish, I say.'

'How is Maud?'

'Took some aspirin and sleeping like a baby. Arty's with her, poor little devil. Maud and her kid are very close. It's nice to see them together. I told Arty he was to stay off school and look after his mum.' Nan gave her worldly-wise half smile. 'Took to that idea like a duck to water, he did.'

'She's going to have it hard, Nan, now Arthur's ceased to bring his wages home.'

'She's got a nice house. She'll have to get a lodger, or

scrub a doorstep or two. She'll manage because she's got to. When the chips are down something always turns up.'

In spite of Nan arguing, Poppy went to work. Not before Charlie had put in an appearance, though. His grin all but split his face in two.

'My Gawd, ducky,' he exploded, 'I always knew you was a good'un. Had a squib up your arse last night, I hear. Give Ewebank a right bashing, eh? I do hear as how your aunt's saucepan's got a dent in it the size of an 'ouse! Good on yer, kid.'

'I only tried to stop him from beating Maud,' she said primly. 'I didn't enjoy it, Dad. In fact I feel ill when I think of the mess I made of the man's face.'

'Lor' love yer, you done us proud, ducks. I don't hold with blokes beating up wives. But you shouldn't have done it in your state of 'ealth. Better take things easy from now on, eh? Clary reckons –'

'That I should put my feet up?' She laughed and kissed him. 'Not on your life!'

He just doesn't understand, she thought as she walked slowly along the lane that led to Bill's land. Neither does Nan. They simply can't realise the peace and joy and wonder of it all here. The marshes are just a stretch of grass to them, a few bushes and trees. Rabbits are just things to buy from butchers, to skin, clean, cook and eat. To them the marshes are empty splodges of nothing. They don't see the birds and insects and little furry things all getting on with it. Poppy thought of a poem she had been thrilled by at school, by John Masefield. Entranced, she had told her aunt about the lines that made her most excited.

'And it goes on, Nan, "It comes from the westlands, the old brown hills. And April's in the westlands and daffodils." Oo, doesn't it sound lovely?'

'You don't half carry on,' Nan had replied, giving poetry short shrift. 'Filling you and Ros' heads with rubbish. Living in the country would drive me stark staring mad.'

The East End is her world, Poppy thought. It's mine too, my birthplace, but I know Paradise when I see it! Perhaps my dad and Nan are the lucky ones. They are content with their lot. Unlike me.

*

274

That evening, on the way home, Poppy bumped into Harry, who was bouncing along, hands in pockets, in his cocky I'm-a-good'un way. Harry Peel wasn't so bad, not deep down, when you came to understand him. His little sister seemed to have grown up into the one with most to say for herself. She was like a little bantam-cock for real, whereas her brother mostly put it on. Julie had a will of iron and she was only a little older than Lenny, in fact. She was a worldly-wise kid already. Lenny still looked a child.

'Wotcher, Poppy,' Harry said and grinned. 'I hear as how you had a right old do last night! You half killed Ewebank, they say. Nan's been singing your praises to my mum and everyone all day. Why don't you let me take you to the Blue Diamond tonight, just to celebrate?'

'No, thank you, Harry. Too done in. Why don't you go and pay Beth a visit? You know how she feels about you – and you feel about her. Oh yes, I can see through you. I've a sneaking suspicion that if you'd only forget trying to be a kind of clever-dick like Jay Wray, you'd tell Beth the truth.'

'Mind your business,' he said gruffly. 'Women don't talk to me like that. I'm not me dad, you know.'

'I like your dad a lot, Harry, and more important, so does your mum! She told Nan once that she'd do murders for him, and that she'd make a hole in the River Lea if anything happened to him.'

'As he would for her, I reckon.' Harry's good humour returned. He leaned forwards in a conspiratorial way. ' 'Ere, Poppy, do us a favour? Jay's missus is away visiting her parents in France. At least, that's what she says. She's about as French as my arse, but Jay believes her, so there you are. Anyway, she'll be back home in about another three weeks. She's a lovely woman, and the only one in the world to have Jay by the short and curlies. Been carrying on about her homecoming and boasting that she'll look like some kind of queen. Queen of tarts, if you ask me! Anyway, she'll be wearing all the latest Paris fashions and that.' He snorted with disgust. 'That's the only time she comes slumming down in the club – to show off her clothes.'

'I'd have thought the man would insist on having her

around at all times,' Poppy observed. 'If he's so proud of her, I mean. What's the favour you're asking for?'

'You're the tastiest bit of crackling I know. You're the only one what can hold a candle to her. If you was at my table when she arrives, it'd get me some respect from Jay. Know what I mean?'

'Harry,' she said earnestly, 'in three weeks' time it's on the cards that I'll look like a barge. Besides, respect from that sort is as good as a big fat nothing! Jay Wray is a crooked person and from the looks of things, you're going the same way. Harry, you're breaking Beth's heart! And don't think I don't know why you're not asking her in my place. It's because you don't want her to actually see the rotten dump where you hang out most of the time. Go right down in her estimation, you would. And you know it!'

'Arseholes! I can't ask her because she'd miss the last bus and wouldn't be there for that old bloke she looks after. She's like living on another planet, being stuck out there. There ain't nothing ever happening in no-man's-land, like there is here.'

'That old bloke's name's Bill and he's done more for Beth than anyone. What's more –'

'Oh, I reckon ol' Bill's a good'un, and I've seen his place. To be honest, I wouldn't mind planting out things and that myself, when I'm too old to want to do anything else. But like I told Beth, I'm gonna get rich quick, and Jay's the one who's showing me the ropes. Stow all that crap talk, Poppy, let's get back to the point.'

'Which is?'

'How about in three weeks? If you look like you do now, will you come with me? It's a dead cert that Jay's wife is going to come swanning in like God's gift, and I want to make a good impression.'

'Don't be silly. I'm going to have a baby and it won't stop growing just because you want to show off. Besides, I wouldn't want to be there when Mrs Wray arrives. I wouldn't want to see Jay Wray shaking in his shoes.'

'Do what?' Harry was puzzled. 'Jay ain't the sort to shake in his shoes, not now nor never. Cool as a cucumber he is, and he knows all the tricks. I don't get you, Poppy!'

'No?' She looked surprised. 'I understand that he has all the women he fancies. Quite a lady-killer, they say. Shouldn't he be a bit bothered in case one of his fancy ladies turns up? You say that Mrs Wray holds the whip hand. So shouldn't Mr Clever-Clogs be feeling just a little uneasy?'

'Are you crackers?' Harry crowed. 'That'd be more than they dared do. Oh no, they all know their places and what side their bread's buttered, make no mistake. Now, how about you and me in three weeks?'

'Sorry, truly I am, Harry. But I really do feel all in. Of course, since I don't know my place, if I ever went to the club I might just make a scene. I think it best from now on, Harry, you forget all about ever knowing me.'

'Do what?' Harry was startled, then he remembered. 'Gawd! You clocked him one, didn't you? But he took it all in good part, Poppy! Said you was a real woman. Know what I mean? I think he quite enjoyed you sticking up for yourself.'

'I most certainly did, didn't I?' She beamed at him. 'But he didn't enjoy it, Harry, not in the least. He probably put on an act because I made him seem a fool. But I saw the look in his eyes and he was coldly, furiously angry. So you see, Harry, it would be a very good idea if you kept a million miles away from me. Besides, I rather fancy that Mr Wray has a long memory, and if you want to keep in with him –'

'I get you,' Harry said and winked, then swaggered on his way.

Harry's crazy, Poppy thought, as she walked the few steps home. He actually wants Jay Wray's respect? The man's a crook, an oaf, a bullyboy with lots of sheeplike fools all fawning round to do his bidding. He'll come a cropper one of these bright fine days. And as for his fancy floozies being frightened of him, I'd drop dead before I'd let something like him scare me off. Do business with him? I must have been mad! His sort would never scare me!

When she went in there were two letters for her. One was from Sandy, who wrote saying they'd hit bad weather, but all was well. That was it; nothing more. He never answered a thing she had written about. He's just not interested in what's going on round here, she thought, and who can blame him?

The second envelope bore its penny stamp, but this hadn't been franked. Had the post office missed it Poppy thought, or had it been delivered by hand? Its message, too, was brief and to the point.

'Thursday night,' it said. 'In my office. Eight o'clock sharp.' It was signed J.W.

Some hopes! Poppy thought grimly, lifted the hob and threw the letter into the fire. Then she took off her shoes and sighed with relief. She had told Harry no lie. She really did feel all in.

Chapter Sixteen

In no time at all it was Thursday night. In spite of determining not to be browbeaten, Poppy was distinctly uneasy. Jay Wray was a threat, an impossible, posturing threat. She knew that she had to face him, not skulk away and pray that her visit to the club had just been a bad dream. She had mulled things over during the long labour-filled days in the tomato section. The glasshouse had cocooned her; it was even now silently embracing her in a warmly private crystal world. And she busied herself, automatically nipping out side shoots, admiring the sturdy plants with their lovely leaves and clusters of little green buds. They would fruit early, be among the first of the English grown in the shops.

In spite of trying not to, her thoughts again returned to the Blue Diamond. She sensed, deep down, that even though pregnancy suited her, Jay Wray had more than one ulterior motive to his unsubtle approach. She remembered how, for the tiniest fraction of a second, his eyes had dilated when Harry mentioned her name. She had thought it unimportant – till now.

Slowly and surely, previous puzzles were making definite patterns in her mind. And not very nice ones at that. The connection between Nigel and the odious Mr Tilsby was clear enough. They were cousins, and blood was thicker than water any day. She found herself trying to argue that Nigel had never willingly taken part in Mr Tilsby's dealings. He would most certainly never sink to the level of Jay Wray. Perhaps that was it! Nigel was a superior person, a gentleman. Perhaps the egotistical Jay Wray was resentful of the fact, and needed to pull Nigel down a peg – through her! And for starters Jay was trying to make her toe the line by using threats.

Poppy had an ace up her sleeve. Sandy knew the truth, the whole truth. But Charlie didn't know, nor Nan. Poppy was in a trap of her own making. And all because she had fallen in love with Nigel.

She had sinned and she would be like meat and gravy for the Reverend Rawlins' bread. Her dad would disown her and she would see contempt in Nan's eyes. So Jay Wray was a threat – as was the weird, expressionless Reggie Parker, who seemed to be dogging her footsteps these days. Poppy's mouth went dry and she felt afraid.

Then, right out of the blue, Mr Banes' voice rang in her ears: 'Gotta be neat. Gotta be quick. Gotta be right!'

It was a little law she had tried to live by ever since. She used it outside when sowing, thinning, pruning or planting, and when just walking through life. It was a good way, a clear and confident way of dealing with things – and hard to live by when emotions got out of control. She ought to be neat and quick and right about her feelings for Nigel. Nip thoughts of him in the bud, just as she nipped out unwanted side shoots on shrubs. But he was always there, smiling confidently in the back of her mind, daring her to dismiss him, to stop adoring him.

She needed such unrealistic yearnings to be ousted by Sandy. She wanted Sandy by her now, not somewhere out there at sea. Sandy was good, Sandy was strong, Sandy made her feel confident and free of sin. Dear God, she thought desperately, how can I cope? What can I do about Jay Wray? Without Sandy here, in this particular battle, I am so alone!

Again Mr Banes' message cut clearly through her thoughts. And she knew that she had to nip Jay Wray's mischief-making in the bud.

Bill came in then, tall and thin, his trousers tucked into rubber boots. He wore no jacket or cap, but he looked toasty warm. He was wearing the navy-blue woolly jersey that Beth had knitted for him for Christmas. Bill loved that jersey. And whenever Poppy looked at it, she remembered the cardigans Nan had scrimped and saved to pay Flossie for. Poppy felt tears pricking at her eyelids and impatiently brushed them away.

'You should try to rest more,' Bill said in his calm, quiet manner. 'Just coming and going on the bus twice a day must be an effort now. Besides, you're upset. You have been for a while now. Mayn't I know why?'

'I expect it's just because I'm having a baby, Bill. You get over emotional at times.'

'No worries?'

'None at all,' she fibbed, then laughed softly. 'Why, only the other day I was offering to buy Nan's house for her out of the profits we're going to make. And since Nan wouldn't hear of it, I was thinking of a shop. Just picture it, Bill!' She was speaking too rapidly, too breathlessly, trying to hide the fact that she was in a tight corner and getting scared. 'In time we could have lots of shops where we'll cut out the middleman! Instead of buying from the wholesalers we'll stock up with our own produce. We'd go to market for the stuff we can't supply, of course. But in the main we could push the idea of home-grown for all it's worth.'

'That's a very sound idea, Poppy. We'll certainly give it careful consideration.'

'Another thing,' she rushed on, 'we could let door-to-door salesmen buy trays of ferns and other pot plants. Think of all the out-of-works who'd try their hand at anything to earn a crust! Why, the latest thing men are doing is painting people's door knockers for a few pence. So why not let them buy our plants rather than Woolworth's paint? Another thing –'

'Poppy,' he told her gently, 'they are quite splendid plans and we will go into each one very thoroughly. In the meantime –' He looked at her with his clear, honest eyes. 'In the meantime, my dear, I want you to know that I look on you as someone very special and very dear to me. If you ever need help, of any kind, I'm here. I am your friend. Poppy, do you understand?'

'Oh, Bill!' she wept and flung herself into his arms.

A little while later, when she became calm, he insisted she went home. He walked, hand on her arm, along the narrow rutted track. Then they traversed the winding, overgrown

281

lane to the main road and the bus stop. He waited until the vehicle arrived, helped her on and stood there, watching until it was out of sight. Poppy, now seated, leaned back and closed her eyes, for once glad of the excuse to have the rest of the day off.

Once she arrived home, she made a cup of cocoa, added lots of milk and was sipping it when Nan came in.

'Don't tell me you've taken time off,' she observed tartly. 'Is the world coming to an end? I hardly see you these days.'

'It's the natural hours worked on the land, Nan. From dawn to dusk. In any case, you have Edna's company now, so –'

'Edna's as much a will-o'-the-wisp as you these days. Real awkward hours she has to work at that club. Stays there till late, then back she has to go again for early-morning breakfasts. Yes, breakfasts! Some of them what's got more money than sense stop there all night, and then have a slap-up meal. It makes me sick to think of it. Them boozing and living it up all night, then gorging themselves on breakfasts.'

'They have to eat, Nan.'

'Gorge themselves! This when half the world counts itself lucky to get through the day on a slice of bread and dripping.'

'Nan, you're going on again,' Poppy remonstrated. 'Getting yourself all het up over things you can't change.'

'And as for Edna,' Nan went on, unheeding, 'she might as well be working at Temple Mills like Daniel used to. Remember them shifts he did? Nights; days; six to two; two to ten? Mind you, he still works all hours God gives, for them orphan kids. He don't need to get married, he's already got a great big family with them. All heart, he is.' She paused for breath as Poppy set down her empty cup and stood up, and asked sharply, 'Now where are you off to?'

'Nowhere, Nan! I was going to make you a cup of tea and then I think . . . I think I'll have a little lie-down.'

'That reminds me, I was speaking to Mr Styles when I gave him the rent the other day. I put in a good word. You can move in as soon as the Smiths go. It's a nice house, Daisy let me go inside and see. Of course, she's a lazybones and the whole place needs elbow grease and carbolic, but you can make it nice.'

Poppy smiled tremulously. 'Are you that anxious to get rid of me?'

'No. But if things go as I think they will, Edna will be hogtying her Gus very soon now. Question is, who'd like a house all to herself? Who'll pretty it up and make it a nice home for a new husband? Who'd be downright fed up if someone else nipped in and took it? Anyway, Mr Styles said you can have it and that's how it should be. Edna don't mind sharing, and you do.'

'Nan! I never said, never even thought –'

'No? Well, I know you, my girl, probably better than you know yourself. So don't stand there telling me you don't want your own place.'

'I do, I do!' Poppy couldn't tell Nan that of course she wanted her own house – but not in Jezebel Street! She heard herself saying, 'Thank you, Aunt Nan, thank you very much for thinking of me.'

'You'll make it into a palace and much too grand, and you'll bring your child up to have ideas above its station.'

'Nan!'

'Still, that's your business. At least I know it'll be as neat as a new pin. Now don't bother yourself making me a cuppa. I know the smell of tea makes you go green.' Nan smiled her thin smile. 'Though I promise you, it'll be the first thing you'll ask for when it's born. You'll look at me with them eyes of yours and say, "Nan, I couldn't half do with a nice cuppa!" Be funny, won't it? You having a baby. I hope as how it's a girl.'

A girl? Poppy hadn't thought that far. Not of the baby as such. Up until now it had been a . . . a condition! Yes, just a kind of condition that had to be accepted, to do right by, to see through. The only time she had thought about it, and then only fleetingly, had been on the day Maud had been moaning about her one and only.

'Little shit!' she had said when Arty had been particularly cheeky. 'Blimey, talk about being lumbered! Made a rod for me own back, I did, having him. To think they reckon boys take after their mums and girls take after their dads. If that's the case, I ain't got no excuses about my Arty, have I?'

And even while thinking that, for all she moaned and

groaned, Maud would go through fire and flood for her Arty, Poppy had found herself praying for a boy that would take after her. It just wouldn't do to have a girl. She might look like Nigel and thus give the game away.

'I think Sandy would like a girl, Nan,' she said and fled.

The High Road was quite empty as Poppy walked towards the Blue Diamond. Her mid-green herringbone-tweed coat felt tight as a sausage skin about her, though it looked well enough. It was the one item of clothing she had not skimped on while working at Farringdon's and she was glad of it now. Underneath, she wore a let-out black skirt and a loose-fitting V-necked pale-green jumper. Nigel's little heart-shaped locket hung round her neck. Seeing her reflection in a shop window, she felt she looked her best. She lifted her chin, more confident now, and continued along until she reached the club.

Gus was not yet on duty outside. He sometimes acted as a sort of doorman. Guard in case of cops, Poppy secretly thought, but, because of Edna, she never said it. She walked to the doors, swung them open and found herself inside the place she had sworn never to enter again. Her fragile spurt of confidence oozed away. The long space before her, set with tables and chairs, was already half full. To the left, at the far end, a man played a piano on a dais. The man looked bored. The music was boring. No one was taking any notice at all.

Not sure what to do or where to go, Poppy stood there, waiting. At last one of the penguinlike waiters lowered himself sufficiently to approach. She inhaled, then said regally, 'I have an appointment with Mr Wray. In his office, at eight.'

'You are Mrs Swift?' The waiter's expression gave nothing away. She inclined her head. 'Please follow me.'

She followed him through a bamboo-and-bead curtain at the right of the dais, to a door which bore the word 'Office'. The waiter knocked, nodded to Poppy, then left. She turned the handle and went in.

Jay Wray was sitting behind an overlarge desk, reading some papers. He was immaculate in a dark suit, white shirt and bow tie. He was smoking a cigar, his face screwed up against its curling smoke. His attitude was arrogant and he remained seated. With cool deliberation, Poppy picked up a chair that had its tall back against the wall, and set it directly in front of the desk. Then she sat down and waited with a contemptuous expression on her face. When he deigned to glance at her and saw how she felt, he stared back, his face cold. Then he began deliberately looking her over, all but undressing her with his eyes. It was a silent, calculated put-down. She felt the hot colour rush to her cheeks.

Noting this, he leered and said in an oily way, 'You seem too warm. Shouldn't you take off your coat?'

'I was waiting to be helped,' she replied coolly. 'Most gentlemen offer such assistance as a matter of course.'

'Ah! But I'm not gentleman,' he retaliated. 'And you're no lady.'

Her head jerked up at that and she glared, saying, 'I did not come here to be insulted! What's more, I –'

'You're here because I ordered it,' he cut in. 'Don't forget the fact.' Jay Wray had very dark, velvety eyes, yet there was a spiteful glint in them. Poppy found herself believing all the rumours she had heard about him and felt her heart beginning to beat too quickly. Even so, she made herself continue to stare back at him, outwardly cool, calm and in control. He went on, 'You're here because you were scared not to be since you know damned well I'm not a man to be messed with.'

'I think you will agree,' she told him, 'that you deserved everything you got, since you were the one trying to do the messing.'

'No one shows me up,' he told her in a malevolent voice. 'And so I'm about to show the world how under my thumb you really are.' His tone changed, became crisp and authoritative. 'To begin with, take off your coat!'

'And after that?' she enquired politely, not moving.

'You will undress.'

'Are you waiting for me to scream and cry fainites?' she drawled. 'Oh, dear! Are you intending to be boring? Mete me out a fate worse than death? You honestly believe that will salve your hurt pride? Good heavens, Mr Wray!'

His face went liverish. He half rose from his chair, then controlled himself and sat down again. He smiled wolfishly.

'It's as clear as mud who you've been with. Trying to ape Carson, are we? But it won't wash, not to me nor him – nor his missus. Didn't know about his wife, did you?'

She smiled and shrugged, pretending to be casual. 'I knew. Of course I did.'

'Then you're also wise to the fact that to their sort, specially to the wife, you're a nothing! They're snobs and deserve each other. Just as you deserve everything you're going to get. Smacking my face is going to cost you, believe me.'

'Oh dear, did it hurt so much?' Poppy raised her eyebrows, her lips curved in a smile that held all the contempt in the world. 'I mean, having someone hit back for a change?'

His expression now held such an evil triumph that she felt sick. She knew in that second that he was about to deal her his most vicious blow. She held her breath in apprehension.

'You needn't put on airs and graces,' he sneered. 'They don't sit well on someone whose mother got slung out by her lover and finally went through Tilsby's hands. Oh yes, I've got all the proof, even to the manner of her death. They found her, a real old crone, among her methy mates near the docks. They say she was clutching a bottle in her hands even then. Dead as a dodo, a filthy old bitch in rags. So what's happened to your high and mighty ideas now, eh?'

'I never knew my mother,' she replied, white to the lips and now ocean-deep cold. 'If I had, she might have stood a chance. It was probably people like you who made her what she was.'

'Exactly. And now I'll see to it that you go the same way as your old girl. Starting with me!'

She sat there shocked, mouth dry, heart pounding. She wanted to spring to her feet and run, but couldn't because her legs had turned to jelly. As if from a million miles away she heard Nan's never-ending cry of all those years ago: 'If you ever bring shame to my house, if you ever act like that whore of a mother of yours, I'll swing for you!'

Poppy heard a laugh, a cool, superior sound that tinkled like chips of ice round the room. She realised that the laugh had come from her. That one tiny part of her, the proud, Nan-instilled part, was fiercely hanging on to self-control.

'I'd drop dead before I'd let you lay your paws on me,' she heard herself say. 'Believe me, Mr Wray, I find you quite repulsive. What's more, I refuse to sit here and listen to any more of your lies.'

'Stay where you are,' he told her menacingly. 'I haven't finished with you yet. You will do as I say, and try to remember that you're on the downward path already, and that to the Carsons of the world, particularly to the woman, you're a peasant.'

'Really? Well, Mr Wray, it's common knowledge that it takes one to know one!' She stood up, her green eyes sparkling with defiance. 'And now I'm ready to leave this place, with or without your permission.'

She was out of her chair and heading for the door. Quick though she was, he was faster. She fought him and, before he could stop her, had opened the door and entered the club. She was pulled to a halt violently as he caught and held her from behind. His grip was vice-like.

The people at the tables nearest were watching curiously. A group of men, clearly Jay Wray's cronies, were leering and whistling as he looked at them from over her shoulder. He must have grimaced in some way because they began laughing coarsely.

'Tasty bit of crackling here, mates,' Jay Wray began to boast. 'Knows a trick or two as well. Even better, she believes in sharing among friends! A ducky little redhead that actually managed to put Lady Carson's nose out of joint!'

Raucous laughter rang out from the group. Other people smirked, even some women. Others looked down their noses, seeing her as nothing but the dregs.

Poppy stood very still, quietly staring over their heads, waiting for them to tire of the game, trying not to hear the disgusting remarks and lewd jokes at her expense. Jay Wray was enjoying his revenge to the extent that he released his grip in order to make a gesture of some kind. In an instant Poppy had broken free. She ran towards the exit, past the table with their shadowy occupants, her humiliation knowing no bounds because Reggie Parker was there. He had seen and heard everything. He was sitting at table, drink in hand, fish-eyed, his face tight and empty, like a Guy Fawkes mask.

Outside she had a swift impression of Gus, with his back to her, dealing with a crowd of rowdy youths. He was refusing them entrance and they didn't like it one bit. Then she was away, running out of the area called the Blue Row, along Leyton High Road as though all the devils in hell were after her. She was sobbing and gasping as she reached the railway arch; stitch seized her and she stopped, panting and clutching her sides. A flame of fury grew within her until it burned more fiercely than her sense of degradation and shame. She swore an oath to pay Jay Wray back in kind. Then fresh tears flowed, tears of mortification.

'Dear God,' she heard herself whispering, 'Don't let it be that Nigel knows about my mother going through Mr Tilsby's hands. My mother who is dead. Yes, she is dead and I'm glad!'

I've sinned, she thought drearily, as pain receded and she again continued home. I have sinned greatly, but I didn't think it mattered because I was in love. But now I really am wicked! I should feel sorry for that woman who died drinking methylated spirits, but I don't. I don't care at all!

Poppy was exhausted by the time she crept up to her room, undressed and slipped into bed. As she hugged Sandy's pillow she was comforted to feel two gentle plops as Josh and Jo joined her. They curled up, purring loudly.

Poppy cried herself to sleep.

She woke and lay still. She could hear the world waking up and wished that she couldn't. The world was a wide, misty window of shame and she wanted no part of it. But she needed someone to talk to. She needed Sandy, but he was miles away in foreign seas. She dared not confide in Edna; the less she knew, the better. If Jay Wray found out how close they were, he'd probably give her the sack and Gus, too.

Poppy decided to wait until the coast was clear and Nan had gone off to the Home, then she'd slip across the road and have a chinwag with Maud. Moving mouselike, Poppy washed and dressed and, having heard Nan leave, slipped across the road. She knocked on Maud's door, then went in straight away. There was no standing on ceremony where Maud and Poppy were concerned.

Maud was in the kitchen as usual, enjoying a slanging match with young Arty. Tousled hair, jam round his mouth, eyes bright, he looked at Poppy as she entered and winked before running out of the house. Poppy saw some really lovely paper roses in Maud's dresser. There were dozens of them, in pink, yellow, white and red, waiting to be put on stems.

'Maud, I don't half like those flowers,' Poppy said. 'What are they for?'

'To flog round doors when I'm finished with them – and when I get up the nerve.' Maud winked. 'I know quite a few gippo tricks, believe me. And them women don't have to put up with sarcastic old cows what live in posh Woodford houses neither – which makes them one up on me. Honest, Poppy, Mrs Rowe-Lewis treats me like I'm the lowest of the low.'

'What gipsy tricks?' Poppy asked, intrigued. 'And how did you get to know about them?'

'Learned a lot from distant relations. You make your flowers – I'm a dab hand at chrysanthemums too – and bag them. Make sure you've got plenty of thin wire and go out looking for nice stems to wind them on. Most houses in the better-class areas have bushes in their front gardens, or, best of all, privet hedges.' Maud laughed. 'I've known of housewives buying a bunch of roses stuck on their own privet!'

'And you're thinking of going into business?' Poppy teased.

'Anything's better than being a slave to Mrs Rowe-Lewis. Here, why don't you come over tonight? We can have a right old jaw and I'll let you into a few road secrets. I've got millions of them. Them relations of mine are a real mixed bunch. They follow the markets, travel with fairs, tramp the roads. You know the kind of thing.'

'Sounds fun.'

'Can be. On the other hand it can be hard, but you're never lonely unless you choose to be.' Maud's laugh was bitter. 'Know something? Arthur really thought he was doing me a favour when he married me. Took me off a hoopla stall, he did, and I found myself stuck in a dump in Walthamstow. Promised me the earth, he did. Well, I hope as how he gets given the earth – all bloody six feet of it! Gawd! Is that the time? That old moo will have me guts for garters if I miss the bus.'

Poppy and Maud left the house together. Maud ran to the right, into Skelton Street and on to the High Road; Poppy went in the opposite direction, down the road to see Charlie and pinch some of Clary's toast.

Surprisingly the shop was shut and everything was deathly still. Poppy walked into the kitchen. Charlie looked a broken man. He was kneeling on the floor, unashamedly sobbing and holding a limp Rags. Clary was standing by the table, helpless and ashen-faced.

'Dad!' Poppy was down beside her father in an instant. 'Dad, what happened?'

'He – he'd been out all night,' he said choking. 'He sometimes does that, specially when Mother Mason's bitch is on heat. I –I thought the old devil was having a good time! I went to market on me own because he didn't turn up, an he'd never done that before! Like clockwork, he is. Then I said to Clary, "I'll go an' have a look for the old sod," an' I did.'

'Oh, Dad!'

'He was down the bottom end of Beaumont, crawling along so slow. So bloody slow! He . . . he was trying to come home, Poppy. I ran up to him and I kneeled down there on the pavement, begging of him not to go. He looked at me out of his wise old eyes and I swear he tried to tell me . . . He just put his fluffy old head on me hand and – and he died. I dunno what I'm going to do, Poppy. I just dunno!'

'You're going to cherish his memory, Dad,' she told him quietly, feeling her own throat tightening with grief. 'And you're going to be grateful you had the privilege of his company for so long.'

'He . . . he was family, and –'

'He was old. You gave him a full and wonderful life.' Poppy looked up sadly at Clary, whose heartbreak was as great as Charlie's.

The pair seemed to be withered and too vulnerable in their

anguish. Rags had been like their child. Poppy began wildly searching her mind for something comforting to say. What mere words could ease such terrible grief? None. None at all. But she had to try. For Clary and Charlie, she had to!

'Dad,' she murmured, 'I'm remembering how Ros used to nurse him when he was a pup. How she adored him and how he made her laugh. She insisted that he was almost human, didn't she? He was the apple of her eye and always stayed so, even after we had Josh and Jo. And now, Dad? Now I'm convinced she's up there somewhere waiting for Rags. Just standing there all smiling and loving, and waiting for him with open arms.'

Choking, she left them, two lost and lonely people grieving over their dog. And as she walked down Jezebel Street, Poppy thought of life and death and loneliness. And she thought about birth, and wondered about the baby growing under her heart. Sandy would make a most marvellous dad. She suddenly remembered that he wore a chain round his neck with a little round medal on which was embossed an ancient man carrying a child.

'It was a going-away present from my mother,' Sandy told her once. 'It's real silver and is St Christopher who looks after travellers. He looked after Jesus once, so they say. That's who he's carrying.'

'Do you always wear it?' she had asked, intrigued. 'I like the idea of that old man, though I don't know much about saints.'

'Me neither,' he'd replied, grinning. 'And most sailors are sinners. Still, Mum bought it for me even though we're not Catholic. I'll always wear it and think of her and you and home.'

Now, as she walked steadily along Beaumont Road, Poppy made up her mind. If she was carrying a boy, she would name it Christopher. Sandy would like that and so would Meg, and Vi could do the other thing. Cyril! Over her dead body. It didn't suit Sandy and it certainly wouldn't suit her son.

She continued, determinedly telling herself that it was her life that mattered, hers and the coming baby's. She had pulled herself together before knocking on Vi's front door. Vi, fat and mean-looking, answered. Her lips went down when she saw Poppy standing there.

'You're early!' Vi's tone was acid. 'You'll find your mother-in-law in the kitchen, doing something for her keep, which makes a change.'

Poppy found Meg on her knees, cleaning the floor. She was white-faced and strained. She wiped her forehead with the back of her hand. Dirty water dripped from the scrubbing brush, down her arm.

'Here, let me do that!' Poppy said quickly, but Meg shook her head and smiled.

'No, dear, I'm managing very well. But I would like a nice cup of tea.'

'We're nearly out,' Vi snapped, 'and a new packet costs –'

'Money?' Poppy asked sweetly. 'It's a good job Freddy sends such a nice little sum home then, isn't it? I don't know how you'd manage else. After all, your pension can't go very far, can it?'

'What are you trying to say?' Vi asked nastily, her cheeks, always high-coloured, now beetroot red.

'I think I've already said it,' Poppy replied. 'Now there's something else on my mind. I've just come along to say that I'm thinking of taking a house for Sandy and me. It's three doors away from my Aunt Nan, and there'll be plenty of spare space. And if you must now, I've half a mind to kidnap Meg and take her to number ten to live with us. Her life might be rather more comfortable there.'

'You cheeky, sarcastic little bitch,' Vi began, but Poppy was smiling down at Meg.

'I mean it, you know. We would love you to come and live with us.'

'Oh, my dear!' Meg was glowing with pleasure. 'What a nice, kind thing to say! I couldn't of course. I mean, Freddy's used to me being here with his mother and –'

'There's no hurry,' Poppy told her. 'Just give it some thought, eh?'

'The cunning cow's after your allowance,' Vi snapped. 'D'you hear me, Meg? It's plain as the nose on your face, she's after your money!'

Meg carefully placed the scrubbing brush in the pail of

water, where it floated among swirling grey froth. Then she got to her feet. She was looking her mother-in-law directly in the eye.

'No,' Meg said in a quietly distinct manner. 'No, Vi, she's not!'

'Thank you,' Poppy told her and chuckled because Vi looked as though a despised lamblike person had changed into a lion. 'I won't stay for tea because I have to make another call before I go home. I just wanted you to know about the house, that's all.'

Vi was still mouthing like a fish when Poppy left.

How I loathe that woman, Poppy thought as she cut through the alleyway to the left which led through to Skelton Street, but I can handle her. She was on her way to Daniel's cottage in the grounds of the Devere Home.

Daniel, looking serious, opened the door. He stood back to let her pass. She entered his kitchen, which was warm, old-fashioned and cosy, and saw all the papers he had been working on.

'I'm sorry,' she said, 'I've come at the wrong time, haven't I? I'll go!'

'No, matey, you won't.' His arm went round her shoulders in a friendly, companionable way. 'Sit yourself down, you're looking done in.'

'I've just been crossing swords with Vi Swift, that's all.'

'Then you need a break,' he told her and his hyacinth-blue eyes twinkled merrily. 'Though it's a pound to a penny you wiped the floor with her. But there's something else, isn't there?'

'How is it that I can never hide things from you?' she asked quietly.

'Come on, out with it.'

'I've just left Dad and Clary. You see, it's Rags –'

'The poor old devil's snuffed it? And I thought he'd go on for ever, too. They doted on that dog, didn't they?'

'Yes,' she whispered. 'We all did.'

'Well, remember that Rags had a damned sight better innings than the kids had before they came here,' he told her bluntly. 'I tell you, Poppy, it makes my blood boil sometimes. You can tell, just looking into their wary young faces, what

293

they've been through. Starvation, whipping, abuse, and being just plain bloody unwanted! I need to do so much! I've been there, I know how the poor little tykes feel. I wanted to take them to the seaside. See them get some colour in their cheeks, chew a stick of rock. But that's water under the mill now.'

'What happened, Daniel? What's wrong?'

He shrugged and had a wry expression on his face. 'It was decision-time – and I've been outvoted, damn it.'

'Outvoted?'

'We have some funds, quite a nice little sum, to spend. Of course the others have always had their eye on the old factory building opposite Loweries. It's been empty for years. As you know, it used to belong to Loweries, but they use the main building now for both pickles and jam. They're prepared to let the old place go for a song – and we have enough. It's been proposed and agreed by the board that we grab the old factory and use it as an extension, for girls.'

'That's wonderful! I don't see why you're not happy about it. Have you something against needy little girls?'

'Lord, no, matey! It's just that I wanted us to do more for the kids we've already got. We're being forced to let Lenny go, now he's well and old enough. No, don't glare at me like that. You never change, do you? It wasn't my idea. Besides, it's all settled: Lenny will stay in my old room at Flossie's. She and Bert have agreed. That's not bothering me. I'll see the kid all right, believe me.'

'Then I don't see –'

'The seaside,' he cut in. 'I had my mind set on getting a place for them, an old barn we could call our own, a run-down building, anything would do. I wanted us to have a holiday home. We could take the nippers away in groups and give them the time of their lives. But you're right, of course you are. It is time we did something to help girl children.'

'Yes,' she told him. 'And I'm sure you'll get the holiday home as well. That is, if you want it enough.'

'I know exactly the kind of place I'd like.' He was all enthusiasm now.

'Could it be in Kent?' Poppy suggested. 'I know there are

hundreds who enjoy going hop-picking out there. A real cockney holiday that is.'

'I was thinking of another place a world away, matey. I was thinking of the West Country. I'll never forget how you kept spouting that poem you learned at school. How wistful you looked about a place you'd never known! I'd like my kids to see it, that's all.'

'Oh,' she breathed, 'how lovely that would be! I remember the poem and always will. It goes, "There's a warm wind, the west wind, full of birds' cries. I never hear the west wind but tears arc in my eyes."'

'Shut up!' Daniel said. 'You'll have me blubbing in a minute. Tell me what's going on at Bannerman & Swift. Better still, tell me all you know about how Sandy's doing. He's a damn lazy letter writer, that I do know.'

'You probably know as much as me. He wrote to say that they were having dirty weather. He calls the *Vanessa* a real rusty old lady, but says she's a gutsy old girl just the same.' She smiled ruefully. 'That seems to be the way with sailors. They look upon their ships as living creatures. Sometimes, Sandy says, they love their ships above everything else.'

'Well, we all know that Sandy doesn't love his ship over and above you, matey, so that's all that counts.'

'Yes,' she replied thoughtfully, knowing that Sandy loved Ros and always would. Ship or no ship, Sandy was a one-woman man, it was as simple as that.

As she walked home, Poppy conceived a plan. She wouldn't wait to write about it to Sandy . . .

It was the early hours, it was raining and cold. The streetlamps, widely spaced, stood like tall, thin men on guard along Leyton High Road. The only human beings to be seen were a male and a female. They were bowed under the weight of their burdens. The woman held a spade, the man carried something in a blanket as carefully as he would a child. They moved silently, in the brooding stillness of a borough asleep, eventually disappearing round a secretive, ivy-shrouded corner wall.

The cemetery gates were never locked. They groaned mournfully as they were pushed aside, and the two people walked steathily along the gravelled driveway that eventually led to the church of St Catherine's. They progressed more rapidly now, every so often looking fearfully about them. A pale moon came from behind a cloud and floated like a cold blind eye. A chill wind gusted and caught at the hem of the woman's coat. She followed the man along the turfed pathway that wound between the graves. He stopped at the spot a little beyond the place where a rose bush was already swelling with the sap of the renewal of life. He gently set his burden down before taking the spade from the woman.

Quietly, methodically, gnarled hands lifted the turf of the path. Then the digging began, while the woman watched with tears in her eyes. The night wind soughed among branches and crackled among laurel leaves in a ghostly way. A bird wailed, high and weird, leaving a silence behind.

The digging was finished at last, and Rags was carefully laid to rest. The long narrow grave was filled, the turf replaced. The man and woman knelt down, fluffing out edges, disguising, blotting out all trace.

'The rain will do the rest,' Charlie whispered hoarsely. 'No one will ever know.'

'They will walk on him!' Clary sobbed. 'They'll tread on him. I can't bear the thought.'

'No, they won't, old girl. They'll walk over him, not on him, and he won't never feel nothing at all. He'll just lie there for ever, looking after our Ros. Should we say something?'

'You just tell him to behave himself and . . . and ask Ros to open her arms wide like Poppy said. Then let's go home, Charlie. For God's sake, let's go home!'

After a little while they walked forlornly back to Jezebel Street.

Chapter Seventeen

As the days went by and work continued with nothing out of
the way happening, Poppy began to relax. So, Jay Wray was
all mouth and trousers and that was all. She had upped and
lipped him and he had humiliated her in turn. Now it was
over and done with, but she could not forget. One day that
man would pay dearly for what he had put her through,
shaming her before all those sneering faces. Thank goodness
it was no one she knew apart from Reggie who was always
close-lipped. Neither Gus nor Edna had mentioned anything.
Harry Peel had gone a bit red and looked ashamed when he
saw her two days after the incident.

'Sorry, Poppy,' he'd said gruffly. 'I heard what happened.
You should never have gone to that place. You're a cut above
that crowd.'

'It wasn't your fault, Harry.' Then anxiously, 'You – you
won't say anything?'

'Me lips are sealed, luv. When you see Beth you might say
as how I'll be over one day soon, eh?' He grinned sheepishly.
'She don't belong anywhere near Jay, neither! I'm beginning
to think you and her have got it right. Truth is, I don't see
how I can get out and –' He shrugged his shoulders, then,
hands in pockets, cap at jaunty angle and whistling shrilly, he
went on his way.

That same evening she had bumped into Reggie Parker. He
looked at her in his strange empty way, but that was it.
Nothing! Poppy could have fainted with relief.

The normal pattern of her life resumed: the long lovely
days with Bill, the evenings with Nan, Maud, Meg and – not

so good – with Vi. She saw Edna in between shifts, but the hours were difficult; even so, their friendship deepened.

'The Smiths have gone,' Nan said one bright morning. 'Now we can get started. I'll need plenty of elbow grease. I'll rope Flossie in and anyone else I can grab hold of. Leave it to me, girl. Leave it to me!'

Tight-lipped, feeling ungrateful where the reverse should have been the case, Poppy nodded, smiled dutifully and went off to catch her bus.

After that it was all a mad scramble. As Sandy would say, it was all hands on deck. Nan was there, all bright-eyed and bossy, as well as Charlie, Clary, Edna and Maud. Dear frizzy-haired, jolly old Flossie and her little bald Bert went along, and even Gus was roped in. Meg never came, which was sad, but then neither did Vi. Poppy found herself caught up in the hustle and bustle, and joined in all the activity. She worked until too tired to carry on, then watched as the others continued with the scrubbing, cleaning and lino-laying. The second-hand furniture Poppy had selected, all rich dark oak, and a three-piece suite covered in brown Rexine for the front room, were delivered to the door by Bill, with the help of his horse Bo-Bo and the green grocery cart.

Poppy had an eye for a bargain and it showed. Everyone oohed and aahed at such luxury. Only Poppy couldn't get excited about the move. Perhaps unreasonably, she felt she had been pushed out from number two.

Poppy had chosen plain paint for the walls: peachy pink for the front bedroom, sunshine yellow for the back. The kitchen walls were a pale creamy orange, the colour of Nan's crysanthemums; the scullery was whitewashed, the wood painted mid-green. Only the downstairs front-room walls were covered with a lustrous wallpaper, closely resembling that in Nigel's flat.

Flossie had made curtains from the materials Poppy had chosen: various jazzy patterns picking up the wall colours on backgrounds of white. These flanked the white lace, essential for blocking out the miserable view of the street. Most of all, Nan envied that expensive white lace.

'It's all light and real lovely,' she said. 'A palace, girl! You've got a home to be proud of already, and when you've worked on it for a year or so, got yourself a nice carpet for the front, and kitchen rugs and lots of bits and bobs, you'll come to love every inch of it.'

'I know,' Poppy agreed dutifully. Inside she was thinking, It's all right, I suppose – for a stepping stone.

Poppy continued to take the bus to Bill's. Up to now they had made good profits. They decided to plough two-thirds back into the business.

Delighted about how well things were going, agreeing that they must prepare for winter's quiet months, Poppy made regular visits to the bank, putting in small amounts. The rest she spent on important things, like little presents for her relatives and friends, not forgetting the children's home. They always needed lots of things there.

'You're spoiling us, matey, you really are!' Daniel said. 'The kids love the books and toys.'

'I'll be a very, very rich lady by the end of the year,' she told him, mentioning the millions of seeds one got in a pound, and that it was the labour, time and effort put in that put up the costs. She omitted to mention the hazards – the weather, the insects, the birds, the rabbits that chomped merrily through everything and rapidly multiplied. Poppy and Bill also had to pay the wages of the people they employed, and there were overheads: the maintenance of the greenhouses, the heating, the sacks of fertilisers, even old Bo-Bo's hay. So they hardly made a fortune, but given time . . .

Poppy left the tomatoes in favour of working outside. It was heavier going, but she welcomed that. Labouring under glass had come to feel claustrophobic. She was slowing down and at last her condition was beginning to show. It was a nuisance, just one of those things, she told herself firmly; and activity helped. Nan said it wasn't hard work that killed, worry was worse. Poppy's greatest worry was that the baby would look like Nigel, which might bring suspicion to people's minds. It would also be an everlasting reminder to Sandy. His back was broad, he was a very nice man, but deep down he might be hurt. She didn't want that.

It grew warmer. Flowers were blooming; runner beans

grew tall; globe beetroots, lettuce and raddish were ready to be pulled. New things were put in, old things taken out, and there was an incessant hoeing of weeds. Birds were fussing and fretting in the trees. The marshes stretched into the distance like a gently ruffling green sea. It seemed impossible that a place like Jezebel Street was only a bus ride away.

Bill had a secret place where he would sit and think. It was lush and green, a little buttercup and cowslip world near the river. Here forget-me-nots grew, and jolly little ducks swam in and out among the reeds. Further out, swans glided along like silent snow queens, regal and remote in their watery world. Bill took her there one sunny midday. They ate cheese and onion sandwiches together, and Bill said, 'Come here when you need time to yourself, Poppy. Try to rest more than you do. This lovely spot helps, just by sitting and listening to the music of the Lea.'

'I'll do that,' she replied gravely. 'Thank you for sharing this sanctuary with me.'

A few evenings later Edna came knocking loudly on the door of number ten. Poppy, not long home, smiled when she saw how bright-eyed and bushy-tailed her friend was. Dear Edna was pointedly waving her left hand in the air.

'Don't stand on the step grinning like a Cheshire cat,' Poppy teased. 'Come in. I've just made tea on my lovely new gas stove. I always envied Clary hers.'

'I'm engaged.'

'Really?' Poppy raised her finely arched brows. 'I would never have guessed.'

'Bloody marvellous, innit?' Edna crowed. ' 'Ere I am as large as life an' twice as natural, and Gus really thinks I'm luverly! Nutty as a fruit cake, he is. We're engaged, Poppy, and when he asked would I mind marrying him very much, I said when? How soon? Would tomorrer do? Said it all in a rush, I did. Forgot to act all coy, and just about slung myself at him. I don't care, though. I'm getting him down that office just as quick as I can! Can't have him changing his mind, can I?'

'He'd never do that, he adores you. Congratulations, Edna. I'm delighted for you both.'

Edna was beaming all over her well-scrubbed, shiny face. She had done things to her hair and appearance since she had set eyes on Gus, and was now like a young woman transformed. 'Poppy,' she gasped, 'this is the happiest day of my life. Just look at the ring he bought me! We chose it together. We went to the jeweller's at Baker's Arms.' Poppy looked at Edna's engagement ring, with it's three minuscule diamonds that could barely be seen, then at the sublime joy in Edna's eyes, and hugged her friend. 'They mean, "I love you"', Edna rushed on, 'that's what the man told us. And Gus went all gooey and said, "We'll have that one then, if it fits." And it did! I'm so happy I could scream!'

'It's wonderful, truly wonderful, Edna, and I'm so thrilled for you, I could scream too,' Poppy said joyously. 'This is wonderful news.'

'If only Burney was here it'd be perfect! When did you hear from him last, Poppy? And have you been back to see him yet? You said you would.'

'I haven't been to see him, yet,' Poppy replied and went red with guilt. 'Because I've been so busy. Besides, buses go two ways, you know. Burney could just as well come to see me.'

'You know he works early mornings and late nights, same as me,' Edna said indignantly. 'You're the best one to go, seeing as how you can more or less please yourself. Burney can hardly get down here, can he? There ain't enough time in between, except on Sundays, of course. Then he must be fair wore out. We've gotta do something about our Burn.'

'I invited him here, yes, even to stay.' Poppy was on the defensive. 'I wrote and said come any time. That he'd always be welcome. If you cast your mind back, I wrote the same to you, and you took me at my word, thank goodness. The fact that Burney hasn't bothered, and doesn't reply to my letters half the time, shows he's all right. I haven't heard from him at all recently.'

'And you ain't worried?'

'Not really. You know men! Sandy thinks he's written a masterpiece if he sets down more than three lines every two months. Burney sent me a postcard, a pretty vulgar one too, about three weeks ago. He just scribbled to say all was going well, and that's about it.'

'I've got to show him my ring, Poppy!' Edna said urgently. 'And he's got to meet my Gus. I'll never forget as how it was, you, me and Burney against the world. Who'd 'ave thought in them days that you'd marry Sand? And that I'd get engaged to Gus! Now we've just gotta get Burney settled.'

'How?' Poppy groaned. 'Come off it, Edna. Love's turned your head. Burney is someone special to us, but we mustn't try to interfere with his personal life. He must be happy where he is.'

'No, he isn't, and we've gotta get Burney away from Tony's at least. They're still gunning for him, but I don't think it's all to do with you and creepy Carson. My aunt lives near there and hears all the gossip. She knows Burney's our mate, and reckons that the real cause of his trouble is that he's delivered meals to lots of people living in Coopersale Place. In other words, he knows too much! They want him out of it, Poppy, and won't stop at nothing. Trying to force Tone's hand and all, they are. The café windows have been smashed again, did you know that? When Gus and me went home, the place was closed and Burney was nowhere to be found. Tone said he was all right, but he looked worried. He's a real decent bloke what won't give in to bullyboys, no more'n he'll turf his nephew out.' Edna, hypnotised, was again glancing down at her diamond ring, as she added, 'I think I'll go over Hackney way on my next day off. I want to see Burney. Coming?'

'Yes,' Poppy replied instantly. 'When shall that be?'

'Next Tuesday. We'll make a day of it, and go and see my mum. My lot adore Gus, by the way, and Gus is soft about them. He ain't got no parents. He told me that his mum was a tough old bird. She used to clump his dad round the ear'ole with a rolling pin if he got out of hand. She died a couple of years ago. Gus reckons she went up to heaven, still after her old man with her rolling pin. Gus liked her a lot. Gus said that the day he lost her was the only time in his life that he cried. Anyway he's been adopted by my crowd, who'll be over the moon to see him and you –' she stopped in full flow and grimaced. 'Oh, shit!'

'Now what's up?' Poppy laughed. 'Honestly, you don't half rabbit on. I can't keep up with you.'

'I've just remembered that us lowly workers can't bank on anything now that bloody Mrs Wray's back. She's a cow. Queens it over everybody, she does. Jumped-up, painted tart. Gus says it's a right old turn-up for the book. The woman never wanted to be within a mile of that place before, now she's always there. Gus reckons she's heard about that scene between Jay and you, and all of them daft things Jay said about how good at tricks you are and stupid stuff like that. She's probably putting the screw on him. She's certainly all ready with teeth and claws.'

Poppy's stomach turned and she felt sick. She tried to pretend that she wasn't caught unawares, and heard herself saying, 'I hope the woman makes Jay Wray suffer. I'll never forgive that pig for humiliating me. But I'm sorry everyone else is having to pay for it.'

'She sacked the pianist, you know. Said he wasn't polite enough. Probably looked through her when she tried to blind him with her charms. She's the sort that's gotta to be the be-all and end-all, so far as blokes are concerned. Pity about the pianist, though. He needed the job. Jay thought he had class, but there you are, the poor sod's gone.'

'I would have thought a man like Jay Wray could handle a wife!'

'Ha! Like her little lapdog, he is. Makes you sick to see him. The meanest, cruellest old shit around, but wax in her hands. Us kitchen lot hear all the goings-on, we do, everything!'

'Well,' Poppy cut in, wanting to run away and hide, whereas Edna looked set to burble on all night. 'Just let me know if it's all right for Tuesday. I'd like to let Bill know if I'm off for the day. He'll worry else.' She paused, looked Edna straight in the eye and had to add, 'It seems to me you hear a great deal in that kitchen.'

'Nothing passes us by!' Edna was still drooling over the ring on her finger. 'We get it from all directions, but mostly from the waiters that don't miss a trick.'

'Not a single one?'

Edna's face went beetroot. She blinked, then looked over Poppy's head and went dumb.

'You get to know everything?' Poppy insisted. 'Everything, Edna?'

'Well, you know how it is!' Edna brightened and mischievously tweaked Poppy's hair. 'A bit of gossip helps to pass the time and that. Anyway Gus saw you run out, but he didn't let on. It was easy to find out all the rest.'

'Yet you've never told Nan,' Poppy said quietly. 'And not even me. Edna, you're a gem.'

'No, I ain't.' Edna's face creased up as she giggled. 'I'm just waiting to see what you're going to do about it, that's all. That's what I told Gus. "Just you wait and see her get her own back," I said. "Knowing her, she won't take that little lot lying down. She's too much like Nan."'

'Let's just say that I'm going to get me an engagement ring,' Poppy told her, and chuckled in spite of herself. 'In fact, the shiniest diamond that Woolworth's has got.'

'Do what?'

'It doesn't matter, Edna. Now for that tea . . .'

On midday Tuesday, Poppy and Edna walked to Burney's flat. They were pleased and happy, excited to surprise their friend. They saw that the café window had been replaced and the frontage spruced up. Inside it was crowded as usual. They walked round to Burney's street door, which opened at a touch, up the stairs and into Burney's place.

'Burney!' Poppy gasped and ran to him.

'Bleedin' hell!' Edna snapped. 'What 'ave the toerags been and gone and done to you?'

He looked forlorn and wilted, lolling back on his bed. It was clear that he had been beaten up. His face had been bruised, his arm was in a sling. When he saw them, his eyes came alive. He tried to grin, but grimaced with pain, still managing to joke even so.

'You oughter see the other bloke, Princess!' he said, then, 'Wotcher, Edna, what are you both doing here?'

'For starters,' Edna replied firmly, 'I'm off downstairs to get us all a cuppa. And then, because I'm starving hungry and you look like you've not eaten for years, I'll buy us some meat pies. D'you want mash and mushy peas?'

They both nodded.

Poppy, now kneeling at the bedside, kissed Burney very gently on the cheek. 'We shouldn't have left it for so long before coming to see you,' she said guiltily. 'Who did this to you?'

'Don't rightly know, Princess, but I can guess. It's something to do with that Mrs Carson, and the beans getting spilled about the goings-on in Coopersale Place. Right old sort-out there's been there. Even old Flanty's been given the elbow. But it looks like they're really gunning for me.'

'Because of me? How mean! Hasn't anyone stuck up for you, apart from your uncle Tony? What about your friend?'

'Things got too hot for him, sweetheart. He . . . he had to go.'

'I see. Why didn't you leave with him?'

'Wasn't invited.'

'You could have left this place, Burney.'

'And gone where?'

'You jolly well know where!' she exploded indignantly. 'Burney, why on earth didn't you come to me? To us? You can live in my house, where they won't find you. Why didn't you let me know?'

'Didn't want to bring trouble with me.'

'Ha!' Edna jeered, returning empty-handed. 'You ain't seen my fella, Burn. 'Built like a battleship, he is. Just you stick with Gus and me!' She held out her left hand. 'What d'you think about this, eh? Me and Gus are getting married soon and you've gotta be there. Help with all the fancy grub and that – if your arm's better by then. Talking of food, I'll get ours in a minute. They're three deep down there.'

'You're engaged?' Tony was genuinely pleased. 'Good for you, Edna. Really jammy! The ring is very, very nice.'

'I know! Now, Burn, it's "make your mind up" time. Pack enough to carry on the bus, we'll get the rest of it later on. You're coming to Jezebel Street. Poppy's got her own place now and –'

'She lives by herself?' Burn asked quietly. 'Sorry, mates, but wild horses wouldn't drag me there. The neighbours

305

would have a beanfeast tittle-tattling, a man and a woman together alone! Besides, Sandy's a good mate, so I'm not going to hand him any grief.'

'Burney,' Poppy put in firmly, 'stop arguing. You're coming to live with me.'

'Sorry, Princess,' he told her. 'Not on your Nellie.'

'Then what about the room she's just left, in her aunt's house?' Edna put in eagerly. 'That's going begging right now.'

'That's for you and Gus,' Poppy said. 'It's all been agreed by Nan. You're going to have a bedroom up and a living room down.' She turned to smile into Burney's face. 'Don't worry about anything. In the meantime, have you any money for rent?'

'Of course. I haven't stopped working, even in spite of my arm. There's always plenty of running about to do. And I've been saving for my own café, as you know.'

'Well, I'm sure my friend Maud would just love to have you.'

'I'm not exactly,' he began hesitantly, 'the kind of person that strangers might welcome, and –'

'If you're trying to say that you're not big and tough and a real man's man, don't worry yourself.' Poppy laughed. 'Maud's had enough of the Bill Bash'em types to last her a lifetime. I'll have a quiet word if you insist, but providing you keep on the straight and narrow in and around Jezebel Street I know she's going to adore having you.'

Within a week everything was settled and Burney was living in Maud's house. He had his own private room. Maud changed her double bed for two singles and Arty shared her room. Later on Arty would move downstairs. Maud began kidding Burney to try his hand at selling paper flowers from door to door.

'You'll be good at it,' she told him. 'Just the sort all the old girls will go for. G'won, have a try! Come with me and we'll give it a go. It'll give me more courage if I'm with someone like you.'

'You might as well give in to 'er,' Arty groaned, having taken to Burney from the word go. 'You're gonna be sorry you ever got to be our lodger. She goes on and on and on!'

Poppy left them all laughing and teasing each other. Happy and relieved for Burney, thrilled to bits for Edna, she now began to concentrate on her own plan . . .

The dress shop that stood two doors away from the huge Woolworth's store on Baker's Arms corner was the best in the area. Glass-fronted, its windows crammed with mannequins wearing beautiful things, it was a woman's Paradise. Poppy went inside. She left an hour and a half later, well pleased.

That evening she popped in to see Nan, then waited for Edna. It was easy to do some general questioning, and Nan thought nothing of the fact that the two girls were having such a long conversation about the Blue Diamond Club. The place was like Hades to her and she didn't want to know. She got fed up with it in the end and went to see Flossie next door. Poppy got down to brass tacks. She had to make sure of the times when Mrs Wray put in an appearance at the Blue Diamond. She also wanted to know the busiest and best night in the club, and when the four regular Jay Wray cronies would be there.

'Fridays and Saturdays are the busiest, and them four prats are there practically every night. Why?' Edna asked, eyebrows high, eyes sparkling.

'Wait and see.'

'Been down Woolies lately?' Edna asked archly.

'Of course. It's a three-stone, like yours.'

'Exactly like mine?' Edna was aggrieved.

'No – bigger and better!' Poppy teased, then ducked and ran as Edna playfully lunged towards her.

The following Friday, at precisely nine o'clock, Poppy walked out of number ten and into a waiting taxi. She breathed a sigh of relief because the driver was unknown to her, and got in. She wore a flowing apple-green dress of moiré silk. It was cunningly simple in cut and design, a classic that screamed expensive. Poppy's hair was swept up and pinned in curls on top of her head. She wore court shoes the colour of copper and carried a matching evening bag and gloves. A wide moiré-silk stole a shade deeper green than her dress was slung loosely round her shoulders. Her only

307

jewellery was the heart-shaped locket Nigel had bought her and a sparkling ring on her engagement finger. The ring wouldn't stand close inspection, but it looked impressive enough at a distance. Ignoring the curious children and frankly gawping neighbours, Poppy, looking regal, swept out of her house and into the taxi.

'The Blue Diamond, please,' she said and leaned back against the upholstery as the taxi moved away.

Reaching the destination, Poppy paid the man and asked him to pick her up in one hour. Turning, she all but bumped into the serious-faced Gus. She gave him a half-smile and allowed him to open the door for her. She wanted to giggle. She wondered fleetingly whether Gus would shortly be called to chuck her out. Outwardly calm and looking lovely, she walked inside with the air of a queen.

As she entered, all eyes fell on her. A waiter showed her to a table near the dais, where a trio of elderly gentlemen in evening dress and bow ties earnestly played 'Roses of Picardy' and other popular melodies. Poppy sat down, smiled at the four men who had found her such a joke before, and ordered a bottle of red wine.

Without being too obvious, she tried to see where Jay Wray and his wife were. The place was dimly lit, the air thick with the smell of cigar and cigarette smoke. Poppy felt queasy, but maintained her calm and sophisticated air. Her self-assured manner had the desired effect. Jay's cronies were looking at her, all but drooling.

They're probably wondering about all those sexy tricks I'm supposed to be so good at, she thought contemptuously. What a lot of rotten stinkers they are! She let her stole drop casually from her shoulders and managed to smile across at the men again, in a teasing, provocative way.

The waiter returned, bearing the wine on a tray, a glass and a napkin. Poppy, who had ordered red because that was what the men were drinking, now said softly to the waiter, 'Please go to Mr Wray's friends and invite them to my table. Say that I am not happy sitting alone.'

The waiter delivered her message, discreetly, and the men looked over. One, the fat, balding one, openly guffawed. Two others, obviously twin brothers, had short prison-cropped

308

hair and long oval faces. They glanced swiftly over their shoulders, then stayed firmly where they were. The fourth man, slim and handsome stood up. He bore a faint resemblance to Jay and Poppy wondered fleetingly whether he was a relative. He certainly had more courage than his companions. He smiled, bowed in a rather mocking way, and walked towards her. Poppy waited, her pulses racing. The uneasy look the brothers sent over their shoulders had shown her where Jay Wray sat. He was alone! No, she thought, the woman's got to be here. If she isn't, my plan will have failed.

She looked at the man who had joined her and smiled. 'How nice of you to take pity on me. It is always so embarrassing to sit in a place like this on one's own. And more particularly since Jay behaved so badly the last time I was here.'

'He's a law unto himself,' the man replied, then added suggestively, 'Like we all are under the skin. My name's not Mario Maleni for nothing.'

'And I'm Poppy. I understand that you and Jay have been friends for rather a long time?'

'Long enough.' He leered in a greasy, suggestive manner and added, 'On the other hand, you're a bit of a new'un to the game, eh?'

She opened her eyes wide, pretending to be puzzled, acting the part of a young woman innocent about the way things actually were. She leaned nearer to Mario and half whispered in a conspiratorial way, 'I'm new to all this kind of thing, believe me. My condition came as a complete surprise to us both!'

'Oh?' He was eyeing her up and down, confident one minute, confused the next. He gave several nervous glances over his shoulder, towards the side table nearest the wall where Jay Wray sat. She felt rather than saw Jay Wray looking over. The three cronies who had remained at their table were openly watching their chum now, the brothers with admiring expressions, the fat man exuding unease.

It was going along the way Poppy had planned, but too quickly. The woman hadn't arrived. Mrs Wray had to come, to perfect the revenge. Poppy wanted Jay Wray to suffer at his wife's hands just as Poppy had suffered at his. If the woman didn't come – feeling in a cleft stick, unable to stop herself now she had begun, Poppy pressed on.

'As you can guess, Mario,' she told him, 'Jay and I go back rather a long way. We have been discreet because that's how he wished it to be. But now! Things are very different. Jay must come out into the open. He's fighting shy of this, and that's the reason for the very public row we had a while ago.' She looked at him earnestly and reached out to put her right hand over his, careful to allow only a very brief glimpse of her diamond-encrusted left hand once in a while. 'Mario, I'm sure that you understand.'

'No,' he said, uneasy, 'I don't. Are you telling me that you and Jay are –'

'Seriously involved? Of course we are! But, well, let's put it this way, things happen in life that catch us offguard. I was not prepared to find myself in this condition.' She paused significantly, inwardly thinking, that bit's true, at any rate. She wanted to giggle like a naughty girl scared of being found out. But giggling wouldn't fit the picture she was trying to present, of a young lady who had been fully taken in by a two-timing rat. A young woman far above the social level of Jay Wray and his wife.

Mario was watching her, his near-black eyes glinting with curiosity. 'Tell me, did Jay expect you?'

'Oh no!' she confided. 'He never does. He doesn't like me here. He says it's not a very nice place for a lady. But I must make him see that from now I'm going to be a part of his life in the fullest sense. We must both make sacrifices and do the right thing.' She looked round, then went on in all innocence, 'I expected Jay to be here, but he doesn't seem to be. That's why I'm so grateful to you, Mario. I would have hated having to sit here alone.' She looked at him wistfully. 'You don't know where Jay is, I suppose?'

She was about to turn and directly face Jay when the bead and bamboo curtain to the right of the dais swung open. A young woman intent on making a dramatic entrance came through. Dark and fiery-looking, wearing a dress of flamboyant red, she was exotic with thick mascara on her lashes and heavily painted scarlet rosebud lips. She had a most arrogant air. So this, then, was the queen of the Blue

310

Diamond. Mrs Wray, the one person in the world who could, so Edna said, crush Jay with a single glance.

All eyes were now on Mrs Wray, and she knew it. Every man in the room admired her, and every woman was envious of her looks, her clothes, her bangles, beads and earrings of gold. Clearly Mrs Wray knew that too. It showed in her confident, insolent walk.

Poppy wanted to laugh and shout out 'Gotcher!' Instead, as Mrs Wray went to Jay's table, allowing a waiter hold back her chair, Poppy breathed to Mario, 'Who is that?' and, still watching, pretended sudden astonishment – 'Oh, there's Jay!' Continuing to act her part, she asked again in an agitated manner, 'Mario, I asked you, who is that?'

Mario's eyes were cruel as he drawled, 'Don't tell me you didn't know? That's his wife.'

'Never!' Looking shocked, Poppy rose majestically from her chair. The people at the nearest tables fell quiet, watching as she walked slowly and deliberately towards the married pair. She came to a halt beside the table. Completely ignoring the woman, she looked directly into Jay's eyes and said in her poshest tone, 'Jay, I have been waiting for you all this time. I did not know that you had already arrived.'

His voice held venom. 'Get out!' he said. 'Get out before I have you thrown out!'

'Jay!' She forced herself to laugh coolly and speak in an icily superior way. 'Don't put on an act with me, and don't speak to me in that tone.'

He growled furiously and made to leap up, but his wife stopped him. Looking feline and vicious, she almost purred in a foreign accent, 'Let 'er say her piece, chéri, and then 'ave her thrown out.'

Poppy turned to her, brows raised. 'How dare you be so familiar? Sherry indeed!' she drawled arrogantly, 'So you're the person my fiancé mentioned? The one always dogging his footsteps and making a nuisance of herself.' She turned her back on the woman and faced Jay Wray. 'Now I believe you, sweet,' she told him. 'She really does show off, doesn't she? And she really is full of airs and graces. How embarrassing!'

Jay Wray, poleaxed and spluttering because his wife had wickedly snapped at him to 'Sit down!' when he'd started to rise from his chair, was mouthing on about liars and stupid bitches, and goggling at his wife, who had all her attention on Poppy.

'Who do you think you are?' She grabbed hold of Poppy's arm and swung her round.

'Mr Wray's fiancée,' Poppy replied, looking down at her, her lip curling. 'Who else? Hasn't he told you about me?' She turned back to Jay Wray. 'Really, my dear, you should tell this – person to go!'

'You mare!' Mrs Wray screeched. 'You bloody stuck-up mare, I'll –' She leaped up and sprang furiously, painted nails flailing.

This was child's play to someone like Poppy, who had been born in Jezebel Street, and who was muscular from working in the fields. She caught hold of Mrs Wray's waving fists with effortless ease and smiled, pretending an amusement she didn't feel.

'Clearly Jay has been leading you on,' she told the panting woman, whose wide-open mouth in her powdered face made her look like a clown. Looking beyond her to the now standing Jay, Poppy snapped, 'Really, you should not lower yourself to your little Gipsy playmate's level. I heard from Mario and the other three that you had found yourself a flashy young tart.' She seemed to reach twice her size as she took command of the situation, still holding firmly on to his wife. 'No, don't move! I've not finished yet. That is how your friends described her, tart! That's what they said. But then they are all very crude and so are you. Our engagement is off!'

He was mouthing every foul epithet he could think of as he lunged towards her. She pushed Mrs Wray in his way. He tried to disentangle himself from his wife as, furiously yelling, she stumbled against him and hung on. Jay Wray's expression as he looked over his wife's shoulders showed that he was ready to kill. But Mrs Wray stopped him from going after Poppy. Her voice high and shrill, she wanted some answers about just what he'd been up to. Oh yes, she wanted some answers right there and then!

The gawping, sniggering club members watched Poppy as she walked towards the exit with her head held high. And

312

with every step she took she was waiting for someone to leap at her, grab her from behind, attempt to kill her. But nothing happened except low murmurs and meaningful looks, titters behind raised hands. From the table by the wall she could still hear the vociferous shrieking of Jay's wife.

Poppy reached the exit and safety, heart thumping. Her face now creased in a smile more wicked than any of Nan's, she winked at the wondering Gus and was coolly waiting by the kerb when the taxi showed up.

Jay's going to cop it, she thought and wanted to hug herself. And when his wife's done with him, he'll start on his four lovely friends. Have I done it, or haven't I? Talk about killing five birds with one stone!

Once safe indoors, undressed and in bed, she closed her eyes and listened to the noises of the street.

'You filthy old sod!' Liz Parker was yelling. 'Them girls were only 'aving you on, but you don't see that, do yer? You really think as how you're God's gift. But you're only a rotten, evil, stinking old swine!'

'Hark at 'er!' Vic yelled out. 'My lady, my wife. The mouthy bitch what's been a millstone round me neck for donkey's years.'

The door of number seven slammed shut and the yelling and screeching faded, but carried on inside. Shortly afterwards there came the roaring of Reggie Parker's motorbike. It stopped, the door was opened again and loudly slammed.

'Gawd 'elp us,' Vic roared. 'You're an arse'ole, Reg. Must you wake up the whole bleedin' street?'

'Shut it!' Reggie growled. 'Or else!'

There was no reply.

Poppy was grinning wickedly to herself as she fell asleep.

They were dancing and Sandy was holding her close, smiling down into her upturned face. She was drowning in his look of love, but someone had wrenched her away. Nigel! His mouth went over hers, he was gripping her too tightly and something was wrong. His lips were over her mouth and her nose. She couldn't breathe. She was being smothered by

313

Nigel. She was beginning to choke! She was calling to Sandy to save her and fighting for breath as she woke.

The bedroom was filled with smoke.

Poppy scrambled out of bed and ran to the door. Opening it, she wanted to scream. The wall of swirling black and suffocating fumes was such that there could be no escape by the stairs. She saw the orange glow of flames and fell back, slamming the door behind her.

'Oh, God,' she was moaning desperately in her mind. 'I'm going to be burned to a crisp. No, no, no!' For the very first time her hands clutched over her stomach, to protect the little thing that had been making butterfly movements in there. Horror filled her streaming eyes as she again croaked frantically, 'No!'

She stumbled towards the washstand and poured water from the jug onto the pretty new pink towel. Once it was sodden, she held it against her face and ran to the window. As she tried to open it, the sash cord broke and the frame came smashing down on her hand. She gasped and shuddered with fear rather than pain because suddenly the window glass flew in. It smashed to smithereens around her. A face appeared: an empty sort of face, with expressionless eyes.

Reggie Parker pulled himself through.

'There's a ladder outside,' he told her in an everyday tone of voice. 'Climb out and get yourself on it.'

'But —'

'Do as you're told. Take your time, don't look down, and don't worry. I'll follow you.'

She had reached the pavement when the fire engine, its bell clanging, swept into Jezebel Street. And Poppy was in Reggie Parker's stiff arms, weeping and thanking him and needing Nan. Then Nan was there, and so was the whole world, it seemed, all yelling and shouting. Most were cheering on the helmeted men who, busy with their hoses, were putting out the flames.

And Reggie just had time to say in Poppy's ear, 'It was Jay Wray and his mates. You'd better watch out from now on.'

'Thank you, oh, thank you!' Poppy stuttered and fell backwards into Nan's arms. Then the whole world went spinning.

314

She woke up in her bedroom in Nan's house. Dr Fox was there looking pink-faced and kindly, and smiling in a confident way.

'It's rest for you, Mrs Swift, and lots of care from now on. Inhaling smoke can be the very devil, you know.'

'Thank you, doctor,' she said huskily, aware of a pain in her chest and an agony in her hand, but above all of fear. 'And, and . . .?'

'You're baby is alive and kicking,' he told her. 'And when it's born the first lesson you must teach him is not to play with matches, my dear. In the meantime it's rest for you. Lots of rest and quiet, and I have asked your aunt to make sure you obey.'

He bustled out of the room and she lay there in bed, tears slipping down her cheeks. Her throbbing hand had been bandaged. She wondered if she had been out for a long time. Nan came then, with hot milky chocolate and a stern expression on her face.

'I'm going to see that you do as you're told for once, my lady,' she said. 'No arguing! I reckon I'd 'ave gone mad if I'd lost you, too.'

'You won't lose me, Nan,' Poppy whispered huskily. 'I'm never going to leave you. And . . . and, Nan?'

'You sound like a frog, so don't talk.'

'Nan, Reggie Parker saved my life. Will you –'

'He's the hero of the street, make no mistake,' Nan told her. 'And it's decided we're going to have a collection for him. If he hadn't looked out of his bedroom window when he did, and seen flames leaping out of your letter box, you and the whole lot of us could have gone up in smoke.' Her face crumpled up and then she looked mournful. 'Your curtains have had it, and bang goes all your white lace.'

'Never mind, Nan. Nan, I –'

'Here, take this tablet, drink your cocoa and get to sleep. Doctor's orders.'

Poppy obediently did as she was told.

Chapter Eighteen

'Of course,' Poppy said shakily to Nan the next day, 'it's always the same round here. Everyone gets together when the chips are down. But I never dreamed that they would want to help get number ten back to rights. I mean, Liz Parker was always mouthing on about my posh ideas, even when she was helping to scrub the place the day the Smiths moved out. Yet you say she's down there again!'

'Everyone mucks in when it matters, my girl,' Nan said sententiously. 'I thought you knew that!'

'Yes, but you know they've always looked on me as too sniffy, a kind of outsider because I've tried to speak well and –'

'It's you,' Nan told her crisply, 'not them. You've always wanted to be an outsider. You've always hated our street and didn't care who knew it. No one was surprised when you left with young Jessica. The biggest shock to the people round here was that you came back – married to Sandy. Have you heard from him at all?'

'Not recently. I know the *Vanessa* is old and always having parts going wrong. She takes longer than estimated to get to her various ports of call, so his letters aren't regular at all. I expect he gets mine by the sackful. I'll write and tell him everything that's happened to number ten. Just think, I was crowing about all – the colours, the furniture – just a day or so ago!'

Nan gave her a quick look. 'You didn't love him proper when you got married, did you?'

'Nan!'

Poppy felt herself going hot and cold. Nan can see inside me, she thought wildly. She knows things about me – and she's got such direct piercing eyes!

'I ain't daft!' Nan told her. 'It strikes me that you're getting very fond of him now. All I hope is that you can tell real gold when you've got it.'

'Sandy has always been a part of our lives, Nan,' she insisted. 'Even when Ros and I were kids in school.'

Nan smiled her meaningful smile. 'Still won't commit yourself, will you? Well, I hope you stay the good girl you've always been, and remain faithful. I'm not sure I like the way you're for ever turning to Daniel.'

'Nan!'

'All right, I'll shut up, but just you remember what I said. Besides, there's a nice young woman as likes him a lot. Nurse Bittlestone what adores children. I think she's been taken on because she's an expert on dealing with kids in shock. She'll be working with the girls at the new place. They're getting on with that new building like a house on fire.' Nan grinned then. 'I expect the girls will be called the Devere pickles. That old factory's quite a size. I've put in a word for Maud to help with the cleaning there. I hope she gets it, since she hates the woman she works for at Woodford. Well, I'm off!'

Nan bustled out and Poppy sat there in bed, surprised how taken back she was at Nan's news. Daniel and a nurse? How lovely! She was pleased, of course she was! But Daniel? She wondered how it could be that she had taken it for granted that part of Daniel would belong to her for ever. She had always turned to him, even as a child. Yes, she had looked up to him as she would a big brother. And like a big brother he would always be.

She heard footsteps pounding up Nan's stairs and Charlie bounced in. He was carrying grapes and grinning his lopsided grin.

'D'yer want to give me any more heart attacks?' he teased. 'Gor blimey, ducks, you could have got killed!'

'I know. I just went upstairs to bed and woke to find the passage on fire. Reggie Parker said he saw flames coming through the letter box. I owe him my life, Dad.'

'And don't think I ain't shook him by the hand! Said he

317

wasn't a bit surprised to hear that the firemen found several lighter-fuel tins inside your front door. Did Nan say?'

Poppy shook her head.

'And to top that lot off, Reggie's told the cops that he saw two blokes running hell for leather down the street. Made a statement, he has, about he recognised them. But you know the rozzers. They've gotta have proof. What I can't understand is why they did it. Have you got any ideas?'

'No,' she fibbed and bit her lip. 'Unless someone was jealous about all the work done on the place. I mean, everyone made quite a to-do about the painting and decorating. Then there was the furniture going in.'

It was a weak enough reason and Charlie shook his head.

'No, it weren't nothing like that, I'll be bound. Still, it don't matter. That's the coppers' job, not ours. What's really important is that you're all right, also that little unborn bread-snapper of yours. You'll have plenty to tell him when he gets older, eh?' He bent down to give her a great smacking kiss. 'Well, me little cock sparrow, I've gotta go. Clary will be in to see you later. Ta-ta for now.'

He kissed her! For the first time in her life, Charlie had actually kissed her! She put her hand against her cheek and felt so emotional, so absurdly happy, that she cried.

It seemed that everyone came visiting after that. Burney sat with her, then later Edna, Clary, Flossie and Maud. Even Vi was half decent, and Meg was almost in tears. In the end Poppy began to feel it had all been worth it, just to be so fussed over and spoiled.

Two evenings later Edna burst into the kitchen where Poppy had been sitting, talking to Nan. Edna was white to the lips and trembling, hardly able to get the words out of her mouth.

'Jay Wray and lots of others as well as Harry Peel have been arrested,' she stammered. 'The police raided the club. It was awful, all that shouting and noise, and that woman screaming. But the most terrible thing is they ... they've taken my Gus! Oh, bleeding hell, Poppy!'

She threw herself down to kneel before Poppy, then, hiding her face in Poppy's lap, she was choked with deep racking sobs.

'Edna, oh, Edna!' Poppy whispered. 'I'm so sorry, love!'
'Stop that caterwauling,' Nan said crisply. 'And listen to me, the pair of you. The police won't want no truck with Gus. He might be as thick as two planks, but there's no harm in him. They had him that den of iniquity just because he looks like a bruiser, but we all know he's a little lamb at heart. There ain't no harm in our Gus!'

Edna lifted a tear-stained face. 'We know that, Nan,' she wept. 'But the police don't!'

'Well, I might be an old fool, my girl, but even I don't think our police are daft! They'll send your Gus packing, believe me. Pull yourself together and don't upset Poppy no more than you have. Doc Fox says she's to be kept very quiet and calm. She's not even supposed to be out of bed, but we all know how pig-headed she is!' She pulled a handkerchief out of her sleeve and handed it to Edna. 'Wipe your tears, go on! I'll make you a nice cup of tea.'

She busied herself at the range and Poppy told her, 'I think you're right about Gus, Nan. Everyone knows and likes him. But it's not the case with Harry. Poor old Beth! She's had such dreams about her and Harry, ever since they were kids. I expect that'll be over and done with now.'

'Ha!' Nan snorted. 'And p'raps the young Parker boy will give Julie Peel the old heave-ho, now it looks like her brother's to be kept inside. Been sweet on him for quite a time, she has, but she's always trying to take his family down. The biggest problem's Liz. Her and Julie don't get on and Julie also reckons Reggie's weird – though no one can name-call him now! But young Julie's a proper little madam these days, and acts all toffee-nosed about Grant's lot. Now she's got a gaolbird in the family, young Grant can give tit for tat. And, knowing him, he will!'

Edna sniffed and continued to cling to Poppy, who sighed. 'It all happens in Jezebel Street, doesn't it?' she said. 'Thank goodness for Leyton Marshes. At least the air smells fresh over there.'

'I thought that was where you had horse dung up your nose all day long.' Nan was incensed and it showed. 'Give me strength!'

*

They kept Gus for twenty-four hours, then let him go. And the way Edna carried on you'd have thought he'd been shut away for years.

'We're both out of work,' Gus said, gruff and shamefaced once the kisses, cuddles and tears were ended. 'P'raps we'd best put off them plans we made.'

Edna reared up like a turkey cock. 'I ain't having none of that!' Her glare made Gus deflate even more. 'We'll get everything sorted at the registrar's up Baker's Arms. If we go back to Hackney my mum will make a worry of it all. And there'll be all the relations and their millions of kids squabbling about who comes and who's got left out and – oh, my Gawd, it don't bear thinking of!' She swung round to her friend, who had been sitting in Nan's chair, beaming. 'What d'yer think, Poppy?'

Poppy shrugged and raised her brows, having no intention of being pulled into this particular discussion. Gus was frowning.

'But wouldn't you like to be with your family?' he asked in his slow, careful way. His voice held longing as he added, 'I really like your mum and your poor old dad.'

'D'yer think I don't?' Edna was on her high horse now. 'That's why I'm thinking things over now. They can't deal with wedding fuss. And we ain't got a fortune to spend.' She smiled up at him and held his huge hand lovingly against her cheek. 'It's all right for the rich, innit? But bloody hard cheddar for the rest of us. So, if Nan says we can, we'll get wed all quick and quiet. You can move in here with me straight away. At least we'll be able to save the money you've been forking out for your digs.'

'You can't half handle things, Edna.' Gus's eyes held admiration. 'I don't now what I'd do without you. You're real clever. No one could ever tie knots round you.'

'You neither now,' she told him and gave him a great big hug. 'Not now I'm looking out for you. Brain and brawn, that's what we are. Brain and brawn! And now we'd better get on. We're supposed to be helping with Poppy's place. As soon as she's settled back in number ten, we'll have our very own two rooms!'

'Then it'll be my turn to help you two do everything up,' Poppy said. 'Oh, I'm so happy for you both!'

Daniel folded his arms and looked down at Lenny, who stood before him in the Home's business office, balanced on his crutches. Lenny was over his last bout of illness and seemed to have turned the corner at last. His face was rounded and healthy-looking, his eyes were bright and he had a quick and intelligent way of looking at things. Strange, how so many assumed a cripple was also stupid, Daniel thought. Lenny was far from that. Now the boy was watching Daniel beseechingly.

'So how does it feel to be your own master at last, eh? I bet you never believed you'd get to be fourteen and all grown-up.'

'I don't want to leave here,' Lenny said quietly. 'I don't want to go back to Jezebel Street.'

'You've got to, chum. You're managing very well now, even better than most kids your age do with two legs. You're quick on the uptake and you'll go far. Now Miss Wells is a very nice lady and she used to look after me. And, if you remember, she used to be very nice to you in the old days. She's given you her front room downstairs and she and her Burt are going to look out for you from now on, so don't look so scared.'

'I'm not!'

'Well, come on then! You'll like Burt, he's Flossie's man friend, and he's a bit of all right. Works in the office in Duke's coal yard. Remember Vic Parker, the coalie? He's at Duke's too. They're all people you'll know, Lenny.'

'I won't fit in. They'll call me Charity and ... and I just won't fit in.'

'My money says you will – and Poppy says so, too. She'll only be a couple of doors away. And Flossie will love hearing you play your mouth organ and all the merry tunes you blow on that whistle of yours. You can be a big help to Flossie, if that's what you want. Make her the odd cup of tea, things of that sort. You can manage to do that, eh?'

'I can manage a lot of things,' Lenny replied, brightening

321

at the thought of Poppy. 'Can I come back here and visit sometimes?'

'All the time, old son. All the time. We're mates! It's just that the powers that be reckon we need your space for some other poor bloke. Honestly, Len, you're better off than most. So come on, boy, let's get cracking.'

Daniel and Lenny began making their way along Skelton Street, the boy swinging his legs along, handling himself very well. Every so often he glanced up at Daniel.

Daniel was angry. The look in Lenny's eyes had reminded Daniel of himself long ago. It infuriated him that the boy had to leave, but Daniel had been outgunned every step of the way. Money, he thought bitterly, it all boils down to money. Spondulicks are too thin on the ground. Now they're insisting on a girls' section! Wouldn't it have been sensible to use our assets to better the lives of the kids we already have? Jam spread too thinly is worse than no jam at all!

'Daniel?' Lenny asked uncertainly. 'What's made you so mad? Are you worried?'

He grinned then and ruffled the boy's hair. 'Not at all,' he said. 'It's going to be a piece of cake, old son.'

' 'Course it is,' Lenny replied.

Very soon they were in Flossie's kitchen. Bosomy, frizzy-haired Flossie was warm and motherly, and all but smothering Lenny. She was telling him that he was 'her dear little ducks' and 'her own brave little soldier' who was now really and truly 'safe in his own home'.

Lenny's cheeks flushed, his eyes smiled and suddenly, quite brilliantly, joy flooded through him. He knew then that he didn't mind Jezebel Street after all.

A week later Poppy found herself storming into Daniel's cottage, all guns blazing. She knew she could speak to Flossie directly, but Daniel stood for officaldom where Lenny was concerned. He was the one who had promised to look out for the lad even though he had now left Devere's.

'Daniel?' she called out. 'Daniel!'

He came out of his kitchen, loaf in one hand, jam in the other.

'Hello, matey.' He smiled at her expression. 'You're back

on form, I see, and by the looks of it, in a fine old state. What's up?'

'Do you know what's going on? What Lenny's doing?'

'Well, it's not up to me these days. Flossie's taken him on. Hey! Shouldn't you be keeping yourself calm?'

'I've just been to the library.' Poppy was almost choking with indignation. 'And Lenny's outside the picture house. He's sitting on the kerb, his cap's on the ground in front of him, and he's playing his whistle for all he's worth. He's begging in the street, Daniel!'

'What?' Daniel's brows were raised, then his eyes sparkled with laughter. 'Well, I'll be damned! The gusty little blighter's thought of something. Good for him!'

'Good for him?' She was outraged. 'Good for him? I'm going to see Flossie here and now, and I'm going to tell her –'

'No!' His voice cracked out as hard as a pistol shot. 'Mind your business, old girl.'

'I am! And I'm going to tell that Flossie that she –'

'If you dare put your oar in,' he told her in a tone she had never heard from him before, 'I almost think I'll strangle you. Are you listening to me?'

Poppy was so angry she was near to tears. It might be decent weather and Lenny was indeed old enough to work for his living at fourteen, but to be out there begging! It just wouldn't do! She opened her mouth to argue, but Daniel snapped at her.

'You'll keep well out of it. The little tyke's after getting money behind him. Flossie's birthday's coming up, for a start, and he wants to do something about it.'

'There must be –'

'Remember the old Lenny, do you?' Daniel cut in. 'The fragile, mournful waif who was practically glued to the doorstep of number one? Remember the drunks falling over him, the kids teasing him and the crowd of pigs that got a kick out of piddling over him? Do you recall all that?'

'Yes,' she flared. 'Which is all the more reason –'

'To clap your hands and tell him, "Well done!" Lenny's having a go, Poppy. He's doing something for himself. In short, Lenny's doing a great deal for his own self-respect.'

323

'I don't think –'

'Forget it, Poppy. Just keep away from Lenny. Allow him to run his own life, as I run mine and you run yours. I didn't know what the kid was up to, and I'm sure Flossie will have kittens when she finds out, but no one's going to stop that boy! D'you hear me?'

He was glaring down at her and she glared back. Suddenly he pulled her roughly towards him and kissed her fair and square. Then he held her away and smiled into her eyes.

'That's for caring so much,' he told her. 'My God, matey, I wish they were all like you.'

'Well, well,' she told him, rosy-cheeked and glowing. 'Life's full of surprises. What with my dad and now you! I reckon I'm getting quite kissable in my old age.' Then her mood changed because the smile had gone from his eyes and his face looked strained. 'What's wrong?' she asked quickly. 'Goodness me, Daniel, what is it?'

'I wanted so much more for my boys!' he told her. 'It's not to be, I'm afraid. I can't help it, Poppy, but I don't feel good about the cash going for a place for girls! Nurse Bittlestone thinks otherwise. She's heard of a case and she wants me to go along, see for myself and take control. She wants me to get involved! Barbara certainly has a way with her, and when she sparks up she reminds me of you!' He smiled ruefully and shrugged. 'Well, I'll do as she asks and see to it, of course. I certainly have all the authority I need.'

'Then it's settled and my thoughts will be with you.' Poppy twinkled at him, her anger gone, having accepted Daniel's previous words of wisdom. 'But although I'm prepared to go along with you about Lenny, I think you're dead wrong about the other thing. I'm on the side of the poor little orphaned girls.'

'Women!'

'We're a breed apart.' She laughed. 'And I like the sound of your Nurse Bittlestone. 'Bye for now, Daniel.'

Daniel strode along the dark, urine-befouled alleyway, his face grim. He came to the brown peeling door he was looking for. The house he was visiting was large, dilapidated and disgusting. Daniel went in and found himself inside a filthy passage. The air was thick with the greasy smell of frying sprats. The first door to the right had a brass lion handle that was mildew-green. Daniel turned it and entered the near-dark single room rented by the Elms.

First to hit him was the stench, then the cold. One small window was covered with yellowing newspaper. As his eyes became accustomed to the gloom Daniel noted how squalid the room was. Against a bug-infested wall there stood a sagging sofa with great tufts of horsehair spilling out. On this, looking like grotesque bookends, there lolled a sleeping man and woman. She was foxy-faced and dressed in rusty black clothes. The heavily built male was open-mouthed and snoring. His cloth cap was pulled down over his eyes, the top button of his trousers was undone. His braces and leather belt were hanging loosely over his vast stomach.

The only other piece of furniture was a large table covered with torn and dingy oilcloth. On this was dirty crockery, opened tins, an empty beer jug, old newspapers and other rubbish. More refuse spilled over the fireless grate and onto the hearth.

There was no sign of a child.

Daniel stood very quiet and still, his eyes raking the room. Then he saw her, cowering under the table: a small creature, her underfed body barely covered by a dirty cotton dress that was in rags. She was staring at him, her eyes wide in her swollen and bruised face. Daniel went down on his knees.

'It's all right, sweetheart,' he said gently. 'I've come to take you away from this place.'

She was trembling violently, too afraid to cry. Then she froze as the woman woke and yelled, 'Who the bleedin' hell are you? Piss off out of here.'

'I've come for the girl,' Daniel told her as he rose to stand at full height. 'So it's no good making a fuss.'

'You dirty bastard, what d'yer want with her?' she yelled. 'Leave her alone! Ernie, wake up. Ern, wake up, you stupid sod! We've got a nutcase in here.'

'I'm taking the child,' Daniel reiterated, 'and there's nothing you can do about it.'

'Who d'yer think you effing well think you are?' The

325

woman leaped at him. 'Ernie, come to, for Gawd's sake, Ern!'

Ernie Elms awoke, took the situation in at a glance and let out a roar. Daniel had time only to shove the woman out of the way before defending himself against an animalistic attack. The ensuing fight was short, sharp and owed nothing to the Queensberry rules. Daniel let all his pent-up fury and disgust go, and when Ernie went down he stayed down. The woman, hand raised, began to leap at Daniel, but suddenly froze. She was staring at the tall, uniformed young lady who had just arrived and was now standing inside the door. Neat and trim, the newcomer had bobbed brown hair and a stern expression on her comely face. Her large, luminous eyes held such a warning that the woman whimpered, then knelt down beside her Ernie.

'You'll be having a visit from the authorities, Mrs Elms,' Daniel told her evenly. 'Your cruelty has been reported by the caretaker here. Do you hear me? It's all taken down. If anyone asks, tell them that Daniel Devere took matters into his own hands and that your niece has been taken to a place of safety, the Devere Home for Girls. The place that the officials agreed on. Do I make myself clear?'

With a single forceful movement, he pushed the table away so that he could reach the shivering child. He lifted her rigid little frame and, holding her as gently as possible, walked out of the house. Once in the alleyway, Barbara Bittlestone asked Daniel to stop while she wrapped a light-weight woollen blanket round the little girl. She smiled into a pair of very frightened eyes.

'You're nothing but a bag of bones,' she said in the false bright tones used for an invalid. 'But never mind, sweetheart, we'll soon alter that.' She looked up at Daniel, adding, 'Your left cheek's bleeding and I think you're going to have a black eye.'

'It's worth it,' Daniel told her, then a wry grin creased his face. 'I know I asked you to stay where you were, but I couldn't have fought off that bloody awful woman. As for the bloke, I wanted to kill him! Have you noticed this youngster's legs and arms?'

'Leather strap, I'd say.' Barbara's voice was bitter. 'Along

326

with festering cigarette burns. You know, Daniel ...' Her large brown eyes were fiery and Daniel found himself thinking that anger made Nurse Bittlestone rather beautiful. She went on, 'I can't help thinking that murder is clean and final against something as monstrous as this. By the look of things, this child has been deliberately put through hell for years.'

He was staring down at her, a gentle expression on his face. 'You remind me of someone I know,' he told her. 'A very special young chum of mine. Her name's Poppy, and she's rather like you, in so far as she always wants to champion the underdog. If she saw the state this young nipper's in, she would go mad.'

'She's very special?' Dark velvety eyes looked searchingly into hyacinth blue.

'She's married,' Daniel told her, 'and expecting her first within a few weeks from now. I can see you and her becoming great friends. Now, where's that taxi? I won't rest until we got this young'un back safe.' He paused, then added sincerely, 'Point taken, Barbara. You're right. It is very necessary to have a place for needy little girls. Poppy reckons that, too. She told me so in no uncertain terms.'

'Then your Poppy and I are bound to get on,' Nurse Barbara replied. 'There's our taxi waiting as I asked, by the corner in the main road.'

Both Barbara and Daniel were silently fuming over the state of the tiny May Elms as Reggie Parker stoically drove them back to Devere's.

Poppy sat daydreaming before her own kitchen range. Magically everything was once again shipshape and Bristol fashion. The greatest damage had been in the passage. The fire, smoke and fumes spreading to the front room had caused havoc, but everyone had chipped in. Now she had her things around her, as well as new curtains, including the white lace.

It was all very quiet.

Sometimes, at moments like this, she imagined she was in the flat again, waiting for Nigel. She would see him walking towards her, his eyes smiling from behind those extraordinary white eyelashes of his. Then her whole being

327

would be gathered up and carried along with such yearning, her memories holding such poignancy, that her heart would swell and all but burst.

And then she would whisper Sandy's name, needing him, wanting to feel his strong arms around her. Being held by Sandy was nice, familiar, and, oh, so comforting! Now she was remembering her husband, his smile, the way he lifted his chin when he let out his great roar of a laugh. Sandy gave her courage and made her feel strong. Where was he now? Why hadn't she heard? She was missing him even more these days, she had so much more time on her hands. Dr Fox had insisted that she must rest. She felt fat and ugly, and hated doing nothing.

Geraniums stood like little scarlet soldiers outside the front window of her house. Poppy had treated Nan to the same window boxes, and Flossie and Maud. Until now the hordes of kids had left everything alone. So an old promise had been kept, she told herself. Flowers were blooming in Jezebel Street – for Ros.

Sandy would like them, and like her, he would remember. But should one always remember things – about losing loved ones, about giving birth, the things people said? In spite of herself she was remembering all the gory tales women had told her about childbirth. Did they really cut you open from the chest right the way down? Did it split you apart so that doctors had to stitch you up again underneath? Was it honestly worse than hell on earth?

Poppy again found herself wishing rather desperately that Sandy was with her now. She tried to picture him, somewhere out there at sea . . .

Right aft, in the cramped, stuffy crew's quarters, Sandy lay awake on his bunk. Out there, in the broad reaches of the ocean, where below only the threshing of the *Vanessa*'s propeller disturbed the night, Jezebel Street might as well be on the moon. He picked up his favourite wedding picture of Poppy. God, how she could get under his skin!

Unsettled, he went up on deck and looked out. There was something quite awesome about the sea, he thought. It had turned to never-ending black ink from the burnished red and gold it had been at sunset. Then it had all been calm, too calm. Ominous! He wouldn't have been surprised to find crew called upon to batten down hatches. But the moment passed.

Now, out here on the main deck, it was a quiet time, a thinking time, when a man came to terms with his own insignificance. All around lay vast ocean and silver-tipped waves. High above, unimaginable numbers of stars twinkled in the purple basin of the sky. It filled a bloke with a sense of awe, humbled him before the greatness of it all. Sandy lit a Woodbine cigarette and inhaled, enjoying the comforting way the smoke filled his lungs. He found himself wondering at what point, precisely, did a chap cease to be an individual and become a woman's other half? Poppy!

He heard himself swearing, and then Les clowning around as he came to join him at the rail. Rascally old Onions was always good for a laugh.

'Gawd 'elp us,' Onions exclaimed, 'you're a right moody old sod. Let's go below decks. Murphy's raking it in. You'd think the scatty buggers would have learned not to try and beat him at cards.'

Sandy went below, where the air was thick with tobacco fumes and foul language as the game progressed. Sandy was not in the frame of mind to join in. Leaving them to it, he lay on his bunk and listened to the ceaseless beating of the waves against the ship's sides. There were other noises also: the rattle of steering gears, the whine of fuel pumps and the constant creaking of fixtures straining against the *Vanessa*'s motion, which grew more agitated as time went on.

An hour later there was a fair-sized sea running and the wind was up to force 7. It could get worse, and the *Vanessa* was not in good nick. Sandy was watching the light swinging rapidly backwards and forwards.

'Bleeding hell,' Onions swore as he joined him. 'It's getting real nasty. Is what why you're like me, unable to sleep?'

'Not specially.'

'Then what's up, cock?'

'I feel uneasy, that's all. Can't settle. Keep thinking of Poppy.'

'Get under your skin, don't they?' Onions grinned. 'I wouldn't be without my Annie, but thinking about her don't half get in the way of things.'

'What things?' Sandy jibed and he and Onions had a mock battle before finally turning in.

Sandy slept at last and dreamed of Poppy.

The sun was still more than an hour below the horizon, the darkness was absolute. The four-to-eight watch settled down to wait the coming of a new day. At 4.40 a.m. the sleeping *Vanessa* was rocked by a massive explosion. The compass light went on, the quartermaster was thrown to the deck by the wildly kicking wheel, and the alarm bells of the fire detector set up a strident clamour.

Immediately the ship was alive with crew running, feet pounding on ladders. Men half dressed, bleary from sleep, tore to their posts. Another explosion increased the heat of flames and the crazy rocking of the *Vanessa*. Clouds of dense black smoke were billowing in from the forward 'tween decks. From behind the wall of smoke came the crackle of flames and the screams of trapped men.

With his ship and all on board now in great danger, the master ordered his radio officer to send out an SOS and then sounded the emergency signal on the alarm bells.

Sandy, Onions and the others rushed to the boat deck. The fire followed them, and by the time the order was given to abandon ship, most of the lifeboats on the starboard side were unapproachable because of the flames. In no time, the *Vanessa* had been turned into an inferno, from which it seemed few would escape.

'I can't see a bloody thing,' Onions yelled. Suddenly he was lifted by a great force, then sharply released to fall against the deck. Sandy saw him, head bloodied, mouth open wide, trying to hold on, but the *Vanessa* was tilting, and Onions's grip was weakening. He was sliding away, swept to doom in what he used to call the 'sodding drink'.

'No!' Sandy croaked and, making a superhuman effort, grabbed him and held on. The whole world was reeling, the storm raging, the winds howling as good men died.

Sandy fought to stay calm. He held on to Onions, refusing to let go. Something hit the back of his head and sent lights zigzagging before his eyes. He felt rather than saw the tremendous waves that fell on him like black mountains. Yelling for Poppy in his mind, he felt he was drowning, falling beneath the depths. He knew no more . . .

The floorboards of number two Jezebel Street were throbbing under the weight of stamping feet. It was Edna and Gus's wedding day.

'Knees up, Mother Brown,' guests roared out, lifting their knees high and holding on to each other as they pranced round. 'Knees up, Mother Brown. Under the table you must go, ee-i, ee-i, ee-i-o. If I catch you bending, I'll saw your legs right off. Knees up, knees up, don't get the breeze up. Knees up, Mother Brown.'

Faster and faster they went, a wild flailing of legs and feet, skirts and hair ribbons flying, braces bare to view, ties and jackets long since cast aside. Edna was in the thick of it, wearing forget-me-not blue, white daisies in her hair and twinkling stars in her eyes. And big, clumsy Gus was holding her as if she was fashioned from crystal, delicate and wonderful, something he must be very careful to cherish and never to break. Edna's folks were there, and as many of the neighbours as could cram themselves in. Lenny had a special seat and Flossie and Burt were guarding him, adoring him, loving him as deeply as they would a son of their own. Lenny had it made and it showed.

Arty was having the time of his life, stuffing himself with sandwiches, jellies, blancmange, cakes and crisps, all set out in grand kitchen display. In the scullery, huge jugs of beer never seemed to empty; there was even some wine and, for the kids, lemonade. Everything had been bought and paid for by Poppy. 'My wedding present,' she had insisted. Just as Burney had insisted on making a white wedding cake, arm in a sling or no. Edna's two mates had decided long ago that she must have a very special day.

Poppy sat and watched all the merry goings-on. She felt content and excited, too, because Bill had popped in to tell her that things were going very well. He had arranged to rent a lock-up shop quite near Leyton Town Hall. It would be their very first! He couldn't wait for her to come back, he had told her. He missed having her there cheering him up. He hadn't stayed long; jollifications were not for him. But he had drunk a toast to the happy couple, and given them a cheque for twenty pounds. A fortune! Bill had also promised to try and find Gus a job. Both bride and groom were over the moon.

A motorbike drew up outside.

'Wedding greetings,' Nan said, beaming. 'Talk about posh!' She bustled outside, then came back looking worried. She handed the telegram over to Poppy, saying, 'For you!'

Poppy could not take it in. The *Vanessa* sunk? Hands missing, including Sandy! Searches were going on . . .

An agony shot through Poppy, racing from the crown of her head to her toes. It was a terrible pain that went through her heart and soul and every fibre of her being. She bent double under the shock, and felt her legs weaving beneath her watery and useless. She was suddenly aware of a change in herself. She was going hot and cold, and sensing all her previous energy and eagerness draining away. The excitement of life dried up, dead and done for, and there was only Nan to hold on to, to keep her sane.

Nan took the telegram out of her nerveless fingers, then said, 'Oh, my God!'

'Nan!' Poppy whispered urgently, 'take me back to my house. I've got to be alone!'

Everyone had stopped shouting and singing. They were standing still, just staring, looking like frozen statues with wide-open mouths.

'What's wrong?' Edna asked sharply. 'It's something horrible, innit?'

'No,' Poppy gasped. 'It's just a message saying that Sandy's ship is in dry dock again, so he won't be back very soon after all. Oh!' A piercing knife-thrust made her bend again. When it faded, she smiled and gasped, 'I think I'll be better off at home, don't you? Nan will take me back to number ten. You carry on! Please have a very good time.'

Shooing everyone away, Nan put her arm round Poppy and helped her along the street.

'It's not true, Nan,' Poppy whispered, 'it can't be. I was so looking forward to – oh!'

'I'll get Mrs Hodges,' Nan said. 'You go on in, put the

332

kettle on and make sure you've got all the necessary things to hand. I won't be a tick.'

'You mean I'm . . . I'm having –'

'Well, you ain't been eating green apples,' Nan said tartly and forced herself to grin her wicked grin. 'Now forget everything except making sure that your little'un gets into the world all safe and sound. Do everything proper – for Sandy's sake.'

Nan gently pushed Poppy inside number ten, then hurried down Jezebel Street and into Beaumont Road. Now there was no one near to see, Nan's tears escaped, falling like hot blisters onto her cheeks.

Time had no meaning for Poppy after that. It was all gnawing, burning, then knifelike pains that seemed to be cutting her in half. And the lull between the stabbing torments lessened every time so that in the end there was no respite. During the later stages Poppy cried out for Sandy, screamed for Sandy, begged him over and over not leave her on her own. At the very height of the excruciation, at the moment Poppy knew she could stand no more, tiny Rosemary Nan Swift was born.

Filled with an adoration she never thought possible, Poppy looked down at the shawl-wrapped scrap Mrs Hodges handed to her. Nan was weeping and whispering, 'We have a new Ros!'

'With masses of black hair!' Poppy whispered, and kissed the little screwed-up face again. 'Who on earth is she like?'

'My gran had black hair,' Nan sniffed, 'lots darker than your dad's. And don't forget Meg.'

'She probably takes after Meg!' Poppy breathed, silently thanking God. 'If only Sandy was here!' Then she broke down and cried.

Chapter Nineteen

Jezebel Street basked in the sunlight. Little girls holding rag dolls clopped about wearing their mothers' shoes. Boys played cricket with a lump of wood for a bat and an old jacket for bails. Women stood on their doorsteps, arms folded, empty cups on windowsills, either jawing or just watching the world go by.

A shabby cripple limped along the street, dodging the mounds of horse dung, begging for farthings. Four farthings would buy him enough chips to see him through the day. He was trying to sing, but the sound he made was toneless, the words as useless as the roof of his mouth. 'Moun, moun,' he went, 'moun, 'o mourn.' A group of scruffy urchins skipped after him, mimicking, arms waving, lips grinning, eyes cruel. They had followed him from the moment he had been ousted from his corner on the High Road where the organ grinder and his monkey now stood – and had already collected a copper or two.

A Lamb boy shot down the road with spade and bucket, just beating a King. They fought over the dung, which would sell for three halfpence to any of the allotment men. An old codger pushed his piled-high barrow round the scuffling boys. He was grinning and ready to hand out toffee apples or goldfish for rags.

'Hany ol' rags,' he yelled. 'Hany o-el rags?'

'Rags?' fat Mrs Peel bawled out heartily. 'Rags? You'll be lucky to get mine. I'm pissing well wearing 'em!'

Ribald laughter followed this, and filthy jokes, and one blowsy woman lifted her skirt, showing her nakedness underneath, and yelled, 'Come over 'ere, Sunshine, and give me some of your ol' rags. I could use 'em!'

Others joined in the fun. 'And me!' – 'Me too!' – 'Got any drawers to tickle me ol' man?' – 'She means them as don't have no crutch, Raggy!'

The women went from bad to worse, screaming with laughter, and the jolly old ragman gave as good as he got, threatening to have his way with all of them.

Poppy, holding the treasure of her life in her arms, went to the window to peep behind her white lace. She looked ill, there were dark shadows under her eyes, she was still far from strong, but restless just the same. She felt that she was only the husk of a person, because inside she was dead, and now distrusting of fate, or the Almighty. He was wicked and cruel, not merciful. The hard lesson Poppy had learned was that loving meant losing through either death or abandonment – Ros, Nigel and now Sandy.

One couldn't bank on a single thing as being a certainty in this life, Poppy grieved. The whole of existence was merely one huge and frightening void. It scared her to bits. She wanted to run away and hide, but didn't know why or where. All she knew was nameless terror. She feared for her baby, her wondrous new love who was to her more precious than the biggest diamond in the world.

'Nerves,' Doc Fox had told her when she couldn't stop weeping. 'You just need a sedative or two. Things will be much better later on.'

She looked down at Rosemary, peacefully sleeping, and knew that she wouldn't let God take her baby away. She would fight for her, go through fire and water, kill for her, die for her. Give up every last drop of her own blood.

She gently kissed Rosemary, who slept on, then looked out of the window again. Trouble was coming in the shape of Liz.

Liz was marching down the street, her basket filled with potatoes and other vegetables. When Liz saw Aggie, her lips curled. Aggie stiffened, ready for a fight.

'How's Julie feeling now, eh? Eh?' Liz yelled at the top of her voice. 'Us Parkers ain't good enough for you Peels, eh? Got a nutty son in love with his bike, ain't we? And an ol' man what's a sex maniac? Not forgetting me what's a regular, sozzled, mouthy ol' cow! Ho, yers! Heard it all, I have. Ha, bleedin' ha! Got your comeuppance, ain't you? Now what have you got to say for yourself?'

Aggie knew what was coming. Her moon-face went white. She turned, intending to go back inside her home, not wanting to hear. But Liz was triumphant. Liz was filled with unholy joy. At last she had a banner to wave in the face of the 'preening little moo what 'ad made her life a misery'. Liz was on the rampage and not about to let go.

'You come back here, you big fat bitch!' she bawled. 'Just you come here and listen to what I've got to say! You can tell your stuck-up tart of a daughter that I'll lean over an' lick me own arse before I'll let my boy take on the likes of her. My old chap's always been in work, and married to me for over thirty years, so he's every right to eye up pretty girls.'

Aggie Peel pulled herself to full height and sneered. 'An' I reckon he'd see a bit of cold cod as something better than you.'

'Cold cod's better than a fat, hignerant old whale! All mouth and trousers, you Peels are. What's more, I'm going ter show you a thing or two!'

'Shut your cake'ole, you boozy mare.'

Liz grew in stature. She was at battle stations now. Her straw hat was tilted back, her sparse bosom heaved under her floral pinafore. Her shopping basket was raised in readiness to swing. With or without drink, Liz in a fury was a frightening foe.

'Shut your gob and listen for a change,' she screeched. 'My Reggie's a war hero what fought for the likes of you. And what's more, he's now a hero down this street! An' my Greg's too bleeding good for a family what finishes up in gaol. So put that in your pipe an' smoke it till you sodding well choke, you big fat cow!'

'Belt up!' Mrs Peel lunged forwards, ready to crush and destroy. Then she stopped short, hand raised.

'That's enough, you two.'

Poppy, regarded by most of them as a stuck-up little snot, faced them. She was holding Rosemary close, and her eyes

336

were blazing. She stepped determinedly between Aggie and Liz.

Everyone fell quiet. This was the first time she had stepped out of number ten since she had delivered her child. She looked too young to be a widow, and very fragile, for all she was in a towering rage. They could have given her a tongue blasting, roughed her up and shoved her back inside her ponced-up house, but they didn't. A puff of wind could have blown her down, they knew it, and so did she. Poppy didn't know what had made her run outside to face them; she couldn't even remember doing so. So she stood there, glaring and quivering, all knotted up inside. She heard herself carrying on.

'How dare you?' she told them, her voice holding scorn. 'You should be ashamed. You've got husbands to squabble over, haven't you? Gaolbirds or heroes, it makes no odds. At least your men are alive!'

'More's the pity,' a woman with curlers in her hair replied with wry humour. ' 'Ow are you, luv? Can we see your little'un? Can we 'ave a peep?'

Liz and Aggie's row was forgotten as the women surrounded Poppy and oohed and aahed at the perfection that was Rosemary. And Poppy, proud that her baby was receiving so much affection and praise, began to pull herself together at last.

She needed to work, to get on, she decided, as she stood there surrounded by smiling women. And not waste any more time weeping, or at least not letting her grief show. If she was fated to stay in Jezebel Street for a while, then she would make the best of it. She had to stop moping and hiding and letting herself go. She had to pull herself together, be a help to dear old Bill, who made such a point of visiting her. Bill had been filled with awe when he first saw her newborn child.

Poppy had Rosemary to fight for, she told herself, as well as her own life's plan. She had to be up and about, work hard to try and drown all the bitterness and grief.

'We're sorry about your Sandy,' Mrs Peel said. 'Real sorry and that.'

'Bloody shame, luv.' – 'Life's a cow.' – 'It's the shits, innit?'

They all murmured their sympathies, then there was a moment when they all went quiet and looked at her with pity in their eyes.

She stood among them, trying to smile and be brave. But she kept remembering Sandy, hearing his voice, seeing the light and laughter in his eyes. It was even worse than having lost Nigel, she mourned. At least Nigel was still around. Fate could take away and, in Nigel's case, even bring back. About Nigel she could hope and dream and fantasise. But Sandy, her dearest friend, was no longer part of this earth.

She couldn't stand the thought, and tearfully left the small group and went back inside her house.

Late that night a knock came on Poppy's door. She was taken aback to find Reggie Parker standing there.

'Can I come in?' he asked in his rusty voice. 'I've got a message.'

'What kind of message?' she asked, feeling suspicious and never quite comfortable with the man, still unable to come to terms with the cold, flinty look in his eyes. 'Can't you tell me here?'

'Not on the step,' he replied. 'So am I in or out?'

She stepped aside, allowing him to enter. He walked along the passage, freshly painted in chocolate brown and cream, and into the kitchen, which was warm and light. He looked around, nodded and sat down as she requested, saying, 'You've got this place nice again.'

'I like it,' she told him, 'It's good to be able to suit yourself. I'm amazed that you stay with your mum and dad. They're always yelling at you. I'm sure you could afford a really decent flat of your own.'

'I'll buzz off when it suits me,' he told her, then added, 'thanks for that leather jacket you got your aunt to buy me. It's perfect, but you shouldn't have forked that much out.'

'You saved my life and therefore Rosemary's life too. I can never thank you enough.'

'I was just doing what I was paid to,' he told her, his voice rasping like a saw. 'Mr Tilsby asked me, for his cousin, Mr Carson's sake. I was ordered to keep my eye on you.'

338

'Mr Carson?' she stammered, not comprehending. 'I – I don't understand.'

'I've been watching out for you from the word go. Mr Carson's been told what you've been up to, everything! Yes, especially about them Saunders twins setting your place on fire. Jay Wray told them to do it. Out to get you, he was.' Reggie grinned. 'His missus went bananas and put him through hell that night. She didn't care that the clients were all ears. She wanted to know all about you, too right! And all her hollerin' and smackin' him in his gob made him look like an old wore-out dishcloth. You ought to have seen his face. All dirty-looking it was. Grey!'

'Which is exactly how he makes other people feel,' Poppy said quietly. 'He got what was coming to him for a change.'

'When the fire didn't take hold proper and do for you,' Reggie continued, 'he had them twins roughed up.' Again that icy smile. 'They'd already bashed up Porky, so they were for it anyway. Not surprising, after what you said they'd told you about his missus.'

'Oh, Lord, I didn't mean that to happen! I just wanted to get back at them, but I didn't want –'

'When you muck in with Jay you know you're asking for it. Them three's lucky. Mario Maleni's vanished off the face of the earth. Anyway, Jay Wray swore he wasn't finished, and began getting even more open about going in for cold-blooded murder. I let Mr Carson know quick. So Mr Carson shopped him, he did. Sent the rozers all the proof they needed to put Jay Wray behind bars. Mr Carson made you safe.' Poppy noted the flicker of Reggie's icy grin. 'From now on he'll have enemies, seeing as how he's turned copper's nark. Gawd, you must have what it takes.'

'No.' The white lie was forced from her lips. 'I . . . I knew his wife! It was because of her! I – I didn't know that Mr Carson . . .'

'I should say he is!' Reggie remained unconvinced. 'Wants to see your kid. How old is it now?'

'She's five weeks, but –' Poppy was confused, then scared. 'No!' she gasped. 'Not here. Mr Carson must never come here.'

'He knows your old man's gone down with his ship, so he

339

wants to see you and the kid. Says he must and will. You can tell me where and when, and I'll send a message to him by the guvner, who'll phone.'

'I can't!' She was anguished, yet thrilled. Nigel did love her. He really and truly did! He loved her enough to save her from Jay Wray. At least she should let him see his – No! Sandy's child.

'He mustn't come here!' She faltered. 'The neighbours will see and –'

'There's the Blue Diamond, what Mr Tilsby's thinking of buying. Else Mr Carson could come here. He could make out he was something to do with your husband's shipping line. That's what he said.'

'His car! I don't think a messenger from a shipping line would own a car like that. Besides –'

'He'd leave that outside the club and walk here. Mr Carson's message is that he'll do anything you ask.'

'He wants to see me that much?' she whispered, her heart in her eyes.

'Looks like it,' Reggie said. He stood up, cold, efficient, detached. 'I'll call in tomorrow night and you can tell me what's what.'

The following night, sweating because Nan and Edna and then Burney all chose to drop in, Poppy waited for Reggie to call. They left, shaking their heads and carrying on about her nerves.

It was quite late when Reggie finally returned.

'Tell Mr Carson to come here, next Saturday,' she whispered nervously. 'Wild horses wouldn't get me back inside that club! And, if possible, tell him to wait until it's dark.'

He nodded and went on his way.

'Well, mate,' Onions said. 'Looks like we made it – thanks to you.'

'I don't remember,' Sandy said, 'but from what you've told me it was thanks to the *Tehuti* and her crew.'

'No! You!' Onions insisted. 'It was you that wouldn't let me go. Oh, shit! You don't know, do you? Mate, they had to prise your hands off me, you hung on so tight! Me and Annie will owe you all our days.'

'Shut it!' Sandy grinned and they both waited for the ambulance that was to take Able Seaman Les Pickles back home. 'I'm going to miss you, old son. It's good of them to promise us all new berths, eh? I suppose you'll be off and away after your leave?'

'Of course. I'll have a young whippersnapper to look out for from now on. So, for a while at least, it's goodbye and cheers for you and me –'

'Well, you come over my place as often as you can – and as soon as they let me, I'll be with you on the *Rodale.*' Les' grin widened. 'Gawd, it's good to be back, eh? Good to be safe. Gawd, what a how d'yer do! Just when we was making better time an' all. Now my Annie's going to 'ave the time of her life being bossy, seeing I ain't up to defending myself.'

Onions began going over it again, for Sandy's sake more than his own. Wanting to make sure that his mate had everything truly fixed. And Sandy, realising this, went along with it.

The *Vanessa* had been making good time for the Cape when a mountainous sea had rolled in and slammed over her port side, throwing spray high over the bridge. When the water receded it was clear the *Vanessa* was not hurt. She had staggered as though smashing into an unseen wall, as the first explosion occurred. Fire broke out and held, taking some unlucky crew members as well as lifeboats. When the second explosion happened the *Vanessa* was in serious trouble. The seas were now sweeping right over her deck, dousing the fires, and each time the ship slid down the sides of the waves, she seemed to find it harder to rise.

Her distress call was heard by the *Tehuti.* Unable to increase speed because of the heavy weather, she changed course in response.

Knowing nothing of this, Sandy had held on to Les all through the shrieking darkness of that terrible night. The *Vanessa* was sinking by the time the *Tehuti* reached the scene. Survivors of the *Vanessa's* crew watched from aboard the rescue ship as their rusty old girl went down.

The weather worsened, and the *Tehuti* hit trouble. The

ocean swept over her, beating down, smashing and destroying all in its path. The *Tehuti*'s number-one hold was awash, the pumps working overtime. Her wireless station was smashed and made useless: there could be no SOS calls. It looked possible that the *Tehuti* might follow the *Vanessa* to a watery grave. The fact that she made it, and safely limped home, was a credit to the master and all hands.

For Sandy, suffering amnesia caused by the wound on the back of his head, and Les, in agony from a broken hip and internal injuries, the voyage to port was more or less a blur. Having reached Port Arthur, they were separated, needing individual medical care.

Arrangements were made for survivors to be shipped home in double-quick time. It was not until Sandy and Onions were reunited on English shores that Sandy's memory began to return. Unaware that Poppy thought he was dead, he had no notification of his safety sent home. Now he was feeling quite elated and satisfied, wondering whether Poppy had had the baby yet, and whether it was a boy or a girl.

The ambulance men began lifting Onions' stretcher in. The driver looked at Sandy and enquired, 'Where to, mate?'

'Leyton.'

'We'll take you and drop you to the nearest point, if you like. Then you needn't wait till tomorrer, like they said. That's if you don't mind getting back late?'

'Better late than never,' Sandy replied. 'Thanks a lot.'

Poppy's heart was thumping crazily as she went to open the door for Nigel. He was holding parcels and a massive bunch of red roses. He stepped into her passage, dropped the things he was carrying and held out his arms. Then she was laughing and crying and being cradled against him, and listening to his tender, loving words. She was his sweetheart, his precious, the jewel in his crown. And she was whispering his name over and over. Loving the faint tang of his tobacco that clung to his clothes, breathing in the clear odour of the hair cream he used.

At last he held her away from him, admiring her with his eyes, and asked, 'Where is she? I must see her!'

342

And Poppy led him by the hand into the kitchen, where Rosemary was sleeping in her pram, petite, dark-haired and all dressed in white, a newborn cherub.

'Oh, my God!' Nigel said hoarsely, staring down at her. 'I've got to have her, darling. She's mine!'

'No,' Poppy said quietly, dismayed at the yearning she saw in his eyes. 'No, Nigel. She's mine!'

He shook his head, moved almost to tears, unable to look away from the baby.

'She belongs to me,' he reiterated. 'I can give her everything she needs. Poppy, be sensible. She belongs with my wife and with me.'

'Your wife?' She couldn't believe what he'd said. 'You mean that you would like to take Rosemary and – and give her to your wife?' She laughed bitterly. 'Are you mad? If having a child's that important, why don't you give her one?'

'She's barren, Poppy! Look, sweetheart,' he was coaxing now, 'I could give this baby everything. A wonderful home –'

'She has a home.'

'A good school.'

'Skelton School was good enough for me.'

'But this street –'

'Is none of your business.' She was standing as tall as she could now. 'And to think I believed you came here to see me! That you loved me!'

His expression held sincerity. He took hold of both her hands and held them against his chest.

'Poppy,' he told her, 'I swear I have never loved anyone as much as I love you, and I always will! But our paths lie in different directions, sweetheart, don't you see that? It has to be!'

'No!'

'But I would see you more than all right for money if you let her go. I want my daughter to share in all the good things in life.' He was trying emotional blackmail now, adding, 'She will always be the living reminder of our love, Poppy.'

'Love?' she whispered, ashen-faced. 'How can you love me and yet want to steal my child?'

'But what can you offer her, darling?' he argued. 'Nothing!

343

And now your husband's dead, your situation will be much worse. Don't you see?'

'You will never take my baby,' she said fiercely, feeling as if iron hands were squeezing her heart. 'Never! Do you understand?'

'I can fight for her, Poppy.' He was desperate now. 'Don't make me do that! The courts would have to side with me, because of all the good things I can give. Poppy, I don't want to have to go to the law!'

'You pig!' She sprang at him, but he caught and held her, and his lips closed fiercely over her own. His physical attraction was such that for one split second she melted against him. He held her fast, his cheeks against her hair.

'My precious, my sweetheart,' he was groaning. 'How can I let either of you go?'

At that moment Sandy walked through the door.

Poppy felt her life draining from her head down to her toes and into the cold, cold ground. She could not believe the evidence of her eyes. Caught against Nigel's heart, she tried to whisper her husband's name, but her lips merely formed an O. Then with a stifled gasp she slipped into a faint and knew no more.

Consciousness returned, and with it memory, and fear picked at her brain with fingers of ice. She gasped Rosemary's name and sat up, terror in her eyes. Then she saw Sandy. He was sitting, statue-still, at the table, the sleeping baby in his arms.

'Thank God,' she murmured. 'Sandy, he came to . . . He came to . . .'

'I think I saw why he came,' Sandy replied calmly. 'It was all very plain. And since you were hardly holding him at arm's length, it's as clear as day how things stand. But I made him shove off, girl, my pride being what it is.'

'Sandy, you mustn't believe –'

'I warned him,' Sandy continued tonelessly, 'what would happen if he ever dared show his face here again. I dismissed what he said, and told him that this baby is mine. He won't dare try to take her – unless it's your choice.'

'Sandy, I –'

'Whether you choose to take him on, and grab all he told

344

me he can offer, is up to you.' He was speaking in a stiff, mechanical way, not like the Sandy she knew at all. 'My back's broad,' he went on, 'but not that much! So for the time being I'd prefer you to keep on with the story that I'm missing at sea.' He stood up and carefully laid Rosemary back into her pram. 'It's late, no one will see me, so I'll be on my way.'

'No,' she gasped, and pulled herself shakily to her feet. 'Sandy, please don't go! Why do you use that tone, and carry on about me taking what Nigel can offer? Sandy, you don't understand!'

His face remained inscrutable as he replied, 'Fool I may be, but even I can accept the evidence of my own eyes.'

She had never seen him so coldly, bitterly angry. He looked ill, drawn and strained, a bit dazed and out of true. Sandy was always well-mannered, yet tonight his navy-blue peaked cap remained on his head. He should have taken it off the moment he stepped inside the house. Why, she wondered wildly, was she thinking about such a trivial thing? Was she going mad?

Poppy couldn't believe the way Sandy was looking at her. His eyes held loathing and hurt. She stumbled over to the table and frantically poured the tea that had been waiting and ready for Nigel. He refused it, pushing away her outstretched hand.

'Sandy?' she began again. 'You simply don't –'

'You have always made it perfectly clear that you loved that man, and exactly what your life's ambition is,' he told her. 'So I reckon that cuts me out. I understand that Carson's willing to set you up for life, which will be a damned sight easier than slogging your guts out with Bill. Well, the choice is yours, and I've made mine. There's no point in my staying here.'

'Sandy, don't leave. You're my husband. You are –'

'No longer a blind fool,' he cut in roughly. 'To think there was a time when I actually trusted you! I could hardly believe it, even while I was shaking the stuffing out of Carson. He told me that it was your decision to have him visit you here in your house. That you fixed the date and time. You! No one else! Can you look at me and say that isn't true?'

'I did say, but –'

'Well, now it's my turn. I have decided not to stay in your house, nor use your daughter for any kind of excuse. I shall see to it that the marriage allowance continues. Yes, even though to all intents and purposes I'm dead. You can tell all those nosyparkers you so detest that I paid an insurance policy. I will not show my face here again. I shall stay with Onions and his wife-to-be. Don't breathe a word to my mother. I'll cut your tongue out if you do. Goodbye.'

Too numbed and shocked to argue with him, she stood there helplessly and let him go.

All fight beaten out of her, Poppy went back to work with Bill. She took the baby with her everywhere she went, fearful of letting her out of sight. Nigel had looked so strange when he saw Rosemary, so greedy! He might even now try to snatch her away. So it was that Beth minded Rosemary while Poppy worked. An astonishingly blooming Beth these days, because the police, having no evidence against Harry, had let him go.

Harry was now a regular, very chastened visitor. He looked to Beth for moral support. Gaol, he said, was like being shut up in hell. He'd top himself before he'd let them take him again. And Beth, loving him, was for ever sticking up for him and making excuses. She wheedled round Bill to give him a handyman's job. Harry leaped at the chance. He began whistling again and looking at big, motherly Beth with different eyes. It really looked as though Beth would have her happy ending in all good time.

Bill's main concern these days was his carrot crop. Every autumn he remained undecided whether to lift and store them, or leave them in the ground. He swore the flavour was best if they were left, but in heavy soil like this, slugs, maggots of the carrot-root fly, and even rats, left behind an almost empty shell. Rabbits left even less! The sprouts were doing very well, their lush tops having already been sold.

After the rush of the full season, Bill enjoyed quieter times. He made up onion ropes and bagged and dried fruit for the shops. His greatest passion was for growing ferns and wallflowers. Young plants of the latter had already replaced the geraniums in Poppy's window box.

Quietly introspective, Poppy went through the days working all hours God gave. Evenings she preferred to stay alone in her house, having to hide her discomfort when Nan, Charlie or friends insisted on paying calls. Meg managed to come out of her shell at last. She would stand on the doorstep of number ten, looking lost, holding parcels of newly knitted baby clothes. Rosemary had innumerable pairs of bootees.

'Vi's even worse now we've lost Sandy,' Meg said sadly one evening. 'I don't think I can stand much more of this.'

'Sandy hasn't died,' Poppy told Meg, white to the lips and feeling as guilty as hell. 'You mustn't ever think that! He's gone missing, that's all.'

She broke into a storm of weeping, and it was shy, fluttery Meg, who comforted her.

They were all worried about Poppy, but she couldn't even rake up enough interest to mind. She couldn't tell the truth. She wanted to, but Sandy had said she must let sleeping dogs lie. She dared not let him down again. He would never forgive her if she did. All she was able to do was tell Meg over and over again to have faith. As far as she was concerned, she insisted, Sandy was not dead. Until she had official notification, they must all believe, as she did, that Sandy was rescued and safe in some foreign land.

She thought of going to Stratford, to the Pickles house, but decided against. Sandy would not yet be in a mood to listen to her.

Devastated, desperate, Poppy began her letter writing again, addressing her mail to Sandy in care of Mrs Pickles.

'Sandy,' she wrote, 'you're being wicked. You should at least let your mother know. Tell her the truth. Tell her what you saw! Let her loathe and detest me, I just don't care any more! Please, please put her mind at rest.'

There was no reply and she had expected none. But she was not prepared to give Sandy up, and her only way of reaching him was the letters that he had always said he loved to receive.

She wrote and told him of Edna and Gus' wedding, and how the news of the shipwreck had started off the baby's

347

journey to the world. Gus now worked in the stables of a friend of Bill's, and seemed immediately at one with the animals. She told Sandy of Maud and of Arty's escapades. She told him of Burney, who was now trying to sell paper roses going from door to door. She was hoping that Burney would run the Bannerman & Swift new greengrocery shop. It wouldn't be like having his own café, but he would earn regular money, which would at least be a start.

More letters followed: about how Flossie and Burt fussed over Lenny; about Daniel and the Home. Barbara was smitten and, from where Poppy stood, it looked as though Daniel was now something of a dead duck. She scribbled anything and everything. She wrote as if she was speaking face to face with the husband she dearly cared for and missed.

Christmas came and went. Even though everyone made an effort, the loss of Sandy put a blight over the season. And the secret she bore, the shame and guilt, made Poppy feel ill.

Poppy sent cards to all the Pickles, and photos of Rosemary to Sandy inscribed 'To Daddy with love'. To Sandy from herself there was a St Christopher identification wristband inscribed 'To a dear Husband', and a plaintive letter begging him to come home. There was never a reply.

Early in the new year Bill's glasshouses got the full treatment and there was early seed planting to do: broad bean, cauliflower, onion, summer cabbage, lettuce. There were rooted cuttings still to plot up, a million and one things to do. Then Bill showed her the statements of the profits they had made and Poppy looked at him with wide, amazed eyes.

'Then we're on our way, Bill? Really and truly on the way! Shall we plough most of it back in?'

'That's what we have been doing and I'm more than happy to continue if that's what you wish, my dear.'

'It is, it is! Oh! Bill, there is one thing I'd like some money for next time around.'

'Something more for our baby?' he teased.

'In a way. Bill, I adore old Bo-Bo and I'd like to see him have a companion, too. But I would also enjoy seeing us owning a van.'

348

'Agreed,' he replied, ready to indulge her as always. 'Bo-Bo shall have a new companion from me, and Special Deliveries, a van from you. Will there be anything else?'

'Driving lessons?' she said mischievously. 'Or shall they came out of my monthly pittance too?'

'We will have to think about that,' he teased back, and they smiled into each other's faces, as always, very close.

The following weekend Poppy made her way, as usual, round to see Daniel. She was going to fib to him. Even though they were only little and white they were untruths just the same. Yet she didn't care. Not at all!

Rosemary's future was assured. Now that the baby would never need to go short, she could discard Nigel's money. She had been waiting to do it with an easy conscience, and in the knowledge that it was working for the greater good.

It was a relief to find Daniel alone. These days Barbara was there during most off-duty times. Poppy ran up and gave him a great big hug.

'Got a surprise for you,' she teased. 'A great big marvellous surprise!'

'Matey!' He laughed. 'Have you won a fortune?'

'Earned it!' she declared. 'I've just received a profit statement from Bannerman & Swift and guess what? My half is for you!' She waved a cheque already written out in front of his face. 'Yes, Daniel, for you to make a dream come true. Take it!'

He took it, looked, and his mouth dropped open.

'A thousand pounds? A cool fortune, Poppy? I can't believe it – and I can't accept it, of course! You could buy your own house, and Nan's, and finish up Charlie's mortgage too with money like this. I wouldn't think of –'

'I'll never buy a house in Jezebel Street, Daniel, and Nan's dared me to lay eyes on hers! As for Dad, he's doing very nicely, thank you – he gets most of his stock for next to nothing, for a start! No, this is for your dream, for the kids, and . . . for Ros.'

'Look, little'un, you've got to take time out to think about this. I can't just –'

'Not even for your kids?' Poppy asked in mock surprise. 'Not for all the little boys and girls? Children who, you said, so desperately needed a nice place to go for holidays and such? Come off it, Daniel!'

He was looking at the cheque and then staring at her, his face strained, his very blue eyes unsure.

'It's no go, Poppy,' he said and it seemed as though the words were torn unwillingly from his mouth.

'I swear that this is what I want,' she told him, then added, 'and I promise you that Bill and I are certain of earning this sort of cash again, perhaps even more for next year. So where's the harm in taking my cheque? After all, Daniel, you've practically given up everything for this place yourself. Given till it bleeds, in fact. Remember what Nan always says, that it's gracious to give and also gracious to receive.'

'You . . .' He hesitated, then went on. 'You said for Ros?'

'I want you to buy that nice holiday house for the children, Daniel! A lovely place with grounds, something near the sea, and I'd like it to be in the Westlands where the daffodils and violets grow!' She looked down. 'I took her violets, you know. On that day. But she'd gone before I could give them to her. I've not been sure I even liked them ever since. But I know Ros would love to be remembered where wild violets grow. I hope the trust will go along with it, because the fares to take the children there will be sky-high, but the actual place for the children needn't be in the West Country. It will really be up to you. There's just one thing, Daniel. One little thing.'

'What is it, matey?' he asked, his expression still very unsure.

'I want the holiday home to be known as Ros House. Could – could that be arranged?'

'Oh, matey!' he muttered. 'Pinch me! I can't believe this!'

Life after that became brighter for Poppy. She now accepted that dreams could come true. She had helped to make Daniel's wish be granted, and somehow, some day, she had to believe that Sandy would forgive her sufficiently to come home. And over and above all, she had her beautiful, solemn, quite enchanting Rosemary to adore.

Poppy still thought of Nigel with hurt and regret. Loving him as she had, she could sense his feeling of loss even now. He had been quite unable to hide his absolute longing when he had looked at his child. But through his own actions, right at the beginning, he had given up the right to be Rosemary's father. To Poppy as to the rest of the world, Sandy was Rosemary's one and only dad. She was absolutely determined about that.

'Sandy,' she whispered his name, staring up at the sky through the lacework of bare silver birch branches. 'Sandy, forgive me, my dearest and most beloved friend.'

Though the weather was still freezing, and Bill's lonely sanctuary by the Lea quite remote, Poppy often found herself there, praying from her soul. This was something she could never do in church. Such buildings were surrounded by graveyards and for that reason were repugnant to her.

Late one night Meg pounded on Poppy's door. Hysterical, in shock, she gasped, 'It's Vi! She's dead!'

Poppy sat opposite her parents-in-law in the carriage that followed the hearse. She was aware of the magnificent ebony horse so proudly bearing its dark plumes. He was progressing at a snail's pace, sedate, held on rein, as much a prisoner as she felt in her sombre black clothes.

She looked out of the carriage window. It was a wild morning. Clouds, low and black, were being herded across the sky. They were heavy with rain as she was heavy with guilt.

She should have told Meg about Sandy, his reason for keeping away, but her unspoken promise to him had kept her quiet. Then, just as she had been on the point of telling the truth, Freddy had turned up. From that moment on Meg had needed no one else. In grief and desolation, Meg and Freddy were one. Freddy never once mentioned Sandy's name. And in a way it was a good thing they knew nothing of their son. Although she had sent him a telegram about Vi, there had still been no message. Seemingly, Sandy had made no effort to be with his own on this sad day.

Poppy also reproached herself because she did not miss the departed. She could not! She had not even liked the woman and was now mainly conscious of the cold.

By the time they reached St Catherine's and were walking sedately along the pathway, Poppy's heart was filling with

351

dread. Now, at last, she would be standing in the one place she had been avoiding all these years. She wanted to scream and cry and run away.

Carefully maintaining a remote and dignified expression, she followed Sandy's parents under the stone-vaulted porch and entered the holy confines. She was fiercely glad that she had left Rosemary at home, watched over by an adoring Edna.

Ahead, on draped trestles, the coffin faced the altar, ablaze with early spring flowers. Everywhere there were violets. The cold was cutting to the bone, but the church was old and rather beautiful. Poppy felt awe as she looked around her and breathed in the odour of old leather, hymn books, polish, and the sweetness of violets and mimosa, so fluffy and yellow.

Poppy took her place with Meg and Freddy, and stared ahead. Behind her she could hear the shuffling feet of various distant relatives, acquaintances and a curious neighbour or two. Vi had had no real friends.

In the moment before the service began, Poppy heard the sudden gusting of rain against the stained-glass windows and the scratching of ivy against old porous walls. And then tears sped down Poppy's cheeks and she was crying for the lonely person she now was, and for that long ago heartbroken young girl who had so tragically lost Ros.

There came a spate of coughing as the organ music began, sombre and heavy like a ponderously wheezing lament. There came a scraping of shoes as the congregation stood up to sing. The whole oppressive ritual continued. Poppy sang hymns, listened to wise, comforting words and knelt in prayer, willing the time to pass so that she could go.

At last the closing of hymn book pages whispered round the church like a sea of sighs. There was a hollow reverberation as someone pulled back the great oaken door. The congregation began following the pallbearers out to the churchyard.

Spotting Nan, who had come to give her support, Poppy left Freddy and Meg, who were leaning against each other. She went to her aunt and took hold of her hand. They walked in silence until they stood side by side, looking down at Ros' grave.

'So long ago,' Nan whispered. 'So long ago!'

'She isn't here, Nan,' Poppy said gravely, and there was a wealth of care in her voice. 'Don't you understand even now? Ros isn't here! She's somewhere up there, floating and smiling and counting the stars.'

Nan took a hard, sharp breath. 'I ain't going back to their place. Meg don't need us now she's got Fred.'

'Then shall we leave, Nan?'

'Yes, and go to Jezebel Street. You and me will have a cuppa or some of my pearl-barley stew. We need something to warm ourselves up.'

'Stew, of course,' Poppy said and smiled into the older woman's eyes. 'A lot of water's gone under the bridge, hasn't it, Nan?'

'Too much if you ask me,' Nan replied. 'Come on, Poppy, let's get back home.'

The night was raw and cold. Tired, hungry and depressed, Sandy hurried towards the entrance of the station. He had not been able to get back in time for the funeral, and was glad to have escaped seeing his father, who he knew would have been there. Poppy was a different matter. She would believe he had deliberately let his mother down. She had a way with her that made a man feel she could see into his soul. Even worse, she knew him so well. When she was angry she could give him looks that just about said it all.

Oh, damn Poppy! Why on earth did he have to bother with her? But he did, and that was the hell of it! Somebody had to. This even though, in spite of what she said, he felt she still mooned over that slimy fancy-pants bloke. He clenched his fists and swore under his breath. Damn young Poppy for so getting under his skin! He lived for those letters of hers, could see her, feel her, all but reach out and touch her. He was a weak-kneed knuckle-head for so needing to get back to her and home.

He forgot everything then, except the need to get his ticket and run for his train. No one got in the way of the huge, weather-beaten figure.

Strong again and immensely fit, he made it, just seconds before the whistle blew. He took a seat, closed his eyes and thought of his mother. His sweet, loving mother would have been unable to cope with losing the daughter-in-law she adored, and the grandchild she worshipped. Meg couldn't have borne the scandal, the upset, the terrible rows that would have ensued if the story about Carson and that bloody awful night had become known.

At least Poppy had stayed put, safe in number ten, and there had been no hint of the truth coming out. Poppy's letters had shown how she kept an eye on his mum, was fond of her and had never ceased to champion her. She had been loyal to the last. Poppy had been the only one able and willing to keep his grandmother Vi at bay. His gran was no threat now. Because of the grinding grief the old woman had caused his mum, Sandy was not sorry to see her go.

Leyton Midland at last. He left the station, his long legs stretching as he walked along the High Road, turned into Skelton Street, then finally Jezebel and home. He hung up his blue serge jacket and peaked cap on the hall stand, and went along the passage.

Poppy was sitting in the kitchen, by a range that blazed out warmth. The kettle was steaming lazily, the teapot nearby. She looked up as he walked in, crimsoned, then started as though to rise, but changed her mind and stayed where she was.

'I . . . I thought you might have made it sooner,' she said carefully. 'Your mother needed you.'

'Correction, she needed Dad.'

'But he – you –'

'She needed Dad!' he told her bluntly. 'He's a rotten lousy swine, but she still wants him. Women all swoon over bastards, it seems.' He noted the fresh wave of scarlet flooding her cheeks and the hurt in her eyes, but did not comment. 'Now, do you suppose you could get me something to eat?' he asked her masterfully. 'I've spent hours on the train from Scapa and I'm starved!'

Poppy leaped up and ran into the scullery to grab up bread, butter, cheddar and a large onion. She could hear him making tea and she felt the excited pounding of her heart. There had been no warning of his sudden appearance, but all that mattered was that he had come home.

'Where's my daughter?' he called out. 'Upstairs?'

'She sleeps in the yellow room now,' she replied and joined him breathless and smiling. 'She's a wonderfully placid little thing, and you won't recognise her, she's so grown.' She hesitated, then said nervously, 'Sandy?'

'Yes?'

She felt like a kid up before the head, he looked so stern.

'I – are you still at Les' house?'

'No. I've come from Scapa Flow. I've been there a little while now. Your letters have always been sent on, though. Why?'

'You never wrote back and – are . . . are you, I mean, are you alive now? To other people, I mean?'

'I think it could be known that I was rescued from a remote island,' he told her casually. 'Now I've calmed down. We'll just have to wait and see.'

She could feel his eyes on her as she cut thick slices of bread and buttered them. The cheese dish was set in its place, the onion swiftly peeled for him to cut and come again as he chose. He sat at the table, raised one brow and she hastily swung about and opened the dresser drawer to take out knife and fork. As she handed them to him, their fingers touched. She felt a thrill racing through her, and unable to look into his eyes, she stared down at her toes.

'Tea's poured,' he told her. 'Have we any decent milk? None of that tinned rubbish, I have plenty of that at sea.'

'Yes, I have some cow's milk,' she said and fled back into the scullery to pick up the half-filled pint bottle from the stone floor, the best place she knew to keep it cold. She went back to him, feeling daft and embarrassed, hardly knowing why. She poured milk in the tea, then sat and joined him at table.

'At least you . . . you don't hate me quite so much,' she said quietly. 'I mean, at least this time you've taken off your cap.'

'What?' He was frowning, puzzled. Then the penny dropped. 'Oh, I see.' He grinned. 'That was vanity, my girl. They'd shaved the hair off half of my head at the back. Took a bit of a bashing, you see. I'll tell you all about it some other time.' With cool deliberation he pushed the untouched bread and butter away.

'I'm not hungry after all. Got to be a skinny little thing, haven't you? No one would dream that you're such a bossy-boots. Always made the decisions, haven't you?' He looked round appreciatively. 'I mean, I was told, never asked, about the move to this house. I was told about you going in with Bill, never asked. Got a strange way of showing a bloke that you need him around, haven't you, eh?'

'Have I?' She faltered. 'I'm sorry. I didn't know.'

'What else don't you know?'

'I . . . I don't understand what you mean.'

'No?' He stood up, towering over her. 'Don't you know what I want, Poppy? Honestly? Come here!' She sat very still, hope flaring through her in waves. 'Stand yourself up,' he ordered, 'and come here.'

Shaking, she did as she was told and stopped before him, wide-eyed, wondering what he would say next.

'It was a good thing you did,' he told her roughly. 'I read your letter when I got back, and yes, it was a very good and kind nice thing. A memorial for Ros. Also it showed me something I wasn't sure of before. I'm proud of you and I know Ros would have been, too. So – you're not so crazy about money after all.'

'I've never wanted money for its own sake, Sandy,' she told him gravely. 'Only for what it can achieve. Then – you like the idea of the name?'

'Ros House?' he said quietly. 'Trust you to have such a decent idea. But then that's you, eh, Poppy? Come here!'

He swept her into his arms and carried her upstairs. She lay her head against his shoulder, glorying in his strength.

He undressed her, staring down at her dim outline which glowed faintly from the streetlamp outside. He kissed her stomach, murmuring that it was incredible that once Rosemary had been inside there. That now there must be another one, a boy, a Christopher. That he'd give her babies, lots of them, all looking like her. That he would place inside her all his strength and power. That come hell or high water, she belonged to him, and only him. That she was his wife.

His lovemaking was passionate, fierce, almost brutal, but

marvellous. She gloried in surrendering to his lips, his tongue, his strong brown hands, and finally his masculine self.

She whispered his name, groaned his name, matched movement for movement, knew ecstasy, then for zinging stunning moments of time, he took her on high to Paradise.

She spent all that night clinging to him, feeling young and feminine and satisfied as never before.

It was still dark when he told her that he had to go.

'No!' she gasped, shocked and distressed. 'You haven't seen our daughter yet. You haven't seen your mum or got in touch with your dad. You haven't –'

'I'm making my escape before the streets are aired,' he told her. 'It's back to Scapa for me. I'll send you a telegram from there. Do you understand? We've got to make everything shipshape, eh? Got to make everything seem right! Dad might suspect it's not all as it seems, but he won't bother to find out. He's been on dodges himself long before now. He just might think I'm my father's son.'

'You'll be back, Sandy?' she asked desperately, suddenly scared. 'You'll not leave me again?'

'Never,' he told her. 'Except when I'm at sea.'

Before he went downstairs, he popped his head round the door to see the baby and grinned.

'Yes,' he whispered. 'She's going to be the dead spit of my mum!'

He ducked as she made to hit him.

He ate the eggs and bacon she insisted on cooking, but was anxious to leave.

It was still dark but she stood on the step and watched him walking down the road. A large man with the gaslight glinting on his hair, for he had not put on his cap. He walked jauntily, like a man happy with his lot, and she wondered if that was really the truth.

And what about her? Was she happy? Was Nigel really pushed out of her heart once and for all? Yes, she thought, yes, yes, yes! and wanted to dance. At long last she was able to let the past go.

Sandy stopped and turned to wave. She blew him a kiss. He grinned and waved again before turning the corner. He was out of sight and she was missing him already. Did not want him to go.

Does he still love Ros' memory? she thought wistfully. Will he always be in love with her? And – and will he ever truly trust me again?

The thought hurt. She sighed and told herself that she had time to make him love her. All the time in the world! Then she went inside her nice little house. She felt squiggles of excitement curling her toes. Number ten Jezebel Street. Not bad surely – for a mere stepping stone . . .

You have been reading a novel published by Piatkus Books. We hope you have enjoyed it and that you would like to read more of our titles. Please ask for them in your local library or bookshop.

If you would like to be put on our mailing list to receive details of new publications, please send a large stamped addressed envelope (UK only) to:

Piatkus Books: 5 Windmill Street
London W1P 1HF

PIATKUS

The sign of a good book